Winner
2025 Maine Literary Award for
Crime Fiction

DYING

FOR

NEWS

Maureen Milliken

Nevermore Mystery Press
Belgrade Lakes, Maine

Dying For News/Maureen Milliken – 2nd ed. July 2025
ISBN 979-8-9894515-6-2 [print]
ISBN 979-8-9894515-7-9 [ebook]

COVER BY DISSECT DESIGNS

ALSO BY MAUREEN MILLIKEN

The Bernie O'Dea mystery series
Cold Hard News
No News Is Bad News
Bad News Travels Fast

DYING FOR NEWS is set in Franklin County, Maine, a real place, but Redimere, Maine, is not a real place. Any resemblance of the town or its people to any real places or people, living or dead, is a coincidence. Most of the geography is real, but some liberties have been taken, so if things aren't where they're supposed to be, or there are rivers or highways in the book that don't exist, it's simply because it's a work of fiction. While there is a Wesserunsett Stream in Somerset County, Maine, the Wesserunsett River that runs through Redimere is a figment of the author's imagination. This book is not intended to be a reflection on the fine people of the real Franklin County, Maine, or of any law enforcement entity in the state.

Anthony Wilson generously donated to the central Maine Neighbors Driving Neighbors auction, winning the right for his name to be used in the book. He had a choice of characters, and the one bearing his name is not meant to resemble the real Anthony Wilson in any way, shape or form.

CHAPTER 1

THE SNOW HAD started falling sometime after midnight. Bernie hadn't noticed when. The big, soft flakes hissed as they landed on the remains of what was once her house, a counterpoint to the snap and crackle of the burning timbers.

She took off her glasses and put them in her pocket. A month before, when she'd become a full-time glasses wearer, she'd been astounded by the clear, detailed world she'd been missing. Now she'd just as soon go back to not seeing it. It was too real—the flames, the cascade of spray from the fire trucks and hoses, the plumes of gray and black smoke filling the cold night air.

"What a great way to start 2011," she said.

"Look at it this way, Bernie," said her brother Sal, shivering next to her. "Nowhere to go but up."

She almost agreed. She didn't say so, though. That would be tempting fate. She and fate had been in an unhappy standoff for a couple of years. She didn't want to rock the boat.

"You might as well go home," she said. He'd been there for hours. "There's no reason to stay."

"You sure?" He asked it the way someone does when they're trying to sound reluctant but hoping the answer will be yes.

"Yes."

"Anything you need?"

"Yeah, track down Stephanie and kill her."

"On it." He laughed, then kissed her cheek. "Happy New Year."

He jogged away, past the volunteer firefighters' pickup trucks, the Red Cross van, the handful of neighbors still hanging around watching the show. The only thing missing was Bernie's tenant, who'd been ghosting her since Christmas Eve. Bernie wasn't worried, she was pissed off. Beyond pissed off. She'd been stewing in a rising mix of rage and despair since Sandy called four hours earlier to tell her that her house was on fire.

She and Pete didn't have the police scanner on like they normally would. New Year's Eve was a tricky night and both of them—the newspaper editor and police chief—would normally be half-listening to the static and crackle of mundane calls just in case there was that big one. Not tonight, though. Bernie knew something big would happen since they weren't listening. In a weird, out-of-body way, the fact that it turned out to be her house on fire almost didn't surprise her.

Maybe the fire was an accident. Maybe not. Either way, she knew who was to blame. Stephanie had apparently ridden out of town, owing Bernie rent and oil money and carrying a giant load of unearned resentment. The fire felt like a final giant middle finger raised in triumph.

A Red Cross volunteer appeared at Bernie's side. The volunteers had been nothing but kind, offering coffee, doughnuts, blankets. They knew how she felt, how traumatic this was. Their empathy was sincere. Bernie wasn't in the mood. She was tired. Pissed off. She wanted to be left alone to stew.

"Since you have a place to go, maybe you should get out of the cold," the volunteer said. "There's nothing you can do here tonight. No need to get sick too." He was ancient, probably eighty. Yet here he was, in the subfreezing post-midnight cold, on New Year's, no less, telling her, almost forty years younger, that she shouldn't be. He was trying to be nice, but she was tired of hearing it.

"Thanks, but I'm going to stick around."

She could feel him practically vibrating with the need to convince her to leave, could feel his eyes sliding over, bathing her in fatherly concern, as she kept hers on the fire. She took a step away from him, hoping he wouldn't notice.

"Okay, let me know if you need anything, dear." He patted her on the shoulder and walked away.

It was perverse, she knew, that she wanted to stay. She'd been told that there was nothing she could do about a thousand times in the past few hours. By her brother. By Pete. By Sandy. By the volunteer. By half a dozen friggin' guys on the volunteer fire department who'd briefly left their duties just to say it, as though they were sharing unique, vital information.

They didn't get that the one thing she *could* do was stand in the cold and watch her house die. It was penance. It wasn't a sentient being. She knew that. She'd let it down anyway. The fire was the final indignity. Even though it wasn't her fault—at least directly—she owed her house this final attention.

Pete separated from a clump of men, first responders from different law enforcement and emergency agencies who'd raced to the scene. The smoldering remains of the house behind him made his approach seem staged. Not so much staged as ominous, maybe. It felt like a metaphor—him approaching, her house disappearing.

"How are you doing?" he asked.

Same as I was when you asked ten minutes ago. She bit it back. She'd already snapped at Sandy when he'd asked her the same thing fifteen minutes before. "You're the fire chief—don't you have something more important to do?" He'd flinched. She felt bad. Now she felt like snarling at Pete the same way.

"You don't have to stay," he said. He wrapped her up in a bear hug. He smelled smoky, not his usual woodsmoke smell, but rancid and toxic. He squeezed her tight, his warm mouth against her ear. "You're frozen. There's nothing you can do here."

"I know." A couple of minutes before she would've snapped it. Now it was almost a sob. "I don't feel like I can go."

He gave her another squeeze, then took her hand as they stepped aside to let a couple of pickup trucks go past, bumping over hoses as they headed for home. "Sorry for your loss, Bernadette," Ken Parent said out his open window as he slowly rolled by.

"Thanks. I appreciate it." She felt a pang, pathetically grateful that this guy was here, the other guys, too, in the wee hours of New Year's Day, to get wet and freeze and breathe in smoke in a losing battle for someone they barely knew.

The remaining fire crew, lit by the pulsing lights of the trucks, sprayed hot spots and raked embers, masked by a gray smoke veil.

"Good thing Stephanie wasn't here," Pete said.

"Yeah, because I'd kill her."

He squeezed her hand. Hard. "Look," he said. She tensed.

"Look what?" she asked when he didn't say more.

"Sandy's calling the state fire marshal."

"I knew it. She burned my house down."

"Don't jump to conclusions. The fire was fast-moving and substantial. He's just being careful. You know that. You write fire stories all the time."

"Not about my own house."

"Don't get all excited. We don't know anything yet."

"Do I look like I'm getting all excited?"

He didn't answer.

"Even if I am, don't I have a right to?"

"You don't know what caused it. Wait for the investigation."

"This would be a great time for you to be more boyfriend and less police chief."

He kissed her temple. "I love you, but it's an old house. It could've been a lot of things."

It *was* an old house. Old and poorly built. She'd owned it for five years but never had the money to turn it into much of a better house. "What a mess."

He kissed her again, on the cheek this time, his lips warm against her snow-wet face. "So much for our resolution that the new year would be quiet and drama-free."

"That was *your* resolution. I knew better, remember?"

"Seriously, why don't you go home and get warm? I can get a ride back. Things will look better in the morning."

My house will still be gone, she wanted to say. *A pile of smoldering, charred rubble. All my stuff lost forever.* Maybe it wasn't a great house, but it was hers. She didn't say it, because she *had* made a New Year's resolution. A secret one. She was going to start being the person Pete seemed to think she was rather than a cranky, drama-attracting, anxiety-filled snark queen. This was the first test. Hopefully the biggest.

"There's nothing you can do here tonight."

"One advantage to going home is that I'll stop hearing people say that." So much for her resolution.

"Exactly." He cupped her chin in his hand, kissed her on the lips, then said softly. "Go home."

This is home, she wanted to say.

He kissed her again, long and soft. Pressed his car keys into her hand. "Happy New Year. See you at home."

****

The lights were still on when Bernie got back to Pete's house on the lake. Their half-finished beers and sticky plates of buffalo chicken dip sat on the coffee table, next to the scattered pieces of the jigsaw puzzle. When Sandy had called, Bernie didn't even have time to get annoyed that he'd called Pete instead of her. She had no memory of putting on her coat and boots, grabbing a hat and gloves, but obviously she had. Then they were in Pete's car, the blue lights beneath his grill flashing, roaring toward her burning house.

Bernie dumped out the beer. She scraped the remains of the dip off the plates, fighting the urge to scoop up some with a tortilla chip and chow it down. She threw everything into the rubbish, even the dip from the bowl, which would probably be okay if she put it in the fridge. The sight of it made her sick, mixing with the smell of the acrid smoke that clung to her clothes, her hair.

"Another festive New Year's Eve comes to an end," she said to Dubby. He gave her a happy doggy grin as she opened the slider to let him out. The snow had stopped and the clouds were drifting away, revealing the Milky Way in high definition, spread out across the sky

5

over the lake. On summer nights when the lake was flat glass, the stars reflected like a second sky. Now, in the wee hours of the first day of the year, it was frozen, covered with snow. It could be a huge meadow surrounded by pine trees if she didn't know that under that white windswept expanse was the first iffy layer of ice. Within days, if not hours, just like clockwork, the scanner would spit out its first call of the year that someone had plunged through.

"A pleasant thought to start 2011 with," she said to Dubby as he scurried back in, dancing on snow-crusted paws. She wiped them with a towel, not only to ease his discomfort, but to avoid paw prints on the clean-as-a-whistle rug, the polished hardwood floor, the couch, the bedspread.

"Different rules for Pete's house," she reminded the dog as he tried to pull his paw away. It hit her with a force it hadn't earlier. Now there was only Pete's house.

She knew she wouldn't be able to sleep. The sharp, toxic fire odor seemed worse now. She stuffed her clothes into the washing machine, hoping they didn't leave a permanent smell before Pete's could join them.

She took a long, hot shower, washing her hair three times. She couldn't tell if the smell was her imagination, or if it had somehow embedded in her nose.

She climbed between the cool sheets, trying to turn off the running commentary in her head. It ran on several tracks.

There was the fire, wondering what caused it. *Goddamn Stephanie.*

There was logistics—if Stephanie left a cigarette burning or dumped hot pellet stove ashes on the porch, would insurance cover it? She'd made some minor improvements when she knew she'd be renting it out. Her agent had told her there was no rider or anything extra she needed. The insurance was for the house, not the person. But what if that person was a vindictive slob whose carelessness, or something worse, had sparked a fire?

Bernie still had to pay the mortgage. She knew that. She also still had to pay the equity line of credit she'd taken out less than a year before. A lot left to pay.

What had she lost? She'd moved some of her stuff into a self-storage unit when it became clear she'd be at Pete's for a while as his injured leg healed. At the time, she assumed she'd help with living expenses, something she couldn't afford unless she rented out her house. He wouldn't let her—"You're here because of my leg, it wouldn't be fair." So she started making a monthly deposit into a savings account. She'd make him take it sooner or later if he didn't change his mind. How much was in there now? Maybe $5,000? Would that be enough to cover things if she had to wait for insurance to pay out? Cover what things?

Her brain spun around that one for a while until it landed on another topic. Where was her insurance policy and any other documents she'd need? They hadn't been in her house, because she didn't want them accessible to a stranger, even before it became clear how boundary-challenged Stephanie was. She didn't want them at Pete's, for reasons she knew were unfair to him, but whatever. They were either at the storage unit or her office. Her brain was too fried to remember. It'd been a long day. Actually, even though it was only hours old, a long year.

She jerked awake to the sound of the front door opening, then quietly closing. Pete greeted Dubby with a whisper. She found her glasses, and the red blur on the clock came into focus: 4:17 a.m.

Pete, moving around in the dark, was trying to be quiet, as always. She was a light sleeper, and, in what was basically a one-room house, it was always more disruptive than if he just turned on a light and clomped around, like Steve used to. Not that Pete ever clomped.

"You can turn on a light," she said.

"Sorry, I didn't mean to wake you up." He sat next to her on the bed. A bubble of bile leaped into her throat at the sharp fire smell on his flannel shirt.

"It's okay. I wasn't sleeping."

"Bernie." He said it softly, like a sigh. *Uh-oh.* She sat up. Whatever it was, she didn't want to be lying there, like a little kid, as he hovered over her in the dark. It was more than sympathy. That scene had played out hours before. This was something new. New and somehow more serious, if that was possible. *She knew it, knew it, knew it.* Hadn't known what it was going to be, but knew there was going to be some bigger shit, because there always was.

"What's wrong?" she asked.

"They found a body."

Her mind went blank. "In my house?"

"They can't tell who it is. Can't even tell the gender."

"Oh."

"Bernie." He rested his hand, hot and dry and mercifully not smelling like smoke, on the side of her neck. Rubbed gently, almost absently. "They think it's arson."

"Oh no. Stephanie."

"Maybe. Maybe not. Where's her car? Where has she been? She was gone when you went by this afternoon, right? No sign of anyone?"

It felt like an interrogation even though his tone was still gentle.

"Hat hair." She smoothed it, mostly to remind herself this was Pete her boyfriend, not Pete the cop. "She must've come back. Maybe she was watching me earlier, waiting for me to leave. She's been avoiding me for more than a week."

He didn't say anything. In the moonlight she could see his eyes go from her face, which he'd been watching intently—*reassurance, compassion, not suspicion!*—to the window, the lake, the moon and Milky Way through the skylight. She knew what he was thinking. *There goes Bernie again, fucking up again.*

"Which room?"

"Your bedroom."

"Stephanie didn't sleep in my bedroom," Bernie said. It'd been a weird annoyance as well as a relief. Her tenant didn't even sleep on the daybed in the tiny guest room. She slept on the couch. She'd complained to Bernie that the bedrooms were too cold. The house was too cold. Maine was too cold. She cranked up the pellet stove and slept in the living room, going through two bags of pellets a day, twice what

Bernie burned, while still somehow using an astounding amount of heating oil.

Pete's tone was tender. The words, though, were all cop. "The investigator from the fire marshal's office wants to talk to you in the morning. He'll have some tough questions. Get some sleep. I need to take a shower." He kissed her, his fingers pressing on her temple, his palm hot against her cheek. He got up and started undressing.

"Go ahead and turn the light on," she said, irritated that, after that sleep-destroying conversation, he thought the light would bother her.

He walked to the bathroom. He didn't turn on the light.

****

Dawna pulled the cruiser off the road as much as she could so anyone still at the scene could get by. She wasn't worried. At four-thirty in the morning on New Year's Day there wasn't going to be much traffic. Of course someone would complain. They always did. That was going to be the least of her problems in the coming days.

She walked past the remaining fire trucks, stepping over the hoses that still crisscrossed the icy street. She'd have to get the public works crew up here to salt and sand. She added it to her mental checklist.

The snow had stopped, but the air was wet, as though the spray from the hoses froze in the air, hung there for hours, and now was slowly, invisibly melting. If that's how she was thinking, she told herself, she could use some sleep. It was still a long way away.

"Get Pete home all right?" Sandy asked as she came up beside him.

"Yeah. I'm in charge of the local investigation, by the way."

"Just when one shit show is over, another one starts up."

"Number two is all set, Chief," said a guy rolling a hose.

"Gotcha, thanks."

"At least this is more Bernie's problem than his," Dawna said. "Though I can't believe we're talking about a possible arson and a dead body as simply a problem."

"It's his by association."

They turned at a shout of greeting.

"I know he's mayor, but he couldn't wait for morning?" Sandy said.

"Great start for the new year," Ryan Grant said as he slide-walked on the ice toward them, then ducked below the crime scene tape. "What's the story? I was here earlier, but everyone was busy, so I went home and got a couple hours sleep."

"You didn't miss much," Sandy said.

"What a mess." Grant looked from the smoking ruins down to the brown mush where they stood. Hours before, the dooryard had been covered in snow, now it was an icy bog. "What do we know, Chief?"

"Total loss," Sandy said. "Took a while to knock down. Unusual for such a small house, but there you go. Been putting out the hot spots since."

"I heard it was arson. Murder too."

Sandy laughed. "Jeezum crow. They haven't even started an investigation. Possible arson. Maybe. And yeah, there was someone inside, sadly. But we don't know jack. Where'd you hear that?"

"Told you, I was here earlier. Anyway, I'm the mayor. People tell me things." He chuckled, friendly and casual.

"It's not something we've made public," Dawna said. His tone didn't fool her.

"Sergeant." Grant gave her a surprised look, like he'd just noticed her. "Where's your boss? Given it's his girlfriend's house."

"They were here earlier," Sandy said before Dawna could answer.

Grant's oversized head bobbed in a nod on top of his bull neck. His ears were bright red from the cold, his Irish tweed hat for fashion only. Too proud to be smart, Dawna's mom would've said.

She'd let Sandy, great at being Mr. Nice Guy, deal with him. It was before dawn on a freezing cold night and Bernie's house was a pile of smoldering rubble, a dead body inside. She wasn't in the mood.

"The house is no big loss," Grant said. "I was the broker. Good bones but needed a lot of work. She got it cheap, though. She'll probably make out okay with the insurance. Rebuild, get some instant equity."

"A little too soon, isn't it?" Sandy said, softening it with a smile. "Embers are still hot, you know? Let's get the body out first."

"Oh, gee," Grant said. "Sorry. Always thinking like a broker. The body is her tenant?"

"When do you think your guys will be clear so I can open the road?" Dawna asked Sandy. She was too cold and tired for morbid chitchat.

"Shouldn't this be a crime scene?" Grant asked her.

"Actually, it is." He was a big guy, but she was a big woman, and right now it took everything she had to keep from grabbing him by the faux fur collar of his parka and giving him a good shake. "You ducked under the crime scene tape right behind us. Officer Myers is over there making sure no unauthorized personnel go into the house until Major Crimes arrives and removes the body."

"Sgt. Mitchell's in charge of the criminal investigation on the Redimere end," Sandy said, cutting off Grant's response. "State fire marshal investigator is already here. I can get you a report on the fire tomorrow. You might as well go home and get warm."

"Thanks for your concern, Chief," Grant said, no longer friendly and casual. "One thing I want to remind both of you. I'm your boss. You"—he jabbed a gloved finger at Sandy, then Dawna—"and you, too, Sergeant. Not Novotny; I'm his boss and I'm your boss."

Dawna waited for his point.

"You both report to me. The police chief has a lot going on, and frankly I don't trust him to handle this well. I know he's your buddy, MacCormack, and I know you're inexplicably loyal to him, Sergeant, but I'm your boss. Don't forget it. Got it?"

He waited for them to nod. Dawna didn't have an issue with the loyal part, but *inexplicable* pissed her off. She kept her eyes on the burned house, afraid her annoyance would show.

Grant ducked below the police tape and slipped and slid past the fire truck toward his car, parked down the street.

"Like I said," Sandy said. "Fucking shit show."

CHAPTER 2

PETE HIT THE ALARM button at 5:59, one minute before it sounded. He got dressed in the predawn semidarkness, pulling on his uniform pants, a navy-blue long-sleeved T-shirt, his official Redimere PD sweatshirt. He knew he could get away with jeans and a flannel shirt. It was New Year's Day and a Saturday, no one would care. It was necessary, though. He wasn't going to be allowed much control as this played out. He wanted to make sure those guys remembered who he was.

The cold morning air hit him like a punch as he let Dubby out. It was going to be one of those gray days when the light never changed as the sun came up and then disappeared, barely making its presence known. He liked the cold. The way it stung his face and the sharpness when he took deep breaths. His socks stuck to the metal frame of the slider as he watched Dub scurry around, sniffing and peeing in fast-forward, getting his morning routine taken care of double time so he could get back to the warm house. Pete wiped his paws with a towel as the dog whined and pulled away, some bad memory from his previous life.

"It's okay, buddy. I know how you feel."

He got the coffee going, then fed the cats, who'd been watching from the couch with disdain as he dealt with the dog.

"I love you guys too," he whispered as he filled the dishes. Poopoo slow-blinked, but Becky and Billy stared, green eyes wide, tails high and swishing. They bent to their food, unmoved.

"Today is going to suck," Bernie said from the bed, separated from the living area by a shoulder-high partition.

"We'll get through it." She had the blankets pulled over her head. He gently pulled them back to be met with her big brown eyes, wide and fully awake. He sat down on the edge of the bed.

"That's Stephanie," she said. "I can't believe this whole thing. Was it smoking? But they think it's arson. Why do they think that? How did it happen? Even knowing it's her just means more questions. Who did it? How did she not get out? Where did the fire start?" Bernie's voice rose with each question. Pete waited for her to run out of steam. "How am I going to get through this fucking day?" Her voice broke.

He put his hand on her forehead, brushed back the hair that clung to it, still damp from her shower hours before.

"We've had worse days," he said.

She took a deep breath. He braced for her to start crying. Instead, she said, "Oh yeah? Name one. Oh, right. That one. And that one. Oh, and that one."

He laughed. Kissed her lightly on the lips. "Oatmeal, waffles, or French toast today, my little ray of sunshine? Or maybe scrambled eggs and bacon?"

"As much as I'd love French toast with a pile of bacon drowning in maple syrup, I feel like it's an oatmeal day. I need something healthy to sustain me."

"Your wish is my command."

"I can make it." She slid out of bed and reached for the mukluks she used as slippers.

"Coffee's already started," he said, heading to the kitchen. "I can make breakfast."

"This house has too many cooks and not enough whatever the rest of that saying is."

"You're getting 'too many cooks spoil the broth' mixed up with 'too many chiefs and not enough Indians.' "

"Probably." She sat down at the table, and he put a mug of coffee in front of her. "That's one of my dad's sayings."

"Mine, too. Probably should be put on the shelf."

"Definitely. I heard Dubby yelping. I wish he'd get over that issue with his paws."

"We could just not do it."

"Right and have paw prints all over the house."

"You know I don't care about that."

She swallowed some coffee. "Actually, I think you're just being nice about it, burying your resentment. One day you're going to freak out on me."

"How many times do I have to tell you that my need for neatness and order only applies to me?"

"That's the therapy talking."

"Thank mercy for therapy, right? You want blueberries in this?" He was facing the stove, and when she didn't answer, he turned around. She was staring into her coffee cup, wiping tears from behind her glasses.

"It's going to be okay, Bernie."

"I know you didn't want me to move back home, so it's going to be okay for you. You know, since I don't have a home to move back to."

"It doesn't feel like a win. I'm putting some maple syrup in the oatmeal, okay? That sound good? Some sweetness for my sweetness?"

She laughed. "God, I'm awful. You can stop torturing me. I'll stop being a bitch."

He put the bowl of oatmeal in front of her. "You're fine. If ever you had a reason to be a bitch, today's the day."

"What time is my interrogation? Why are you in uniform?"

"I'm sure it won't be an interrogation." He sat down across from her.

"You said last night they'd have tough questions."

"Nothing you can't answer."

"There's a lot I can't answer. I know how cops are." She paused. "Except for you, of course."

"Thanks."

"Why are you in uniform?"

"No rest for the police chief."

"That's not an answer. Do I have to ask a third time?"

"The state police and fire marshal are investigating. Dawna is the town's lead, but I'm still the chief, right? I want to make that clear. I have a job to do too. Speaking of which, I need to leave in a minute, so we'll go separately, okay?"

"This whole thing is going to suck."

"It'll be over soon."

"I might as well look at my phone." She went to her coat and took it out of her pocket. "I didn't want to last night."

She sat back down. "Seventeen texts. Twenty-three phone calls. Not all of them left voicemails at least." She took off her glasses. "I fucking hate these things. I can't believe I have to wear them for the rest of my life."

He reached across the table and took her hand. "Bernie, I'm here for you, okay? You know that. You don't have to worry about facing this alone."

****

Bernie's dread and confusion as she drove down Main Street was at DEFCON 5 or 1, or whatever the biggest DEFCON was. She could never keep it straight. But she went hyper-DEFCON, if that was a thing, when she saw the fleet of vehicles in the parking lot at the public safety building. The sight of Pete's car, parked in between Sandy's pickup and Dawna's Jeep, was slightly reassuring, a sign the cavalry was there for her. Small and likely ineffectual, though, she thought as she drove past the state fire marshal investigation response vehicle, a giant RV. Next to it was a pickup truck with the state fire marshal's office badge on the door. Beyond that was an obvious unmarked Maine State Police car that Bernie recognized as Lt. George Libby's. Then another state police car, marked. Then the state police Major Crimes vehicle, another repurposed RV that took up three spaces.

Despite the fleet outside, the police department reception area was

15

empty when she used the key code to let herself in. She went to the back, where Pete's office door was open.

He looked up from his computer and gave her a big smile. Either a sign that things weren't as bad as she thought or, more likely, Pete heroically trying to manage her impending meltdown.

"You've got hat hair." She reached across the desk to smooth it down. His cowlick popped right back up. She sat down. "Sorry, I did my best. It'll give George Libby another reason to hate you. Your pretty brown locks against his 'I used to be a Marine' buzz cut. I saw his car out there. That's all I need."

"Nothing we can't handle, right?" Pete came around the desk. He'd obviously been waiting for her. "Everyone's in the conference room. Let's go."

"Give me a minute." She took off her glasses and wiped off the fog that had coated them when she'd entered the warm building. "I'm fifteen minutes early."

"You know how these things are. Let me hang up your coat."

"Actually, I don't."

He tugged at her arm. "Up and at 'em." She stood up and he maneuvered her coat off as she continued to wipe her glasses.

"Let's go." His hand was firm on the small of her back as they walked down the short hallway, like he was making sure she didn't stray off course. *It's an ambush.* She fought back the impulse to bolt.

"It'll be okay," he said softly. His hand flexed slightly, gave a little rub. The impulse faded.

A low babble of conversation stopped as they walked in. Four sets of eyes watched as they sat down. Dawna and Sandy. George Libby, of the state police. The state fire investigator, whose name Bernie didn't know. Her face went hot.

"Good morning," the guy she didn't know said. "I'm Ed Michaud, state fire investigator."

Bernie put her glasses back on, one lens smeared with a sweaty palm print. She took them off and wiped them on her shirt. Put them back on. No one said a word. They all had that serious look that meant they knew what was in store for her but were playing like they didn't. Even Sandy and Dawna. She felt exposed and stupid. It *was* an ambush. *I didn't do anything.* She wanted to yell it.

"You don't have to stay, Pete," George Libby said. "We're here to talk to her."

"I'm sitting in," Pete said.

"As police chief, or as her…" Libby let it trail off.

"I have a name," Bernie said.

Pete, at the same time, said, "As her partner. Sgt. Mitchell is the Redimere lead."

"There's no reason for you to be here, then." Libby's scalp under the spray of tiny steel-gray bristles was turning pink.

"I think there's a pretty good reason."

Sweat formed under Bernie's flannel shirt, along the bottom of her bra and under her arms. The heating system pinged and hissed. The longer they bickered, the more time she'd have to adjust her brain to what was coming, but she hated it when people talked about her when she was right there. She glanced down the table at Sandy and Dawna. Sandy made a little gesture with his hand. *Hold up.* Not bloody likely.

"I have a name," she said, louder. "I'm sitting right here."

"We'll get to you shortly," Libby said. "Chief Novotny—"

"He may be able to answer some questions I can't," Bernie said. She had no idea what questions, if any, Pete could answer. But if he left, the cold vacuum that replaced him would suck her right up.

"Oh, really?" Libby asked.

"It's fine," Michaud said. "Let's get to it. As you're aware, we found deceased remains."

"Totally aware," Bernie said. *The fact they're remains means they're deceased.* She kept her mental eyeroll from becoming a physical one. Ignore the jargon. Just get through it. "In fact, it was annoying to see that a press release was sent out about it this morning before anyone bothered to let me know officially."

"We told the chief," Michaud said, nodding to Pete. He seemed confused by her annoyance.

"I would appreciate being communicated with directly," she said. *Not through my boyfriend.* "It's my house, my problem."

"Okay," Michaud said, still confused. "It just seemed easier—"

"Thanks. Appreciate it." It was a fragile wall that she and Pete had built between their personal lives and their jobs. Even if she'd wanted to explain it, lack of sleep and shock would have made the words impossible to find. Pete's hand on the back of her chair, his thumb softly pressed against the bottom of her shoulder blade didn't help.

"You can't have it both ways," Libby said.

"Meaning?" Bernie asked.

"People," Michaud said, holding up his hand to stop Pete from saying whatever he'd been about to add. "This isn't helping. I don't mind having the chief here. It's fine. We have some questions about what was going on with your house before the fire so we can figure out what happened. It's an arson, tentatively." He smiled apologetically. "As I'm sure you saw in the press release. Our canine Brody found evidence of an accelerant."

"That doesn't make sense," Bernie said. "Arson, not the dog."

"That's what the questions are for."

"Okay."

"I'm told you've been renting the house out?"

"To Stephanie Woodbury. Since the beginning of August."

"Do you know if she was home last night?"

"No idea. I've been trying to reach her for days."

"Calling?"

"Texting." She braced for what was coming next.

"Why texting instead of calling?"

"I wanted our conversation to be documented."

"Why?" Michaud asked.

Libby was practically bouncing in his chair. Michaud shot him a glance. Bernie knew what it meant. *You'll get your chance.* She knew then, with a certainty she felt deep in her gut, that this was not a simple interview. It was the interrogation that she'd half-joked with Pete about. The ambush that she felt when she walked into the room.

Dawna and Sandy were on her side, she knew, but there was nothing they could do. Her father's voice came to her, a lesson pounded into all eight of his children before they could even understand the concept. *Most of the people I defend are there because they couldn't keep their mouths shut. No one has to talk to the police if they don't want to. Ever.*

Pete's thumb pressed harder, right where the muscle always balled into a hard rock. *He knew all along.* Her eyes met Sandy's again. He looked down at his hands. Dawna wouldn't look at her either. Libby, on the other hand, looked at her like he was about to take a bite out of a sirloin steak.

Bernie drew in her breath. Apologized mentally to her father and her three lawyer siblings and to the gods of common sense for all the life lessons that she was about to throw out the window. She knew what she *should* do. Knew it well. Would be screaming it at the TV if this were *Dateline* or something. But, like countless innocent people before her, when confronted with a law enforcement interrogation, she could no sooner shut it down and ask for a lawyer than she could pull off her shirt and show them her boobs. Anyway, she rationalized, it isn't bad. They're asking reasonable questions. Easy questions she could answer with no problem.

"Why did you want your conversations documented?" Michaud repeated.

"I've been trying to get her to move out for a month, and she wasn't," Bernie said. "I didn't want to take legal action, but if it got to that, I wanted documentation of what was said."

"Why did you want her to move out?"

"I wanted to move back in."

"Okay," Michaud said. Four sets of eyes moved from her to Pete. His thumb beat a tattoo against her back.

"I moved in with Pete in July because of his leg injury. To help," Bernie said, faster than she'd intended, her need to protect him taking over. She didn't want the other guys to think he couldn't keep his woman, or whatever macho guys thought about stuff like this. She didn't want them to hear the anxiety and insecurity, all those things that had absolutely nothing to do with anything except her. Certainly nothing to do with her house burning down. Nothing to do with Stephanie dying in the fire. She knew how cops could twist things around. *That's why you need a lawyer.* This time it was her sister Theresa saying it. The no-nonsense "when I say jump you say how high" presence Bernie had shared a bedroom with and, truth be told, feared, even as an adult. *Tell them that you want a lawyer.* She corralled her courage. *Not yet.*

"He's getting around better, so it was time to move home," Bernie said.

"You're in a relationship," Libby said. "Why would you move out? People usually don't move out once they've moved in if the relationship is good."

None of your fucking business you fat asshole.

Pete's thumb pressed, painfully, into the muscle that had become more knotted in the past minute. It could be to shut her up—he had to know what she was thinking. Or, maybe, because he'd been wondering the same thing for two months.

"Our relationship is fine. It's great," Bernie said. "In fact, we're engaged." She felt Pete shift in his seat. His thumb didn't ease up.

Dawna smiled. Sandy, too, though it was strained.

Michaud smiled. Nodded. "Congratulations."

Libby smirked.

"His house is small. Smaller than mine." She was rushing again. *Slow down.* "I have a lot of pets. It's easier to live in two houses until we figure out how it'll work." She was getting to that nervous point where she was babbling. She took a deep breath. Smiled. *Everything is fine! Normal!*

"The remains were found in the bedroom at the northwest corner of the house," Michaud said.

"That's my bedroom," Bernie said. "But Stephanie slept on the couch. She said the bedroom was too cold." Unlike this room, which was hot and close. Her head pounded. She was going to lose her ability to rationally answer questions soon, to think and process what they were saying. Then they'd pounce. She'd taken her pill that morning, but it wasn't enough.

Michaud waited a beat, then said, "You were at the house yesterday afternoon, correct? What were you doing there?"

Pete's thumb pressed. Hard. It stayed there.

"Looking for Stephanie. No one was there. Particularly in my bed."

"We'd like to look at your cellphone," Libby said. "We can get it back to you Monday or Tuesday."

"No thanks."

Libby looked surprised, like no one had refused to hand over their phone before. He raised his eyebrows, looked around the table—*can you guys believe this?*—then turned his glare on Bernie. "It would help if you'd cooperate with the investigation."

"Get a warrant." She tried to ignore the increasing pressure of Pete's thumb.

"It'd be easier if you'd cooperate," Libby said. "If you erase things, we can easily find what you erased. You might as well just give it to us now." He was mad. She didn't care.

"Are you charging me? Because if you're not, I'm leaving."

"We have more questions," Michaud said.

"Are you charging me?" She stood up. She didn't look at Pete, it would kill her resolve.

"Of course we're not charging you," Michaud said. "We do have more questions, though. If you could sit down—"

"And let us borrow your phone until Monday," Libby added.

Michaud shot him a look.

"I'll answer questions with my lawyer present," Bernie said. "I'm done for today."

"Bernie," Pete said. She turned. His eyes, that dark shade of green they got when he meant business, bored into hers.

"I'm done," she said to him.

"Novotny, talk some sense into her," Libby said. He was standing up now, too, his face red.

Pete didn't look at Libby. His eyes were still on Bernie. Unwavering.

Hers didn't waver either. The room was dead quiet. Even the pinging of the heating system had stopped.

Pete turned to Libby. "It's not up to me to tell her what to do. She's a grown woman who makes her own decisions."

"Don't be a pussy," Libby said.

"Wait a minute, there's no need for that," Michaud said before Pete could respond. "I'm not sure what's happening here. We're just trying to do an investigation. We don't need to act like it's the schoolyard."

He took a card out of his wallet. "Ms. O'Dea, why don't you contact me later today with a time when you and your attorney can sit down? I'd appreciate it."

"Fine." Bernie took the card and walked out of the room, feeling their eyes on her back.

****

Bernie heard the door open behind her. She knew it was Pete. She kept moving toward his office so she could get her coat, even though what she wanted to do was run from the building. He took her elbow as she got to his door.

"Bernie."

She shook him off, grabbed her coat and scarf, and pushed past him to the outer office, toward the reception area, and freedom. Now that she was out of the conference room, she felt uncertain and panicked. She was going to cry, which she didn't want to do in front of Pete. He'd see it as an admission she'd overreacted or been silly, which she hadn't done and hadn't been.

"Bernie," he said with more urgency, following her to the parking lot. "Wait a minute."

"No," she said, walking toward her car.

"Hang on. Wait. Bernie." He didn't sound mad, he was pleading.

She looked at him for the first time. He didn't look mad either.

"I'm glad to hear we're engaged." He smiled, a small one, but enough to reveal his dimple.

"That's your takeaway from that shit show?"

"It's the thing that struck me. Yeah."

He got points, as always, for gently dismantling the time bomb. "I never said we weren't," she said. "I've always said we had to get stuff straightened out first. Is this what you followed me out here—without a coat—to talk about?" The flashing time-temperature sign at the parking lot entrance said twenty-two degrees.

"No. But it seemed worth mentioning. Even though I know you only said it to shut down that line of questioning."

"I'm not going to apologize for asking for a lawyer and not giving them my phone. First of all, I need my phone for work, since that's how the staff contacts me. Second of all, as a journalist, I don't want them seeing stuff they shouldn't. It's not like my old flip phone. It has access to my email, internet history. All sorts of things."

"I know—"

"Third of all, do you really want them to see some of the stuff I've texted you?"

"They'd just be looking at things relevant to the fire and Stephanie."

"How can they figure out what those are unless they look at everything? Do you really want George Libby reading those?"

"Not particularly, but it has to happen if they're to get what they need for the investigation."

"Great." She moved to get into the car, angrily wiping away tears. *Dammit.*

"Wait." She hadn't zipped up her coat, and he put his arms inside and hugged her tight. His heart beat against her chest, strong and faithful, as always. "Here's what I came out here to say." He pulled her closer, whispered, his mouth against her ear, "It'll be okay. I love you."

"Right. Thanks." She pulled away, wiping her nose.

"Maybe we can play a little text roulette tonight when I get home. You know, take a look and see what comes up."

"That's probably the dorkiest sexy thing you've ever said. Or the sexiest dorky thing."

"I know you find my dorkiness sexy. I'm sure there's a text to back it up, too."

She laughed. "I love you too." She tried to sound breezy, like it *would* be okay. "Just so you know, I'm keeping my last name."

"I wouldn't expect anything else." He kissed her again, this time long and deep, his lips hot against hers in the cold air. "I'll call you when I know more about what's going on."

She started the car, watching him walk away, his limp more pronounced than it had been that morning. She wondered if the text roulette suggestion was really him trying to lighten the mood, or if it was him being a cop, a way to see what was on her phone. It's not that she didn't trust him. She knew he trusted her too. But he'd want to see what was coming so he could protect her. She loved him for it, but it chafed at her. She had his back, too. One thing that had poked into her fogged-up brain during the meeting, but now hit her fully, was that she wasn't the only one who was in their sights. She wasn't that worried about herself. She was like a Weeble, wobbling but never falling down. This whole thing was probably some tragic Stephanie screwup. But if it wasn't, who was it about? Her? Or Pete? She cranked the heat, then sat, thinking about her next move.

CHAPTER 3

PETE SAT AT HIS DESK, hoping that Libby and Michaud would leave soon. Ideally, without checking in on him or busting his butt about Bernie's recalcitrance. He didn't blame her for being cautious. He'd seen way too many people get railroaded when he was a Philadelphia detective—as a patrol cop, a narcotics investigator, then during those long years in homicide. No one blinked at using anything—whether it had to do with the case or not—against a suspect. He'd done it himself.

Dawna knocked on his door, then opened it. "Got a minute?"

"Why aren't you in the conference room?" he asked.

"I needed a break."

"Me too." Sharp pain pulsed from his thigh up his back and down to the bottom of his foot. He pulled the bottom drawer of his desk out and rested his leg on it. What he really wanted to do was lock the door and lie down on the couch with his leg elevated and an ice pack on his forehead.

"Can I get you some ibuprofen?" Dawna asked.

"Thanks, no. Is it that obvious?"

"Only to me because I know you too well. Don't worry, your secret is safe."

"So."

"Yeah."

"Fucking mess."

"I don't think the focus is going to be on Bernie for long," Dawna said. It was gentle, tentative. He knew what she was really saying.

"The implication being she should just lighten up and cooperate?"

Dawna shrugged. She never pushed Pete unless she thought he was seriously off track, but this was different. He knew what could happen. He'd seen it more than once, including with George Libby. He and the department had clashed in the past two years, and Libby was gunning for Pete. Bernie was going to get caught in the crossfire.

"I'm not her father. I don't own her. Bernie makes her own decisions, no matter how I may feel."

"This could be bad if she doesn't cooperate."

"It could be worse if she does."

"What are you saying?"

"She didn't do anything, obviously," Pete said. "But I've seen plenty of cases where some guy like Libby gets tunnel vision."

"We can make sure that doesn't happen."

Libby appeared in the open doorway. "Make sure what doesn't happen?"

"The vending machine running out of Cheez-Its," Pete said. He shifted his leg off the drawer and sat up straight.

Libby settled next to Dawna. "Your problem, Novotny, is that lies come way too easy."

"*That's* my problem?" Pete hated banter, if that's what this even was.

Libby turned to Dawna. "You're discussing the case with an involved party?"

"I'm talking to my boss."

"I need to talk to him privately. A fresh pot of coffee wouldn't hurt, though."

Dawna's black eyes flashed and her face turned red. She stood up. For a second Pete hoped she'd put her two hundred pounds of muscle to work and pummel Libby into the carpet. Of course, she'd never do anything like that, but the thought of it made him feel a little better.

"The supplies are on the table in the squad room," she said. "It's a Keurig. I'm sure you can figure it out."

Good for Dawna. Two years ago, she probably would've made the coffee, then apologized to Pete later for doing it.

"Close the door," Libby said after her, but she'd disappeared down the hall. He blew out an exaggerated sigh, and closed it himself.

"I don't know where to start," he said.

"Why start anywhere?"

"I give you credit, you have chutzpah," Libby said, pronouncing it chutts-pah. Pete fought the urge to correct him.

"What's the problem, George?"

"Well, *Pete*, for starters, your lead on this case should have autonomy since you're involved. She shouldn't have run to you for advice or instructions or a pat on the head."

"She didn't."

"Your involvement is a huge issue. The fact you're fucking a possible arsonist and murderer is a very good reason for you to go on administrative leave, which I plan to have a conversation with your boss about."

"Yes, Bernie and I are in a relationship. Probably not unlike the one you have with your wife."

Libby snorted. "I doubt—"

Pete knew Libby was trying to bait him. He wasn't going to bite. "Arson and murder have yet to be officially established. It was her house, but she wasn't living there at the time. I can vouch for her whereabouts."

"Of course you can," Libby said. "I just want to point out that in the past two years, every time the shit has hit the fan in this town, you two have been involved."

"We've been involved because she's editor of the only newspaper for miles and I'm the police chief and it's a small town."

"I can shut your girlfriend down in a heartbeat if you stand in the way of this investigation. Now, if you were as smart as you think you are, you'd tell her to get her head out of her fat little ass and cooperate."

"Don't talk about her like that."

Libby smirked.

Pete cursed himself for letting his anger show. "Say what you have to say that's relevant to the case, or get the hell out of here," he said.

"We're going to get a warrant for her cellphone, and the fact she didn't give it up means we'll be looking at it very, very closely. Innocent people don't need to lawyer up. I don't have to tell you. That doesn't help her either."

"She certainly has a right—"

"Shut up." Libby, face flushed, stood up. "I'm not here to argue with you. I'm here to tell you what's going down if you don't get your girlfriend in line."

Pete closed the door behind Libby, quietly, just to show he hadn't gotten to him, then turned the lock. He lay down on the couch, a pillow below his left leg. He'd planned to take some aspirin but was too pissed at Libby to remember it. Now he didn't have the energy. He took a deep breath and held it for four beats. Let it out slowly. Put his arm over his eyes. *We've been through worse.* He used it as his four-count as he breathed deep and let it out. Then again. As a mantra, it sucked. Still, it was a reminder. He made a silent promise to Bernie. *We'll get through this one too.*

****

It was New Year's Day, Bernie knew that, but she kept forgetting. How could people be taking it easy, watching football and parades on TV and eating great snacks, when her world was spinning into chaos? She needed people to not give a shit that it was the holiday. One person in particular.

A former client of her dad's once told her the best advice he ever got when he needed a lawyer was to hire "a pissed-off little Irishman." Bernie's dad and Kermit O'Neil didn't have much in common, but they did have that. She looked up Kermit's number. Easy-peasy with her new smartphone. Another reason not to give it to the cops until she had to.

He told her to come on over, and she drove the half mile from the police station to his place feeling better than she had in twenty-four hours.

He opened the door as she climbed the wide front steps of his restored Queen Anne. She stepped into the scents of cinnamon and a wood fire. They wrapped around her like a hug.

"Thanks for seeing me, especially since it's New Year's."

"I just want to warn you, I'm overloaded," he said as he led her through the reception area to his office. "Since Henry left, I'm the only lawyer in this part of the county doing criminal cases."

"The rural attorney shortage continues," Bernie said. She'd done an article on it. "Sorry about you and Henry. It must be hard to lose both your law partner and your life partner at the same time." Boy, she needed coffee. "Sorry, that came out much lamer than how I meant it."

"It's fine. When someone is so easily lured away by better weather, more money, and who knows what else, maybe we weren't meant to be. Anyway, I hear Miami Beach is awful this time of year."

"Yeah, who can take that humidity?"

Kermit sat down on a comfy-looking armchair. He nodded at an identical chair for Bernie. A box of tissues sat squarely in the middle of an antique-looking coffee table, polished to a retina-destroying shine. It matched the chairs. All of it was on a rug that even to her untrained eye looked expensive. She'd deal with how much his excellent counsel was going to cost her later. Assuming he took her case.

"Coffee or tea? Water?" Kermit asked.

"No, thanks." She *could* use a giant honking mug of coffee, but she didn't want to spill it all over Kermit's beautiful furnishings. She was that jittery.

He leaned back and opened a drawer in a credenza, took out a legal pad and pen and placed them on the knee of his pressed jeans. "Ready when you are."

She laid it all out—the fire, the body, her fraught relationship with Stephanie.

"The good news is, I don't see much of a case for them," he said. "They don't even know for sure it's arson, which is incredibly hard to prove. Sniffer dogs aren't evidence. They can't testify in court. The investigators still have to figure it out. Sure, maybe there was an accelerant. Maybe. There's still a lot of junk science around arson that's easy to shoot down. If there wasn't a body, I'd say you had nothing to worry about."

"I'm freaking out a little." Bernie tried to keep her voice from shaking. "A body. In my house. My house that burned down. I know it's Stephanie. I haven't been able to reach her. I mean, it's bad enough that it's her. But the fact we were at odds…"

Kermit slid the box of tissues toward her.

"Her car wasn't there, right? You said you hadn't been able to reach her since before Christmas. It may not be her. That's still bad, of course, but if it's someone else, this could be all about her and nothing to do with you."

"What, though? She overshared and bombarded me with texts and phone calls and popping into the office for months. It got so I'd hide in the back to avoid her. This was even after I asked her to move out, though it kind of got more hostile and less desperately friendly, you know? Shit, that's awful to say. Anyway, then, all of a sudden, there's nothing. Not a word. Not a peep." She balled the wet tissue up in her hand, the tears gone. It felt good to talk about it with someone who didn't have a stake in her emotional well-being. It made her feel less emotional.

"Game plan," Kermit said. "You should talk to the investigators, but with me there. Be careful about what you say about the case to anyone, even your family and friends. Maine's one big small town. Even more so Franklin County. You don't want things to get back to them they'll take the wrong way."

"Does that mean you're taking my case?"

"Yes."

"Oh, thank god."

"Being careful means with Pete too," Kermit said. "I like him, but he's a cop."

"On this he's my partner, not a cop. Anyway, he and George Libby hate each other, so it's not like they're going to share information. He's good at keeping a secret too. Much better than I am."

"Okay, just use your judgment." He seemed more resigned than convinced. "You guys have managed to maintain a Chinese wall between your jobs and relationship for, what? How long have you been together?"

"Since a year ago Thanksgiving, with that one month off in June, which—"

Kermit waved it off. "The point is, for well over a year you've been able to separate work and your relationship. Keep that up, only on steroids."

"This is different. It's not work, it's my life. It helps that he's a cop, especially a former homicide detective. His input matters. I've never been a suspect before."

"Just be careful."

"What about my phone?"

"Wait for the warrant. It will spell out exactly what they can retrieve and look at."

"But they'll see everything."

"That's something you'll have to live with. They can't use anything for their case that wasn't on the warrant or it can get thrown out."

"I don't want—"

"Don't tell me you've sent Pete vijayjay photos."

Bernie's face burned. "No. But some stuff is still embarrassing. And what about my job? Contacts? Folders and notes for stories? I don't want them snooping through private job-related things."

"We can try to negotiate a limit to what they can see, but they're going to argue they have to look at everything. Forensic cellphone investigation is just beginning to evolve, and face it, Bernie, we're not at the point yet where they can parse, for instance, what texts they see and what they don't."

"Great."

"Anything that can be used against you?"

"Probably." She was beginning to see the futility of it. She wouldn't be able to stop the tide of accusation. Of humiliation. "I didn't do anything. But you know me. My sense of humor..."

"I don't want to know until I have to. Don't delete anything from your phone. *Anything.* Even if you think it's incriminating. Or, conversely, even if you think it's perfectly innocent but don't want them to see it. They'll still find it and it'll make things worse."

****

Dawna was almost home, looking forward to eating lunch, maybe even catching a nap, when she got a text from George Libby: "See me in conf room ASAP."

She turned her Jeep around and headed back. She knew an order when she got one. Libby's unmarked cruiser was the only vehicle in the lot. The fact he'd waited until the building was empty to summon her didn't bode well. But she'd done two tours in Afghanistan and could handle whatever he had in mind.

"This should just take a couple of minutes," Libby said as she sat down. He seemed almost friendly, like their exchange in Pete's office never happened.

"No problem."

"I'm going to have to find a new center of operations," he said. "I don't trust this room, or the building for that matter."

Dawna nodded. The building was new but definitely wasn't soundproof.

"Normally, it's fine, working with local law enforcement, but this case is different."

Dawna nodded again.

"It's problematic that the homeowner in an arson and a likely murder is intimately involved with the police chief. Problematic is the best case."

Dawna had learned from Pete how to develop a good poker face, to not react. It was part of the job, and she was proud of her progress. It had never come in as handy as it did now. "They're the two most honest people I know, and I'd stake my career on the fact that they've done nothing criminal relating to this case."

Libby's poker face was working too. "Oh, you would, would you?"

Dawna held his gaze, as hard as it was, cocking her head in a way

32

that she hoped said she was listening but wasn't concerned.

"Your chief is soft." He tapped his temple with a large finger. "I'd be surprised if he still has a job by the time this is done. I'm surprised he still has one now, but that's local politics for you."

"What's the bottom line?" She was tired. She wanted to go home, where she could think and figure this out.

"The bottom line, my dear, is that you keep your mouth shut about this investigation as well as adjust your expectations as far as Novotny goes. You can help your career by being an asset and helping us solve this case. If you don't help, your career will go right down the shitter with your boss's."

"Understood." She stood up. "Is that it?"

"That's all for now. I'm glad we're on the same page."

She nodded, feeling Libby's eyes on her as she closed the door behind her. Crossing the parking lot to her car, she still felt them even though the conference room was on the other side of the building.

****

Bernie waved to Dawna as they passed on otherwise empty Main Street, but Dawna didn't notice. Bernie got it. She had a lot to deal with too. Bernie turned up School Street, marveling, as usual, how smoothly Pete's old car shifted down to third gear, unlike her old clutch-challenged rust bucket. It had lurched and whined up this hill thousands of times. She missed it. Now her house was gone too.

When she got to the top of the hill, she pulled over across the street from what was left of the place that had been home for nearly five years. Yellow crime scene tape flapped in the wind. It stretched from the pine tree marking the corner of her lot, across the gravel patch of driveway that barely accommodated two cars, past her little dooryard that was now a trampled mess of frozen mud, to the other side, where a steep wooded hill began. The message was clear: Stay out.

The bedroom end of the house was a black debris pile. The only things recognizable were pieces of the roof she'd paid thousands for months before lying in a heap in the snow. The kitchen and living room end was more intact, though partially collapsed. What wasn't black was scorched, the remaining vinyl siding drooping in thick melted ripples.

She sat there with the engine running, itching to get out, cross the yellow tape, and sort through the rubble to salvage some piece of her life. No one was there, no one would see.

She couldn't, though. Just like she couldn't delete the texts from her phone that she was dying to delete.

Not that I'm guilty of anything. She kept reminding herself of that. Still, she knew about consciousness of guilt. Investigators, and later a prosecutor, could use her actions, even innocent ones, as evidence that she was guilty. If you deleted texts or computer history, took this route instead of that one. Or slipped under the crime-scene tape to check out your house. Her father used to rail about it back in the day. Now her lawyer siblings did.

Even though it was Saturday—*New Year's Day, for chrissake*—she looked up her insurance agent's number online and left a voicemail. "My house burned down. Not a joke. I need to know how this works. I should tell you they're investigating it for arson. Sorry, I know that's a hassle. I know you won't get this until Monday, but wanted to let you know." They'd been nice in July when she wrecked her car. Got her as good a payout as possible. Maybe they'd be nice now too.

Her phone buzzed. A text from Pete. "Going Frm groc str Chck 4 dnnr. Bk by 2." It took her longer than normal to decipher it. *Damn his flip phone.* He was going to the grocery store in Farmington and Chuck, his dad, was coming for dinner and he'd be home by two.

She hadn't recovered from that morning's grilling and needed to process. She was relieved he'd be gone for a while. She turned at the end of her driveway, almost knocking down the crime scene tape, and headed for what she was going to have to learn to call home.

CHAPTER 4

BERNIE COLLAPSED ON the couch with her phone, scrolling through and answering the dozens of texts that had piled up. The ones expressing sympathy were the easiest. "Thanks!" The ones that asked questions about arson or the body from people who'd seen the news online were also easy. "No idea what happened. They don't know much. I can't talk about it."

The ones from her siblings were the worst. The lawyers and doctors demanded details, wanted to know how she felt, what was going on, whether Pete was helping or was a liability. She responded the same to all of them: "I'm fine. I don't know. I'll keep you posted." She ignored the Pete questions. Her responses resulted in more texts demanding more details as well as phone calls she didn't answer.

There was a voicemail from Fergus Kelley, which she deleted without listening to. He'd texted too: "Doing fire story whether you talk or not. Call me." She deleted it. *Franklin On Call* and its feckless reporter would just have to manage their story without her.

She returned calls from Carrie Beals and Guy Gagne, her staff at the *Watcher*. Both were sympathetic but, pros that they were, focused on coverage. Cover it like it's any other story, Bernie told Carrie. Ask questions, talk to people, get information, ignore that it's my house, though you have to say in the story it's the newspaper editor's house.

Bernie also gave her a quote: "It's distressing beyond words that someone has died in a fire in my house. I don't know who it is, but all my loved ones are accounted for. I haven't been able to reach my tenant, but there's no evidence that it's her. I can't comment further because it's an ongoing case. I wish I could."

It was a fine line, trying to say the right thing while knowing people would parse every word for hidden meaning or guilt. She felt a flicker of empathy for the people over the years she'd interviewed in tough situations.

Guy told Bernie if she wanted to take the week off to deal with things, he could put out the paper. She appreciated the gesture, but there was too much work for one person.

She also answered her mom's call.

"I called Pete, and he said you were home," her mother said.

"With a cellphone it doesn't matter where I am."

"If you don't pick up, it also doesn't matter where you are," her mother said.

Bernie brought her up to date—the light version—though apparently Pete had already told her most of it. She was happy when her mother moved on to family updates and the weather in Florida.

After Bernie hung up, she sat back on the couch, one cat on her lap and another behind her neck. The wind whipped snow from the lake against the big picture window and slider. Normally she'd love this. An afternoon off, the pellet fire burning, her dog's snout on her foot, the cats purring as they nestled against her. Not today. Her body felt like it was made of wet concrete, but her brain fought it. She wanted to get up, get out, and do something to fix things.

She scrolled through the photos she'd taken the afternoon before of the squalor Stephanie had created. Piles of garbage bags in the kitchen—Stephanie had an aversion to the dump. Belongings taken from Bernie's closets and basement—things she hadn't bothered to put in storage—inexplicably stacked on the kitchen counter and table. Half-filled dog bowls for Stephanie's two little terriers in every room, despite the fact Bernie had told her not to leave dog food out because it was a mouse buffet. And, of course, mouse droppings on the floor to back that up. One thing she wished she could've captured was the smell: cigarette smoke that Stephanie had tried to mask with the equally cloying, sickening odor of air freshener.

Would she delete those pictures if she could? She wasn't sure. Did they make her seem guilty? Did they make Stephanie seem guilty? Even if she deleted them, she'd texted them to her brothers Sal and Tommy, her friend Carol, her sister-in-law Robin—all with messages that had varying degrees of sarcasm and hyperbole. She'd also texted a couple to Pete with the message, "WTF. I want to cry."

She needed a change in mood. She found her favorite photo. Not really embarrassing, since the context was private. Even so, she cringed at the thought of George Libby scrolling to it with his sweaty, fat fingers. His knowing smirk.

Bernie had been annoyed Pete was considering buying a climate-killing gas guzzler when he started driving again. Then he texted her to come out and see his new car. She walked out of her office that sunny October day, and there he was in jeans and open flannel shirt with a T-shirt underneath, aviator sunglasses, hair ruffled by the breeze, leaning against his brand-new Inferno Red Dodge Charger. The combination of the car that she would've sworn was so not Pete, and him leaning against it like the biggest badass in town? She couldn't wait to finish work and get home.

Even his semiapologetic, wonky explanation for buying it, launched when she was barely in the door a couple of hours later—much earlier than she'd planned—didn't cool her down.

"I got the Charger because it's really good in the snow, with the 3.5-liter V-8 engine, 250 horsepower, and all-wheel drive, and the seat is comfortable with my leg. Since I have to use it on the job, it's the best for my needs."

"Best for *my* needs," she'd practically growled as she dragged him to the couch. He didn't understand why she was so worked up, but he'd been happy to oblige.

Libby and his buddies would probably think the photo was just a guy with his car. They wouldn't see what she did. Still, it was private, special to her. She didn't want to share it with them.

Until four months ago, she didn't even know, or care, what a V-8 engine was. But now she knew the sound of a 3.5-liter V-8 engine like Pavlov's dog knew his bell. A car crunched on the gravel and ice outside. It wasn't the Charger.

****

"I've been sent," Tommy said, giving her a hug. "How are you doing?"

"Great for someone whose house burned down in a possible arson with a dead body inside that's probably my tenant, who I was feuding with."

He followed her into the house. She felt a deep, hard clench in the pit of her stomach every time she said *dead body,* but was trying not to show it.

Dubby danced around his legs. Tommy bent down to pet him. "Oh right, I forgot you got a dog. Didn't you name it George W. Bush or something? Mom had a fit."

"His previous owner named him, and it was Dubya. As in dub-a-you. Get it? W. I got tired of explaining it. He's Dubby now. He doesn't seem to know the difference."

"Nice spot you have here," Tommy said. "Kind of small, but the appreciation will be good."

"It's Pete's."

"Nice renovation. I bet the fish don't fry in the kitchen, beans don't burn on the grill, am I right?"

"I don't even know what you're talking about."

"You do so. *The Jeffersons?*" He sang, "Movin' on up…"

"What are you implying?"

"You finally got a piece of the pie."

"I'm some gold digger?"

Tommy laughed. "If you are, you need to find a guy with a bigger house. No, this is just nicer than yours." He made the sign of the cross. "May it rest in peace."

"Want a beer?"

He looked at his watch. "New Year's Day, it's after noon, sure."

She got one for herself too. "What do you mean you've been sent?" She already knew what he meant, but she wanted to make him say it.

"A jigsaw puzzle. Fun." He took a gulp of beer as he scanned the scattered pieces and partially done puzzle, which took up most of the large coffee table.

"We do those," Bernie said. She didn't want to explain. "Use a coaster and put your beer down on that space at the edge, not on the puzzle. You know how I hate it when people say something is fun when what they mean is that they think it's weird or stupid."

"No, I don't know." He was poking through the pieces. "You have so many things you hate when people say, it's hard to keep track. I guess you've rethought your disdain for couples who say *we* for subjective things." In a falsetto, he said, "*We* don't like restaurants that serve bread, then explain how you're supposed to dip it in the olive oil. *We* don't like TV shows with time travel. Blah blah blah."

"How is doing a bad imitation of me doing something I hate representative of my point?"

He picked up a puzzle piece, tried it, then rejected it. "Your boyfriend really knows how to ramp up the excitement, doesn't he? Jigsaw puzzles. A house big enough for him and maybe one of your cats."

"You should be happy I'm with someone solid and honest who loves me for who I am."

"Yet ever since you met him, you've been in some deep shit or another. Did you notice how that shade of purple is only in this one part? Crap, that one doesn't fit." He sifted through the pieces. Bernie wanted to tell him to stop—the purple part was Pete's section—but she didn't want to take more crap.

"Why don't you get to the point of why you're here?"

Tommy was sorting pieces into piles of similar colors. "If you're going to do a puzzle this size, it needs to be better organized. I thought you were going to start dating Bobby Dolan. Didn't you guys go on a couple of dates recently?"

"More than a year ago. One dinner. It wasn't a date," Bernie said. "We're in the process of organizing the pieces. We just started. It's fifteen hundred pieces. It takes a while."

"We just started," Tommy said in the falsetto. Then in his normal voice, "Blubby Dolan. I don't blame you for not dating him. God, that guy would cry at the drop of a hat. Though he's a good lawyer and could come in handy right now." He picked up a piece. Put it back down. Chuckled. "Remember that time we were going to some Halloween party, and he was dressed in this Indian headdress and your friend had to sit on his lap because the car was so crowded? He got a boner and she freaked out. We started calling him Poker-Hardness, you know, like Pocahontas?"

They both laughed. "That's probably racist," Bernie said, just as Tommy said, "Can't say that stuff anymore."

They sat in silence for a few minutes, Bernie thanking whatever gods may exist that she was with Pete, not Bobby Dolan.

"Aha!" Tommy fit a piece into the puzzle, then lifted his beer in a salute to himself. "I *knew* that purple went there."

"Say whatever it is you've been sent to say. If part of it is to convince me to hire Bobby, you can forget it. I've already hired Kermit O'Neil."

"Okay." He turned his attention to her. "That's good about Kermit. You obviously need a lawyer. So, forget Bobby. Yes, they thought he'd be a good choice. Aside from that, the powers that be, namely the law firm O'Dea & O'Dea, have sent me here to lend my expertise."

"Don't you have work to do in Portland?" Tommy wasn't part of the family firm in Augusta, he was one of many partners in a firm in Maine's biggest city. "Why didn't Theresa and Pat consult me about this? When I talked to Mom a little while ago, she didn't mention anything."

"Mom doesn't know. Theresa and Pat thought it would be a good fit for me, since I'm taking some time off." He raised his beer bottle to her. "Someone needs to look after our troubled sister."

"I just said I already have a lawyer."

"Kermit's great, but I have arson defense expertise."

"The bigger issue is that someone's dead. Just so you know, I didn't do anything. I didn't commit arson. I didn't kill anyone."

Tommy looked serious for the first time since he arrived. "I know you didn't. Of course you didn't. Jesus. But we decided—"

"You, Theresa, and Pat—"

"Let me finish, for chrissake. What do you think? Something like this happens and we're not going to talk about it? You need family support. Here, on site. Sal's not any help, and not only because he's a part-time art professor trying to open a restaurant and not a lawyer. I'm sure his puppy-dog devotion to you is ego-boosting, but in practical terms, he has nothing to offer. You've gone through a lot of weird shit and acted like it's business as usual. Well, this isn't. It's serious. We're not going to have it."

"*We're* not going to have it? You three decided?" She stood up, hands on hips, glaring at him. "How about asking *me*? I'm used to getting this condescending shit from Theresa and Pat, but I outrank you—"

"Calm down. Sit down and listen."

"Sit down? *You* sit down." She knew it didn't make sense, since he was already sitting, but she was too pissed off to care. "The three of you can go fuck yourselves. I have a lawyer. I didn't do anything wrong. It's going to be fine without your overbearing, paternalistic so-called help."

"Hey, what's going on?"

Bernie hadn't heard the siren call of the V-8 engine or Pete opening the door. He put two grocery bags on the counter, then hung up his coat and took off his boots as Bernie glared at Tommy, who smiled at her, then stood up as Pete walked over.

"Good to see you, Tom," Pete said.

"You too."

They shook hands. Bernie watched the manly exchange with annoyance.

Pete turned to Bernie. In his uniform, with that calm, I'm-in-charge look, she had an irrational flash that he was there on official business, to sort out the sibling fight that could at any second explode into physical violence. Except, of course, it wouldn't. Words were the O'Dea family's weapons, and they prided themselves on using them with deadly precision. He was smiling at her, cheeks ruddy from the cold and wind. Loving partner, not cop.

"What's up?" he asked.

"Tommy's here to help me with any legal issues that may crop up. Against my will."

"Legal issues may crop up against your will?" Pete's eyes danced.

"Him being here." She gave Pete a fierce cut-the-shit glare. He should be on her side, not teasing her.

"Glad you can help," he said to Tommy. "I think that any legal issues for Bernie will blow over pretty quickly. She hasn't done anything wrong."

"That's good to hear, *Chief,*" Tommy said. "But as we both know, jails are full of people who haven't done anything wrong, but are the victims of tunnel vision and confirmation bias."

Pete's smile didn't waver. "Not *full of,* but I understand your point. Just so you know, I have Bernie's back. My love for her supersedes any loyalty to law enforcement or false belief in the superhuman powers of investigators." He turned to Bernie, kissing her quickly on the lips. "I'm going to change, then I'll get dinner started." To Tommy, "You're staying? My dad's coming over, but there's more than enough."

"Sure. Your dad?"

"He moved here from Wisconsin last summer," Pete said as he disappeared around the partition.

Tommy rolled his eyes at Bernie and said, sotto voce, high and nasal, "My love for your sister supersedes my head being up my ass."

"Don't be an asshole or you can leave," Bernie said at normal volume. She knew Pete had likely heard him. Unlike an O'Dea, though, he wouldn't feel compelled to one-up the snark.

"Want another beer?" she asked Tommy. She sure did.

"I picked up some more." Pete, unseen, sounded as though he were right next to them. "It's still in the car, along with seltzer for Chuck."

"I'll get it," Tommy said.

When the door closed behind Tommy, Bernie went around the partition. "Don't worry, he's not staying with us. In fact, I'm trying to convince him to go home to Portland ASAP."

"I'm not worried," Pete pulled on jeans. The ugly scar on his swollen, discolored thigh still made her wince more than six months after his accident. "Why do you want him to go? Is it such a bad thing for you to have family support on hand?"

"I have you." She gave him a quick peck on the lips as Tommy came back in.

"Nice car," Tommy said. "A little *Starsky and Hutch*, though, isn't it?"

"They drove a Ford Gran Torino," Bernie said. "Duh."

Pete, who'd followed her into the kitchen, handed a beer to each of the siblings, then opened one for himself. It felt to Bernie like a peace offering. She patted him on the butt in approval, making sure Tommy didn't see. She didn't want to give him any more ammunition by engaging in a PDA, which Tommy knew she disdained. Her feelings for Pete overrode any control she had over things like that—also something Tommy would use against her.

"I needed something that was good in the snow that also had some power, since I have to use it on the job," Pete said.

"You don't have to explain," Bernie said. "It meets our needs." She gave him another stealth pat on the butt, adding a squeeze for good measure.

"We should talk about what's going on," Tommy said.

"That's up to Bernie." Pete squeezed Bernie's hand, then started putting away the groceries.

"If she's going to be charged with something, she needs as much help as she can get. We all need to pitch in."

"My lawyer's the best arbiter of that." Bernie's cellphone vibrated in her pocket. "Speaking of which, it's him."

She looked up from the screen. Her brother and Pete were both looking at her expectantly.

"I'm going to take this outside." She grabbed her coat and went out into the cold.

****

Pete unwrapped a ham and put it in a roasting pan as he waited for Tommy to say whatever it was he was dying to say with Bernie out of earshot. Pete had only recently met him, but it wasn't hard to figure out he liked to take charge.

"Hope you like ham," he said. "It's going to be a couple hours." He sat down in the easy chair across from the couch. "We'll have roast potatoes and asparagus too."

"Sounds good." Tommy gave Pete a long look. "How are you doing?"

"Pretty good," Pete said with a smile he hoped looked genuine. Bernie's family obviously knew about his leg. He wasn't sure how much they knew about his PTSD. He hoped not much. He was going to assume Tommy was asking about his leg.

"Good. Since my sister's welfare is a top priority, your welfare matters to me. You need to be at the top of your game."

Pete wasn't sure if Tommy was being sarcastic. The guy was an uncanny copy of his sister—despite the blue eyes, slightly rounder physique and halo of salt-and-pepper curls around a shining bald spot—but unlike her, he had a good poker face.

"Thanks. I am," Pete said.

Tommy saluted Pete with his beer bottle. "Don't worry, I don't underestimate you."

"I'm not worried."

"We both want to make sure Bernie comes out of this okay," Tommy said.

"Definitely."

"We just have to figure out the best approach, since she's going to fight us every step of the way."

Loyalty to Bernie collided with agreement. The night before, as the fire roared, he'd started wondering how to walk the fine line between loving her, supporting her, allowing her to make decisions about her life, while also keeping her on a straight line, rerouting her tendency to veer into unexpected, dangerous territory, and leading her to safety.

Tommy watched him, steady, assessing. Like he wondered if Pete was up to the task.

"Bernie isn't stupid," Pete said. "If she feels like she's being handled, she's going to react poorly. Then we have a disaster on our hands."

"Don't I know it."

"That said," Pete continued, "while you and I are experts in criminal conduct and investigation, we can't discount the fact that Bernie has a unique mind, a way of thinking that can leave us in the dirt. If we don't let her figure it out and do things her way, we could miss something important. I'd advise against a heavy-handed approach in favor of more of a firm guiding hand. One she doesn't realize is there."

Tommy took a long swig of beer. "You know we're Irish twins, right?"

"I know you're close in age."

"Right. Irish twins—that must be pejorative now—two kids born within less than twelve months. In our case, ten months."

Pete knew what it meant. Bernie's annoyance at being older than Tommy, but his classmate throughout grade school and high school still burned strong. He was as talkative as she was, as full of ideas and the desire to share them, but he charmed teachers while she annoyed them. At least that was her version.

"What does being Irish twins have to do with anything?"

"I think I know her better than anyone on this planet."

Pete was confident that no one knew Bernie the way he did. It went way beyond the intimacy of a relationship. When you opened yourself raw to someone, the way he'd had to do the past six months, you truly found out who the person on the receiving end was. He knew her right down to her rock-solid, true-blue soul. Her smart-ass brother, more caught up in his life than anything Bernie was up to, didn't hold a candle.

"So you think."

His steel-cold cop voice did its job. Tommy nodded. "Gotcha. Maybe we should just agree to put the whole who-knows-Bernie-best thing aside in the interest of making sure she doesn't end up in a pile of steaming shit."

"I'm not sure that the two of us—"

"You've known her for what? Two years? In that time, I can't see how you've done much to keep her out of shit. In fact—"

The door opened with a blast of icy air as Bernie came back in.

"We'll finish this later," Pete said quietly. Tommy nodded. They turned to Bernie, smiling.

Nothing to see here.

****

"Zip up your pants fellas, the dick-waving contest is over, and I don't give a shit who thinks he won. Which I'm sure is each of you."

Bernie knew exactly what had gone on while she'd been shivering in her car talking to Kermit. She'd cursed the fact she hadn't brought her keys, but she didn't want to go back in and walk in on the verbal carnage.

"That'd be a little sick, your brother and your boyfriend comparing dicks," Tommy said.

"You'd think. Yet I'm 100 percent positive that's exactly what was happening." The fact that Pete put his hand on her thigh and squeezed as she sat down next to him, showing Tommy he was the alpha male with the most influence over her, confirmed her suspicions.

"What did Kermit say?" Pete asked.

"He said that my brother and my boyfriend could screw everything up if they engage in a death match over who will get to control my every thought and action because they care more about who has the biggest dick than they do about me going to prison."

"How prescient of him," Tommy said. "And how odd that he words things just the way you do."

Pete laughed. He squeezed Bernie's thigh again.

This was going to be a nightmare with these two. "Okay, he didn't say that in so many words. He *did* say that a lot of people would weigh in on what I should and shouldn't do, but since I retained him, I should listen to him. He and I will make the decisions."

"I tell my clients that too." Tommy had been sorting through the puzzle pieces but looked up to make sure she saw the eye roll that accompanied his statement.

"So it counts when you tell your clients but doesn't count when my attorney tells me the same thing?" Pete's hand was back on her thigh, this time as a calming signal. She tried not to let it annoy her.

"What did he say about next steps?" Pete asked, taking his hand off her thigh and picking a puzzle piece out of the pile. He put his forearms on his thighs, piece in one hand, beer bottle in the other, staring at the puzzle. She knew that he was paying attention to her. That was one of the points of the puzzle, according to his therapist. A way to engage part of the brain so the discussion part could open up more freely. Bernie didn't totally get it, but they were on their third puzzle, and it seemed to work.

"I have a meeting with Kermit at nine, then we're meeting with the fire investigator at ten," she said.

Two heads swiveled from the puzzle to her. Two sets of eyes—one blue and round, one green crescent moons—both intense and focused on hers. Bernie wished she didn't have to say what was coming next. She didn't want to give them the satisfaction.

"Kermit said that he'd welcome you guys at the 9 a.m. meeting." They both, as she knew they would, looked at each other. She half expected them to high-five. "But with the fire investigator it'll just be Kermit and me."

She'd argued with Kermit after he'd suggested including them. "They're going to try to take over. They're going to be in a constant male ego war with each other, and it's going to distract from the task at hand," she'd said. Kermit said it was better to let them in. He could more easily control them, and they could actually help.

"We should be in with the fire marshal too," Tommy said. "As members of your legal team."

"Did I say you're members of my legal team?"

"If we're going to be at your meeting with Kermit, we are," he said.

Kermit told her not to stress herself out by arguing with them—he'd handle it. Easier said than done. As calmly as she could, she said, "The fire investigator, Ed Michaud, is going to be alone. Having three guys beating their chests at him won't help."

"I wouldn't say beating our chests," Pete said. "At least not me. When do I ever beat my chest?"

"If you guys love me as you claim to"—she glared, first at Pete, then Tommy—"you need to make decisions based on what's best for me and not your male egos."

"I don't think ego—" Pete said.

"Case closed," Bernie said.

CHAPTER 5

KERMIT'S CONFERENCE ROOM, in the former dining room of his house, plusher and fancier than Bernie's taste, was still soothing, which she needed badly at this moment. She wished the guys would get over it and start focusing on how to tackle whatever was going to happen to her so she could eventually get back to normal life. Right now, that seemed like it was never going to happen. Kermit, at least, was winning what had turned into a three-way dick-waving contest.

"I've been trying to make the point that Pete can't help because he's the police chief," Tommy said. "Even if he wasn't, he hasn't passed the Maine bar. I mean, you got your night school law degree how many years ago?"

"I'm also a graduate of the FBI National Academy at Quantico," Pete said. "That alone—"

"Guys," Bernie said. "The clock is ticking. Can we talk about the fire investigation meeting?"

"Good point," Kermit said. "As I'm sure you know, Bernie, arson is the most serious property crime you can commit in Maine. It's considered the second most serious crime in the state after murder. One good thing is that it's hard to prove beyond a reasonable doubt."

"I didn't set my house on fire."

"I know. But we have to approach it from the viewpoint of the case they may make, which I would have to defend you against. Whether you did it is beside the point. You know that."

"Hear, hear," Tommy said.

Kermit continued. "One of the biggest factors is culpability—did you, as an arsonist, want the outcome that resulted, namely the destruction of your home?"

"If I didn't set the fire, then obviously not."

"They're going to try to prove culpability if they charge you. That means they need to determine motive. I don't usually ask clients for a lot of details until I get the case from the DA, but in the interest of nipping things in the bud today, why don't you give me your version of events?"

"I have no clue what happened," Bernie said.

"That's fine. In fact, if the fire marshal or state police ask, that's your answer. Don't let them draw you into speculating. Fortunately, I'll be sitting there to shut that down, but in general, keep it in mind."

Bernie knew that intellectually. She also knew how easy it would be to be drawn in. She nodded.

"Tell me about your tenant, your living situation, and what you did Friday afternoon."

Bernie tried to mentally sort what could be a long, tangled story into a quick synopsis. "When Pete hurt his leg last summer, I moved in to help him. I still had to pay my mortgage, so I had to find a tenant."

"He was charging you rent even though you'd moved in to help him?" Tommy said.

"Hold on," Pete said.

"I'm playing devil's advocate," Tommy said. "This is what the fire marshal would ask. As a cop, you should know that."

Pete was close enough to Bernie that they were almost touching. She could feel him thrum with tension.

"He insisted on me *not* paying for anything," she said. "I didn't agree. It made me feel, not compromised, but more dependent than I wanted." She'd had trouble explaining it to Pete. Explaining it to anyone else while not embarrassing Pete in the process felt impossible. She'd seen that at the meeting the day before. "I put $600 a month into a savings account. I figured if there was an issue, I'd give it to him." She'd never told Pete this.

"What kind of issue? In what scenario would I suddenly demand money from you?" Pete asked.

Bernie's cheeks burned. "It just felt important to do. I also didn't like the idea of my house being empty. Even though I was right here in town. It felt wasteful."

"You're leaving out an important point." Pete's voice was strained. She'd annoyed him. "You hadn't even fully decided to rent your house out when Stephanie contacted the paper to put an ad in because she was having trouble finding a long-term rental that would take her dogs. That's what tipped the decision."

"Is this true?" Tommy asked.

"Of course it's true," Bernie said. "Does it matter?"

"Don't bite my head off," Tommy said. "I'm just thinking that if this same scenario played out with the cops, it wouldn't go over well. Totally forgetting an obvious and explainable point, then having your cop boyfriend jump in with a logical explanation you should've made in the first place."

"Why don't you let Kermit do the talking?" Pete said.

"I'm just doing what any good lawyer would do."

Kermit sighed. Loudly. "I hate to sound like a schoolmarm, but if you two can't behave, you're going to have to wait outside. I really need to have this discussion with Bernie. I don't have time to referee your squabbles."

"Sorry," they both said.

Kermit looked at his watch, pointedly. "Bernie, continue. This time without interruption. Please tell me about your tenant."

"Stephanie had a contract to work for Sturgis, the fabrication company that just built that plant. She'd been in the military, but recently had been a home health aide in Arkansas. She looked for rentals all over Franklin County, but no dice. She called the paper to take out a classified ad. Annette had heard me talking about maybe renting out my house, so she told me."

"The term of the lease?" Kermit looked up from taking notes.

"Month to month. I didn't know how long I'd be at Pete's, but a few months at least. She said she wanted to find something more permanent. We agreed to monthly, and I drew up a lease—"

"I drew up a lease," Tommy said. "Remember?"

"Tommy drew up the lease," Bernie said. "If she wanted to move out, or I wanted to move back in, we'd give the other person thirty days' notice. I left a full tank of heating oil, and she had to fill it before she left. What else?" Bernie tried to think of the provisions. It seemed so simple at the time. She should've known better. "Since the electric was in my name, I added $50 a month to the rent for that, and if she went over, she had to pay me the difference. A month's rent as security deposit. No smoking in the house."

"How much did you charge her?"

"My mortgage is $578, so I charged her $625. That's the rent, plus the electric."

"So, you actually were only charging her $47 for electric," Kermit said.

"Does that matter?"

"Probably not. It shows you were a little forgiving. That can work in your favor if it comes to circumstantial elements. How about insurance coverage?"

"We ended up increasing the replacement amount. I'd put a new roof on in July and added more insulation. Then, when I knew someone else would be living there, I did some fixing up so I'd feel okay about charging enough to cover my mortgage. I replaced the windows, front door, stove, washer and dryer."

"That sounds expensive."

"I took out a home equity loan last spring to help match that grant for the newspaper building, and there was enough left for the repairs. I was going to do the roof and windows anyway." Now she would be paying it back for a house that no longer existed. It was a crushing thought.

"It increased the value, even with the market depressed?"

"Yes." Bernie hadn't thought about any of this. "Is it a problem?"

"Probably not, but it's not unheard of for people with debt to burn down their property for the payout. I'm not saying you did, but the cops might."

"That's nuts. I talked to my insurance agent yesterday—she called me back even though it was New Year's Day. I have a replacement policy, which means they pay if I rebuild. It goes directly to the contractor. I don't get some big check. I could've gotten an actual cash value policy, which would've meant they'd hand me a check when it's settled, but with the way the market is, I didn't. It's all moot since I get nothing until the investigation is done."

"I understand all that," Kermit said.

"If you rebuild—which I'm sure the bank holding your mortgage is anxious for you to do—you'll end up with a ton more equity than you had before," Tommy said. "You don't have to build a shit shack like what you had. Your coverage will pay for something nicer."

"Thanks for the mansplanation," Bernie said. "My agent already told me that. The insurance company wants to send an adjuster over but can't as long as it's a crime scene."

"You've decided to rebuild?" Pete asked.

Kermit rapped his pen on the table. "People. Back to your tenant. How were things with her?"

"Okay at first, but issues cropped up. She burned through heating oil and pellets for the stove like there was no tomorrow. I didn't put in a provision for pellets since I bought my usual two tons in July—they come in forty-pound bags—so I figured that was all set. She wanted me to refill the oil tank in November, and I was like, 'No, that's on you, since it's different from electric. You can call any oil company and pay right then for it.' That annoyed her. She said my house was too cold and drafty. I guess it is, but this is Franklin County, Maine, and it is what it is. I guess living in Arkansas made her not used to cold. In August, she complained there was no air conditioning. I'm like there *is* AC, it's called opening the windows. She's originally from New Jersey, so you'd think she'd have some concept of seasons."

Bernie paused to think. "She texted me all the time and showed up at the office, not just with questions and complaints, but also to gripe about the neighbors, the crappy hours the store keeps. It almost began to feel harassing, but not the kind of harassment you officially complain about, you know? Just like, geez, leave me alone, I have to work for a living."

"Wasn't she at work during the day?"

"She worked second shift. Three to midnight."

"What did she do?"

"Some technical thing. Something that needed security clearance, because they do defense contracts. They seek out military people because it's easier as far as clearance goes. That's what she told me. She couldn't talk much about it, which was fine with me."

"Did you say anything to her about the harassment?"

"Not really. I felt bad. She'd moved here from 2,000 miles away and didn't know anyone. I felt like she had anxiety and other issues. How do you tell someone to get out of your hair without hurting their feelings?"

"I said something," Pete said.

"What?" Bernie said. Not as in, *What did you say?* but rather, *What the hell are you talking about?*

"She showed up at our place Thanksgiving weekend. You were out shopping with Angie."

"That's my sister in Skowhegan," Bernie said to Kermit.

"Stephanie came by wanting to talk to you," Pete said. "When I told her you weren't there, she said she'd wait. I asked her what it was about, and she wouldn't say. I told her you wouldn't be home for hours, and she got irrationally pissed off. Accused me of turning you against her, which was bizarre. Then she went off on what a shitty house you have—her words, not mine—how you won't take care of issues with the house, you're overcharging her rent, you're a bad landlord, all sorts of stuff. At that point, you'd said you wanted to only communicate with her by text, so I told her to text you. I also told her what she really needed to do was find a new place to live and get started on moving out, since you'd given her notice almost a month before and wanted her out by December 1."

"Why didn't you tell me?" Bernie asked.

"You were already worked up about her not making any move to leave. I didn't want to add to it. Your anxiety was like this." He held his hand about a foot above Bernie's head. "Also, the fact she showed up there was inappropriate. I told her if she ever trespassed on my property again, I'd arrest her. I didn't want you to be upset. More upset, that is."

"Great."

"Wait a minute," Kermit said. "When did you give her notice?"

"At the end of October. Pete could drive again. He'd recovered enough from his second surgery that he didn't need to stay off his leg. It wasn't necessary for me to live there anymore. I went to the house when I knew she was there, because I wanted to be sure she got it, and handed her a letter saying that I was moving back in on December 1. That gave her more than the thirty days we'd agreed to. It was October 27. I remember because Pete had a doctor appointment the day before and was told he was doing well. It seemed like the time was right."

Pete tensed next to her. Tommy watched them with interest. Bernie gave him a look. *What's your problem? Shut the fuck up.* He shrugged.

"What next?" Kermit asked.

"She seemed stunned. I reminded her of our agreement. I hadn't been inside since early August, a little after she moved in—I went to check the window installation and the new appliances, make sure they were all set. After that I wanted to respect her space. In October, I didn't go in, but I could see from the door, even though she stood in the opening and didn't open it far, that it was a mess. I could smell cigarette smoke. Not fresh, like she was holding a cigarette, but that stale, gross smell. I didn't say anything, but I was thinking 'there goes your security deposit.' I got a long, rambling voicemail from her the next day, crying and saying she didn't have anywhere to go and blah blah blah and didn't have the money to put down a deposit on another place. I felt bad for her, so I told her she could use the security deposit as November rent as long as she was out by the end of the month. I decided to suck up the cost of cleaning and getting rid of the smoke smell and everything. I just wanted her out and to get my house back."

"That was a mistake, the security deposit," Tommy said.

"Thanks for your awesome input," Bernie said. "Like I said, I was doing what I thought was necessary to get her out. The day before Thanksgiving, I texted to ask if she was going to move out over the weekend or if she needed until November 30, which was a Tuesday. I wasn't trying to push her, it's just that most people move on a weekend, especially a long one, right? She texted back she'd need as much time as she could, because she was cleaning. Then, I guess, a few days later, she visited Pete's." Bernie glared at him. His eyes met hers, his expression unreadable.

"To make a long story short—"

"Too late," Tommy said.

"To make a long story short," she repeated, with emphasis, "she did not move out November 30. Or December 1. She kept asking for extensions. I ended up doing a day-to-day thing, charging her twenty dollars a day—basically a per diem of the rent—but with a verbal agreement that she'd leave as soon as she could make arrangements. She was going to leave me the lump sum when she left as well as what she owed for heating oil."

"I told you that wasn't going to work," Tommy said.

"She stopped answering my texts for the most part, but I know she was there because I drove by every day and her car was there, usually cleared of snow, lights in the windows, all that." It had been soul-crushing, driving by her house, the windows bright, wishing she could go in, collapse on the couch, sleep in her own bed. "She texted about a week before Christmas, with a photo of the bathroom and the comment 'Look how clean!' No response to my questions or anything. The last time I texted her was Christmas Eve. We were at our family party at my brother and sister-in-law's in Winthrop. She never responded. I wanted to give her space for the holiday. I didn't drive by to see if anything was going on. I texted her again the day after

Christmas. Nothing. I was pretty pissed off by then. I left a voicemail, figuring her not responding to texts was a way to get me to engage differently. She didn't call back. Both in the voicemail and final few texts, I threatened legal action. Finally, New Year's Eve, I went over. I planned to record the conversation on my phone."

"She didn't tell me she was going over there," Pete said to Kermit.

"No, I didn't. You would have insisted on coming with me, and I didn't want her to feel ganged up on. Now that I know about how pissy you were on Thanksgiving weekend, I'm glad I didn't."

Tommy jumped in. "It probably would've helped to have Pete there. It would've made her feel like this was serious."

"What? Maybe wear his uniform and gun too? Right."

"That's not what I meant."

"Even if he were in his pajamas, it would've made her feel threatened and escalated the problem." It figured Tommy would finally team up with Pete when the topic was how she'd fucked up. "It's a moot point, since she wasn't there."

"What happened next?" Kermit asked, looking at his watch.

"When I got there Friday, her car was gone. She obviously wasn't home. No barking dogs, even, which is something the neighbors had complained about a lot. I figured she took off when I sent the text to avoid me. She said she was estranged from her family, so it's not like she was going anywhere for the holidays. She even told me a couple months before she'd already signed up to work the holidays because it paid double time."

"Back to you going to the house New Year's Eve," Kermit said.

"I let myself in. It was a mess. It reeked of cigarette smoke and dog piss. It was too warm—the thermostat was up to seventy-two. When I lived there, I kept it on sixty-two so I wouldn't waste oil. When the pellet stove was going, which it wasn't that day, it warmed most of the house up pretty good, though not the bedroom—"

"What next?" Kermit asked.

"I checked the oil, and the tank was almost empty, which means she never called for a delivery. I checked all the rooms. No one else was there. I'm absolutely positive. My bedroom was like I'd left it, including the same linens and quilt on the bed, but there was dog food and piss on the floor. The guest room was a mess. Waist-high in crap. She'd apparently gone through my stuff. Boxes and stuff I'd stored in the closet were piled on the bed and floor. I guess I should add that since she arrived with no furniture and few belongings, she said she didn't care if I left my stuff there. I'd moved some things to self-storage—anything valuable and stuff I didn't want anyone snooping through."

"What next?"

"There were weeks' worth of garbage bags, full, on the kitchen floor. I already heard she'd never picked up a dump pass, but when I asked her about it months ago, she said she'd found a dumpster at work she could use."

"You must've been mad," Kermit said.

"Are you kidding me? Livid." The horror and despair Bernie had felt when she'd walked into her house two days before were almost as traumatic as the fire. She'd been so anxious to get back in, picturing the cozy nest, all hers. Stephanie had laid it all to waste.

Pete took her hand where it rested on the table. When she'd texted him as she stood amidst the carnage, he'd called her immediately and hadn't said a word about her going over there, even though he'd warned her not to engage with Stephanie on her own. He just listened to her cry, told her he was sorry. That he loved her. "I'll get home as soon as I can, and we'll talk about it," he'd said. She couldn't tell him that she *was* home. Home but homeless. That's how she'd felt.

"What next?" Kermit asked.

"I texted my brother Sal, because he knew I was going over and wanted to know how it went."

"Sal knew you were going over but not me?" Pete said.

Bernie ignored him. "I texted Tommy. I texted my friend Carol to vent. Texted my sister-in-law Robin, who I'd complained to a lot about Stephanie. I texted Stephanie, of course. I told her it didn't look like she was ready to move out and that she needed to text me back ASAP. I said I was going to pursue a legal remedy."

"Then?"

Bernie shrugged. "I went to Pete's. No, wait. I stopped at the store to get some stuff for the night, since it was New Year's Eve. I chatted with Walt, asked him if he'd seen Stephanie. He hadn't in a while, but couldn't remember how long. The store was busy, so we didn't talk long. I got home a little before five."

"Okay."

"That's it?"

"Yeah, we'll see what the fire investigator has to say, then go from there."

CHAPTER 6

AS PETE PREPARED a cup of coffee for Tommy, he tried to figure out the best approach to get him on his side. Being at odds wasn't good for Bernie or her case. It also made him feel like an asshole.

"Boy was Bernie pissed when she saw that cop's car in the parking lot," Tommy said as Pete handed him his coffee. He was sitting in front of Pete's desk, his feet up on the other chair.

"I wasn't surprised to see Libby," Pete said, sitting on the couch. "He isn't going to let Ed Michaud handle the interview on his own. Let's hope Kermit keeps it from being a shit show."

"He just needs to keep Bernie from saying too much. A lot of the things she told us they can twist around and make her feel like she's a suspect. We don't even know for sure there's a crime."

Pete shifted to sitting sideways and put a pillow under his leg.

"We don't, right?" Tommy asked.

"I know as much as you do."

"Sure."

"What's your problem with me?"

"I'm looking out for my sister."

"So am I."

"Like I said yesterday, ever since she's known you, there've been problems."

"I haven't caused them."

"Wow. You're saying it's all her fault?"

"Of course not."

"You come across like Mr. Perfect. You sure have the women in the family fooled. I saw how you worked them at Christmas, helping the girls with the dishes. They have that damn 'Sexy Sheriff' video of yours on speed dial. I can see through it all, though."

"I helped your sisters with the dishes because that's how my mother raised me. As far as that video, I was just singing karaoke to Bernie on her birthday. I didn't know anyone was filming. I have no idea who put it on YouTube. I don't even know why I'm arguing with you. None of this will help Bernie."

"Yeah, why *are* you arguing? If you're so intent on looking out for my sister, you're doing a shitty job."

"I can't win with you, can I? If that's how you argue in court, then remind me never to hire you."

"Good one. I'm *so* offended."

"Can we get along? The only reason I care what you think is because Bernie loves you and I'm part of your family now."

"You are? Sounds to me like she was ready to run in the other direction until her house burned down. It takes more than singing a cheesy song to keep a woman."

"Thanks for the relationship advice. Oh wait, you're single, right? 'Between girlfriends' is how Bernie puts it. I don't get how a guy with five sisters is so clueless." Pete desperately wanted to end the stupidity, but it had sucked him in. He waited for Tommy's next jab, ready to counterpunch. Instead, Tommy cracked a big smile.

"Touché, my man. Nice to see that Mr. Perfect can be as petty as any O'Dea."

"Does that mean we're done acting like twelve-year-olds?"

"Oh no, we're just starting. I haven't even touched on you working for years for the most corrupt homicide department in the country. I can't believe she doesn't have an issue with that. How many innocent guys did you send to death row? Philly had like the third highest death row population in the country, right? Half of those guys were railroaded into a conviction. She has to have mentioned it. It's one of her big topics. Not just Philly, but in general."

"We haven't discussed it."

"I find that hard to believe."

"Why don't we spend our energy helping Bernie? After that, if you want to go all in, I'll meet you anywhere, anytime, and wipe that condescending smirk right off your face."

"This from the guy lying down with his leg up."

"I only need one leg to kick your ass." His leg pulsed with pain. He took a deep breath. Held it.

"I guess you haven't heard the one about the one-legged man in the ass-kicking contest," Tommy said.

Pete let out the breath. "I haven't had much sleep. Can we call a truce? Talk about something else?" He was exhausted. He needed aspirin but didn't want to limp to the desk with Tommy there.

Tommy looked like he was going to resist, but then he smiled again. It was similar to Bernie's—open and genuine. "Totally. This is wearing me out."

"Thanks."

"You get that I'm just on edge because I'm worried about my sister, right?"

"I'm worried too. You can believe whatever you want, but nothing is more important to me than her being okay."

Bernie's voice approached from the hall. She wasn't happy.

"It's way too soon," Pete said.

"Can't be good."

Pete felt a burst of panic, small, but enough to propel him off the couch to meet the voice, leg forgotten. For a second. When he put his weight on it, it gave way, and he was falling. He reached for the chair Tommy's feet were on, but it was inches too far. He braced to meet the floor with his face.

Tommy, quicker than Pete would've guessed, was out of his seat, hands under Pete's arms. He pivoted and lowered Pete into the chair.

"Whoa," he said. "You okay?"

"Fine. Thanks. It does that." He bent to adjust a nonexistent issue with his shoe to hide his embarrassment.

The door burst open and Bernie, her face red, eyes wet, blew in, followed by Kermit.

"That was short," Pete said.

"They took my phone," she said, her voice shaking. She collapsed onto the couch. "They—"

Kermit held up his hand. "Let's talk at my office. They're still here."

"Don't give them the satisfaction of hearing how upset you are," Tommy said.

Bernie's eyes went from Tommy to Pete, where they lingered, then narrowed. "What's going on with you two?"

"We heard you coming and were girding for it," Pete said. He forced a smile.

"It was too soon," Tommy added. "Seemed like trouble."

Bernie looked from one to the other. Pete slid his chair a little farther from Tommy, though he knew it was too late. He could always count on Bernie, no matter how deep her distress, to read the room and notice every detail.

She held his gaze, shook her head. "Whatever. I'm too upset to deal with you two."

"Let's go," Kermit said. He took Bernie's parka from the coat rack and held it for her as she put her arms in, then put on his own. Gloves and fedora in hand, he looked expectantly at Tommy and Pete.

Pete wasn't ready to stand. "You guys go ahead. I'll meet you there. I have a quick paperwork thing I need to take care of."

"Bullshit," Bernie said. She walked to the back corner and reached behind a bank of filing cabinets. "Here you go, Superman." She handed him his cane.

It wasn't going to help. They'd left their cars at Kermit's and walked the few blocks to the police station. The walk over, a minefield of ice patches and clumps of frozen snow, was a challenge. Now, with his leg giving out, he wouldn't be able to manage it at all. His physical therapist was a broken record about using crutches when it was acting up, but they were tucked away in the closet at home. Bernie already knew he couldn't walk. He knew she was waiting for him to say it. He couldn't in front of Tommy and Kermit.

"You know what? I'm gonna get my car and come back for you guys," Tommy said. "I know it's a short walk—it's just too cold and windy. Why should everyone suffer?"

"You don't have to do that," Pete said.

"Not a problem." Tommy nodded at the window. "Anyone notice how the weather's turned?" The sky beyond the pine trees was dark. Hard pieces of snow slapped against the glass. "I'll be back in a jiffy." He was out the door before anyone could respond.

"Well, okay," Kermit said. He unbuttoned his coat and sat on the couch.

Bernie sat next to him. "I have a question," she said to Pete. "Does it hurt your pride more to be seen in public on crutches or to have my brother pity you? Just curious."

"It's a toss-up." He lifted his leg to the chair Tommy had vacated.

"You need some aspirin, right? All friends here, you don't have to pretend."

"Thanks."

"Wouldn't ibuprofen be better?" Kermit asked.

"That's what everyone tells me," Pete said. "But aspirin is the only thing that works."

Bernie got the aspirin and small bottle of water from his desk drawer. She took a handful of Goldfish crackers out of the bag that she made him keep there, insisting he at least eat something if he insisted on aspirin.

"Working on the budget already?" she asked, nodding at the papers spread out on his desk.

"Never too early to work on the budget. Town meeting's only two months away, and the budget committee is anxious for numbers."

"Yeah, I know, it just seems…whatever. My brain isn't working this morning."

Her eyes told a different story. Her stare was unnerving. He hoped putting the handful of crackers in his mouth at least partially covered whatever his face was giving away. He and the mayor had been getting along all right recently, but that had changed in an unsettling way Friday afternoon. Bernie seemed better than when she'd walked into the room, but it was still the wrong time for that piece of news. She'd find out soon enough.

"How do you keep cashmere so pristine with this weather?" she asked Kermit, sitting down next to him. "Not just the snow, but I have salt and sand all over my coat and can't get it out, and that's with Gore-Tex."

Kermit launched into a detailed explanation of cashmere care. Bernie listened, apparently intently. But Pete knew she'd figured something was up. He hadn't heard the last of it. His problems were small potatoes compared to what she was facing, but she wouldn't see it that way.

****

The spitting snow that had started while they were in Pete's office turned into a storm while they sat around the table in Kermit's commercial-grade kitchen, the snow a white blur outside his floor-to-ceiling windows. He'd whipped up omelets and found the remains of a Waldorf salad in his giant refrigerator.

"Nothing fancy, but it's lunch," he told them.

"Just what the doctor ordered," Bernie said. She was in mental turmoil, but it wouldn't stop her from eating. Watching her phone disappear into George Libby's sweaty, fat hand felt like a violation. The tension between Tommy and Pete also had her on edge. And she didn't buy Pete's explanation that the financial printouts on his desk were because of the budget. It wasn't so much that his explanation didn't make sense—this was the time of year departments usually started that work—but she'd become an expert on his deflection tells. His face gave it away. She just had to figure out why he was deflecting.

"How long are you in town?" Pete asked Tommy.

"A week, maybe two. I have to find cheaper digs, though. I'm at the Four Seasons Lodge, and even this time of year it's pricey."

"No way," Bernie said. "I thought you were here for just a couple of days, to check on things."

"He's a good attorney," Kermit said. "Would you rather have Tommy running interference or have Theresa and Pat on the phone every day demanding information and ordering us around?"

Pete shot Kermit a warning look, which Kermit ignored. "They're all looking out for you."

Bernie's face got hot. "I get it now. This was all some big plan you cooked up with them. 'Oooo Bernie fucked up again. Oooo Bernie is an idiot. Oooo she has to be bailed out by the smart people.' "

"Bernie—" Pete said.

"Don't you Bernie me." She turned to him. Her voice rose and cracked, but she was too pissed off to care. "You knew too. That's what you and Tommy were talking about."

"There's no conspiracy, Bernie," Kermit said.

"Let me," Tommy said. "When I got here, after you told me you retained Kermit, I called him to find out what was up. I offered to take some of his cases so that he can focus on yours. I can do most of it from Portland, so don't worry. I'll just pop up once in a while to check in."

He smiled, innocent. She wasn't sure whether to buy it.

"And I play hockey," Tommy said.

"Yes, I know. You *are* my brother. That's going to be so fucking helpful."

"I heard you guys talking about the pond hockey tournament earlier," Tommy said to Kermit. "You're down a player? I was varsity in college. Brown."

"The answer to the age-old question, 'What's the color of shit?' " Bernie said. Her burst of anger had sapped what little energy she had, but she couldn't help herself.

Kermit practically bounced in his seat. "Great! We're all attorneys. The Advo-Cats."

"Worst name ever for a hockey team," Bernie said. "How are you going to play hockey from Portland?"

Pete elbowed her. She didn't want to look at him, but if she didn't, he'd just keep doing it. He mouthed *I love you*. She rolled her eyes.

"Let's talk about what we learned from this morning's meeting," Kermit said.

"Thank you," Bernie said.

"They're not officially calling it arson, but they're treating it like one. As you know, arson is tough to prove since they've rejected a lot of the junk science surrounding fire investigations."

"A lot of prosecutors are still happy to use that junk science in court," Tommy said. "A lot of juries are still bamboozled by it."

"We'll tackle that once we get their discovery, if charges are brought. Police will naturally say the person who was found inside is a victim of murder if it's arson and if the remains are too degraded to determine cause of death. We haven't heard from the medical examiner yet. There are obviously other things they know that we don't. The meetings yesterday and this morning didn't last long enough for them to reveal anything."

"Not that they would have," Pete said. "Particularly about the remains."

"Stephanie," Bernie said. The hard knot she'd previously felt when considering the body in her house had turned to waves of nausea now that George Libby had shown her photos that would live in her nightmares for the rest of her life—a grotesque, twisted black form that didn't even look human.

"We don't know that." Pete draped his arm on the back of her chair, his way of showing her he was there with her. He rubbed her shoulder as he took a long swallow of beer. It was some kind of Belgian brew that came in a bottle with a stopper. One sip turned Bernie's stomach.

"More beer?" Kermit asked the guys. "I'm having another." They both nodded. "Water, Bernie? Seltzer?"

"I'm fine." They were acting like this was a casual lunch conversation or some kind of collegial lawyer discussion about some case no one was involved in. But this was her life. Libby, after showing her those horrific photos, had zeroed in on the issues with her tenant.

Kermit had shut it down. Then Libby asked for her phone. The fire inspector hadn't said much at all. Bernie had been willing to proceed with the grilling so she could find out what was going on with the investigation, but it was just another ambush. Her fear, her anguish over the whole thing didn't seem to affect this trio, all of whom professed to have her back.

"I wish they'd just tell me something," she said, trying to sound as conversational as they were. "It *is* my house."

"They're not going to tell you details of the investigation if you're a suspect," Tommy and Pete both said at the same time—slightly different wording, but the same message. Bernie waited for Tommy to say *jinx*. He smiled, his eyes dancing. He was thinking it. Pete was looking down, poking at his largely uneaten omelet with his fork.

Bernie persisted. "If it's not her, that's just as bad but in a different way. I've tried calling her, but her phone is off. The only emergency contact information she gave me is her work supervisor. I called him, and he told me he can't talk because it's confidential, which is bullshit."

"We can pursue that," Kermit said. "If it's not Stephanie, and we can track her down, she may have information that will help. Be prepared that they're going to look at your insurance coverage and your financial situation. I'm surprised they didn't ask for your laptop, but be prepared for that too."

"I can't do my job without my laptop."

"Download anything you need for work to a thumb drive ASAP," he said, holding up a hand to stop her protest. "Please don't delete anything. Anything. If they want to go after you, they can use that as consciousness of guilt, even if it has nothing to do with the case."

"There's nothing on my laptop that I'm embarrassed about," Bernie said. *Unlike my phone.* "I'm concerned about them seeing work-related things that aren't their business. I know I'm not Woodward and Bernstein or whatever, but I'm working on stories that I don't want people poking around in."

"We can cross that bridge when, or if, we come to it," Kermit said.

Tommy jumped in. "We can make a case for an injunction."

"*We* can make a case?" Bernie said.

"The biggest issue is that they're going to look for anything in your texts or calls that can help them if they want to go after you," Tommy said. "As you well know"—he was talking to Bernie, but looking at Pete—"it's not about the truth so much as what they can use as evidence to support the theory they think has the best chance of winning in court. Confirmation bias is the rule of the day, not justice. I know your sense of humor, but even if the cops get it too, which I doubt, they'll pretend they don't. They can totally fuck you over."

"I don't disagree," Kermit said.

"I do to some extent," Pete said. "But yeah, out of context, some things that aren't evidence could be mistaken for it."

Tommy snorted.

Bernie knew they were waiting for her to talk about what was on her phone. There were definitely texts that could be taken the wrong way, but she wasn't going to go into it with the three of them. Maybe Kermit, next time they spoke privately. Maybe.

"I guess we'll find out," she said. She took a forkful of Pete's omelet. She wasn't hungry but didn't want to just sit there doing nothing while they stared at her waiting for her to say more.

Pete squeezed her shoulder. "It's going to be okay," he said. "We'll make sure. You didn't do anything wrong. They'll find out the truth."

She swallowed the food that she'd been holding in her mouth while she thought. "Hopefully they'll finish with me fast and move on."

She avoided Tommy's eye. She knew what he was thinking. Their dad had said it so many times that it was burned into their consciousness. "Cops are like a cat with a pork chop once they have a good suspect. The only way to win it is shut down, shut up, and hope they give up and start looking for a juicier piece of meat."

CHAPTER 7

BERNIE WAS UP by five the next morning. Actually, she'd been up all night. She couldn't get the photos of the charred body that Libby had shown her out of her head—he'd looked so smug, knowing the effect it would have. Old cop trick. She already knew it, but that's what Pete said, trying to reassure her. Maybe cops could shrug it off, but she couldn't. She'd seen some bad photos as a journalist, but this was someone she knew. It didn't look like Stephanie, of course. It didn't look like anyone. It was a twisted tangle of unidentifiable pieces framed by the black twist of metal and debris that had been Bernie's bed. The photos played like a slideshow as she lay awake. Pete's arm around her all night was like a vise, pressing her back against his warm chest, his bad leg thrown over her thigh.

"There's not enough coffee in the world," she said as she opened the slider. The blast of subzero air jolted some life into her.

"Quick, Dubby," she said to the dog as he pushed past her legs onto the icy deck. He didn't have much choice. He was too short to venture off the path she'd dug for him in the snow, a small oval around the short stretch of yard between the deck and the lake. He double-timed around it, a frenzy of sniffing and leg-lifting, then charged back up the deck and into the house.

She sank onto the couch, feeling heavy and sluggish. She powered on her laptop. She'd spent hours the night before transferring work files to a thumb drive. If they took her work computer as well, she'd be sunk. She tried not to think about it. She was determined to pretend it was a normal day right up until things went to shit, which they surely would.

She went over the notes for the staff meeting she'd planned for that morning, back when she was excited about the coming year. The *Watcher* was in the black despite the fact newspapers all over the country were shutting down or shedding employees. Sure, the high circulation and advertising numbers were largely because of the mind-boggling amount of tragic news the town had endured, but the paper's small staff had met the challenge. You couldn't do good journalism without resources, and resources cost money. The content of the news was beyond her control, and as awful as things had been, she wasn't going to feel guilty about the benefits.

She could even afford to hire another editor, someone who could fill in when she was on vacation, allowing Guy to slide further into retirement. The Affordable Care Act had kicked in, so she could help her staff get health insurance. She knew she wasn't required to, but she could, so she would.

Things were good! What a great way to celebrate the paper's one-hundredth anniversary, she'd planned to tell them. A new century! A new era!

"Yay," she mumbled. She went through her PowerPoint, making small tweaks. None of the good things had changed, but now they had a big asterisk. Everything would be fine *if* she didn't go into a financial tailspin because of it. *If* she didn't get charged with a crime. And the most immediate concern, *if* they could figure out a way for the newspaper to cover the whole thing without compromising her and her job.

"I'm hitting the shower, unless you need it first," Pete said, leaning down to kiss her. "Happy New Year, by the way, in case I never said it."

"It's off to a great start," Bernie said. "Nowhere to go but up. Did I wake you up?"

"No. I have to go in early."

She watched him walk to the bathroom, trying to assess if his limp was better this morning. What she really needed was a similar indicator for his mental health, but she hadn't fully figured that one out. She knew he'd be solid and supportive through all this, hiding the mental toll it was taking.

"Too bad he didn't fall in love with a normal person," she said to the dog, curled up on her legs. Her wet legs. *Shit.* She hadn't wiped the snow from his paws and Velcro-fur belly. She scanned the floor for paw prints. A wet trail led across the polished hardwood and onto the rug. She pushed Dubby away and got up. "You're going to get me into trouble."

"What?" Pete said. The bathroom door was open, the shower not yet on.

"Nothing. Talking to the dog."

She wiped up the prints, wishing she could focus on her work. *Oh right.*

"Forgot to take my pill," she said, walking into the bathroom. Pete was reading the back of one of the many containers that lined the shower shelf.

She took her seven-day dispenser from the medicine cabinet, necessary because, no surprise with ADHD, if she didn't use one she wouldn't remember if she'd taken it and would spend all day obsessing. Pete kept his three prescription bottles neatly lined up on the dresser. He never mentioned them, but also never forgot to take them. Never lost track.

Give it forty-five minutes, she told herself as she tried to get her hair gathered better into its scrunchie. The nonstop thoughts about the fire, the charred human remains, the gnawing insurance and financial issues would fade from paralyzing rumination into concerns and challenges to be tackled. The accompanying thoughts of how many ways her life could come crashing down after she'd worked so hard to get exactly to the place she'd always wanted to be—and hadn't even known she was there—would seem like the mental hyperbole she hoped they were.

"What's this?" Pete stood in the tub, sniffing the contents of a jar.

"Body sugar. I got it at that new Maine-made consignment store."

"What's it for?"

"It's like soap, only an exfoliant too. It also has lanolin in it, which helps protect skin from the wind and cold. It's organic. The woman who makes it has a farm in Industry, I think. That's mango-peach-coconut. I liked the smell." She didn't add that, even though she liked the effect, the smell had become too cloying. She'd bought it, now she had to use it up.

"Is it just for women?" He rubbed some on his forearm, then smelled it again.

"Yeah, it's just anecdotal, but research shows your penis will turn black and fall off if you use it. Either that or you lose interest in the NFL. I can't remember which. Maybe both."

"Right." He was reading the label again.

"Whoa, tough crowd. I'll leave you alone to make that big decision. I'll have another pot of coffee ready when you're done.

"Daddy's being weird today," she whispered to the dog after the water started running.

She hadn't done much but stare at the PowerPoint by the time he finished.

"All set for your meeting?"

"As set as I'm going to be," she said. "My, you smell nice. Like a tropical drink that's been out in the sun too long. If you like it, I'll get you some with a more manly scent so the guys at the station don't beat you up."

Normally, he'd laugh or make a joke. Today? Nothing.

She closed the laptop and thought about getting dressed, but couldn't find the motivation. She considered it a victory when she moved to the table.

Pete came out of the bedroom, buttoning his long-sleeved navy-blue uniform shirt, the matching tie he rarely wore loose around his neck. It was the first time she'd seen him wear either in months.

"What's with the monkey suit? I thought you liked the sweatshirt." She watched him flip the tie through his fingers as he knotted it.

"I have a meeting with Ryan Grant, and even though the sweatshirt is a quarter-zip with a collar, he says it makes us look like slobs."

"Since when do you care what he says?"

"This *is* my uniform."

"Is it about the budget?" She did air quotes around *budget*.

"I really am working on the budget."

"I know, but there's also something you're not telling me."

He joined her at the table, putting his tie over his shoulder so he wouldn't get coffee on it, a habit even though Bernie had never seen him dribble coffee in all the time she'd known him.

"I have time to make pancakes before I leave," he said.

"Don't try to distract me with food. We're out of maple syrup anyway. I'm just going to have toast, maybe a fried egg if I can get the energy."

"I'll make it. I could use some too."

"I fear for the day the honeymoon is over and I have to wait on myself. But sure, go ahead. I'll enjoy the ride while it lasts."

"I love feeding you, because food makes you happy." He went to the refrigerator.

"Well-fed, compliant, and docile. Maybe you're trying to make me so fat that I can't leave the house. At least it would keep me from having to face the horror that my life outside the house has become."

"Bernie, everything is going to be okay. I promise. Not just with the investigations, but with you. And me. Us. Everything." He kissed the top of her head.

Unexpected tears filled her eyes. "I appreciate the thought, but no one can promise that." She wasn't sure which thing she meant.

"I don't know what's going to happen with the investigation, but I do know that you have 100 percent of me, everything I can do, to make it all right."

"What if I get arrested? Convicted? There's not much you can do about that."

"That won't happen."

It happens all the time. She didn't need to say it. He knew how she felt. They'd argued about it many times before agreeing to disagree. Every time it had come up in the past two days, she'd braced for reaction, then was surprised when he'd let it pass.

"Look at me."

She turned.

"I guarantee 100 percent that it won't happen. I will not let it." He stood there in his police chief uniform, his face set with resolve. But she also saw the tie thrown over the shoulder, his still-wet brown hair sticking up in tufts, the eggy spatula clutched in a white-knuckle grip. She took off her glasses and wiped her eyes on her sleeve.

"I love you, Bernie."

"I love you too," she said. "Don't think I didn't notice that you totally dodged telling me what the deal is with the mayor today."

"Yeah, that." He turned back to the stove.

"Yeah, that."

"As you know, my contract is up in August. He wants to discuss it. That's what the council executive session tomorrow night is about."

"Really? It's eight months away. That's not good."

"Not good," Pete said. "Almost definitely not. I don't have anything to apologize for. We're doing a good job. The department is. The council has my back."

"Is that why you seemed so weird earlier?"

"Was I weird? Sorry."

"Distracted. Not my level of distraction, but noticeable."

"Probably lack of sleep."

"I know things have been rocky with Grant on and off, but I thought you basically got along. This isn't about *Real Rural Justice* is it? Because you don't want that stupid TV show coming here?"

"He's got a bee up his butt about a couple things. I don't know what sparked it. I guess I'll find out today. It's probably, as you would say, a dick-waving contest."

"Right." It felt like more.

"You know who'd win that." Pete gave her an exaggerated wink.

She laughed, but she wasn't reassured.

****

Bernie took a detour on her way to work, driving up the hill to the corpse of her house. The yellow crime scene tape still flapped in the wind. Just like last time, she longed to duck under it and go in even though she knew that anything that wasn't burned or smoke-damaged was a soaked mass of uselessness. It was all gone—her books, clothes, the few pieces of art she owned, furniture. All the stuff she'd left there, thinking it would be safe, even cared for, by her ridiculous fantasy of who a tenant would be.

People had been reassuring her that it was just stuff. They couldn't, of course, add to that cliché that no one's life had been lost, because someone's had. You can't really say to someone, "At least *you* didn't die! Too bad for that faceless, lifeless, twisted tangle of burned bones who did!" She didn't wish that on anyone, even Stephanie. Even if it was Stephanie's fault.

In the end, though, the fact the trappings of her life were now a pile of stinky, destroyed, useless crap was her fault. She'd betrayed her house by putting it in someone else's hands. Maybe it was just stuff, but it was her stuff. She wasn't materialistic, but she took comfort in her things. They made her feel good. The colors, the textures, the *being there* of them.

She'd asked Sandy the morning after the fire if it looked like there was anything worth saving. "Sorry, Bernie," he'd said, sweet and compassionate, as always. "Looks like everything's gone."

At least he didn't try to make her feel better with platitudes. He had decades of experience talking to people who'd lost their homes, and he knew the trauma it caused.

"It's going to hurt a while," he said. "But eventually it'll fade from being a horrible trauma to a bad thing that happened that you got past."

Three days and the needle hadn't moved. On top of it, she could end up in prison. *Even though I didn't do anything.* The flapping tape mocked her. It wasn't a locked gate, wasn't an electric fence. The only thing keeping her from getting out of her car and ducking under it was the knowledge that doing so would make things worse.

She was startled by a knock at the window. She started the car so she could lower it, watching her neighbor jump back, then shake his head in annoyance.

"Hi, Dean," she said. She didn't smile. She wasn't in the mood. They'd never had a relationship that was anything more than cordial. He was meticulous about his well-manicured lawn, hedges, and color-coordinated flower garden, so much so that a lawn crew showed up every week from April to October. The fact they blocked the road and ran their climate-killing machines for hours was a major irritation. He had some pet peeves about her, too, including his claim that her cats got into his garden, despite the fact they were indoor cats who only escaped occasionally then hid under her bushes until she found them. He also complained that when she listened to the Red Sox on her screened porch it was too loud. He was also nosy, making comments on visitors, where they parked on the street. She wanted to tell him that if he paid less attention, she'd be less of a problem. Now here he was, ruining her silent reverie with her destroyed house.

"I wondered who was over here," he said. "Then I recognized your boyfriend's car."

Bernie's car now, but that wasn't Dean's business. "Can I help you?"

"When do you think you'll get this cleaned up?"

"Thanks. Yeah, it *is* traumatic. But I'm handling it. Appreciate your good thoughts."

"Sorry for your loss." He didn't sound it. "But it must be obvious to you it's an eyesore and public nuisance. I don't want to make a complaint, but…"

She wasn't in the mood. Didn't have the energy. "As soon as the insurance company gives the word, I'm going to take care of it. I'm as anxious as you are."

"What do the police have to say?"

"Not much. You know the police." She smiled. She knew he knew it was fake.

"I thought, given your boyfriend, you'd know."

"Nope." She put the car in gear. "Good morning."

He put his hand on top of the window before she had a chance to shut it. He leaned in, blasting her with coffee breath. "That girl you rented to was a nightmare. This used to be a nice neighborhood. I won't report you further, keep what I know to myself, as long as you don't plan on rebuilding and moving back. Don't think you'll get away with it because of your boyfriend. This time I'll go above his head."

"Report me? For what? *Further?* Renting to someone whose dogs barked too much?" Bernie was taken aback. It was partly the way he said it—creepy in its matter-of-factness—but also that it didn't make sense.

"You already know."

"I don't."

"The male visitors? She was obviously selling something. I could smell cannabis, even from my yard. I'm sure that wasn't all she was selling. Didn't your boyfriend tell you? I'm not surprised nothing came of it."

"I have no idea what you're talking about."

"I'm not going to go back and forth. I strongly recommend that you don't rebuild. Cut your losses and sell the property. Once you've cleaned it up, of course."

Her brain whipped from *guys* and *cannabis* to the nerve of this guy telling her what to do. "I'm definitely rebuilding. The insurance company wants me to, and the bank does too. *I* want to. I can't wait to move back." She'd move back just to spite the guy.

He straightened up but still clutched the top of the open window. "You clean it up, I'll buy the land from you."

Chrissake, the embers were barely cold. "Sure." Her tone said the opposite.

"Think about it. Seriously." He was semifriendly now. "I'll make a fair offer."

She raised the window and did a three-point turn in the empty street, grinding the gears, silently apologizing to Pete for destroying his car.

She felt Dean's eyes on her. She looked in the rearview mirror, watching him watch her drive away.

CHAPTER 8

DAWNA WASN'T SURPRISED to see Pete's car alone in the parking lot when she pulled in at seven. She knew about the meeting with the mayor. Between Bernie's fire, the possible murder, new hires at the station, a new year, a budget to prepare, she was surprised he wasn't sleeping there.

He gave her a weary smile when she stuck her head in his office. "I'm going over these budget figures even though I know Grant isn't going to want to talk about them. Not much else I can do."

Dawna sat down. "It's tough to fight bullshit. How's Bernie?"

"Dealing with it. She hasn't melted down or anything, at least much."

"That's good to hear. It's a tough thing."

"You know her, just keep moving forward, like a shark, as she says. I feel helpless, though. There's not much I can do."

"The fact that you're there for her is huge."

He shrugged. "I feel like my issues hang over everything. I'm sick of everything being about me."

"Look at the bright side. The fire evens it out."

He laughed. "There's that. Can you close the door?"

When she sat back down, his smile was gone.

"I've decided I'm saying no to *Real Rural Justice*. The last thing we need is a bunch of people with cameras following us around."

"Good. But doesn't Grant have the final say? He really wants that stipend. He's got people convinced that it'll be good publicity after all the bad publicity. Help spur economic development and all that. They're buying it. People want to be on TV."

"They should be careful what they wish for. He has the final say, but if the department doesn't cooperate, there won't be much of a show. Hopefully the producers will decide we're too much trouble and go somewhere else."

"People are going to say you don't want it because of the editorial Bernie wrote."

"Let them," Pete said. "Her reasons and mine aren't the same. I don't care what people say anyway."

"If you need me to back you up with Grant, I'm happy to."

"Thanks. That brings up the next thing. Did you know that Harry Truman didn't know they were working on an A-bomb until twelve days after FDR died?"

"No. That sucked for Truman." She could guess what his point was going to be. She didn't want to hear it.

"Lucky for you, I'm not FDR."

"Don't tell me we're developing an A-bomb."

"I know I ask a lot of you, but lowering yourself to meet my sense of humor isn't a job requirement." His smile wavered.

"Sorry. I have a feeling what's coming. I'm kind of nervous."

"Maybe this'll blow over. I hope so, because we're just getting up to speed. With Mandy starting today, we'll finally be fully staffed for the first time since I became chief. We have a great crew."

"You'd think Grant would appreciate that."

"I'm not worried about keeping my job," Pete said. "The council has my back. They did before, when they had every reason not to. Now, when there's no reason, I can't imagine they'd change course. But we need to be prepared."

Dawna nodded. Hoped he didn't see her swallow the lump in her throat.

"Can you make time this afternoon so I can go over the budget with you and some other administrative things? Just in case. I know we can't go over everything, but I can give you the tools to handle things. You're already familiar with a lot of it anyway. I'd still be around if you had questions. Unless they take me out back and shoot me."

Dawna didn't smile. She knew just as well as he did that no matter how much the council had Pete's back, Ryan Grant had the power to fire him. "I don't get how this suddenly came up."

"I don't either. He and I were doing okay. Not great, but okay. Then Friday he called and said we had to meet today. He didn't sound happy. Gert told me about the executive session. Boom."

"It can't be just about the TV show."

"Bernie said the same thing. Who knows?" Pete's phone buzzed. "Speaking of Bernie. She's amped up to an eleven with everything going on."

"If you need to talk to her, we can finish this later."

"I'll call her back."

"You don't think he'd just fire you today, do you?" Dawna asked. "Not wait for the council meeting tomorrow?" She hadn't wanted to say it, but she had to know the answer.

"I wondered, but I don't think so. He knows it would be bad, politically. I don't think he wants to fire me, or suspend me, or whatever. I think he just wants to jerk me around. But today's meeting isn't going to be a happy one, and like I said, we ought to be prepared, just in case."

She felt marginally better. "Libby wants me in Augusta this morning to talk about the investigation, but I should be back by early afternoon. I guess he's abandoned our conference room."

"Yeah, by a good sixty miles."

"You know, Libby's not a bad investigator," she said. "He just doesn't like us. He'll get this solved soon."

****

No one was at the office when Bernie arrived. This was her favorite time of day. She could relax and get her shit together before the interruptions, the frenzy. She needed it more than ever this morning.

Running into Dean had messed up her morning even more than it already had been. Every single thing about the conversation was off-kilter. The mention of guys and cannabis, his reference to a police report, his push to buy her property. For what felt like the millionth time, she cursed George Libby and the fact she didn't have her cellphone. She needed to call Pete but couldn't remember his cell number. She called his extension at the police department, punching the numbers on her desk phone with more force than was needed. It's great that cellphones had taken away the need to remember numbers, but when Armageddon came and the grid shut down, they were all going to be screwed.

She got Pete's voicemail. "Welcome to my personal Armageddon. Call me as soon as you can. It's important. Call my desk, not my cell." She was about to add, "Or you'll be calling George Fucking Libby," then remembered that calls to the station were recorded.

She hooked her laptop up to the wall monitor she'd been so excited about when she and Pete had installed it the week before. The high hopes she'd had for the staff meeting now seemed small and foolish. Didn't she know by now that looking forward to something, being excited that the future held nothing but good news—*No bad news! None!*—meant disaster was around the corner? She was Pat O'Dea's daughter after all. When someone had a run of luck, he'd caution, "Don't use up all your good luck." Like there was a limited amount of it just waiting to be sucked away and replaced with misery. Part of her wrote it off to the potato famine and all the other affliction that had befallen her Irish ancestors. Part of her believed it.

Her desk phone rang. It was her friend Colleen, calling to see how she was doing. Bernie caught her up on everything—she hadn't realized there was so much until she went through it. It had been a long two days.

"I'm also calling with a tip," Colleen said.

"If it's that you've been named head of the new Redimere College Diversity Board, we got the news release. Congratulations."

"They didn't have a choice, since I'm the only Black woman on staff. But that's not it. You know how you asked me if I'd heard anything about the college and that Nakilot Mountain land?"

"Yes, and you told me that as a lowly professor you're not privy to Redimere College's secret development moves."

"I did. But I started thinking about it, and nosed around and they *are* up to something. They may even have acquired the land."

"I knew it. I knew it. I knew it."

"I know you didn't want to say more last week, but will you tell me now why you're asking? I'm nosy, too."

"Do you know Rita Chandler? The real estate broker?"

"I rent my house from her, remember?"

"Oh, duh, right. She wanted to talk about an issue with Normand Ouimette's land, but not over the phone. We never connected, because she was leaving on a vacation to Cabo—where even is that?—but she said if we didn't connect, we'd talk when she got back. As you know, his land includes Nakilot Mountain, which Norm had told me the college had been pushing to buy for years, since it's adjacent to the back end of the campus. I even called Ken Parent, the guy who does a lot of the college's development stuff, to see what he knew—we're kind of friendly—but he never got back to me either. That week between Christmas and New Year's sucks for getting people to call back."

"I wonder's what's going on?"

"Something fishy. Normand Ouimette was committed to handing his land over to the Passamaquoddy Tribe. I did a story on it a few months ago. If he changed his mind, that doesn't make sense. It also happened really fast, if the college has acquired it."

"I'm happy I could help distract you from your fire."

"No medicine like a good story to work on," Bernie said.

Bernie felt more energized than she had all weekend. She had something juicy to work on. She had a newspaper to put out. She'd even figured out a way to track down Stephanie somewhere in between all the other stuff.

"Moving forward, just like a shark," she said to the empty room.

She flipped through the giant ancient Rolodex on her desk that held phone numbers going back decades. She'd added cards, but didn't feel right about removing ones that were in her predecessor Harry's handwriting, or those of his predecessors. The mix of different handwriting, ink, pencil, scribbled out numbers, and notes like "don't call in the a.m. he'll rip your head off," was a part of the newspaper's history. She vaguely remembered putting Normand Ouimette's number on a card. And here it was. A crisp white card with her cramped, barely readable script—a nun in grade school told her she'd be unemployable because her handwriting was so bad—that stood out from its yellowed, smudged neighbors.

His voicemail was full. She wasn't surprised. He rarely answered his phone. One reason he lived where he did was because he wanted peace and quiet, he'd told her. She got it.

Her next call was to the communications director at the college. She got his voicemail and left a message asking if she could talk to Anthony Wilson, the college president, about the Nakilot development plans. The best strategy for not getting jerked around was act like she knew there were plans, not ask if there were.

She went to the shelf where she kept the planning board and town council agenda packets, organized by month and year. Maybe she'd missed some subtle agenda item about the project. Even if the town wasn't involved, the college would need plan approval. Lots of developers got the ball rolling with the town before they owned the land. The college had ramped up development since Wilson became president. They were very proactive about having their ducks in a row.

****

Bernie had just sat back down at her computer again when a notification popped up that the YouTube channel Redimere Raw had posted a new video. She kept an eye on the channel, not so she could watch "Sexy Sheriff" for the millionth time, but because it sometimes broke news. This was one of those times. And it was about her.

The new video filled the Redimere Raw home page. "Strange But Not a Stranger: Burning Down the House on School Street." Bernie gave them kudos for using a lyric from Talking Heads, one of her favorite bands. But the journalist in her gave it a C-minus. It implied knowledge that didn't exist. Not a stranger? The title worked as far as clicks went, though. The video had been posted three hours before, but already had 577 views.

It wasn't an official video from someone involved in the fire investigation, but something from someone's phone, blurry and shaky. Whoever it was, though, was closer to the fire than she'd been. The audio was a cacophony of men yelling, water hissing on hot wood, the crackle of flames, the cackle of static from handheld radios, the occasional whoop of a siren.

After a few seconds of that noise, a voice that didn't sound close enough to be the person holding the phone said something that was mostly inaudible, except for the words "arson evidence," which Bernie heard clearly.

Sandy came onto the side of the screen, looking handsome, as always, even in the dark and blurry phone video. He was talking to someone a few feet away from whoever was holding the phone. It didn't look like he was aware he was being recorded.

"We're not talking about that right now," he said.

The phone shifted lower, like the person holding it was trying to be inconspicuous.

The other voice said something, again mostly inaudible, then clearly, "If she burned down her own house."

Another voice, different from the first one, laughed and said, "[inaudible] do her a favor [inaudible] shit shack."

"I think they need you over on that hose," Sandy said.

A card came up on the screen. "Who knew this fire at 47 School Street was arson even before Redimere's fire chief? Even before the fire marshal was there? This video was sent to us anonymously with the same question."

Another card appeared on the screen. "Someone dead. A house burned down. The owner didn't do it. What happened? Will we ever find out?" It faded to black.

Bernie watched the video several times, looking for anything she'd missed.

When Redimere Raw first started posting in late summer, Bernie asked Carrie to find out who was behind it. She had no luck. It posted videos that it claimed were uploaded anonymously. The administrator put in their own comments and had discretion about whether to use the videos. At least that's what the disclaimer on the page said. Bernie would love to know who was behind Redimere Raw, but it wasn't high on her priority list right now. Especially since they seemed sure she was innocent. She could use all the support she could get.

CHAPTER 9

PETE WAS ABOUT to call Bernie when Sandy knocked, then opened the door and came in. Pete put his cellphone back in his pocket.

"Busy?" Sandy asked.

"It's not even 8 a.m. and I'm sitting at my desk with the budget spread out in front of me. How busy could I possibly be?"

"Gotcha." Sandy sat, inching the chair closer to the desk so he could put his coffee mug down.

"World's Best Fire Chief. Nice. I must've missed the awards ceremony," Pete said.

"Christmas present from a fan. Speaking of which, how's Bernie doing?"

Pete pushed back the annoyance, the stab of pain that had faded but wasn't completely gone. He'd forgotten that Bernie had ordered the mug special for Sandy. They were *just friends*. He couldn't justify being hurt when he'd been the one who'd broken up with her. He was *fine* with their friendship. He didn't hold a grudge against Sandy for moving in on her so fast in that brief window. He'd reassured Bernie so many times that he was starting to believe it. Still, he allowed himself a second to imagine pushing the file folders on his desk forward just enough so the mug would slide off right into Sandy's lap, hot coffee staining his crisp white shirt.

"Bernie's great," Pete said. "You know, moving forward."

"Right. Like a shark. How about you?" Sandy said it gently, his compassion sincere. Pete felt stupid. Guilty. Sandy hadn't deliberately chosen that mug to stick it to Pete. *A small t.* His therapist's voice cooed softly. *Little triggers will happen, let them sit, then shoo them away.* Benjamin always illustrated how to do this by making delicate shooing motions with his massive, pudgy hands. He had Pete do it too. It worked, surprisingly. But he'd cut his hands off before he'd do it in front of Sandy.

"I'm fine."

"Right."

"I am."

Sandy shrugged. Gave Pete his thousand-watt smile. "If you say so. Sorry to bug you when you have a lot going on, but I wanted to talk before your meeting."

"It'll be fine."

"It may not be. The mayor and George Libby were in Grant's office with the door closed yesterday for a long time."

"On Sunday?"

"Exactly."

"And?"

"Someone overheard part of it. That someone passed it on to me because they were concerned."

"Can you get to the point? I have a long morning."

"Grant implied heavily there were likely some shenanigans involving Bernie's insurance, regarding the fire, and that you're likely involved. He said he got a tip from someone who was at the scene."

"Give me a break," Pete said. "How would Grant know? And who at the scene would know or be talking about Bernie's insurance? Even if someone was, and passed it on to Grant, Libby isn't going to believe that crap."

"Even so, Grant's got a bee in his bonnet about you, is my point. Why's he sticking his nose in a criminal investigation and implicating you? You get that's a problem, right?"

"Of course I get that. I'm a cop, remember? It's just not high on my priority list. He's pissed off that I won't agree to *Real Rural Justice* and he's posturing. Libby may be an asshole, but he's not a bad cop. He's not going to let town politics get in the way of what I expect to be a competent investigation."

"Just giving you a heads-up."

"I appreciate it."

Sandy stood up. "Oh, I left a message on Bernie's cell about the insurance adjuster. I'm accompanying him on a walk-through, but she didn't call back. I just wanted to let her know in case they didn't."

"Libby has her cell."

"That explains it. She usually gets back pretty quick. That must be driving her nuts, not having her phone."

"You don't know the half of it."

After the door shut behind Sandy, Pete washed down three aspirin with his now-cold coffee. A headache that had been a flutter when he walked in that morning had bloomed into a pulsing throb. He put on his reading glasses and picked up the budget printout he'd been going over when Sandy came in. He switched his desk phone to answer mode, a signal to Vicki when she came in that he wanted to be left alone. He liked math. Nice clean numbers were easy to understand, easy to figure out. Within minutes he was lost in them, everything else, even the headache, temporarily forgotten.

****

"Pete!" Bernie said it out loud when her phone rang. She'd been about to try him again, desperate to tell him about the video footage from her house. But it was Ryan Grant. She had to think about it for a second. Had she called him earlier? No, but she'd been planning to. If the college had acquired Norm Ouimette's land, he was likely the broker, or at least would know who was.

They exchanged hellos and had the perfunctory discussion about her house burning down that Bernie was getting used to. *Thanks for your concern. Yes, it's tragic that someone died. No, I don't know much else.* At least Grant sounded friendly. The old Ryan, not the one he'd become since he took office a year before. They'd had a good working relationship.

90

He loved to talk about real estate and development and was a good source. When he became mayor, she went from being someone who'd write about his projects and get his name in the paper to a sneaky hack who wanted to make him look bad. At least that's what she surmised. She took it in stride. They love you until they hate you. She'd been doing this a long time and knew that well. This morning, she wouldn't call it love, but it was at least a little less hate. So far.

"I heard you're asking about the college's Nakilot project," Grant said.

She tried to remember how he'd know. Probably the college communications guy. The fact it had pinged from the college across town to the town office told her, yeah, something big was going on. She was happy it was Grant calling, instead of the college guy. She might at least get some useful information instead of a carefully vetted non-information news release that would waste her time.

"I was just about to call you," Bernie said. "Not sure though if I'm talking to you as a broker or as mayor. Is there a town role? Like a special tax district or something?"

"The college hasn't officially come to the town with their plans."

"But you were the broker, right?" He wouldn't be calling otherwise.

"It was a private deal. You should talk to the college."

"Normand Ouimette sold it to them?"

"That's what I like about you—you keep persisting." There was an edge to his voice.

"That's my job." She said it in a bright, upbeat way that made her want to puke, but would be more effective than snapping it at him.

"I can tell you this much. The college acquired the property through a private sale. Ironically, I was the broker. It's not my place to say more unless the buyer and seller give me the okay."

Not ironic. Not even coincidental, since he was the broker on a lot of the college's deals since Anthony Wilson took office. "Buyer being the college and seller being Normand Ouimette?"

"I'd love to talk about it, but I can't say more. I suggest you give the college a call."

"Was it the entire Ouimette parcel? All 146 acres?"

"Talk to President Wilson."

She had a flash of Woodrow Wilson, all wire-rimmed glasses and grim sepia gaze, waiting for her call. Prying information out of the long-dead president would be easier than getting it out of Redimere College's president, he of the expensive suits and haircuts, too-white teeth, insincere smile, and carefully crafted say-nothing news releases.

"I'm setting something up," Bernie said. "Maybe after—"

"Good. A pleasure talking to you, as always."

"Not," Bernie said to the dial tone.

It was obvious that he'd called to see how much she knew. She wondered if he'd learned anything. At least he'd confirmed the college had acquired the land, but it raised more questions than it answered. She hated writing stories like that.

She'd done two features in the past year about Normand Ouimette and his land. He was a retired Redimere College professor whose smart investments had given him enough of a nest egg to buy two adjoining parcels, one from a mining company and one from a timber company, neither of which used the land anymore. Her first story had been about how he planned to donate it to a land trust and open it back up to low-impact recreation, like hiking, fishing, hunting, and snowshoeing. The second story came after that one, when Passamaquoddy officials contacted her to let her know the land had been deeded to their people after the Revolutionary War, then stolen by the mining and timber companies. Normand had been mortified. He pivoted to working with the Passamaquoddy with the goal of giving the land back. That was in October. What had changed? Normand was the only one who was going to give her a straight answer.

****

Bernie was glad Carrie was the first to arrive. She wanted to talk to her lone reporter before the rest of the staff got there. Turns out Carrie wanted to talk to her, too.

"I guess this won't surprise you, but Fergus Kelley is hot on the trail of the real story behind your house burning down and your tenant dying." She did air quotes around *real story*.

"The only thing that would surprise me is if that useless excuse for a journalist actually admitted he's a giant festering boil on our noble profession and lanced himself into oblivion."

Carrie nodded, expressionless, as always. "He had a meeting with the mayor about it, and afterward told Louise Babb, and she told me, that he's sure it has to do with Chief Novotny. Louise was like, 'How?' Fergus said something like, 'I don't know but I'm going to find out.' Don't tell anyone. She'll get in trouble."

"That's a good source you've cultivated." Bernie sometimes wondered if she was patronizing Carrie, but then figured that since she was still in college, any positive feedback was mentoring. She had a couple more years before it became patronizing.

"We're friends, actually. We do computer and tech stuff. Kind of like a tech club. Do you know Julie Gower? She's in it, too. Since she's homebound, she attends using Skype. The virtual technology?"

"Right." Bernie had no clue.

"We're the only members. We meet in Louise's basement. A couple guys came to the first meeting, but when they saw it was run by females, they didn't come back."

"Their loss. On our fire story, get together with Guy this morning and hash out where you are. I can't be in on it, as you know."

"Yeah, but I can tell you at least that I'm waiting for calls back from the fire marshal and state police, so I haven't gotten far with official information. I did want to talk to you about something that I'm not sure we should be talking about, but I feel like I need to tell you. I talked to your neighbors yesterday." Her eyes were their usual unblinking stare. "It's not like it's a big secret. I'm sure the police have, too, and probably already told you about it."

No, they haven't. Where the hell is Guy? "What did they say?"

"Dean Davis? The guy in the house that's kind of a little down from yours on the other side of the street? The cedar shingle with blue shutters?"

Bernie nodded.

"He's the only one who had anything bad to say. The others were all like, 'I feel bad, she's a nice person, blah blah blah, but I don't know anything since her house is the last one before the woods and I keep to myself, blah blah blah.' "

"Nice they think I'm a nice person."

"*He* didn't say you're a nice person."

"I wouldn't expect him to. He's a giant pain in my ass. I was there this morning, and he knocked on my car window and scared the shit out of me. He's the Gladys Kravitz of School Street."

Carrie blinked.

"And I'm Samantha?" Bernie said.

"I don't know what that means."

"*Bewitched*? The TV show?"

Carrie shook her head.

Bernie felt old. "What did Dean have to say?"

"Stephanie hadn't been around before the fire. He wasn't sure, but he assumed she went somewhere for the holidays, definitely before Christmas."

"Nice he's keeping track."

"He said she hadn't been going to work, like, for weeks. He wasn't sure when it started, but he noticed her car was there all the time, not gone during work hours."

"Really."

"Since before Thanksgiving. He said he told the police. Then he added"—Carrie flipped the page of her notebook—"and this is a quote, 'The detective from the state police, not that gigolo boyfriend of hers.' And by *hers*, he meant you, not Stephanie."

"Gigolo. Hmm. That would mean I'd be paying Pete for his services. Intriguing."

"I think it was a reference to the 'Sexy Sheriff' video? Because then he said, 'There was a time police arrested people for that kind of behavior, not put it on the internet for the world to see.' "

"You'd think Dean was an old geezer. He's hardly older than me."

Carrie flipped back a page. "Fifty-three. Political science professor at Redimere College. He has an odd schedule, so he's at home a lot."

"Okay, eight years older. Doesn't he have anything better to do than look out his window and go on YouTube? Did he say anything about reporting Stephanie to the police? That he thought she was selling drugs?"

"Ohhhh," Carrie said. "Maybe that's what he meant by, 'If you don't know, you're as ignorant as you look,' after I asked if he had any issues with Stephanie. Then, 'Ask your boss.' Then he said, like, buh bah, and closed the door."

"Rude."

"*Did* he report her to the police?"

"If he did, no one told me. I'm trying to find out." *When the hell is Pete going to call back?*

"There's another thing." Carrie looked nervous. "I don't know how much credit to give it."

"Pretend it was someone else's house and we're just talking."

"I guess he wasn't home when you were there earlier on Friday. He seemed very disappointed. But he said you were also there later."

"Later when?"

Carrie read from her notes: "My partner, Tetley, and I were watching *Jeopardy!* when I heard a car door slam and looked out the window to see Bernadette's car in the driveway. She was bringing things into the house, so I assumed she was moving back in. Tetley can corroborate this, though she didn't look out the window."

"Tetley?" Bernie had never learned Dean's girlfriend's name. Not surprising, since the woman couldn't even be bothered to say hi when Bernie greeted her.

"Like the tea?" Carrie shrugged. "I asked if he was sure about the time, and he was, because they always have a glass of wine and watch *Jeopardy!* before dinner, and it was the part where Alex interviews the contestants. Tetley was irked he was missing it because he was looking out the window. Irked is his word."

It irked Bernie that a couple as annoying as Dean and Tetley would have a routine so similar to the one she had with Pete. "He's mistaken. It wasn't me. It was dark, and it's not like he's directly across the street. Too bad he's not as observant as he is nosy, because he could solve this whole thing right now."

"A little bit after he saw the car and person, he saw the fire and called it in. That was right after they turned off the TV and were sitting down to dinner," Carrie said. "He did not see when the car left."

"Great."

"So. Um."

"Um?" Bernie's brain was working through the information.

"What do I do with this?"

"Write it up. Just like anything else. If you have questions, talk to Guy."

"I assume our conversation was off the record just now. Do you want to respond to what he said?"

"Yeah. Let me give you a quote for the record."

Carrie waited, pencil poised over her notebook.

"I haven't talked to my tenant, Stephanie Woodbury, since before Christmas and wasn't aware she was out of town. I've been to my house three times since she moved in. Once in August, once in October and again late afternoon New Year's Eve, when I was there for about twenty minutes, leaving before four thirty. No one else was there. I commend my neighbor Mr. Davis for being vigilant. That's what keeps communities strong. But he's mistaken about me being there later on New Year's Eve. I can't say more because of the ongoing investigation."

****

Bernie had a few minutes before the staff meeting, which gave her time to do one final task. One more step toward normalcy. Ever since Carrie had mentioned Louise Babb, the town clerk, an annoying mosquito had been buzzing in Bernie's brain. It finally bit. The previous year she'd received a historic preservation grant to upgrade the infrastructure of the newspaper building. It was a long, involved, and complicated process, with a lot of paperwork, which her accountant needed so he could start her taxes. She'd forgotten all about it until he called her Saturday to express his condolences about the fire, then reminded her. That's when she thought of the pile of documents in a drawer in the hallway dresser she used as a filing cabinet in her house. She'd never removed them with her other documents before Stephanie had moved in, because they were in a different place. Sandy told her, when she'd asked, that the dresser was a goner.

The town clerk had copies, since the town administered the grant. That was the mosquito buzzing in her head. Problem solved. A small thing, but given the past few days, it was a win she'd take. Louise confirmed, yes, they had copies of everything.

"Hey, sorry about your house," Louise added. "Stephanie was a pain, but no one deserves to die like that."

"How did you know Stephanie?"

"The Dog and Pony?"

A smelly closet of a bar behind Blue Seal Feeds. Even though it was two blocks from the newspaper office and they served an excellent brisket sandwich, Bernie didn't hang out there. She got the brisket as takeout, holding her breath as she stood at the sticky bar waiting for her order, feeling decades of cigarette smoke seep into her skin.

"You hung out with her?" Bernie asked.

"Kind of. The way you do if you're regulars somewhere. She actually asked for a job there, but they're like, 'Are you kidding me?' "

What Carrie said about it looking like Stephanie wasn't working finally settled into Bernie's brain. "Do you know what happened at Sturgis? Why she wasn't working there anymore?"

"She got fired. She had a twelve-month contract, but it didn't matter. She was out the door. It was way back in October. She'd only been working there like six weeks. She had no trouble talking about it nonstop. You know, everyone else's fault but hers."

Bernie hung up more convinced than ever that Stephanie, with all her secrets, was the key. If only George Libby would figure it out, too.

CHAPTER 10

PETE PUT ON his coat and went into the outer office. "I have a meeting with Ryan Grant. I'll be back later, not sure when," he told Vicki as he pulled on his gloves.

"But there's no one else here."

Pete pulled his radio off his belt, waved it at her, then put it back. "Everyone's got one of these." *Like he needed to tell her this?*

Vicki's face crumpled.

"Sorry. I'm having a bad morning. I was out of line." He knew that she was buzzing with anxiety, handling calls about a case that was too close to home and they had no answers about, wary about his meeting with Grant, probably wondering if her job was going to collapse under the weight of it.

"It's okay." She'd turned back to her computer. The tremor in her voice, though, told him it wasn't.

"Everything will be all right. You're doing a great job with all this. I appreciate it."

She nodded, her back still to him.

His meeting with Grant wasn't for an hour, but he needed exercise. He wasn't going to heal physically or mentally without it. The cold blast as he walked out the door felt good, scouring him clean. His headache had eased. Even his leg felt okay, relatively, which was good because if Bernie saw him limping by the newspaper office, she'd have no problem coming out onto the street and blasting him about not using his crutches. *Shit, I never called her back.* He checked his watch. She'd be in the middle of her staff meeting.

His walk was going to take him up School Street, where he'd slip under the police tape and look things over at Bernie's house. Pete had been a homicide detective for years. He needed to see the scene for himself, even if it told him nothing. He's the police chief, no one would think twice about it. Libby would throw a fit, but he was down in Augusta jerking Dawna around. He'd stop in and say hi to Bernie before his meeting, after he was done.

He navigated the partially cleared sidewalk, slick with ice and littered with clumps of rock-solid snow, down Main Street, mentally going through the checklist of what he knew about arson and related homicide. He didn't get far. Up the block, two women burst out of Dunkin'. They spotted him and started yelling, terrified.

"There's a guy in there with a knife. A crazy guy," one said as he reached them.

"Is anyone hurt?"

"Vanessa's in there," she said. She had her arm around the other one, who was sobbing. Neither were wearing coats.

"Is she hurt?"

"I don't know."

"Did you call 911?"

"We ran out and saw you." Her voice had started to shake, her calm dissolving. "It just happened."

"Do you know him?" Pete asked as he walked toward the door.

"Not his name."

"You two go over to town hall where it's warm."

Pete radioed county dispatch, a 10-32—assailant with weapon— and 10-74—officer needs assistance.

The women, despite the cold, hadn't moved.

"You need to go get warm," Pete said. "Everything is going to be fine." He felt like his entire day had been telling that to women who knew better. They didn't look any more convinced than Bernie or Vicki had, but holding hands, they ran across the side street to town hall.

Pete turned toward the glass front of the shop, registering the body language of the two figures inside. His gun was at the office, locked in a drawer. He took a deep breath, settled his face into the calm mask he'd perfected over more than twenty years as a cop. Then he pushed the door open.

****

The staff meeting had turned into a chore Bernie wanted to get through rather than a celebration of success, so it was nice and short. Her small staff seemed just as happy to get back to work. Bernie's fingers itched to call Pete. *Why hadn't he called?* She called Kermit instead. The fact that she had to call from her desk phone, instead of her cell from a more private place, got on her last nerve. She practically snapped at Kermit when he answered.

"I need to check in with Libby," he said when she asked for an update. "Until I talk to him, I don't have anything." He didn't seem bothered by her mood. He was probably used to uptight clients.

"The biggest thing is, I want my phone," Bernie said, trying to sound reasonable. "Actually, the biggest thing is, I don't want to get arrested. And I want my phone."

"You won't get arrested. You *will* get your phone."

"I don't mean to sound like I'm obsessed with a trivial thing when someone died," Bernie added.

"You're upset. It manifests in various ways," Kermit said. "It'd be great if Stephanie would reach out. I know everyone keeps saying it, but without her car there, or her dogs, it's very possible it's not her. Dawna told me that they've tried to reach her, but they don't even get voicemail. I don't think they found her phone at the scene either."

"Speaking of cars. My neighbor told Carrie—you know, my reporter—that mine was at the house the night of the fire, long after the real me was actually there. We need to make sure Libby knows that's bullshit."

The hum of work around Bernie had stopped. "Nothing to see here folks, carry on," she called out. She waited for the hum to start again.

100

She said to Kermit, almost whispering, "I wish they'd figure out who it is. I feel bad, but it's weird. I'm not sure what kind of bad to feel until I know who it is."

She'd just hung up when the mundane buzz and static of the police scanner chirped to life.

"All officers be advised 10-32 at Dunkin' in Redimere, 29 Main Street. Redimere 0-1 on scene advises 10-74."

"That means a person with a weapon and the officer needs assistance," she said to the room, which had gone quiet again.

She didn't have to say the rest aloud. Everyone knew that Redimere 0-1 was Pete.

CHAPTER 11

"ANY CLOSER AND I'll fucking kill her."

The guy was off to the side of the counter, near the display case with the travel mugs and pound bags of coffee. He had Vanessa around the neck. Pete knew her by first name only, a friendly woman old enough to be his mother. She called him dear and knew how he liked his coffee without him having to ask. Knew if he ordered doughnuts they were for Bernie, and what kinds she liked. She looked petrified. A flash of panic, a bolt of sheer horror that no meds or therapy could erase, nearly paralyzed him. Cop mode kicked in and it was gone.

"Jeremy, right?" Pete asked. "I'm not armed." He held his hands up, palms out. The guy, the name, came back fast. Pete had responded to a fight outside the Pour House. Jeremy and some other guy, with Jeremy taking the worst of it.

He didn't respond. His eyes, dark under lank brown bangs, skittered across Pete, over his shoulder, up above his head. When Pete took a step forward, they locked on his.

"Get back!" Jeremy shouted again. He was shaking almost as much as Vanessa. He was twenty-five, Pete remembered.

"Are you okay, Vanessa?" Pete asked. He sincerely wanted to know, but it was also part of his training—humanize the hostage and you soften the hostage-taker. Sometimes.

"Yes." Her voice broke.

Pete held her gaze, trying to signal she'd be okay. He'd been here before, with Bernie. He'd failed that time. *Not now.* He pushed back another jolt of panic.

"Jeremy, I know you don't want to hurt Vanessa. Why don't you let her leave so we can talk?" He took off his gloves and ski cap and put them on the table next to him. In that fight, Jeremy had taken most of the beating.

"Oh yeah, that old trick," Jeremy said, but he seemed uncertain. The knife moved a little from Vanessa's neck, not deliberately, but because his hand was shaking. It could easily go the other way. One tremor in the wrong direction and Vanessa could be hurt whether Jeremy intended it or not.

Pete's radio cackled. "Redimere 0-1 this is Redimere 0-7. Eyes on you. Please advise." *Tyler.*

"I'm getting my radio," Pete said to Jeremy. "I'm going to tell him everything is okay in here, all right?" He slowly unzipped his coat. "Look, no gun. Okay?" Jeremy didn't respond. "I'm taking my radio off my belt. I'll do it slowly, so you can see, okay?"

The radio crackled again. Tyler's voice, a couple octaves higher. "Chief, this is Redimere 0-7 what's your 10-101?"

Jeremy nodded. Pete pulled out the radio. "I'm with Jeremy and Vanessa. Jeremy has a knife. I'm going to talk with him about what's going on. When state and county arrive, let them know we're okay. Just talking." Pete knew the lack of 10 codes would confuse Tyler, but he wanted Jeremy to know what he was saying, no tricks or ambushes.

"So, 10-12?" Tyler asked after a pause.

"Yes. Stand by."

Another pause. "10-4." The radio crackled off.

Pete spread his arms, waist-high, hoping Jeremy would get it. *I come in peace.* "Why not let Vanessa leave? I know you don't want to hurt her. I know you don't want to make things worse."

"Like you know about me."

It was the opening Pete had banked on. "You're right. I don't know about you. But I know you don't feel heard or like anyone cares. I understand."

"Yeah. Right."

Pete waited, not taking his eyes off Jeremy's. He kept his arms spread out, relieved they were steady. He knew it was a tough line—connecting without sounding like he was full of shit, waiting for what he said to sink in instead of piling it on. They'd gone over it in negotiation training, but he already knew it from years of interrogating suspects. He could walk that line easily. He was in the zone.

"You're the cop who brought me to the hospital."

"That's right. Pete." A detail would solidify it, prove he remembered. "In March. Cold as hell." Pete smiled as he said it, a slight one. Empathetic. It wasn't put-on. He'd felt bad for Jeremy that night, a sad hard-luck kid who could've been Pete's brother if he'd lived another ten years. Pete brought him to the hospital so he could book him after he was treated. Jeremy had been wanted on a warrant for drug possession with intent to sell. No record for anything violent.

"Turn off your radio and I'll let her go."

It quietly crackled in Pete's outstretched hand. He wasn't broadcasting their conversation, but he wasn't going to waste time and energy arguing about it. Vanessa was stock-still, white with terror.

He raised the radio to his mouth. "Tyler, Vanessa's coming out in a minute. She'll be by herself. I don't want anyone to approach the door when it opens." He'd seen the robin's egg-blue flash of a state police cruiser in his peripheral vision. Blue and red lights pulsed on the ceiling and wall to his left in an awkward rhythm that told him there was more than one. If he turned his head slightly toward the window, he knew he'd see cops with bulletproof vests, long guns ready, just waiting for a sign. He didn't turn. His only focus was Jeremy and Vanessa.

Jeremy couldn't see outside from where he was, but the lights had made him flinch, tighten his grip on Vanessa. The tremor in his hand was worse, and his bangs were plastered to his forehead with sweat.

Pete said a silent prayer that Jeremy would keep from melting down. He nodded slightly, reassuring. *We've got this.* Jeremy blinked. Licked his lips. Pete would have to take that as agreement.

"Vanessa's coming out now," he said into the radio. "Once she's safely outside, I'm turning off my radio so Jeremy and I can talk."

Jeremy didn't lower the knife. He stood, staring. Shaking. Vanessa's eyes were closed, her hands clenched at her sides. Her chest rose and fell under her bright orange polo shirt, the name tag picking up the reflection of the flashing police lights.

"Come on, man," Pete said gently. "I know you don't want to hurt Vanessa. You're not that kind of guy. You want to talk. I'll listen. We can get Vanessa back to her kids and grandkids." He had no idea if she had any, but guessed Jeremy didn't either.

"Bullshit," Jeremy said, but not with the same force as before. "You don't want to talk. It's a trick."

Vanessa made a small noise. To the prayer that had been repeating in his head—*please let this work, please let this work*—Pete added a plea that Vanessa wouldn't do anything to set Jeremy off.

"The night I brought you to the hospital I did exactly what I said I would, right? No bullshit, right?"

Jeremy's eyes stopped skittering. They held Pete's. His Adam's apple bobbed in his skinny, pale neck. The kid was scared shitless. Pete gave a small nod, like before. *Trust me.*

"Okay, but I'm keeping the knife."

"That's fine." It wasn't, but he'd deal with that after Vanessa was safe.

"Sorry," Jeremy said to Vanessa. For one terrifying second Pete thought it was a prelude to him cutting her throat. Then he removed his arm from around her neck.

Vanessa stood still, swaying. Pete reached out, too far away to take her arm, hoping she'd move toward him before Jeremy changed his mind.

"Come on, Vanessa. You can go."

She took a step toward him. His eyes on Jeremy, he took Vanessa's arm. It was ice cold, trembling. He gave a squeeze to reassure her, but also as a signal to get moving. "Vanessa. It's okay. They're waiting for you."

She turned to him, tried to form words. She was paralyzed with terror. He gently turned her, pressed his hand firmly on her back.

"Wait," Jeremy said. "You don't move. Only her."

"Vanessa, go," Pete said softly. He squeezed her arm, harder this time. "Please. It's okay."

She came alive with a jolt. "Oh my god," she whispered. She reached the door in three strides, opened it, and flung herself outside. A smattering of cheers came through the door with the cold wind. A crowd had gathered.

"I don't want everyone watching me," Jeremy said.

"They can't see you where you're standing." Pete turned off the radio, held it out for Jeremy to see, then put it on the table next to his gloves and hat. "Why don't you tell me what's going on?"

Jeremy shook his head, but his shoulders slumped. He looked sad and scared. Defeated.

"Tell me, Jeremy."

"Everything. Nothing."

"Why this morning? What happened?"

"Happened?" His face switched from defeated to angry. "I'm tired of people's shit, that's all. All the time. Just tired of it."

"These women gave you shit?"

"I can tell you don't believe me." He held the knife at his side. Pete wondered if he'd forgotten about it. Pete's leg started to spasm. He shifted his weight.

Jeremy lifted the knife, pointed it at Pete. "Don't fucking move."

"I believe you, that they gave you shit. Tell me what happened."

"They don't like me, some of the girls here. I know that. When I came in, one of them made a face and whispered something to the other girl. I have money to pay. It's not like I come in here and steal. It's not just them, it's everyone. My girlfriend is pissed at me. Everywhere I go I get shit."

"I get it. You're trying hard, but no one gives you credit. It seems like everyone's judging you instead of seeing you."

"It doesn't *seem* like. They are. Vanessa's nice. She didn't do nothing.

I feel bad, but I got pissed, and she was right there wiping a table and just smiling, like she was in on the joke. So, you know. I was just really pissed off. And…" It came out in a rush. He stopped, looked at the knife in his hand. Wiped it against his thigh.

"Want to sit down? You know, really talk?" Pete was desperate to get the knife. Patience and listening were the keys, but he wasn't sure how long his leg would hold up.

"No," Jeremy said.

"It'd be easier to talk if you weren't holding that knife. You don't have to give it to me, but I'd feel better if you put it on a table or the counter."

"I bet you would."

Pete almost smiled. It's what his brother would've said in the same situation. Or Bernie, in a different one. "You've got me there."

"Gotcha," Jeremy said, more to himself than to Pete. His eyes were focused past Pete's shoulder. There was no window over there, just a shelf with napkins, straws, cup lids, the trash can. Jeremy was thinking. Pete was ready for it to go either way.

"You aren't stupid," Pete said once it was clear Jeremy wasn't going to talk. "You must know this is a no-win situation. You were brave to let Vanessa go. It showed you're a good person who cares. If you end this now, things won't be that bad." Pete nodded toward the window. "We both know this could get a lot worse. It's up to you. You don't want that to happen." He was spreading it too thick. He needed to ask the right questions, not preach. "You must feel pretty bad, hopeless, to be here. What is it?"

Jeremy shrugged.

"We're not going anywhere. Tell me."

Jeremy tapped the knife against his thigh, his other hand clenched, then unclenched in rhythm with it. The buzz of the crowd outside had gotten louder. Pete could almost physically feel the growing impatience of the state police, the sheriff's deputies, his own officers, all just beyond that pane of glass. They were only going to give him so much time. He hoped they were paying attention to his body language.

Watching him. Trusting him. He kept his eyes on Jeremy, his hands out slightly, waist-high, the way they'd been since he'd put the radio down. He didn't have to work to keep his face calm, open. His success at seeming—*being*—laid back and empathetic had earned him grudging respect from his fellow Philly cops, many of whom considered mindfucks, lies, and bullying the best ways to get what they wanted out of a suspect.

They stood in silence, listening to the buzz from outside. The Muzak, which Pete hadn't noticed until now, softly played a vaguely familiar pop tune. As he watched Jeremy, he tried to remember what the song was, another trick to keep his impatience in check. The other part of his brain was hypervigilant, Jeremy its only focus.

"Am I going to be arrested?"

"Yeah." Pete relaxed, just a fraction. The fact Jeremy hadn't qualified it with *would I be* or *if I give up* was a good sign. "You threatened people with a knife, right? Held it to Vanessa's neck. I promise I'll make sure you get help, too. What happened here this morning isn't you. I'll make sure that's taken into account."

"I don't want to go to jail again."

"You're going to have to. I can make sure you get a good lawyer who'll help you get the best possible deal, if you want me to. I'll make sure the DA knows you let Vanessa go. You cooperated."

"My lawyer last time sucked. No one gives a shit. I can't go to jail. I have a girlfriend. She has kids. Shit, she is going to be so pissed. I lost my job, now this." He angrily wiped his eyes with the sleeve of his parka.

"Look, Jeremy, I know it's scary. I know you feel like no one will listen, because no one has in the past. I know you're afraid once you let go of the knife, your life will go to shit. But I'll help make sure things are as okay as possible."

"My life already is shit."

"It could get a lot worse, right? The decisions you make now will make the difference. It'll be worse, for a little bit of time, no matter what. Then it can get better. Or a lot worse. You can turn things around, take care of your girlfriend the way you want to. Take care of your kids."

"They're her kids, but I…" He laughed, half bark, half cough. "An hour ago I was worried she'd be pissed if she knew I was blowing money on iced coffee and a doughnut. Now look. She's going to be done with me."

"All you can do is prove to her that you're committed to doing better. She loves you, right?"

Jeremy shrugged.

"Back in March, you were unemployed and using, right? But you got a job."

"Don't you listen?"

"I know you were fired. But you proved you could do it. She understands that. She has faith in you, right?"

He shrugged. "I wasn't even using, because she didn't want me to, with the kids. But since I lost my job. Whatever."

"I promise I'll make sure you get the help you need. With drugs, mental health. I can even talk to your girlfriend if you think it'll help."

"It won't. She hates cops." At least he was listening, his wheels turning. Pete needed to close the deal.

"What's her name?"

"I'm not fucking telling you that. So you can hassle her? Threaten to take the kids away? Fuck you."

Wrong move. "I wouldn't do that."

"Fuck you."

"You obviously care about her and her kids." Pete needed a foothold, needed to gauge the right approach. His time was running out with the guys outside. He latched onto the speech he gave himself in the mirror when he brushed his teeth. "You know how to be the man she knows you are. So, do it."

Jeremy's eyes flashed. The knife tapped angrily against his leg. "It won't be worse if I kill myself. It'll just be over."

Pete's heart sank. How had he lost ground so fast? "I'm going to do everything I can to keep that from happening. I'm five feet away from you. If you try to kill yourself, I'll be right there, and the worst that'll happen is you'll hurt yourself, maybe a little, maybe seriously. You think your life is bad now? It'll be a lot worse if you're in the hospital or incapacitated. Not just for you, for your girlfriend and her kids too." He knew waiting, letting silence do its trick, was important, but he couldn't stop himself. "I know how you feel. You don't really want to die, but—"

"What the fuck do you know? You have no idea how I feel."

"Yes. I do. I thought of killing myself once." *Twice. More.* "I came very close. I didn't want to die. I know that now, but I didn't then. What I wanted was to stop feeling the way I did. I didn't think I ever would. I'm so glad I didn't do it. Things *do* get better."

"Yeah right." He wiped his nose with the hand that held the knife. Pete fought the urge to leap forward and wrestle it from him.

"I have a girlfriend too. Even though I love her more than anything it didn't stop me. I was just thinking about myself. When I think now what that would've done to her, it scares the shit out of me. Nothing that happened to me could be worse than doing that to her. Do you understand?"

"You're different from me. You weren't going to jail. I don't think my girlfriend gives a shit right now what happens to me anyway."

"I don't believe you. But if it's true, I bet you can think of at least one person who you don't want to let down, even if it's not her. There must be someone who cares about you and who you matter to." Pete hoped like hell there was, or this would backfire too.

"I guess." He wiped his eyes with the knife hand again. Pete tried to keep his own eyes from following the knife. "Probably my mom."

"Think of your mom," Pete said. "The end really is the end. There's no chance to make amends. No one will ever love you the way your mom does, right? Do you want to do that to her? No chance to put your arms around your girlfriend, no chance to hang out with your buddies, help those kids grow up. No chance for anything."

Jeremy was full-blown crying. "Shut the fuck up. Get out. Leave me alone."

"Jeremy, drop the knife." He said it softly, a plea. "I'm not leaving without you." He'd inched closer, could probably tackle him. He didn't want to. He wanted everything he'd said to be true, for Jeremy to know that. He felt the eyes through the window. Felt Tyler and whoever else was out there wondering why he was letting it go this long.

"Get out," Jeremy said, a sob, the arm that held the knife covering his eyes.

"No." Pete stretched one hand toward the window, palm facing the watching cops. *Stop.* He lowered it when Jeremy brought his arm down.

"Jeremy, I could've jumped you about a dozen times since we started talking. I could've signaled to those guys outside to shoot you through the window. I didn't, right? Please trust me. I know what it's like to feel like no one cares. But people do. I do." His voice cracked. "I'm telling you the truth." He wanted to wipe his eyes, too, but was afraid to make a sudden move that would startle Jeremy or be misinterpreted by the guys with the guns. He hoped they couldn't see the tears on his cheeks. It was the damn PTSD. This shit was too close.

On the other hand, it worked.

"Okay." Jeremy deflated. All the bluster and energy seeped out of him. He dropped the knife.

"Thank you," Pete said. Inside, he collapsed with relief. He moved toward Jeremy as he took the handcuffs off his belt. "I have to cuff you, okay?"

"Whatever."

"I also have to turn my radio back on to let them know we're coming out."

"Whatever. You were going to fucking talk me to death."

Pete cuffed Jeremy's hands, in front, not behind. He kicked the knife away, out of reach. He held Jeremy by one arm, trying not to grip him too tight, but tight enough. The danger was still there. Jeremy could change his mind and turn on him, even without the knife.

Pete wiped his eyes. He picked up the radio. "I have Jeremy in custody. We're going to come out. I'll hand him off to Officer Anderson, who'll transport him to Redimere PD."

After an acknowledgement crackled, Pete said to Jeremy, "I walked here, so I can't take you. Tyler will take good care of you."

Jeremy shrugged.

"I meant everything I said."

Another shrug.

"He'll Mirandize you at the station. No one will hassle you if you don't want to say anything. In fact, you probably should wait for your lawyer." Bernie would be proud of him. The other cops would crucify him. "Don't tell anyone I said that," he added with a smile.

Pete's radio crackled. "Redimere 0-1, we're waiting." It wasn't Tyler but a state trooper. Pete could see him through the window, a blue-uniformed giant in front of a cruiser that was parked in the middle of the street, lights flashing.

"I'm just talking to Jeremy. We'll be out shortly," Pete said. Jeremy's lawyer would probably have a field day with this if he or she caught wind of it. But he wasn't trying to get information out of him, he was trying to help. "A Franklin County deputy will take you to Farmington later, since we just have a small holding cell. They'll book you into jail. Do you have a lawyer?"

"I had a guy, but he sucked."

"Okay, if you can't get one, I can help you. Ready? Let's go." He squeezed Jeremy's arm and took a deep breath. Jeremy took one too.

Tyler and the state troopers approached as Pete walked Jeremy past the state cruiser to Redimere's. He saw Carrie, camera high to shoot past the police line, taking photos. He was acutely aware of Bernie at Carrie's side. He told himself not to look, to focus on getting Jeremy into the cruiser before someone had a better idea, but he did anyway. Her face was white. Even from yards away he could tell.

"It's okay," he said even though she couldn't hear him.

He opened the back door of the cruiser, and put his hand on Jeremy's head, gently guiding rather than pushing. "It's okay," he repeated, then closed the door.

CHAPTER 12

B ERNIE CAUGHT PETE'S eye as he led the kid to the cruiser. Well, not a kid exactly, but he was skinny, strung-out looking, obviously scared, vulnerable. He didn't look like a threat, but Bernie knew better. Pete gave her a quick nod. *I'm okay.* She knew better about that too. Despite the meds, the therapy, the hard, hard work he'd done, something like this could be a trigger. A Big T, Pete's therapist, Benjamin, called it. Big T's had big consequences. Pete had earnestly repeated it to Bernie. She'd nodded, fake earnestly, hoping that behind the jargon, Benjamin was the cure. For now, though, Big T meant big trouble.

"Let's get back," Bernie said to Carrie. Pete was talking to a couple of state troopers. They didn't look any happier now than they had as they'd stood with their hands on their holsters, their radios to their lips as Pete, just visible through the window, seemed to be having a casual chat with a guy holding a knife.

"I'll give the chief a call in a bit to see what he can tell me," Carrie said as they walked back. "I guess our first edition of 2011 is going to be pretty newsy."

"Newsy. Yeah." Bernie reached into her pocket for her cellphone, feeling the need to text Pete that she loved him and was thinking about him. It wasn't there, of course.

The office was warm and smelled like coffee. Normally Bernie would be soothed, but her heart and mind were back on Main Street in the cold wind.

"We were listening on the scanner, but it didn't tell us much," Guy said as he, Shirley, Paul, and Annette watched Bernie and Carrie hang up their coats.

"Suspect in custody," Carrie said. "Chief Novotny peacefully talked him into submission."

"Good to hear it," Guy said.

Annette clapped. Shirley and Paul, deep into their ad sales and layouts, murmured positive things.

Bernie wanted her cellphone. Wanted it bad. She punched Pete's work number into her desk phone even though she knew he wouldn't be back yet. Vicki picked up.

"Can you ask Pete to give me a call when he can? I don't have my cell or I'd text."

Bernie wanted to leave him a message. Let him know she was thinking of him. But not through Vicki. The convenience of tapping on a name had immediately erased most phone numbers from her memory. Funny how she could still recite her family's phone number from when she was a kid, but blanked on the number of the person she talked to the most.

Wait. She opened her desk drawer and pushed a couple notebooks aside. There, in all its glory, was her old flip phone. She'd considered giving it to Pete to donate to the county domestic violence organization, which repurposed them—she'd written an article about it—but then she didn't. She hadn't totally trusted the miraculous new smartphone technology, so she'd hung on to it in case her new phone failed her. She'd had to change providers and couldn't get the same number since she was keeping the old phone. All of it made the guy at the phone store treat her like an addlebrained idiot. Even though she did her best to make sure everyone had her new number, there had been rogue calls to the old one, mostly from her parents. They'd tapered off, though. At some point she'd put the phone in her desk drawer and forgotten about it as junk piled on top of it.

The problem now was, if she used the old phone to call Pete, it would bring up the troubling fact that she had it. Pete would tell her she had to give it to Libby. She'd gotten the iPhone in October, a birthday present to herself, and of course Libby wanted the one she'd had before that, too. She'd told him she'd given it to Pete to donate. At the time, that's what her brain told her she'd done. It was too full of fire and dead bodies and George Libby's smug judgment to update the information in whatever lobe it was stored in.

The thought of them having access to everything she'd texted for years, everyone she'd called, made her want to throw up. She'd figure out what to do about it later. For now, she'd just feel like some kind of drug dealer or con woman with a secret burner phone.

She scrolled through the directory, surprised the phone still had battery power. She found Pete's number. She put the cellphone back in the drawer, pushing it behind notebooks, a box of paper clips, and some ancient protein bars. She punched his number into her work phone.

"I know you're busy." She tried to say it quietly so her coworkers wouldn't hear. "I just wanted to let you know I love you. Check in when you get a sec, okay? Carrie's gonna call at some point for the story. Talk later."

While she was leaving the message, she had another thought about the flip phone. She dug it out again. It had been weeks since she'd checked the voicemail. There were seventeen, all from people she'd talked to since then. Except one.

Her heart stopped for just a second.

Normand Ouimette left a message on December 20.

"Hi Bernadette, this is Norm Ouimette. Can you give me a call ASAP? It's urgent. I don't want to say anything on the phone."

****

Dawna had not enjoyed her time that morning in Augusta. It was obvious that the investigators were focused on Bernie. She understood. On the other hand, Bernie didn't set her house on fire or know anything about the body. She tried, as politely and diplomatically as possible, to see if other avenues were being pursued.

"Have you considered a second crime scene? Maybe the deceased wasn't killed at that house but placed there?" She tried to say it mildly, almost apologetically, so they wouldn't get defensive.

"There's nothing to indicate that," Libby said. To his credit, he wasn't totally dismissive, more like he was lecturing a rookie about something fundamental. "The lungs were too damaged to tell if they'd inhaled smoke, but even if they hadn't, the deceased was likely killed on-site. I mean, think about it. Why would someone go through the trouble of killing a person somewhere else and then put their body in a house and burn it down?"

Dawna could think of a lot of reasons. The point was exploring the possibilities. Which they weren't.

"Why would the homeowner do that—kill someone in another location, then put the deceased in her own house and burn it down?" Libby asked.

Dawna could think of answers to that too, but didn't want to give them more ammo against Bernie.

"Maybe, if that were the case, it's not the homeowner who killed the person. Or even burned down her house," she said.

Libby looked up from the papers he'd been shuffling. She knew what he saw—someone who he didn't think could contribute much to the investigation. Someone wasting his time. Despite the confidence Pete had given her the past couple of years, she still hadn't figured out how to overcome the Libbys of the world.

She plowed ahead anyway. "I know fires are the worst, as far as evidence goes, with it all being either burned or soaked."

"We have good evidence," Libby said, once again listing everything that implicated Bernie.

Now, as she sat in Pete's office listening to him recount the standoff, she weighed how much to tell him. She'd gone back and forth on it as she drove home. He was her supervisor. More than that, they were good friends. He treated her like an equal. Her loyalty to him was akin to what she'd felt with her fellow Navy Corpsmen in Afghanistan.

He was honest and smart. On the other hand, he was the partner of the main, and apparently only, suspect. Dawna felt an almost physical barrier to crossing that line.

Then there was this: As he matter-of-factly recounted the incident with Jeremy, he'd started shaking. He stopped talking, drew in a long breath. Closed his eyes. When he opened them, he wiped tears. It lasted seconds, but she knew a panic attack when she saw one.

"I'm okay. Just haven't had much sleep. This thing with Bernie…"

"I know." She did know. A lot. He'd been open about his PTSD since he began treatment, something she'd been pushing for more than a year. He'd seemed better, but recently she felt him slipping. It was small things. Subtle. A look. A drawn breath. A panic attack.

"I know today was tough," she added. "But Tyler and Jamie told me you were great. Any day something like that can be resolved with no one hurt is a good day."

"Right." His half smile said otherwise.

"Right. Period."

He smiled wider. "Okay, right."

"Do you want to hear about my briefing?" She didn't know until she said it that she'd overcome her resistance to discussing it with him.

"I'm not sure we should be talking about it."

"Who else am I supposed to talk to? I need a sounding board, and you're it."

"Talking will hurt you a lot more than it'll hurt me."

"It's not like I'm in the loop anyway. I probably don't know anything that you don't. I trust you. I don't trust them. I know you'll always do the right thing." She launched in before he could argue.

"We know eyewitness evidence can be faulty," Pete said when she finished.

"Which doesn't stop anyone from hanging a case on it or a jury from believing it."

"If it comes to that. But a good defense attorney could easily destroy the account of some neighbor looking out his window on a dark night."

"It's officially arson now, by the way," Dawna said. "Tests at the lab confirmed an accelerant and they left two gas cans at the scene."

Pete perked up. "Where?"

"In the garden shed. They'd been placed, supposedly to look like they belonged there, but they were on top of new snow that had drifted in. The issue is, no prints, so maybe wiped clean? They're standard five-gallon plastic ones that everyone has for their lawn mowers and snowmobiles. Libby said that an arsonist other than the homeowner would've thrown them in the fire, not put them back in the shed."

"Speculating on what someone would or wouldn't do and considering it evidence is always a mistake," Pete said. "Someone trying to frame the homeowner would put them in the shed too. The lack of prints means nothing since so many factors play into that. Especially this time of year. No one's going to be doing that with their bare hands. They'd wear gloves."

"Maybe they should check Bernie's gloves. When they don't find gas…" She shrugged.

Pete laughed. "Have you ever seen her at the gas pump? I guarantee they'll find gas."

"The gas cans are the biggest piece of evidence, at least that they told me about. Bernie can't be excluded, which is why they told me, I'm sure. They want to send a message that she's still on the hook."

"The joke's on them. She doesn't own one gas can, much less two. She uses a reel mower. She doesn't have a boat or snowmobile."

"She could still have gas cans in her car, in case she runs out of gas."

"Not her. She ran out a couple months ago. We had a discussion about it, since she's run out of gas many times in her life, which I just can't understand. I told her she should get a gas can for her car, and she took my head off. Upshot is, she didn't feel the need to have a gas can, and if I ever got her one, she'd shove it up my ass. I know the argument wasn't actually about the gas can, but bottom line is, she doesn't have one."

"I'll let Libby know."

"Maybe Stephanie bought them, but there's nothing gas-powered at the house. If they were for her car, they'd be in her car. If it were my case, I'd consider that it could be staged. Why would Bernie, or Stephanie for that matter, put them back in the shed if they'd used them to burn down the house? Throw them in the fire or leave them in the yard, like most arsonists do. It's more likely someone wanted them to be found. My money is on Stephanie as the arsonist. Libby made sure to let me know they haven't been able to reach her. I'm sure he thought it was a dig—that Bernie could have killed her—but all that says to me is that Stephanie's taken off and doesn't want to be found."

"Then whose remains are those?" Dawna asked.

"God only knows."

****

Bernie wanted to get to Stephanie's former workplace with plenty of time to catch second shift going in, but at Kermit's request, she stopped by his office on the way out of town. She almost immediately wished she hadn't. Still, she'd known since Sunday this was coming, that her texts were going to come back to haunt her.

She sank further and further into the soft, enveloping chair as the reality of her idiocy became clear.

"They haven't given me transcripts or told me what the content is," Kermit said. "They *have* given me a heads-up that the texts are incriminating. Which is odd. Usually, they just spring things."

Bernie didn't need transcripts. She knew exactly what they said.

Bottom line is, they wanted to talk in Farmington in the morning.

"It's up to you, but since it's officially arson now, the best course is to explain. If you don't, they may use them to get an arrest warrant."

"Who says they'll believe me?" Kermit had said *arrest warrant* the same casual way he'd said *strawberry cruller* when he'd offered her one ten minutes earlier. Yes, she'd eaten it. Of course she had. Now, she wanted to run, screaming, out of Kermit's warm and elegant house into the cold wind and just keep running.

"If you explain, it makes it harder for them to convince a judge to sign a warrant based on the texts. We would also make the case that they need to talk to the text recipients, as well as provide their responses, to put it all in context. That'd slow them down."

"If the judge signs the warrant, they'd still arrest me, right? You'd be making that case with me in jail."

"I don't believe they're going to arrest you, at least not tomorrow. I don't even know for sure they really believe the texts are significant. I think they want to use them as a wedge to get you to confess or say something incriminating. I'll be there to keep that from happening."

****

The meeting with Kermit sapped Bernie's excitement about her plan to reach out to Stephanie's coworkers. Even without it, though, she had to do it. She pulled up on the shoulder near the Sturgis entrance drive, a straight, wide concrete shot to a building a good quarter mile down, a massive hulk with just a few windows in the front, surrounded by chicken wire topped with razor wire. There was a guardhouse halfway down the drive. She wasn't going to go anywhere near it.

She'd made sure her sign would be easy to read for anyone focused on getting to work on time, so they'd see more than just some crazy lady standing in the snow at the side of the road. She'd printed DO YOU KNOW STEPHANIE? on newspaper page-size proof sheets. Underneath was a photo of Stephanie, enlarged as big as Bernie could make it while keeping it recognizable, and CALL ME with Bernie's office phone number. She'd considered using the number for her old flip phone instead, but if Libby took it, she'd be sunk. She hoped that potential tipsters weren't scared off by her voice message, identifying herself as the editor in chief of the *Weekly Watcher*. On the other hand, it may lend some credibility.

She watched from the warmth of her car as the last of the first shift left. There was a fifteen-minute gap between shifts "for security purposes," as Stephanie had put it. No one seemed curious about her car being there, a good sign. If they weren't curious, maybe the security staff wouldn't be either.

When it was time, she pulled her hood up over her hat and wrapped her scarf around her neck as well as the lower half of her face. She wasn't trying to disguise herself, just stay warm. Sturgis was in one of the rare flat areas among the hills and mountains that ran along the border of Franklin and Somerset Counties. When they'd built it, they'd cut down every tree on their multiacre property. Made it easier for their dozens of surveillance cameras and guards to scope out intruders, but it turned it into an open wind-blown tundra.

She only had so much time, even though she'd stay on the main road. As she stepped into the whipping wind, she sang "And on the sign it said no trespassing, but on the other side it didn't say nothing."

She planted herself in the snowbank at the corner of the entrance to the company driveway. "This land was made for you and me," she sang. The wind whipped her sign, and she had to hold it both top and bottom. She hoped that was enough so they'd be able to read it.

She didn't have to wait long. As a pickup truck came down the road, signaled, and slowed, the driver glanced over, then looked longer. His truck was followed by another, then another, then more, too many for her to rest her arms. She felt the thrill of success, though every minute was excruciating. The part of her face exposed to the wind stung, and her glasses were too cold on her nose, which was running nonstop.

When she'd started, she'd tried to keep her eye out for traffic coming from the plant, since it would likely be security. She'd get shooed away at some point, of that she was certain. But the wind was too much, and she'd had to hold the sign up in front of her face to block it. That's why, a little before three, she didn't see the SUV.

She was startled by a vehicle door slamming yards away. Two men approached. They were in uniforms, the kind meant to make a private security force look like it was legit military or law enforcement.

"Can we help you, ma'am?" one of them asked. Not friendly.

"No, I'm good." She held the sign steady, buying as much time as she could before the inevitable happened.

"You're going to have to leave," the guy said.

"I'm on public property." *On the other side, it didn't say nothing…* She almost sang out loud. The traffic was slowing more now that there was a confrontation to watch. Several cars were backed up at the turn. The guy who wasn't talking waved them on.

"The law states you can't loiter within two hundred yards of our facility." So far, he'd barely glanced at her sign. All she needed was a few more minutes to make sure everyone saw it.

"Really? I didn't know that was a law." She smiled and put on her ditzy-gal act, which sometimes worked, sometimes didn't. "Am I loitering?"

"You need to leave."

"I'm trying to find my missing friend. She worked here up until, I think, the end of October. Do you know her?" She turned the sign slightly toward the guards.

"No," they both said at the same time.

"Did you look closely?" They hadn't looked at all. She desperately wanted to wipe her nose. She also had to pee. She just needed a couple more minutes. An arrest, though, would be a big problem in many ways, including getting the paper out. But they couldn't arrest her, right? They were just security guards.

"Please leave or we're going to call the sheriff's department."

The stream of vehicles had ended. There was no one on the main road as far as Bernie could see in either direction.

She rolled up the poster. "Sorry I inconvenienced you guys."

They watched as she got into the car. The wheels spun in the snow at the side of the road before they caught. She did a three-point turn, waved, and took off for Redimere. She checked her rearview mirror as she hit the gas. They stood, motionless, watching her drive away.

CHAPTER 13

P ETE OPENED THE door to the smell of tomato sauce on the stove. Bernie always said walking into a warm house that smelled like food on a cold day makes anyone feel better. She was right.

"The conquering hero," she said. "We literally have not talked since this morning. And you know how I feel about using the word *literally*."

He put his arms around her as she stood at the stove. Warm and soft. He could melt right into her. He kissed the back of her neck. "Sorry I never called you back. I kept meaning to, but things kept coming up."

"A guy with a knife. Some excuse." She leaned back against him, then slipped out of his arms and went to the refrigerator. "How did your talk with the mayor go? Is this all we have for lettuce?" She dumped a pile of vegetables next to where he was leaning on the counter. "I made the rash decision to break out the final batch of the frozen sauce and meatballs from Mom. I figured we both deserve it. My day was shitty, but you win the shitty day competition, hands down. Want a beer?"

She was doing that thing she did when she was upset but trying to act like she wasn't. Talking about trivial things. Moving around. Not looking at him.

"I never made the meeting. Any updates from Kermit?"

"Yeah." She handed him a beer, then started tearing the lettuce.

"And?"

"It's hard to make a salad when you're practically standing on top of me."

"I'll make the salad. Why don't you relax and tell me about your day."

"Your day is a more urgent discussion topic."

"I'm sick and tired of my day. What did Kermit say?"

"I guess I'll finish off that wine we opened yesterday." She took the bottle out of the fridge. "Tommy left enough for one glass."

As he chopped vegetables, he watched her at the table, chin in hand, swirling the wine in her glass, wheels turning.

"Did anyone report Stephanie to the department?" she finally asked.

"For what?"

"Selling pot? Anything like that?"

He didn't have to think about it. "No. I would've told you. Where'd this come from?"

"My neighbor Dean Davis. He said he did."

"The one with the stick up his ass? I don't know what he's talking about, but I see all the reports, and I would've let you know if I saw something. You know that." She was watching him with a concentrated scrutiny that made him uncomfortable. He still wasn't used to the way her glasses made her already huge eyes look bigger, but this was more than just the glasses. "I know your anxiety is at DEFCON 1. Don't add rumors to the mix. Tell me about Kermit."

"It's not a rumor. He told me he made a report."

"He's lying."

Her look practically pinned him to the counter.

"He's lying, Bernie. I don't know why, but he is. Tell me what Kermit had to say."

She sighed, long and exaggerated. Took a longer drink of wine. "They want to talk to me tomorrow. Kermit will be there, of course."

"I'm sure it's nothing to worry about."

"It's about my texts. Kermit doesn't know specifics, but he figures they're bad enough that they can get an arrest warrant. Talking with them will cut the warrant off at the pass."

Her tone of voice, overly careful, fake cheerful, meant this was bad. He asked the question he should've asked the previous day when they took her phone. "What texts are you worried about?"

"Not ours, though I'm sure Libby has read them. Probably ones I sent to Sal and Carol and Robin bitching about Stephanie."

"Okay."

"There's one in particular that I think they'll focus on." She met his eyes. Hers filled her face. His heart broke. "You know me and my sense of humor."

"Bernie."

"When I went into the house Friday and saw the mess—I think this is probably the worst one—I texted Sal that I should just burn the place down."

He put down the paring knife.

"Then, as if that wasn't enough, I added, 'Too bad Stephanie isn't here to burn with it.' " She took a big gulp of wine. "LOL."

"Oh, Bernie." He was at her side in three steps. He pulled her head against him, her tears immediately soaking through his thin uniform shirt and the T-shirt underneath. "Oh, Bernie," he said again, a whisper. He kissed the top of her head.

She pulled away, took off her glasses, and wiped her eyes with her forearm. "Obviously, if I'd known my house was going to burn down and Stephanie, or whoever, was going to be found dead in the rubble, I wouldn't have texted that."

"I know." He sat down. "It seems bad, but you'd have to be an idiot to text that, then do it."

"Well." She spread her arms in an exaggerated Italian shrug.

"You're not an idiot. If I were investigating, I'd look into it but assume it was likely an unfortunate coincidence."

"Thanks for thinking I'm not an idiot." She drained her glass. "George Libby isn't you. I'm sure he's said more than once in his stellar career that classic cop cliché, 'I don't believe in coincidences.' I wonder how many innocent people have gone to the chair because cops don't believe in coincidences?"

"He's not stupid."

"I know how cops can take something like that and run with it."

"They'd need more evidence. There isn't any."

She brushed tears away in an angry swipe. "Pete, I didn't burn down my house. I didn't kill anyone."

"I know." He wanted to hug her again, but he'd learned hugs came later. What she needed in the initial stages of a crisis was space to process her feelings and repeated reassurances that he was on her side. The space part was hard, but the second part was easy.

Her lips trembled as she looked at her wineglass, twisting the stem between her fingers. She took a deep breath but didn't say anything.

"They'll figure out pretty quick you didn't do it," he said. "I know it's pointless to tell you not to worry, but don't. It'll be okay."

"I know you're mad, so just be mad instead of acting nice."

"I'm not acting and I'm not mad. Well, I am, but at whoever burned down your house. Whoever killed the poor person who was found inside."

"There's another thing, but I don't know if the cops know about it. Dean told the cops he saw—"

"Your car there New Year's Eve after dark?"

"You knew?"

"Dawna told me this afternoon. It obviously wasn't you. I can back that up. You were here."

"The problem is," she said, eyes on him, sparkless and darker than he'd ever seen them. "Are they going to take your word for it?"

****

Bernie was usually at her desk by six-thirty on Tuesday. It was production day, which meant fifteen or sixteen hours of work, at least. This Tuesday was no different, unless you counted the fact that she'd been up since three, when Pete's nightmare blasted her out of bed. She'd left for work shortly after five, since she was going to lose time she couldn't afford to go to Farmington to talk to investigators about crimes she didn't commit and knew nothing about.

"This day already sucks and the sun's barely up," she said at eight, as she settled into the passenger seat of Kermit's incredibly clean, comfortable, and warm SUV.

"Then it can only get better," he said.

As they sped south on Route 27 to Farmington, Kermit kept up a nonstop stream of advice, speculation, and admonishment, but Bernie barely heard it. She was having trouble focusing. She couldn't remember if she'd taken her pill. If she had her cell, she'd call Pete even though he was at work, and ask him. He'd remember.

"What?" she said to Kermit for the millionth time.

"I said, you have to be totally alert and focused. Something you're apparently not."

"Sorry. I had trouble sleeping."

"I'm going to shut up now and let you get your head together. But to summarize: Answer their questions with the truth, no tangents, speculation, or details they don't ask for."

"Should we have a signal if I want to bail? Like I say Blackhawk down or tug my ear?"

"How about you say, 'I need to consult with my attorney,' and we go out in the hall to talk."

"I guess that would work."

"I know it sounds crazy, but yeah."

"I just want my phone back." She didn't know how many times she'd said it over the past few days. It felt like once she had her phone, everything else would be manageable.

"Hopefully that will happen today. They're going to jerk you around about it first, though. Stay focused."

She tried to concentrate on what she'd say about the texts as she watched the snow-covered fields and woods roll past, colorless against the gray sky. Her texts were innocent. Bad jokes. She was sorry, given the circumstances. *Don't say that you're sorry unless they ask if you are.* She couldn't remember if Kermit had told her to show remorse. She didn't have the energy to ask. She *was* remorseful about her stupid texts. The rest of it? She wished it had never happened, but she was otherwise clueless. Isn't remorse feeling bad about something you actually did?

How was she supposed to react to Dean Davis's supposed sighting of her around eight when at the time she'd probably been annoyed at Pete's pontificating on how much the contestants should bet (something that always confused her) and the fact that he once again knew the answer to Final Jeopardy? The annoyance was part of the routine—she enjoyed it. He was so cute, knowing all the answers and doing all that math. It was a mundane night, but special. She'd felt peace as they sat there, doing the jigsaw puzzle, snacking, watching *Jeopardy!*. She felt content. She felt *good*.

Yes, she was pissed at Stephanie. Yes, she wanted to move home. She was also happy being there, having a nice quiet New Year's Eve with Pete. There's no way she would've gone from the warm living room, the pellet stove humming, the dog and cats snoring around them, into subfreezing temperatures and snow unless the house they were in was burning down. Forget about driving across town to burn down her own house. The thought jolted her from her semislumber. *Don't say that. Don't make offhand remarks about fires.*

Her brain felt melted and useless. She probably did take her pill, but it was no match for lack of sleep, ping-ponging anxiety, and the crushing fear for Pete that hadn't faded since his terrorized shouts woke her up. When he'd started talking and thrashing around in his sleep, she knew it was going to be a bad one. Benjamin had said Bernie shouldn't wake him up during a nightmare. Hard as it was, she didn't. Pete sometimes didn't wake up either. But he'd had a similar one Thursday, and she could tell this was going to be the same. She got out of bed, hoping it would fizzle out, knowing it wouldn't.

After he'd headed for the bathroom—his usual retreat after a bad nightmare—she got to work stripping the bed. He'd never peed during a nightmare, that she knew of, until Thursday. Now he'd done it again. He joked about it, but she knew he was mortified. She, on the other hand, tried to imagine the terror that would cause that. She approached changing the sheets matter-of-factly. *Just get past it.*

She wanted to help, but didn't know how. She needed to figure it out since she'd pushed hard for him after his accident to address his PTSD. Instead, all she could do was change sheets and pretend it was normal. Now, while he was at work, likely fighting a migraine—they came like clockwork after a nightmare—and pretending he was fine, she was in a Lexus with heated seats roaring down to Farmington to talk to the state police about texts she'd sent about burning down her house the same day someone set fire to it.

"There's something seriously wrong with me," she said.

Kermit patted her knee. "Join the club, my friend."

"So happy there's a club for that, but I can't imagine it'll help any of us."

****

Bernie and Kermit were shown into a small conference room at the sheriff's department, which had lent Libby the space. Bernie was surprised that it wasn't one of those tight, windowless chambers with metal chairs, like you see on *Dateline*, where the cops lean in and put their hand on your knee as they bark at you to just admit you did it. She scanned the upper wall for a video camera. She found it in a corner, light blinking red.

"They always make you wait," Kermit said. "Part of the power play."

"I'm sure they're really busy," Bernie said, playing for the camera. She would have asked Kermit if it was okay that it was recording, since she was alone with her attorney, but she didn't want to let on to whoever may be watching that she'd noticed it.

Libby made them wait twenty minutes before he bustled in, his suit jacket tight against his muscular chest, his scalp shiny under his buzz cut, full of what Bernie thought of as righteous self-importance. She felt vindicated that she could still see his horseshoe-pattern baldness despite the close cut.

"How's everyone this morning?" he asked.

"Awesome," Bernie said.

"We are well. And you?" Kermit said.

Bernie hated small talk, but with the camera, she pictured a day sometime in the future, in a courtroom, where the video would be played to show how her attitude was a clear indication of her guilt. Maybe it would be on *Dateline*, with a box in the corner of the screen asking viewers to tweet whether they thought she was guilty. "Would you send joke texts about burning down your house? Let us know!" People across the U.S. would gleefully type into their phones and laptops that no, of course they wouldn't. She was either an idiot or guilty. Likely both.

"Thanks for meeting us in Farmington instead of Augusta," Bernie said. "I appreciate you making the drive."

Libby raised his eyebrows with suspicion. Kermit's body shifted next to her. She got the message: *Shut your piehole. Only answer questions.*

Bernie focused on Libby's large fingers as he shuffled his stack of papers. His wedding ring was embedded— painfully, it looked like— in his pink flesh, little black hairs sticking out above and below it.

"Let's get to it," he said, pretending—so obvious!—to choose which paper to start with. He slid one across the table.

It was a screenshot of a text exchange with Stephanie when she was in the thick of trying to get her out of the house. Stephanie wanted to talk in person. Bernie responded, no, she just wanted Stephanie to honor the lease.

"Why not talk in person?" Libby asked.

"I wanted it to be on the record. Stephanie had a habit of remembering things differently than I did." *Didn't I already tell him this?* She couldn't remember.

"Had?"

Kermit broke in. "Figure of speech. Let's discuss the content, not get caught up in trivial semantics or what tense my client is using. It's meaningless."

"I'll decide what's meaningless," Libby said.

"Bernie is aware she can leave at any time. She doesn't have to be here," Kermit said. "She's taking time on a very busy workday in order to cooperate. If you're going to waste her time, we'll have to leave."

"Ms. O'Dea is here to answer questions about an arson and murder, the two most serious crimes on the books in the state of Maine. It happened on her property. She'd be smart not to play games."

Ms. O'Dea herself was getting impatient. Why did every conversation between men about her—*when she was sitting right there, for chrissake*—end up in a dick-waving contest?

"I was referring to my conversations with Stephanie. The conversation was in the past," she said. *Don't challenge me on language usage, pal.*

She was hyperaware of the old-fashioned wall clock ticking as Libby pushed paper after paper at her, texts between herself and Stephanie that got increasingly heated. Stephanie's getting longer, veering from pleading and placating to calling Bernie the worst landlord ever, with specific, ranting criticisms about Bernie's little house. Bernie's got shorter, basically, "Please move out." Then simply, "Leave ASAP."

"I was getting legal advice from my brother, who's a lawyer," Bernie said in answer to Libby's question about why she didn't answer Stephanie's questions. "He said to not engage. Stephanie and I had an agreement. She needed to honor it."

Once that topic was exhausted, Bernie braced for the New Year's Eve texts. Libby shuffled through his papers with the pretense— *again!*—that he didn't know which one to show next. He finally pushed across screenshots of exchanges she'd had with Sal, Carol, and her sister-in-law Robin, all of them featuring Bernie bitching about Stephanie, but not on New Year's Eve.

"She was really getting under your skin," Libby said.

"She wouldn't move out. I'm a verbal person. I have to vent. I'm a vent-prone verbal person." Kermit stirred. She got it. *Don't elaborate.*

The next round of sliding papers were screenshots of texts to Pete about Stephanie. They weren't as angry, there wasn't as much passionate prose, as Bernie liked to think of it, than the others. She'd wanted him to focus on the issue, not her emotions. His responses were all variations on, "Don't engage," "The issue will resolve itself," "She can't stay there forever."

"What's he implying?" Libby asked.

"He's not *implying* anything. He's saying things will work out. That's his attitude generally. That things work out."

"You don't see a more sinister meaning?"

"Sinister? Pete?" She laughed to show Libby it was ridiculous, even though her bullshit radar told her to beware of where this was going. "You know him. He doesn't have a sinister bone in his body."

Libby slid over another one. "What about this, then?"

It was to Sandy. "I'm worried Pete's anger issue is getting worse."

Bernie had forgotten about it. "What's the date on that?" It didn't really matter, just a stall so she could process.

"Why text the fire chief about the police chief's anger issues?"

"I'm texting a good friend about my boyfriend. Sandy knows a lot about PTSD"—she wasn't going to out Sandy's own PTSD issues to Libby—"and he's Pete's best friend."

"I don't care about you and MacCormack and your *friendship*." He said *friendship* with a knowing leer that made Bernie want to punch his large nose. "Describe the anger issues."

"This isn't relevant," Kermit said.

"This is an arson and murder investigation. If someone involved has anger issues, it's relevant."

"Pete's not involved," Bernie said. "He doesn't have anger issues. Not like psycho anger issues. It's just part of PTSD. He gets mad, very briefly, but not physically violent or anything. It's over in seconds. It's frustration at his injury and his state of mind."

"State of mind? You said he's not involved. Involved in what?"

Bernie shrugged. "State of mind, whatever. I don't know the medical terms. He definitely wasn't a danger to anyone. Isn't." She didn't take the bait on the "involved" thing. Let him ask again if he wanted to play that game.

Libby thumbed through the remaining papers before pushing another one across the table. It was a screenshot of a text from Pete to her and her response.

"I'm so sorry. I know I already said it, but I can't say it enough. The thought that I hurt you devastates me. Please, if you are dizzy or in pain, TELL ME. I'll take you to FMH. I am so very sorry. I love you. Please forgive me."

Bernie had responded, "I love you too. I'm fine. It's my fault. Don't worry about it. PLEASE. Focus on work. See you tonight."

She stared, heat rising from her chest to her face to the tips of her ears. She knew she was bright red. Kermit leaned in to read it, so close she could smell his minty-combined-with–hazelnut-coffee breath.

Libby waited while they read. Then waited some more. Finally, he said, "That's a long text for someone with a flip phone. Punctuation, correct spelling, even capital letters for entire words. It must've taken him an hour to write it. It's by far the longest text you have from him."

Bernie shrugged, still looking at the paper.

"Read it out loud," Libby said.

Bernie did, trying to make the Pete part sound gentle and compassionate, the way she'd read it in her head when he'd sent it.

"Well?" Libby asked.

"What's your question?"

"It sounds like someone's anger issues are bigger than you're admitting. Pain? Hospital? We both know women always say it's their fault in order to protect themselves."

"This has nothing to do with anger. It's private."

"Nothing's private in a murder investigation."

"This is."

"I'm sure your attorney would advise you to answer. It's in your best interest to explain it rather than leave it to us to interpret."

"Bernie, it's probably a good idea to answer," Kermit said.

She gave him her most scathing look. Just for a second she considered lying, but just as quickly realized she couldn't think of one. It would be obvious it was a lie. Best to just twist the truth a little.

"We were in the shower together and he…" It was as close to the truth as she could get without telling the full truth. She knew it would be used against Pete even though it had nothing to do with her house or Stephanie. *How did this become about Pete?* She closed her eyes.

"He what?"

She felt like the camera in the corner was zooming in, burning a hole in her. *Sorry Pete. Sorry sorry sorry.* "We were in, um, an intimate position, and his leg gave way. I fell and my face hit the side of the sink. It's a small bathroom."

She bruised easily, and even though it was weeks ago, the faint evidence on her cheekbone and temple was still visible. It throbbed now, like a telltale heart.

Libby held her eyes. Bernie forced herself not to look away.

"That text is a lot of apologizing for a sex accident," Libby said.

"I got hurt. He felt responsible. People don't generally have sex accidents. I mean, you know, right? You're a guy…"

"It sounds like he feels a lot more responsible than for just an accident. It sounds like he's apologizing for deliberately hurting you."

"That's how he is. He feels responsible. He apologizes very well."

"Right," Libby said. He held her eyes for a couple of beats. "Moving on." When he slid over the final sheets, the screenshots of Bernie's texts the afternoon of the fire, she was relieved.

Half an hour later, as she and Kermit were putting their coats on to leave, Libby pulled a Columbo.

"One more thing." He waited for them to stop buttoning and wrapping and pulling. "The skull of the person in your house was fractured in several places. We may not know much else, but we know it was murder. By the number of blows and force, by someone who was very, very angry."

CHAPTER 14

PETE WAS JUST thinking how much he enjoyed this kind of duty—hanging around backstage at the elementary school, waiting for his cameo appearance, as the kids practiced for their upcoming production of "What the Constitution Means to Me"—when he heard a woman shout, followed by a louder male shout. The woman sounded terrified, the man angry.

He ran down toward the source. He rounded a corner to find Sean Speck, who he knew all too well, yelling at a woman, his finger in her face. She was pressed against the tile wall as he crowded her. She was a good twenty years older, six inches shorter, and scared to death.

"What the hell are you doing?" Pete grabbed Speck by both arms and pulled him away.

"Get off of me," Speck screamed. "I have a right to be here."

"You don't have a right to do what you were just doing." Pete slammed Speck, face-first, into the wall. Speck made a gratifying *ooof.* Pete held him there with his body weight as he grabbed his radio and called it in. He had to repeat himself, loudly, since Speck was screaming over him, "Get your hands off of me! You have no right! Get your hands off of me!"

"Are you all right?" Pete asked the woman through gasps as he tried to keep Speck from squirming away from him. The photographer was taller than Pete and outweighed him. Pete had fitness and strength, and a load of rising anger, on his side, but it was only going to go so far.

"Yes," she said. "He wasn't supposed to be back here, just take pictures from the auditorium."

"Pretty ironic that a play about the Constitution results in a photojournalist being suppressed from doing his job," Speck screamed.

The woman said to Pete, her voice shaking, "We weren't—"

"Shut up, bitch," Speck screamed.

"You shut up," Pete said. His rage had been building as he pressed Speck to the wall. All the shit this guy had given Bernie. All the problems he'd caused. All his entitled, lazy bullshit. The small rational part of his brain that was still functioning channeled Benjamin's voice. "What's coming up for you right now? Let's lean into it." The therapist, brow furrowed, face melting with sadness, urged, "Lean in, Pete."

"Lean into this."

"What?" Speck yelled as Pete pulled him back, then slammed him hard against the wall.

"Oh, my." The woman stepped back.

"You may want to go wait somewhere where you're safe, ma'am," Pete said. In reality, he wasn't sure what he'd do to Speck. He didn't want to traumatize her any more than she already was.

"Fuck you! Police brutality!" Speck's high-pitched scream fueled Pete.

"Shut up." Pete leaned his shoulder hard into Speck to hold him in place as he took his handcuffs off his belt. He struggled to get Speck's arms behind his back. He cuffed them. He leaned harder against Speck to catch his breath and saw that a small crowd had gathered.

"Someone move those kids away," he said in his sternest cop voice.

Pete knew he'd have to confess to Benjamin Thursday. Knew he'd feel guilt and shame, deeply and painfully, probably within hours. Knew that Benjamin's sadness and empathy and disappointment would swamp the room and make him want to crawl out of it and curl up somewhere in a ball of self-hate. But that would be Thursday. Right now? He didn't give a shit.

"I'm suing your fucking ass," Speck said.

Pete eased off, and as Speck moved, he body-slammed him. Hard.

"Go ahead you piece of shit," he whispered, so the bystanders, who'd been backed down the hall by the principal, wouldn't hear. "You do that."

He was still pressing Speck against the wall, as hard as he could, five minutes later when Jamie and Tyler came sprinting down the hall.

****

Bernie called Pete the second Kermit's car turned onto Route 27. When he picked up, she felt giddy, almost like those first days of dating. Like she hadn't seen him for a week.

"Either you got your phone back or I'm talking to George Libby," he said.

Bernie deepened her voice. "Yes, this is George. I'm calling to tell you I secretly admire your cop skills and want you to share your wisdom with me. Just don't tell the guys." She knew it was lame, but it was the best she could do after the exhausting morning.

"What's up?" Tense, despite the joke.

"I wanted to let you know it went okay. He seemed to accept my explanation that the New Year's Eve texts were bad jokes. He asked about my texts with Stephanie and some other ones, but it didn't seem to go anywhere."

"That's good."

"The bad news is, it's definitely murder. Head bashed in. I'm not sure what else it would've been anyway, even if they hadn't found murder evidence. I mean, someone poured gasoline right on the person. Poor Stephanie. How's your morning going?"

"Great. I'm at the school for that Constitution thing. There was a little kerfuffle with Sean Speck. I'll tell you about it later."

"Kerfuffle? Not a fracas or a donnybrook?"

"Just a kerfuffle."

"You sound like maybe it was more."

"Did Libby tell you anything else about the body?"

"Other than the bashed-in skull? No."

"It's definitely female. It was so badly burned that they had to do extra tests. The hyoid bone is broken, which indicates manual strangulation. Stephanie's bigger and stronger than you, so that's in your favor. Probably why Libby didn't mention it. Don't jump to the conclusion it's Stephanie until they can positively identify it, though."

"Who else would she be? And how do you know this?" Bernie wasn't a cop. She couldn't call that charred form "it," no matter how unlike a human. "I don't know if I should be flattered or hurt by your assurance I'm too wimpy to strangle someone."

"Friend in the ME's office. It's off the record. For our ears only until it's official."

"I can tell Kermit, right?" Kermit was alternating between watching the road and turning to her, mouthing "What?"

"Yes. Attorney-client privilege."

"I guess I should let you get back to work."

"One last thing."

Fucking Columbo. "The truth about the kerfuffle?"

"What? No. You haven't seen my notebook anywhere, have you? The one I keep for Benjamin? Steno-pad size? Blue cover?"

You mean your feelings journal? Normally she'd tease him, but he didn't sound normal. "No. What's up?"

"I can't find it."

"It'll turn up."

She waited for him to sign off, but he stayed on the phone. Breathing.

"Everything okay?"

"It's just weird. I wrote in it Sunday but forgot to yesterday. I was going to catch up this morning, and it wasn't there. It's always in my nightstand drawer."

"Pete, I never touch it. Ever." She stayed away from it like it was plutonium. She didn't think she could bear what was in there, the raw reality. What she saw as he pretended he was fine was enough.

"That's not what I'm saying."

"What *are* you saying?" She could feel Kermit's interest. She wanted to tell Pete they'd talk later, but he wasn't like her, jabbering on until someone shut her up. If he wanted to talk, he needed to.

"That nightmare I had last night was bad."

"I know."

"I'm sorry. You know, waking you up, having to change the sheets."

"Please don't be sorry."

"I just wonder…"

"What?"

He swallowed. "If something's going on that's affecting my memory."

"You're stressed out. You mislaid it. It's been a crazy few days. Totally normal to be a little scattered. Look at me."

More silence.

"Are you okay?" she asked.

"Yeah, fine. We can talk later."

"I love you." She gave it extra feeling.

"Get a room," Kermit said as Bernie put her phone in her pocket.

"I know. But after all that's happened, it's crazy not to say it."

"I get it. What's his news about the body?"

Bernie told him.

"Libby should've told us," Kermit said. "It could've changed the conversation."

"Maybe that's why he didn't. He wanted to talk about Pete. Don't you think that's troubling? Not just the texts, but how he zeroed in on how Pete and I are the only alibis for each other the night of the fire." Another tidbit Libby brought up as the meeting ground to a close.

Kermit didn't respond.

"Right?"

"This is hard to say," Kermit said. "I know Pete well. I like him a lot. But if there's anything you need to tell me, you can. It comes under attorney-client privilege. I've had many a client everyone thinks is a nice guy, but behind closed doors he's not."

"Jesus Christ. You too?"

He didn't say anything, his eyes on the road.

"Pete's not abusive. Believe me, I know about abuse. I just wrote a series on it, remember? You were quoted in it. I also don't get what

Libby pretending to think Pete is an abuser—and I know he's pretending—has to do with my house burning down or Stephanie being killed."

"I just needed to hear you say it."

Bernie hoped she wouldn't have to have that conversation with anyone ever again. As much as she meant it, how do you not sound like an abused woman in denial?

"The alibi is easy to take care of," Kermit said. "He's the police chief. There are probably things you haven't thought of that can confirm he was home. He's always in touch with the department, right? I'll do a request for the communications records from that night."

"I'm sure he talked on the phone to Dawna or Jamie, I just can't remember because he's always talking on the phone to someone at the department. Though all that does is put him home, and that's only if he was on the landline, which he probably wasn't. Neither puts me there. Libby made it clear he's sure Pete would lie for me."

"You didn't ask Pete about the other phone," Kermit said.

"Oh shit. I'll ask him later." Libby had asked, again, about her previous phone. She said, again, she thought she gave it to Pete to donate to the women's shelter. She'd have to "find" it at the office. Now that she had her new phone back, she didn't care. She was more worried about Pete. His missing journal, Libby's focus on him. The phone issue was nothing, a fly buzzing around among the killer raptors.

"Be sure you ask Pete about it," Kermit said.

"It?"

"Your old phone. Libby isn't playing games. This is his job. Whether it's your phone or whatever really happened in the shower or anything else. Don't screw around or it'll come back to bite you. Bad."

"Okay. I know."

"Bernie, I'm serious. This isn't over until it's over."

****

By the time Kermit dropped her off, Bernie had switched to full work mode. She welcomed the distraction. She also didn't have a choice. She listed in her head the tasks she had to do, how long each would take, what would come next. She knew she had to eat lunch at some point, but didn't want to interrupt her mental list-making to consider what to have, or when. As she walked in the door to a buzzing newsroom, ready to make a beeline to her computer and get to work, she hit her first obstacle.

"Bernie," Annette said in her singsong way. "Louise Babb dropped this off."

It was a cardboard box, the kind a ream of paper comes in. A Post-it on top said, "O'Dea grant documents."

At least she could get her accountant off her back. She'd check to make sure what she needed was there later.

She checked her desk phone voicemail. A couple of readers who hadn't gotten their paper, an advertiser wanting to take out a bigger ad.

Then a young male voice, high and nervous. "Hi, um, okay this is a newspaper. I didn't realize that. If it's the wrong number, just delete this. I saw someone with a sign out in front of Sturgis yesterday? If this is the right person, call me back. I'm Joe." He gave a number.

When Bernie called it, he picked up on the first ring.

"I worked with Stephanie. We're friends. I don't know what you want to know."

"I'm trying to figure out where she is," Bernie said.

"She's not at her house?"

"No one's seen her since before Christmas." If he didn't know about the fire, she didn't want to let on. She wanted any information from him to be without input from her. "She doesn't work at Sturgis anymore?"

"No, not since… Hey, I don't want to talk on the phone," he said. "You're in Redimere, right? I'm just going into my class at the college. I get out at twelve-fifteen if you want to talk."

"That works for me." Actually, it didn't. She was so behind. But if this guy was a friend of Stephanie's, she'd just have to make it work.

"I park in the overflow day lot. You know it?"

"Yes." That's where Bernie usually parked too.

"I'll be in the back row, by the woods. I have a red Corolla with a driver's side door that's a different shade of red."

Of course you do. "See you then."

****

Pete was putting his phone back into his pocket as Tyler and Jamie came out of the building with a still yelling Sean Speck.

"Thanks a lot, Chief," Jamie said with a big grin. "Just how I wanted to start my morning."

"The principal said to tell you rehearsal is rescheduled," Tyler, also smiling, added.

The fact that the guys were on board with Pete's response to Speck—way more than his encounter with Jeremy the day before—didn't make him feel better. The disappointment in himself, the shame, was already starting.

As he went back in to get his coat, the principal and the teacher Speck had been haranguing were waiting. They thanked him profusely, asked if he was okay. Women just like the ones from the coffee shop the day before. Grateful he'd been there. Treating him like a hero.

He didn't feel like one.

"Sorry that had to happen and it interfered with the rehearsal."

"He's a problem every time he comes over here," the principal said. "Very arrogant. Kind of a bully. We're going to say that in our statements too. The boys asked us to come over to the police department later."

"Thanks."

He couldn't get out of the building fast enough.

He walked as briskly as his leg and the partially cleared sidewalk would allow back to the station, not wanting to run into anyone until the red fog was totally gone.

Fucking Sean Speck. That's all he needed, though Pete knew that his lack of control was all on him. Seeing the guy verbally assaulting that teacher—using his size and self-righteousness and misplaced anger to intimidate her—had been a trigger. All he could see was his stepfather towering over his mother, spit coming out of his disgusting mouth as he belittled her. It had been one trigger too much. The morning was already shredded by his nightmare and lack of sleep. Another ruined night for Bernie, too, which compounded his shame. His journal was missing, so he couldn't even assess the shame, the terror from the nightmare, possible triggers, or anything else on Benjamin's one-to-ten scale. Or assess the panic at totally blanking out on where his notebook was. Then there was Ryan Grant and his bullshit.

He'd been scheduled to talk to Grant when he was finished at the school, but that wasn't going to happen. Whatever Grant had to say, he could do it in front of the council tonight.

CHAPTER 15

BERNIE FELT LIKE she was running in place, the morning slipping away as she gained no ground. At least interrupting the day to meet with Joe Walsh might result in some information about Stephanie. It'd be great if it would explain everything.

As she put her coat on, she sang out loud, "Life's been good to me so farrrrrrr."

"Has it, then?" Guy asked.

"Sorry, earworm." The song had been going through her head ever since the guy said his name. It was the only Joe Walsh song she knew. A catchy tune and lyrics that made her smile. Maybe her day *would* get better. Nowhere to go but up. "My Maserati does 185, I lost my license, now I don't drive," she sang as she drove to the college. As she turned in at the entrance, her phone buzzed. It was Louise Babb. Bernie considered letting it go to voicemail, but if Louise was calling, something was up.

She pulled over. She couldn't talk and drive.

"Just wanted to see if you'd had a chance to check the docs I left for you and make sure it was everything you needed."

"Not yet, but I'm sure it's fine," Bernie said.

A long pause. Bernie was about to look to see if she'd dropped the call when Louise said, "Check them when you can and let me know."

Geez, Louise. Give me time. She was as bad as Bernie's accountant.

She spotted the red Corolla, sitting alone in a nearly empty row at the back. She pulled in a few spaces away and looked over to see a pale face looking back.

The guy was out of the Corolla, leaning against the off-color door, sucking hard on a cigarette, by the time Bernie had gathered her stuff and approached him. Unlike Joe Walsh the rock-n-roller, she guessed this guy didn't have a mansion that he forgot the price of. He was too thin, an Army coat hanging open over a T-shirt and jeans despite the cold. No hat, no gloves.

He held out his hand for a shake, and she took it, feeling nothing but bones through her glove.

"I'm Stephanie's landlady, and I'm worried about her."

"After I hung up, I checked the paper online and there's a story about your house burning down. Was that Steph in the house?" Despite his skinny paleness, his wispy adolescent mustache though he looked close to thirty, he watched her with a steely intelligence that caught her off guard.

"I don't know. That's why I'm looking for her."

"You know Sturgis dumped her, right? Couple months ago. She needed money, so I rented a room from her for a while. Thanksgiving to mid-December."

"I didn't know she was renting rooms."

He sucked hard on his cigarette, then held it at his side, tapping it with a finger to flick ashes. "Figures. She said you were okay with it. I never know if Steph is telling the truth or not. It's not so much she's calculated about it, she just doesn't seem to know the difference."

"Have you talked to her recently?"

"No. I found a place in Kingfield and we kind of lost touch. Couple times. Texting, maybe. Not since maybe Christmas Eve? We wished each other happy holidays. I like Steph a lot. She was fun to work with. Funny and everything like that." He held up his cigarette. "Liked the smokes too. You know how it is. We're a dying breed. Sturgis has an outside smoking area, a spot with an ashtray near the parking lot. We'd hang there and freeze our asses off on our breaks. They tried to do a nonsmoking campus, but they had a problem getting people to work there. That's where we talked. Mostly joking around and bullshit."

"Why did they fire her?"

"She showed up late too much. Called out sick. I think she failed the drug test too. They did random testing. It's not like she even smoked pot much. Never had her own, but was happy to bum off someone else. I told her she's playing Russian roulette with that random drug test, especially with her being late and calling out—once they have you in their sights, they're looking for reasons to end the contract. But she was…I can't really think of how to describe it. I don't want to say free spirit, because that's like, too cheerful, you know? I guess more just a victim of her impulses."

Bernie could relate. Not a lose-your-job, screw-over-your-landlady kind of way, though. "Did she sell pot?"

"No. Like I said, she never even had her own." He took a final drag from the cigarette and dropped the butt on the icy asphalt. "Oh, I know what you're talking about. That asshole neighbor. I think he was out walking and smelled it. We used to sit on the screen porch and smoke if it was a nice night. Cold, but you could see the stars and shit, right? I think that, and me hanging out there and my buddies coming by, set him off. You can only fit two cars in the driveway, and that's if someone shovels, which Steph wasn't big on. Guys would park kind of half in the street since there's no shoulder, wheels up on the dooryard, you know? That guy came over and bitched about it once. Then I guess he called the cops. Some asshole jarhead from Redimere PD came over and gave Steph shit."

Asshole jarhead. So, not Pete. Must be either Brent or Jamie, since Tyler, all blond cowlicks and apple cheeks, was no one's idea of an asshole or jarhead. "Do you know which cop?"

"Not his name, but he had that fake military haircut lots of them do. Acting like he's in some war and we're the enemy. The whole militarization of the police thing."

Brent. "What happened after the neighbor reported her?"

Joe laughed, but there was no mirth to it. "You'd have to ask Steph.

She said she made some deal with the guy. She liked a good deal."

"You don't know what?"

"Naw. Look, it's wicked cold. I don't have anything else to tell you. I gotta get home and eat before work. So…?"

"If you hear from her, can you tell her to get in touch? Just let me know she's alive? All is forgiven."

****

Later, when Bernie had a couple of minutes, she went into her back office, closed the door, and called Dawna's cellphone.

"Do you know anything about Brent making some kind of a deal with my tenant?"

"Like what?"

"I don't know. A guy she worked with said Brent responded to a complaint there, stupid neighbor stuff, and Brent made a deal."

"I checked for any reports or complaints regarding Stephanie after the fire and didn't find anything, so whatever happened wasn't recorded. I'm the last person Brent would tell about any deal. If you find out anything, let me know. If he's going off script, it's a problem."

"Speaking of off script, don't mention this conversation to Pete, okay? He's got enough going on."

"My lips are sealed."

Back at her desk, Bernie put her feet up and watched the muted bustle on Main Street as darkness descended. She had hours of work ahead, but had reached a mental firewall. Her stomach rumbled. She'd barely eaten lunch—a sub that she'd nibbled at, then forgotten about, then thrown away. Eating would help, but she was past the point of figuring out how to go about it. Her phone buzzed.

Colleen, checking in to see how she was. And yes, she'd be happy to go out for bite.

They met at the indoor market at the mill, where late afternoon it was easy to find a table in the cavernous space far away from prying ears. Bernie grabbed a lentil soup in a bread bowl, too hungry to figure out what she really wanted. At least it was filling.

"I've got something to run by you," Bernie said. "I'm not sure if this comes under your expertise in social forensics, but it's something I can't discuss with anyone else in the world, even Carol, and you know she and I talk about everything. Except this."

"I'm honored. And a little scared."

"Remember when I fell in the shower?" Bernie pointed to her cheekbone.

"How could I forget? It looked like you went a couple rounds with Smokey Robinson."

"Sugar Ray. Different Robinson. Though I'm wimpy enough, a few rounds with Smokey would probably have had the same result."

"What happened?"

"The state cops went through my texts. There was a big apology text from Pete, and now they think he's a girlfriend beater. Or at least they're acting like it."

"Elaborate."

"Please know Pete's not a girlfriend beater. You know that, right?"

"I thought I did."

"He's not. The day of the shower thing, Pete came home for a couple hours before he had to do the night patrol. Someone was off or something. We weren't going to see each other at all. Wednesday's usually the day we reconnect, because I have such long days on Mondays and Tuesdays. Normally I would've been home by midafternoon, and we'd have some time together, but I had that meeting with the development council."

"Yeah, I remember. We had lunch that day and you were griping about it."

"The meeting got canceled, so I figured I'd surprise him."

"And?"

"I don't know why I thought surprising him would be a good idea, since I personally hate surprises. I've never nailed down how he feels about them. I go in and I hear the shower running, and he's singing 'Tougher Than the Rest,' you know, the Springsteen song."

Colleen laughed. "Oh no."

"Right. I'm like, *oh my god.*" Bernie had a horrible singing voice but couldn't help herself. "'If you're rough enough for love, baby, I'm tougher than the rest.' It seemed like the mood was for a surprise."

"Oh no." She didn't laugh this time.

"I undress, go in the bathroom. He's got his head under the water, back to the door, so he doesn't see or hear me. I step in and put my hand on his hip. It probably didn't have anything to do with it, but it's the hip with the cigarette burn scars from his stepfather." Colleen was the only person Bernie had talked to about that, too.

"Oh no."

"Turns out people with PTSD startle easily." She shrugged. Felt her face go hot.

"They do."

"I startled him. He threw his elbow back. It got me right in the cheekbone. Then he wheels around and"—she wasn't sure she could even say it out loud—"punches me."

"Oh no."

"More like punches *at* me. His leg gave way, and I was already falling sideways, so it kind of grazed my temple, next to my eye."

"I see."

"I can't emphasize enough he didn't know it was me. He thought I was at the meeting. I startled him."

"I get that."

"He slipped and fell, but he also, realizing it was me, was trying to grab me to keep me from falling. He got my forearm, but he was falling too, so he wrenched my arm a little."

"It'd be funny if it weren't so…"

"I know! He was beside himself. I think the fact his instinct had been to punch bothered him as much as the fact he'd connected, more or less. He wanted to take me to the hospital. Who surprises a guy, a cop no less, by grabbing him in the shower when he has PTSD? I should've known he startles easily. My heart broke for him."

"It's not your fault."

"No really, who does that? Me. I do that."

"Don't be so hard on yourself."

"I felt so dumb. He's all whispery and touchy and sexy all the time, and I'm just this big dumb blob that crashes around, even when I try to do sexy things. I really screwed up."

"I can see a lot of ways that this is a problem."

"Exactly. I convinced him I didn't need medical attention. I told him just go to work. He didn't want to leave. He went, but he sent me this wicked goopy apologetic text and again said he'd take me to the hospital, which is what Libby read on my phone. I wasn't hurt that much, but the biggest thing is, if we went to the hospital, I couldn't count on them believing me. They'd report it."

"They would have to."

Bernie ate her soup and watched Colleen pick apart her muffin.

"I know you're being honest, but you should know that in my research, I've seen a lot of ways a perfectly nice and honorable guy can be a danger," Colleen said.

"I know, but I don't feel like he is. My biggest concern is that it set him back, mentally. Or it *was* my biggest concern. Now my biggest concern is they're going to use it against him."

"How did you explain it this morning?"

"That we were having sex in the shower and Pete's leg gave out."

"Plausible."

"I thought so. I'm not sure Libby did."

"If they're focusing on Pete, they must not have enough on you."

"Exactly." Bernie was happy Colleen got it. "The other thing is, both Libby and Ryan Grant are totally on Pete's ass. I feel like it's not a coincidence. I know it just seems like I'm going all conspiracy theory, but it's a strong feeling I have."

"I'm probably the one person you can talk to who would encourage that feeling. Stranger things happen."

Bernie hadn't eaten much of her soup but wasn't hungry anymore. "I'm probably overthinking it, with Pete before the town council tonight. I'm exhausted. It's just a feeling I have. An ill wind."

CHAPTER 16

PETE HAD TO get out of the too-bright, too-hot council chambers, just for a couple minutes. He'd love to leave altogether, but he was there to do penance. The meeting had nothing to do with what happened at the school, of course, but penance doesn't always come with a bright neon arrow pointing to the transgression. Pete hadn't thought about the concept of penance for years, until he started dating Bernie. For someone who, by her own proud admission, hadn't been to Mass in three decades and had stopped going to confession long before that, she talked about it a lot.

The waiting was part of it. He accepted that as the council launched into a long discussion with the transfer station manager. But he needed a break.

As he went into the hallway to get a drink of water, Eli Perry followed him out. "Natalie saw what happened at the school today."

"I'm sorry," Pete said, leaning over the drinking fountain.

"She thought you were great," Eli said. "A big hero."

"I'm not."

"We both know that." He smiled to show no offense meant. "I wanted to give you a heads-up. Speck called Ryan Grant and went off about it. I only know because I was at town hall filling out some forms in the outer office and could hear Grant's end of the conversation."

"Thanks. I appreciate it." Pete already knew it would come up. How could it not? "What are you and Natalie doing here?"

"She has a thing she wants to read during the public remarks session. That asshole Grant knows what it is and put her at the end hoping we'd leave, but he doesn't know Natalie."

"Hey fellas." It was Sandy.

Eli said hi, told Pete good luck, then went back into the chambers.

"Thought you didn't have anything tonight," Pete said.

"I'm here for you, buddy. As the management personnel representative."

"That won't be necessary."

"Better safe than sorry."

When they returned to the chamber, Natalie was marching to the microphone at the front of the room. Eli, a three-hundred-pound clenched fist, leaned forward in his chair as he watched his daughter. Pete got it. He could feel it himself, the urge to stand next to her and stare down Ryan Grant and anyone else who was going to give her shit.

He was surprised when her twelve-year-old voice, usually low and shy, rang out as she read from a piece of paper.

"Distinguished members of the council and Mr. Mayor, my name is Natalie Perry. I am a member of the Passamaquoddy Tribe, part of the Wabanaki people. My ancestors have lived on this land for ten thousand years. As a representative of my people, I am making a request of the town council to read a tribal acknowledgement at the beginning of every public meeting. I would like to quote Wabanaki Reach, which says 'Land acknowledgment is a simple, powerful way of showing respect and memorializing the spirit of the people who were originally here. It is a step toward correcting stories and practices that have erased Indigenous people's history and culture. It is a step toward inviting and honoring the truth—truth-telling.'

"I would like to suggest wording for this acknowledgement, borrowed from the University of Maine, that could be 'We acknowledge the town of Redimere exists on land that has been home to the Wabanaki people, particularly the Passamaquoddy Tribe, for more than 13,000 years. We recognize and honor the current tribes who comprise the Wabanaki Confederacy—the Penobscot,

Passamaquoddy, Maliseet, and Micmac peoples—who have stewarded this land throughout the generations. We respect the traditional values of these tribes and affirm their inherent sovereignty in this territory. We support their efforts for land and water protection and restoration and for cultural healing and recovery.'

"You say the Pledge of Allegiance and a silent prayer at the beginning of every meeting to acknowledge heritage and traditions for some of you here. The tribal acknowledgement would do the same, while also acknowledging the people on whose land this town is built. Thank you for your consideration."

She turned away but then, with a little "oh," went back to the mic. "Also I want the town to acknowledge that it will honor any Wabanaki artifacts and treasures that may be uncovered and condemn any theft, destruction and appropriation of them. Thank you."

Gert Feeney, the chair, smiled encouragingly. Ryan Grant and a couple of his council cronies, on the other hand, looked like they were fighting back laughter. The other members were largely expressionless, probably wishing she hadn't brought it up, Pete figured. Now they'd have to agree and face ridicule, or ignore it and look ignorant.

"We'll take that under advisement," Gert said.

"Good job, Natalie," Pete said as she walked past him, her face bright red.

Eli gathered her in a hug and said, "Good job, Peanut."

Gert called the executive session into order as the Perrys and Carrie, who'd been sitting in the back row, left.

"We're not really going to do that, are we?" one of the councilors asked as the door closed.

"No," Grant said. "It's ridiculous. That kid didn't even write that. Someone put her up to it. Eli's not even Native American. He should know better."

"We'll discuss it at a public meeting," Gert said. "Chief MacCormack, you're here as the representative for Chief Novotny."

"Yes."

"You don't have to stand," Gert said to Pete.

"Thanks. I prefer to." He was being stubborn, but it was also strategic. Their seats were on a platform. He didn't want to have to look up at the council members, or Grant in particular.

"Suit yourself," Grant said, shuffling a sheaf of papers meaningfully. "I have something to say and would like to do it without interruption. You'll get your chance to speak after."

Pete didn't respond. He settled his face into benign non-expression. He was determined to hold that look until this meeting adjourned.

"There's a lot here. Your three-year contract is up for renewal September 1. I know that's eight months away, so I'll just cut to the chase. In the twenty-eight months you've been chief of police in our town, one officer has died, another's in prison for life, and you've been critically injured twice, costing our insurance company more than we've ever paid for town personnel collectively, much less for one person. I think the total is up to"—he made a show of looking for a paper with the figure on it—"$427,019.32. And counting. It has a huge effect on our premiums."

Grant held up the paper, squinted, as though consulting it. "That also includes extensive mental health treatment. As a Navy SEAL in Panama and the Persian Gulf, I've known plenty of men who have good reason to have PTSD and are fine. Where did you serve? Nowhere. So, I—"

"Wait a minute, Ryan," Gert said.

"With all due respect, Gert, I'm the mayor. He's the police chief, in charge of our citizens' safety. We're not going to tiptoe around it. You people did that before, and all it did was cost us money. That's why we have a mayor now. You can say your bit afterward."

"With all due respect, Mr. Mayor, it's a legal slippery slope," Gert said. "We can't discipline a town employee for medical or mental health bills, some of which are due to his heroic work on our behalf."

"With all due respect, *Gert*, you'll get your chance."

Her eyes narrowed and her mouth straightened into a lipless line. She crossed her arms and leaned back in her seat. The other councilors shifted uncomfortably, looking anywhere but at Pete.

The last thing Pete wanted was to have his mental health discussed in this setting. He could barely talk to Bernie, Sandy, and Dawna about it. It was a physical effort to keep his poker face, but he'd had a lot of practice. He unclenched his fists and looked straight ahead.

"That's just insurance costs," Grant continued. "There may be other consequences we won't see until later. You've compromised the department by engaging in a relationship with the editor of the newspaper. In fact, you've flaunted it. We've had multiple reports that you practically engaged in a drunken sexual act at the Pour House a few months ago—"

"Wait a minute," Pete said. Heat rose up the back of his neck.

"I'm talking," Grant said.

"I have a right to know what you're referring to."

"Um." Rene Lambert glanced at Grant, then said to Pete, "I think he's referring to karaoke night? You sang that Madonna song? My wife enjoys the video."

"There was nothing drunken or sexual about that," Pete said. He'd sung "Crazy for You" to a very embarrassed Bernie on her birthday, ending it by taking her by the hand, dipping her back, and kissing her. He had no idea someone with a smartphone was filming.

"I'm talking," Grant said.

Rene's bald head turned pink. He rolled his eyes at Pete in apology.

"It's on a YouTube channel called Redimere Raw, which has no person's name associated with it. It's gone viral and is the featured video, with the title 'Sexy Sheriff,' of all foolish things," Grant said. He did air quotes around *YouTube, gone viral, channel,* and *Sexy Sheriff.*

He looked at each council member in turn, to make sure they got his point. "It's an embarrassment to the town. This from a guy who refuses to sign the release for *Real Rural Justice,* which actually shows police in a good light and can garner needed revenue as well as economic development interest in this town."

There it was. Pete relaxed, just a fraction. If the TV show was Grant's issue, he could easily handle it.

Grant looked around the room again with what Bernie called his

Mussolini face. Lower lip out. Eyes narrowed. Making sure everyone was under control. "Let's move on to the fact that you skipped an important personnel meeting with me yesterday without the courtesy of letting me know you weren't coming, then again today."

"There was an armed hostage situation yesterday." *Could Grant really be that obtuse?*

Grant grinned. *Gotcha.* "A situation in which you had a prolonged therapy session with a known dangerous criminal instead of allowing more seasoned and equipped law enforcement personnel, who were on the scene, to handle it. You didn't even have your sidearm. You turned off your radio, against policy. I've been briefed on the situation. It proves you're not someone we want in charge of our citizens' safety."

Pete took a deep breath. "My training and experience—"

"Chief Novotny, it is NOT YOUR TURN TO TALK." Grant's face flushed. Once he was satisfied Pete was done, he said, "It's not the first hostage situation you haven't handled correctly during your time in our town, which I'd like to point out never had a hostage situation in the two-plus centuries it has been in existence until you arrived. On Thanksgiving before last, didn't you mishandle a hostage situation that put lives in danger? Including your girlfriend's?"

So much for keeping cool. The explosion started in Pete's gut and spread through his veins and out his limbs. The red mist roared in. It burned. Clouded his vision to little pinholes with Grant at the ends. He couldn't have stopped it if he'd wanted to. And, just like earlier with Sean Speck, he didn't want to. As he sprang forward, hands grabbed him from behind and pulled him back. He'd forgotten Sandy was there.

"Cool down, bud," Sandy said.

The anger drained, replaced with the familiar shame.

"You cool?"

Pete nodded. Sandy let go but didn't move away.

Grant smirked. He'd hit his mark.

Gert banged her gavel, though the room had gone dead quiet.

Pete's leg throbbed. He was hit by a wave of exhaustion that almost knocked him over.

"We haven't even touched on your inappropriate behavior today at the elementary school, attacking a journalist and scaring children," Grant said. "Obviously, it's why you didn't attend another scheduled meeting with me later. You didn't want to face the consequences."

"Stay cool," Sandy whispered. Pete breathed in. Held it.

Gert said, "I think it's time we adjourn and revisit this when everyone's had time to calm down."

Grant turned to her, annoyed. "I'm not finished."

"All right, Ryan. Keep things civil and on point."

"All right, *Gert.*" He rolled his eyes. "Chief Novotny, the experiment of you being our police chief hasn't worked. It's within my power to remove you from the position. The council's approval is a formality. You can resign and not make this a public shit show. Excuse my French. Up to you. If you'd bothered to show up today to the meeting that I graciously rescheduled after yesterday's fiasco, we could have avoided this circus that you've created tonight."

"Move to table," Rene said.

Someone quickly seconded.

"All in favor?" Gert asked.

Five hands went up. Grant, who didn't get a vote, shook his head, pursed his lips, and shuffled his papers.

"Motion passes," Gert said.

The motion to adjourn the executive session went just as quickly.

"Pete and Sandy, you can go," Gert said. "Tell Carrie it's okay to come in if she's still out there."

Without looking at Sandy, Pete walked past the three rows of empty metal chairs, trying to limp as little as possible. He grabbed his coat from the last row and pushed open the door to the hallway.

Carrie closed her laptop and scrambled up from the floor.

"You can go back in," Pete said, surprised he sounded normal and could smile.

"Is everything okay?"

Pete wondered if she'd heard him yell. It was hard to tell. Her eyes were unblinking behind her outsized glasses.

"Fine. No vote."

"Let's go to my office and have a beer," Sandy said as they walked down the hall.

It had been an awful day. Year, so far. All Pete wanted was Bernie, as painful as that conversation would be. He checked his phone. She'd texted earlier that she was done for the night and was going home. The text was at 10:30. Too early for her to leave work on a Tuesday. She must be exhausted too. He wondered if she was going straight to bed or was waiting for him.

"It's not negotiable," Sandy said.

****

As Bernie brushed her teeth, debating whether to wait for Pete or give in and go to bed, she got a text from Carrie.

"Exec ssn going long can't hear words voices not good."

A little later, as she lay in bed, fully awake, her phone buzzed again. A text from Pete. "Having 1 beer w Sandy. Home soon. Lv U."

She texted back, "Wake me up when you get home."

Dubby jumped onto Pete's side of the bed. All three of the cats curled on top and around her, their purrs a comforting lullaby. At least she'd have company as she lay staring at the stars through the skylight.

It was 1:27 when she heard the sound of the Charger.

"I'm awake," she said when the door opened. "You can turn the light on."

"It's okay."

She listened as he shuffled around in the dark, taking off his coat and boots. He peed for what seemed like five minutes. *One beer my ass.* She listened as he brushed his teeth. Exactly two minutes. She pictured him placing his watch on the sink, keeping track as he brushed. Eventually he sat down next to her on the bed.

"Sorry," he said.

"About what?" He was a silhouette that smelled like beer, snow, and sweat.

"Waking you up, for starters."

"I was awake."

"Keeping you up waiting, then. I know you didn't sleep last night, and today was a long day."

"I'm fine. What happened tonight?"

"Ryan Grant was a dick." He rested his hand on her cheek, the side that was still slightly discolored. Sometimes she caught him looking at her cheekbone, his expression unreadable. She wanted to tell him to get over it, but they hadn't discussed it since that day. In the dark, without her glasses on, she couldn't see his face clearly. His thumb brushed a slow rhythm, his fingers tangling in her hair.

He didn't seem like he was going to elaborate, so she said, "Just give me the headline, okay? It's obviously bad if it required you to have nearly three hours of beers with Sandy."

"Busted." His thumb, warm and gentle, stroked her cheekbone.

"What happened, Pete?"

"He wants to fire me. We didn't get that far before they tabled it. I got pissed off and wasn't my best self, as Benjamin would put it."

"What did you do?"

"Nothing. Sandy stopped me. My plan was to vault over that ridiculous throne and punch his fucking face. Instead, I just looked like a jerk."

"You just had a long day." She didn't believe that was all there was to it, but it was late and she was tired.

"I'm sorry, baby." He kissed her, long and soft, then sat back up. "I know I'm letting you down."

"You're not. I love you. I just want you to be okay."

"I know." He got up.

"Go ahead and turn on the light."

"No, it's okay." She listened to him undress, his breathing labored. She knew it was his leg, not the beer. She watched his dark shape move unevenly as he hung up his uniform, then think better of it and put it in the hamper. He got into bed, and she rolled over on her side. He curled up against her, his arm around her, stretching his bad leg over her thigh. He kissed her neck. "I love you."

"I love you too. Tomorrow will be better."

CHAPTER 17

ETE PULLED UP in front of the Beehive, a rambling apartment complex that had been created forty years earlier by attaching four triple-deckers to each other with poorly built additions. The result was a dilapidated hybrid tenement with mismatched windows and doors, its once-yellow paint a dirty beige that peeled from beaten-down clapboards.

Its residents were as tired and in need of care as their building. It was central to many of the department's worst calls. At least today wasn't one of them.

He stepped out of his car into the icy pile of snow pushed up against the small dooryard that stretched along the front. A woman sat on the steps leading into the farthest entrance, watching him warily, smoking a cigarette. If the Charger, though unmarked, didn't scream cop, the fact he was in full uniform, including a parka and hat with the department insignia, gave him away.

"Don't tell me it's against the law to sit on my own steps and smoke, because I know it's not." Her tone wasn't unfriendly, but Pete felt the underlying tension. It didn't matter if it was Redimere, Maine, or Philly, anytime a white cop approached a Black resident, it was there.

"Not a problem, Imani." He wanted her to know he remembered her. "I'm sharing some information with area residents."

He held out the flyer he'd taken off the pile on his seat. "Someone's been breaking into cars, mostly unlocked ones—"

"It's not really breaking in then, is it?" she said.

"Technically, it is."

She rolled her eyes.

"Someone's been taking belongings out of people's cars. It's been going on for weeks, and the person has hit a lot of cars. We're asking people to keep their cars locked, not leave anything of value in them, and if they know anything, to let us know. The number's here on the flyer. It's also got a list of the types of things that have been stolen to help people keep their eyes out."

She didn't reach for it or even look.

"I get it. You come to where the poor people live, because obviously we're the criminals."

"I'm going a lot of places," Pete said, friendly. "Downtown businesses too. They're putting this up in their windows." True, he'd just made the rounds at Timberwoods, the trailer park, and his next stop was going to be College Garden Apartments, which had a population similar to the Beehive's. Also true, he wouldn't be going to the million-dollar homes on Shore Drive.

Imani looked him in the eye. "I don't steal from cars, and I'm not gonna do your job for you."

"I know that." His only previous interaction with her had been an unhappy one, nearly a year before. He'd been called to the Country Grocer after she'd been caught by the owner walking out with diapers she hadn't paid for. She was probably waiting for him to bring it up. He wasn't going to.

She took a long drag of her cigarette, her eyes still on him. "You're clueless, aren't you? You arrested Jeremy, and my life is totally fucked." She didn't sound angry, just resigned.

"What do you and Jeremy have to do with each other?"

"He's my boyfriend. I need him to watch my kids while I'm at work. I even changed jobs to a night shift so he could. Now it's pointless."

"You're not at the Country Grocer anymore?" Walt hadn't wanted to press charges, maybe because he and Imani were among only a handful of Black people in town. Maybe because he saw the same thing

Pete did—someone trying to do the best she could. She'd pointed out if she could pay for diapers, she would. If her kids ran around dirty, as she put it, she'd get arrested for that too. Walt was having trouble filling a position, and by the end of the whole thing, he'd hired her.

She looked at Pete with the same angry, frustrated expression she had when he'd asked why she was stealing diapers. "What did I just say? I had to change jobs to make it work with my kids. Now that's fucked up because I've got no one to watch them."

"Sorry. I thought—"

"You thought what? That since I had a full-time job, my life was perfect? I have two kids under two. Jeremy had a day job, so I had to switch to nights so one of us could be with the kids. Then he lost that, and I stayed nights so he could look for another one." She said it with exaggerated slowness, as though he were simpleminded.

"Now he's in jail."

"Bingo, Kojak." She threw her cigarette butt into the snow. "Thank you very much."

"Imani, he held a knife to a woman's throat. Jail's where he needs to be."

She sighed and shook her head. "Men."

He waited while she took a pack of cigarettes out of her jacket pocket, shook one out, lit it. Took a long drag. Looked at the ember, considering. She hadn't told him to leave. He was good at waiting. She wasn't wearing a hat or gloves, and her jacket was worn and thin. She could only sit there for so long.

"I gave up smoking before I had my first baby. So this is your fault too. I can't even afford it." To his surprise, her eyes danced, just slightly. A small smile twitched, then disappeared. She sighed and held out her hand. He handed her the flyer.

Imani looked it over as she took a big drag. "Yeah, okay. Gift cards? Sunglasses? This guy's small potatoes. I'm sure it's some loser who needs it for drugs or something. Just tell people to lock their fucking cars." She held it out to him.

"Maybe show it to your upstairs neighbors?" Pete didn't take it.

"No one lives above me, and the people on the third floor are away visiting family."

"I'd like to think you and your neighbors could help us out."

"Like to think. Ha. I'd like to think I know where my groceries are gonna come from. My diapers."

A baby's cry sounded from inside, audible through the several inches of open window next to the stairs. "Right on cue," she said. She threw her cigarette butt in the snow, where it landed next to her first one, and stood up. She held the flyer out to him. This time, he took it.

"By the way, it's not illegal for me to be out here smoking when the kids are taking their nap." She nodded toward the open window. "I can hear them fine, okay?"

"Not a problem."

Imani closed the door behind her.

Pete looked down the row of bowed apartment fronts. No one else was out. He didn't see any lights, even though the day was dark, or signs of life. He thought he saw someone move away from the window in the apartment above Imani's, but he wasn't going to go knocking on doors. He got a staple gun out of his car and affixed a couple of flyers to the poles lining the street.

"Pete." A happy shout. He cringed. He'd been getting into his car. Almost escaped.

"I thought that was you out here, son." Chuck, coatless, gave him a quick side hug. "What are you doing? On the job I see. Can you spare a few minutes for your dad?"

"Oh my god, he's your son?" Imani, a baby in one arm, was at the window. She pushed it further open.

"My boy," Chuck said.

"I guess everyone has a parent at some point." Then to Pete, "Since Chuck's your dad, I guess I can help you. Only because I like Chuck."

"I appreciate it," Pete said.

"Whoever's doing the stealing, they've done it at Pondside Convenience, that's where I'm working now. Someone saw a guy riding away on a bike right before they saw their car was gone through. I don't think anything was taken, but someone was looking for stuff. Glove compartment open, that kind of thing. Maybe they didn't report it since nothing was taken, but Pondside has surveillance cameras."

"Thank you," Pete said.

"I only did it for Chuck." She closed the window.

****

"Maybe we'll get a paper out after all," Bernie said to the room as she finished another page. No one responded. She said it about fifty times a day. They were used to it.

Carrie got up. "Do you have a minute? Guy too?"

"Sure."

The trio crowded into Bernie's closet-size office.

"Sorry I'm bringing this up so late," Carrie said. "But I feel like we can't ignore the executive session at last night's town council meeting. I don't mean to be awkward, but there's enough information out there that if we don't write about it, we look like we're covering it up."

Carrie, as always, was wise beyond her years. Usually a good thing. Bernie wished now, though, that she wasn't. She was right, but Bernie didn't want to deal with it.

"What do you have on the record?" Bernie asked. "I assume we're not writing about anything you overheard through the door?"

Carrie blinked. "Of course not. Ryan Grant grabbed me after the meeting and said, 'I know you people won't run anything, but we are considering terminating the police chief's contract. I can't say more now. I'm sure your boss knows all about it.' He also said that he'd given Fergus Kelley the same information."

"Why didn't you say something earlier?"

"I should have. I just felt..."

"I know, but don't, okay? By the way I *don't* know about it. I haven't been told anything except Grant is a dick, which we already know."

Guy broke in. "I'm sure he said that—about us not running anything and about Kelley—to force our hand and make us do it. He wants the info on Pete out there even though it was not a public discussion. I know this puts you in a bad position."

"But you agree, right? That we should run it?" Bernie said. "Even if he is using us, he's the mayor, and it's about firing the police chief."

"Yes."

"I'm going to go back out there and get the paper out, and you two can stay here and hash out the story. We only have space for about six hundred words. Eight hundred, tops."

"It'll be short," Carrie said. "Just what Grant said, the public details of the chief's contract, and I've already called Gert Feeney to get the council's response."

"You should get a quote from Pete."

"Left a message on his cell," Carrie said. "I have one more thing to ask you." She looked uncomfortable.

"Okay." Bernie was anxious to get back to her desk.

"Did you say anything to anyone about Louise telling me Fergus Kelley said that the mayor thought the chief was involved in your fire?"

"No. You asked me not to. Why?"

"The mayor gave her an earful about telling me things like that."

"Maybe he overheard her."

"He was out of the office when she called me."

"It wasn't me."

Carrie shrugged. "Louise's problem, then."

Bernie left her office to find her brother Sal standing in front of her desk. He had that fake hangdog expression that told her he was going to annoy her. She didn't have the patience today.

"I was across the street at the store, and I thought I'd drop in to see how you're doing," he said.

"Awesome. And busy. But thanks for checking."

"Good. That's good."

"Anything else?"

"Seriously, Bern, how are you doing? Remember, you're not the first O'Dea to come under the blazing, but misdirected, eye of the law. I know how much it sucks."

"It does suck. But I'm fine. And like you, I did nothing wrong, and hopefully it'll all blow over. I'm thrilled that you care, but I'm not sure why you picked now to have a heart-to-heart."

"Have you talked to Tommy?"

"Not since he went to Portland Monday. He's back sometime today."

"Don't get mad."

"What? For chrissake, Sal."

"I *knew* he didn't tell you. He's here for the long haul. I mean, not a couple weeks or something. He's found somewhere to stay." He rushed the last part out quickly as he pivoted toward the door.

"Wait. What?" Tommy had assured her he was just going to be involved for a couple weeks, tops. Lawyer or no, all he was going to do by being here longer was stress her out more. "Sal, come back."

He waved as he opened the door, then was gone.

****

"Have time for a cup of coffee?" Chuck asked Pete after Imani shut the window.

"No, gotta get back to work."

"I need to talk to you." He stood, coatless in the subfreezing cold, waiting.

They went around the collapsing stockade fence that divided the apartment building from Chuck's little New Englander, one of a row that drifted down the street to the river. The outside was much as it had been when Chuck bought it months before, when he'd decided to stay in Redimere. Chipped white paint, a sagging porch. The tiny dooryard was covered with snow, but Pete was sure it was still a barren patch of hard-packed dirt underneath. Chuck's new pickup truck made the house look even dingier.

"When I saw the story about the guy with the knife online, I actually sat down and wept."

"It wasn't a big deal."

"I hear you had a rough council meeting last night."

"It was an executive session. Private. I don't know what you could've heard."

"I heard you also got into a little tussle at the school with that asshole photographer."

"Boy, you hear a lot."

"I just want you to take care," Chuck said as he opened the door and stood aside for Pete to go in.

Bev Dulac was perched on Chuck's couch holding a coffee mug.

"I'll get your coffee," Chuck said. "Bev brought some lemon cake. Want a piece?"

"Sure." He didn't, but he couldn't say no with Bev right there.

"Just so you know, I'm on my break," Bev said.

"I'm not the post office police," Pete responded. "You probably outrank me, anyway."

Chuck came in from the kitchen with a tray of coffee and cake. "We were talking about Ryan Grant."

Bev nodded. "He should stick to real estate. I knew when he pushed for us to change from a select board to what we have now we were headed for trouble. Count me as the one person who wasn't surprised when he ran for mayor. I don't even know where he has the time, with all his real estate deals. Rita Chandler, you know, his ex, is livid."

"Did the two of you call me in her for a reason?" Pete asked.

"I heard your voice outside, and what we're talking about has to do with you," Chuck said. "Rita was my broker when I bought the house. Great gal. Lots of energy."

"I don't know what she was doing with Grant," Bev said. "I never liked him. He's a slick one. He's got his fingers everywhere. Rita was telling me about that parcel down behind Bernie's that has been on the market for a decade, but now—"

"What parcel?" Pete asked. "I don't know anything about it. Sounds like something you should talk to Bernie about."

"Even beyond what Rita told me," Bev said. "People are saying the arson—"

A car door shut outside.

Bev made the motion of locking her lips with an invisible key.

"We'll talk later," Chuck said. "My new roommate is here."

Footfalls on the steps leading to the kitchen door were followed by a knock.

"Come on in," Chuck called out. "You don't have to knock now that you live here."

"Hey Chuck, Bev." Tommy, his round face flushed from the cold, put a box on the counter. "Hey Pete. Your dad tell you the good news?"

CHAPTER 18

WHEN BERNIE GOT home around three, Pete was on the couch, in jeans and a flannel shirt, working on the jigsaw puzzle.

"You're home early. To stay, looks like."

"Things were quiet. I left early since yesterday was such a long day."

That was unusual, but she was glad. Benjamin was always on him to take more time off to recharge.

"I got some pork chops for supper," he said, not looking up.

"Pork chops and applesauce." Bernie drew it out, as she picked up Poopoo and sat down next to Pete. The cat purred loudly, settling into her lap. The fire in the pellet stove danced merrily. Bernie was overtaken by a surge of comfy happiness.

"I didn't get applesauce, but we might have some in the cupboard," he said. "I'll make mashed potatoes. It's too early to start, though, unless you're hungry."

"That's fine. I was actually doing Peter Brady doing Humphrey Bogart."

Pete sifted through the puzzle pieces.

"You know, *The Brady Bunch?* 'Pork chops and applesauce,' " She tried to say it more like Humphrey Bogart.

"Oh right."

"That was a good quote for that story on your contract," she said. "I can't see Ryan Grant finding one little nook in it to latch onto."

"The less said, the better."

"Thanks for talking to Carrie."

"It wasn't a problem. I can't find that piece, you know with the lime green and red streak that I knew went with the rocket. I'd put it aside?"

He looked at Bernie to see if she was listening. She was. With a sinking feeling.

"I found where it goes, but it's not here," he said.

"It must be there somewhere." Even as she said it, she knew no, it wasn't. She put Poopoo on the floor and leaned over to look, just for show, while she got her thoughts in order.

"Well, it's not." He slapped his hands on his thighs.

"Oh no. You know what? I think I accidentally vacuumed it up."

"You accidentally vacuumed it up?"

She stood up and moved to the other side of the table. "Yeah, I was vacuuming. A couple pieces were on the floor." The cats batting around puzzle pieces was a constant issue. "After I picked them all up, or thought I did, I think I caught a flash of it under the couch, but I was thinking about something else, and it just now registered that I probably vacuumed it up."

"Let me get this straight. You knew you were vacuuming it up, but you did anyway, then just blithely went on with your business?"

"Am I ever blithe?" Bernie asked. "I didn't see it happen, I'm just guessing that's what happened." She didn't understand why he was getting so mad.

"Goddammit, Bernie. I need that piece. What the hell is wrong with you? Are you a child?" His voice rose in agitation, the veins standing out in his neck.

Bernie's brain did that thing it did when confusion overtakes logic—it shut down, unable to process. Even when her ADHD meds were working full steam it could happen, but with no sleep and thirty hours of work in the past thirty-six hours, she didn't have a chance. Her thoughts ping-ponged. She couldn't grab onto anything or find something to say that made sense. She said nothing.

"Well?" he asked, standing up. "Well?" He was full-out yelling, the muscles and veins in his neck throbbed as the skin covering them turned red. "Well?" He practically screamed it.

"For chrissake, Pete, it's a puzzle piece." She couldn't remember him ever being this mad at her. Now that she'd found her voice, she was mad too.

"It's not the puzzle piece, it's the total lack of sense. I need it to finish this part of the puzzle." His voice went up an octave, almost as if he was going to burst into tears. His hands were fists at his side. "I mean, how fucking stupid can you be? Did you vacuum up my notebook too? Is that where it is?"

"You know what? Fine." She tried to keep her voice steady. This was a new development, and PTSD be damned, it pissed her off. She could stand there and trade insults or she could do something. "Wait right there."

She went to the utility closet and got the vacuum cleaner and a section of newspaper from the pile stacked with obsessive neatness, ready for recycling. She took a pair of latex gloves out of the box next to the cleaning supplies. When she came back to the living room, Pete was still where he had been, his face still red, fists balled at his sides, doing that breathing thing. Fine, let him if it kept him from yelling.

She held up the newspaper. "See?" She spread it on the floor. "Just like you like." She held up the latex gloves. "See? Just like you want it." She snapped them at the wrists as she pulled them on. His finicky housecleaning ways had been by turn amusing and anxiety-inducing since she moved in. Now they, too, were pissing her off. She disconnected the vacuum cleaner canister and put it on the newspaper as he watched. His face had faded from red to drained and pale.

"Want your fucking puzzle piece? I'll get your fucking so-important puzzle piece." The absurdity of the situation should've made her laugh, but his outsized anger made it feel precarious, dangerously unsettling. She felt tears start.

"Here." He said it quietly, stepping toward her, his hand out as if to help.

"Stay the fuck away from me!" She hadn't meant to, but she screamed it, her voice breaking.

"Bernie." He practically whispered it, his hand still out.

"Don't fucking Bernie me. I may be fucking stupid, I may be fucking childish, but I can find a fucking puzzle piece in the vacuum cleaner canister. Any moron can do that." She sorted through the dog hair, her hair, the balls of gritty dust, popcorn kernels, the bits and pieces that collect in a vacuum canister, still much cleaner, though, than if they'd been at her house, where she only vacuumed when it became obvious that she should. Pete did it at least a couple times a week. She'd been so proud of herself the other day when she'd noticed two tumbleweeds of cat and Dubby hair and got out the vacuum. No good deed goes unpunished, as her dad was fond of saying.

She didn't look at Pete, but could feel him standing closer, his labored breathing the only sound. What she could see of his hands in her tear-blurred peripheral vision confirmed he'd calmed down. He was wiping them on his thighs, his nervous tell. She felt a little less unsettled and confused, but pissed off was still going strong.

The piece, bright amid the browns and grays of the dusty pile, was easy to find.

"Here's the all-important puzzle piece," she said, not yelling anymore but with a tone she hoped made it clear that she wasn't going to let him off the hook.

"Bernie." He held out his hand again. Not for the piece, it seemed, but for her.

"No, wait," she said, deliberately obtuse about the gesture. "God knows what toxic substances it came into contact with in its thirty-six hours in the canister." She got a disinfectant wipe from the box he kept in the cupboard. It took her a minute to tear the foil packet open with her shaky gloved hands. She wiped the puzzle piece, both sides. Took off the gloves and threw them away.

She turned to Pete, finally looking him full in the face. He was white, stricken.

"Here's your all-important puzzle piece. So much more important than my stupid feelings, right?"

He took the piece, his eyes, wet, on hers. "Bernie."

"Stop fucking Bernie-ing me," she shouted. "And as far as your notebook goes, I've never touched it. Ever. IT'S NONE OF MY GODDAMN BUSINESS. If you ever want to talk to me about what's going on in here"—she pointed to her temple—"I'd love to hear it. It'd be much better than being yelled at and called names. But until then, I have enough respect for you I'm not going to spy."

She stormed by him, angling away as he reached for her. "I'm going into the bedroom and want to be left alone. Pretend there's a fucking door and I just slammed it."

She realized how ineffective that was, given he was right there on the other side of the partition, watching her.

"Don't fucking talk to me," she said as she walked by him. He didn't reach out this time. She went into the utility room, bringing the vacuum cleaner with her. She slammed the door behind her and put the vacuum cleaner away in its designated spot. She sat in her reading chair, which he'd surprised her with the previous summer, hobbling around on his crutches to clear a corner, enough for a small but comfy chair, side table, and lamp crammed in next to the washing machine after he noticed she was going into the bathroom to read while he watched sports. She dropped into the chair, put her face in her hands, and cried.

What the hell just happened? She had no clue. She wiped her eyes. Yes, he was getting better, but the bad parts seemed so much worse. She hadn't helped things with her tantrum. This wasn't one of her siblings fighting over whose sweater it was or what TV show to watch. She was forty-five years old. She knew from decades of experience that once the satisfaction of the door-slamming stomp-off faded, there was never a good exit strategy. Sooner or later, she'd have to go back out there. He'd be repentant and touchingly apologetic. He'd mean it. Nothing like this had ever happened before. There were no guarantees it would never happen again. Apologies weren't going to solve the problem.

****

It was fully dark as Pete drove down Loon Lane. As the lights of his house came into view, cozy and warm, he wondered what kind of chilly

173

reception he was in for. He pulled in next to Bernie's car and turned off the engine. Took a deep breath. Held it. Let it out. Did it again.

He walked in to the smell of food cooking. The pellet stove cast a glow on Bernie, who sat on the floor with some kind of project in front of her. It was spread out on newspaper, something she normally wouldn't do.

"Hi honey, I'm home," he said. It was a line they'd started saying months before as a joke, but he'd come to genuinely feel it. He'd probably never tell Bernie. Certainly not tonight. As he took off his boots, he tried to gauge the emotional temperature before launching into the apology he'd been rehearsing for the past couple of hours.

"How was the thing with Sandy?"

"Fun, actually. We were checking the fire roads to make sure they were plowed. I got some snowshoeing in. The exercise felt good." He'd left her a note saying Sandy had called, he was going out, he was worried, he loved her, and they'd talk when he got back. He waited for her to call or text, but she hadn't.

"You're just in time." She picked up what looked like four long, thin pieces of wood. Molding or something. She gave him a tentative smile. "Check this out." She took each piece and fitted it to a side of the coffee table, the edges of the table fitting neatly into what he now saw were H-shaped rails. "I gave it a lip, but not enough to get in the way of doing the puzzle."

"It's a puzzle cat guard," she said when he didn't respond. "It's so they can't knock the pieces off the table. And the pièce de resistance…" She got a large piece of plywood that was leaning against the wall. "This fits on top. I'm going to poly it later. We can put it on top when we want to use the coffee table for other stuff. I used some of that felt left over from when you made the furniture casters for the bottom, the same outline as the frame, so it wouldn't slide around. We may need Velcro or something." She placed it on the frame over the table, covering the puzzle. "I know the bare plywood doesn't look good, but I'll paint it and, like I said, poly it. I hope it's okay that I used that molding in the shed."

She was nervous. The chatter and flitting around the room made that obvious. It was the way she looked at him, then away, likely afraid he'd start yelling, that got him. He'd hurt her and she was afraid. His heart flipped and melted at the same time.

"What do you think?"

"It's great. I got applesauce." He held up the jar, then put it on the counter. If she hadn't seen his tears, she'd definitely heard his voice crack. She was behind him in seconds, pressed against his back, arms around his waist.

"I'm sorry about the puzzle piece and what a bitch I was. You haven't slept in days, and you have a lot going on."

"I'm the one who's sorry." He turned around and put his arms around her, pulling her in tight. "Someday, I promise, I'll get to the point where I don't have to apologize daily for being such an asshole."

"It's not daily. Anyway, you're the best apologizer I've ever known. Even before we were dating. It's one of the things that attracted me to you. I'd hate for it to stop."

He squeezed tighter. "Don't be so easy on me." He leaned back so he could look at her. "You know how much I love you, right?"

"I do." She kissed him lightly on the lips, then moved to the stove, where potatoes were boiling. She poked at them with a fork.

"I ran into Chuck earlier today," he said. "Is it possible he's dating Bev Dulac?"

"Not likely. She's gay."

"Did I know that?"

"Not sure. Her partner died a couple years ago, I think before you moved here. Why do you ask?"

"She was at his house. They mentioned something about a parcel of land behind your house that's been listed for years maybe getting sold."

"The Perkins parcel," she said. "I doubt it was sold. It's landlocked. Not really *land*, because one side is water. The family has an easement across my property, or had. You know that old lane, right before the woods, where it gets steep?" She turned around. He nodded. "They'd go down on that. It's twelve acres or something. But someone died, the deed no longer allows the easement, or something. I don't know. They listed it, but there've been no buyers because they'd need a deeded easement and there's some issue. Even if I wanted people driving across my property, they can't now. So it's worthless. I'm not totally sure how it works. It was explained to me when I bought my house, but, you know."

She waved the fork around as she talked, caught up in the story. "I never really thought about it much, but Rita Chandler brought it up last summer. I ran into her at Choppy's and she said I should buy the Perkins parcel—it's developable and I guess has a great view—and use my lot for the road down there. I'm like, 'Why the hell would I do that?'" She laughed. "I like my house the way it is. Quiet. Liked, I guess." She turned back to the potatoes.

Her face was flushed from the steam from the pot, her hair coming out of its scrunchie in whisps. She was wearing a large sweatshirt and flannel pants, but underneath she was all curvy and soft. It was everything he could do not to hug her again. The land thing was a stall while he worked up to what he'd really wanted to say.

"I've got a favor to ask. I called Benjamin earlier, before Sandy called. He wonders if you could come to a meeting after my appointment tomorrow so we can discuss some grounding strategies to navigate my anger and how to better lean into the discomfort as I heal. How we can better hold space for my challenges while also honoring your emotional space." He waited for her to make a joke about the jargon. He wasn't a fan either, but it was easier to quote Benjamin than to say, "We need to find a way for you to endure my pain and self-absorption until I can get my shit together."

He watched her shoulders rise and fall as the poked at the potatoes. He wished she'd make a joke, some sign things were back to normal.

"I can do that. I'm happy to." She looked over her shoulder and smiled.

"My regular appointment is at two, then we can meet with him together at three, if that's okay," he said, relieved. "I have to be at court to present to the grand jury, since Dawna can't go. I'll catch a ride down with Kermit."

"Sounds good. These are done." She reached for the handles.

"Let me do that." It was a big pot, her arms were short, and a couple of months before she'd splashed boiling water all over herself doing the same thing. He could tell she wanted to argue, but she stood back.

"It's ironic, isn't it, that the puzzle, which is supposed to facilitate authentic dialogue, was the Big T for the worst argument we've ever had as a couple," she said. "We definitely leaned into that."

"Biigggggggg T. Yeah." He poured the potatoes into the colander, the steam hitting his face. There were way too many for one meal. They'd be eating mashed potatoes for the rest of the week.

He put the pot down and wrapped her in a tight hug, burying his face in her hair.

CHAPTER 19

BERNIE COULD ONLY be responsible for her end of things when it came to good journalism. That's what she told herself as she scrolled with dismay through the *Franklin On Call* article, her coffee going cold beside her. Pete was in the shower, so she had time to gather her thoughts. The *Weekly Watcher* article was benign in contrast to this crap. She did a split screen to compare.

First the *Watcher*'s:

Police Chief Contract Undergoes Early Review

By Carrie Beals
Staff Writer

Police Chief Pete Novotny's employment contract is under early review at the request of Mayor Ryan Grant, who said he's unhappy with how the department is being run.

Novotny's job performance was the topic of a fractious executive session at Tuesday's Town Council meeting. Executive sessions are private, but Grant, Novotny and Council Chair Gert Feeney confirmed the topic was Novotny's contract.

None would give specifics of what was discussed, though Grant said he is "troubled by the horrific violence" in town in the past two years, the health insurance cost increase related to the police department, and "problematic aspects of Novotny's behavior."

Novotny told the Watcher that he can't comment while the discussion is ongoing.

The town switched to a mayor and council form of government on Jan. 1, 2010, and since then Grant and Novotny have sometimes clashed, usually over budget matters.

Their latest disagreement has been over Novotny's reluctance to involve the department in the reality show "Real Rural Justice." Similar to the long-running and popular "Cops," the show follows officers on the job, showing interactions and arrests "in real time." Grant has said the show will highlight the "good things the police do" and "repair the town's image," helping bring needed economic development.

The town was the subject of an episode of the true-crime documentary series "Murdertown USA," which aired a year ago and is available on cable television. It chronicled the events of the previous summer, in which a police officer and three residents were killed. Grant frequently references the episode as damaging to the town. At the time it was filmed, September and October 2009, the town had a select board form of government and Grant, a real estate broker, did not hold a town position.

Novotny has said "Real Rural Justice" would be a distraction and that the department "needs space to do its job." He cited the fact that three officers in the six-member department have been hired in the past six months and are still getting used to the job and town. "We need to focus on keeping Redimere safe, not on whether we're in a good camera shot."

According to Grant, the TV show contract comes with a "generous" annual remuneration, but both Grant and the show's producers have declined to offer specifics while they are still negotiating an agreement.

Novotny's employment contract expires Aug. 31. He started Sept. 1, 2008, after 20 years with the Philadelphia Police Department, much of it as a homicide detective. Novotny, 45, is a native of Milwaukee, Wisconsin, but said that he considers Maine home and owns a house in town.

"I'm the police chief, a job I'm committed
to. I'm also committed to Redimere," he said
Wednesday.

The mayor has authority to terminate
department heads, with cause, without Town
Council approval. Feeney said, though, that it's
"a gray area" in regard to Novotny's contract.
He was hired by the select board more than a
year before the government change. Feeney and
Rene Lambert, who were board members at the time,
are the signatories of Novotny's contract, along
with Lew Kinney, who didn't run for a council
seat when the town government changed.

"The chief was hired by unanimous approval of
the select board, with the backing of our chief
at the time," Feeney said. "He was not hired by
Mr. Grant. The select board, then the council,
has stood behind him as he's guided our town
through unprecedented tragedies. Daily, he shows
intelligence, restraint and compassion. He is an
active and popular member of our community. I
have total confidence in him and will continue
to support him."

Bernie had played no role in the article, but couldn't have been happier. Straight and to the point.

She knew that feckless Fergus Kelley at *Franklin On Call* would take every shot he could, but what she didn't expect was that Ryan Grant would load him up with ammo. She wasn't naïve. She'd been a journalist for twenty years and knew that politicians liked to give their favorites more than they gave others, but this was personal:

Redimere Mayor: Police Chief
Is 'Loose Cannon That Will Blow Up Town'
By Fergus X. Kelley

REDIMERE - Mayor Ryan Grant said this week
that Police Chief Pete Novotny, who has a history
of troubling behavior and mental health issues
in his short tenure at the helm, must go if
Redimere is to be a safe place again.

Novotny's contract expires Aug. 31, but Grant said the town can't wait that long.

"Hiring a guy from away, from an urban area with urban problems, was a noble experiment, but it didn't succeed," Grant said in an exclusive FOC interview Wednesday. "We've seen an uptick in crime, and frankly an element in town that just wasn't here when I started here as a real estate broker 15 years ago."

Grant pointed to Novotny's unprovoked attack on freelance photojournalist Sean Speck, who frequently works for FOC, as an example of Novotny's "unprofessionalism and volatility."

Novotny attacked Speck in the halls of Redimere Elementary School Tuesday morning while Speck was having a discussion with a teacher who was harassing him. Speck said he suffered injuries that had to be treated at Franklin Memorial Hospital and that he plans to sue the police department.

He was removed from the school in handcuffs by Novotny's officers, which he called "another humiliation." He was not charged with a crime.

Grant also pointed to Novotny's physical and mental health as "dangerous and costing the town money."

Novotny has been seriously injured twice in less than two years. Once on the job, in 2009, which put him out of work for two weeks but on "light duty" for two months as he recovered, Grant said. The second was a hiking accident in July under "troubling circumstances" while Novotny was on paid vacation.

Grant also said that while he can't talk specifically about Novotny's mental health, in general his issues make him "not fit for duty."

"I was a Navy SEAL and served under fire in Panama and the Middle East, so I know what I'm talking about," Grant said. "I've seen guys undergo worse than he has, and they manage much better than he does. He's never served."

Grant said that the town's insurance has paid nearly $500,000 in physical and mental health costs for Novotny. "That's more than all town personnel combined since we began providing health insurance," he said.

Grant said Novotny's lack of stability is obvious in on-the-job incidents, like Monday's standoff, in which he put himself and others in danger by not allowing a Maine State Police tactical team to take over as he conversed with the suspect. He said off-duty incidents also show his instability, including the notorious "Sexy Sheriff" video that has "gone viral" on the video internet service UTube…

"He can't even spell *YouTube* right."

Bernie jumped. She'd been so engrossed that she hadn't heard Pete come up behind her.

"You've read this?" She wanted to close her laptop, but you only did that if you were guilty of looking at surprise birthday gifts or cat videos when you were supposed to be working. Or porn, if you were her previous boyfriend.

"Dawna called earlier." He poured a cup of coffee. "You want more? I'll make another carafe."

"You don't seem bothered. She called earlier? It's six."

"She called right after I got up. Five thirty. You were in the bathroom." He measured coffee beans with his usual precision.

He was wearing the starched cotton shirt and black tailored suit he reserved for court appearances or anything fancy and formal. The suit jacket was still on its wooden hanger, but even without it he exuded an attractive professionalism that was distracting. He sat down across from her at the table, smoothing the emerald-green silk necktie she'd given him for Christmas. The color had made her think of his eyes, though it was lighter and shone more.

"The tie looks good, don't you think?" He flipped it over his shoulder.

"Don't try to distract me with your well-groomed ways. Why aren't you upset about *FOC?* It's not even journalism. It's a hatchet job."

"I couldn't care less what Kelley writes. It doesn't surprise me that he and Grant have teamed up. I didn't learn anything in that story about how Grant feels that I didn't already know."

"The rest of Redimere has."

"They know who I am. They can judge for themselves what kind of job I'm doing."

"You could probably sue him over what he says about your mental health. That's supposed to be private. It's not even true. Much."

"You know as well as I, if I sue him, it'll reveal more than I'm comfortable revealing."

Yet there he sat, normal and handsome, his shower-wet hair neatly combed, his hands steady as he sipped his coffee. He *was* normal. A normal guy who had challenges he was working on. She felt a renewed surge of anger at Ryan Grant and Feckless Fergus Kelley.

"I like my job and want to keep it," Pete said. "In fact, I'm determined to keep it. I'm not going to worry about Ryan Grant. We have bigger things to deal with. Getting your case headed in the right direction is our top priority. My thing will take care of itself."

"I don't know how *we* are going to do that when *we* are at the mercy of the Ryan Grant of police investigators, George Libby." She was still trying to find the right time to tell him she'd learned Stephanie was renting out rooms, that Dean Davis had reported Stephanie to the Redimere PD, in the form of Brent, and that Brent had made some kind of deal with her. All according to Joe Walsh, of course. It had been a crazy couple of days. Now didn't feel like the right time.

"You have the top criminal defense lawyer in Franklin County representing you, with help from me and, I hate to admit it, Tommy. You'll be in the clear soon and we can move on."

The sound of a car coming down the road grew louder as Pete spoke.

"Speaking of the top criminal defense lawyer," Bernie said.

****

Cup of coffee in front of him, Kermit got down to business. "Libby has hinted that they don't have anything they can use to charge you with. The texts aren't enough. The gas cans are a nonstarter. He needs more, too, than the neighbor claiming he saw you, though Libby gives that more significance than I do."

"An eyewitness account can be solid evidence," Pete said. "Convictions are built on it."

Bernie snorted. "Eyewitness evidence is notoriously shaky, despite how much cops love it. You said that yourself just the other day."

"It can be good, or it can be bad."

"In this case, it's bad," Kermit said. "You two have an alibi. I haven't talked to the neighbor, but from what I can surmise, it was dark, he saw a car but not a person. It could be anyone's, a silver midsize SUV."

"I haven't driven a silver car since I wrecked mine in July. I'm driving Pete's Forester. It's dark green."

"There you go." Kermit raised his mug in a salute. "Let's assume that our intrepid investigator would've ferreted out that information sooner or later."

"I'm off the hook."

"Maybe. They want you to take a polygraph. Just to be sure, as Libby put it."

"I'm not doing that."

"I agree," Kermit said.

"Why not?" Pete said. "Just so they'll move on."

"You, as a former homicide cop, should know what bullshit they are," Bernie said. "There's a reason they're not allowed in court. They just use them to scare people, intimidate them, and because they're too lazy to actually investigate. On top of it, since I take ADHD meds, I'm probably not even qualified."

"A professional examiner can account for medication effects," Pete said. "Polygraphs are a useful tool when used correctly."

Bernie could tell he was trying to sound reasonable, not defensive, but she knew him too well. The way he pursed his lips, looked at his coffee. The careful, formal wording. All tells.

"*Tool* being the operative word," she said. "Do you want Libby to use a manipulative tool against me? Given my level of anxiety and the fact that the texts make me feel guilty? That the past two months with Stephanie totally stressed me out? How's that all going to read? If my results are inconclusive or I'm lying or Libby just feels like telling me that I failed even if I didn't, that's just going to drag this on longer." She'd avoided topics like this with Pete as long as she'd known him. It was too hard, went too deep into areas where she knew they'd both dig in and not come out any better for it. But this was her life.

"Obviously it's up to you and your lawyer's counsel," Pete said. He took a prim sip of coffee, a blush creeping across his cheekbones.

"I agree with Bernie," Kermit said. "The fact that they're asking means they don't have a case."

"You're right," Pete said to Kermit. "That's fine."

Glad you both agree. Bernie's annoyance rose as the two men nodded to each other with what looked a lot like smug satisfaction.

****

Once Pete and Kermit left for Farmington, Bernie called up the *FOC* article again.

She found the place she'd been in the article when Pete had interrupted her. It was just more bullshit, mostly about how Pete was blocking the town's chances of making money and "repairing its reputation" by allowing *Real Rural Justice* to film. As with everything else, Feckless Kelley got that wrong too. He didn't even attribute it to Ryan Grant.

> The police chief's resistance to the show came after "Weekly Watcher" editor Bernadette O'Dea wrote a scathing editorial blasting the show and other similar shows, which she labeled "copaganda," an apparent made-up word that demeans pro law enforcement television fare. The editorial was ironic given that O'Dea and Novotny cohabitate in an apparently "romantic relationship."

The poor writing and idiotic conclusions would've made Bernie laugh if they didn't piss her off so much. She and Pete had discussed *Real Rural Justice.* They both thought it was a bad idea, but had wildly different reasons. They'd had a good-natured argument, the kind that they both enjoyed and that didn't come with the scary anger and confusion that, say, an argument about a vacuumed jigsaw puzzle piece would. Then they'd agreed not to talk about it.

She hadn't told Pete that her anxiety about losing the business she'd built with care and uncharacteristic patience and planning had ramped up when her house burned down. *With a body inside!* She'd felt it since she'd bought the paper, but it'd gone from a low thrum that she could ignore most of the time to a high-pitched squeal after the fire. Telling Pete would just make him worry about one more thing he couldn't do anything about. But now, fucking Ryan Grant, with help from Fergus Kelley, had pulled her into his Pete vendetta. It was the last thing she needed.

She called Pete's cell.

"Hey," he said in that warm way he had, as though they hadn't been together just twenty minutes before. Kermit's car hummed in the background, windshield wipers faintly swishing away the snow that had started to fall.

"Are you going to clear up with Grant, in a way that will be made public, that I had nothing to do with you not wanting *Real Rural Justice?*"

"I could. I hadn't really intended to talk to him unless I had to, given what's going on."

She heard Kermit say something in the background.

"That TV show," Pete said, responding to Kermit. "Bernie doesn't like the fact the *FOC* article makes it sound like she influenced me."

Kermit murmured something.

"Sorry," Pete said to Bernie. "You're right. I'll make it clear to Grant that we have a separation between our jobs. I wasn't thinking about that. I know a bad reputation can wreck your business."

"Thanks."

"Least I can do," he said, though it was gruff. "We can talk more later. I've got to prepare for the grand jury, so I'm not thinking about this stuff until this afternoon when I talk to Benjamin."

Not thinking about it? How does he do that?

"Okay?" he asked when she didn't answer.

"I guess so."

"Bernie, I love you. Everything's going to be okay."

She wanted to hash it out. Grind it to a pulp. She pictured Pete in his nice suit, the tie she'd given him for Christmas, his curls and cowlicks probably popping as his hair dried, sitting in the ancient, ornate courtroom presenting Redimere's cases to the grand jury, the members of which may be wondering if he was the deranged nutjob they'd read about that morning.

"All right," she said.

"I love you," he repeated. She could feel him relax all the way down the snow-covered highway.

"I love you too." She hung up. She had seven hours until the meeting with Benjamin. Maybe Pete couldn't engage with Grant right now. She knew a public dustup on her part would be self-inflicted damage of the type she was trying to avoid. But he was trying to take down Pete. And now he was trying to take her down. She needed to go to work, take care of payroll and other stuff. But not thinking about it? *Sorry, Pete. That's not going to happen.*

CHAPTER 20

"HOW'S YOUR FIRST week going?" Dawna asked as she settled into the cruiser.

"Good." Mandy said it in that layered way, one syllable a whole sentence, *good for the most part, but there is a lot of stuff.*

"Don't feel like you have to be comfortable and on top of everything right away. This has been a weird week. Any questions, or concerns—*anything*—you can talk to me. The chief is good, too, but try me first."

Fergus Kelley and his article had blown up Dawna's morning. She'd reassured Mandy and Tyler, shut down Brent's snarky asides. Jamie, who wasn't on duty, had called, apprehensive and disappointed in Pete. She couldn't do a lot about the guys, to varying degrees, but she hoped that Mandy, so new, wouldn't let it influence her.

"I like him," Mandy said. "I don't put much store in what that article says. He reminds me of my dad. My dad's more of a hippie, but they have that same thing where you can tell they're listening, and they're looking at you like you're a person, not like, you know, whatever."

Dawna pulled out onto Main Street. "One thing we're looking at today is the thefts from cars over the past couple of weeks. It's adding up to a lot. If the total reaches more than $10,000, the perp is going to be facing a felony."

"If we catch him. Or her. I reviewed the reports to familiarize myself with the case."

"I know all we have is that not great security camera image of the guy on the bike leaving Pondside Convenience, which may not even be him, but you'll find a lot of people who commit crimes don't think things through very well."

"Tyler was saying in this case the victims are stupid, too, leaving their cars unlocked." Dawna could hear the question behind the comment.

"Stealing is against the law. Bottom line. Would you go in someone's unlocked car and take something? No. Would I? No. It's not ideal to leave money, or something valuable, in your unlocked car, but that doesn't mean someone has a right to steal it."

"I kind of tried to say that."

"One thing you'll catch on to quick is that we have a lot of frequent fliers," Dawna said. "People we interact with a lot. We're not always arresting them, but a big part of the job is being like a social worker, or amateur psychiatrist, or Main Street diplomat. Solving little problems." She drove past the three blocks of brick and clapboard buildings on Main Street, past town hall and the elementary school.

"There's one now. That's Zack Staples. He's always up to something. Lots of times, I stop and talk to folks, just in a friendly way, but I just did it with him the other day and don't want him to think I'm harassing him. It's a fine line."

Dawna waved. Zack, in his old parka, the kind with fake fur around the hood, lifted a huge Dunkin's cup in salute before putting the straw back in his mouth. He was bopping along in his usual goofy way, his lanky frame bouncing with each long stride. He was smiling, sunglasses perched atop the brim of a glittery baseball cap. The lumpy rucksack hanging off his shoulder bounced merrily along with him.

"He's stylin'," Mandy said.

"Stylin' all right," Dawna said. "He's living at Timberwoods, the trailer park down there"—she pointed down Main Street—"with his ex-girlfriend. They broke up, but he got evicted from his apartment, so…" Dawna shrugged. "That's his side of it. I'm sure there's more to it. There's a lot of that going on. People bouncing around, living different places. It makes it hard to keep track of the troublemakers, even in a town of two-thousand give or take."

"Did you clock his shades?"

"What?"

"His sunglasses? Those are Kahuna Biggies. Wicked expensive. Very popular on the slopes. Looks like the blue wave edition, pretty high-end. A pair was stolen in those car thefts."

"Good work." Dawna pulled into a driveway and turned around.

"A lot of Dunkin's gift cards were stolen too. He's got that iced coffee," Mandy said.

Dawna pulled up next to Zack.

"Hey Zack, talk to you a minute?" She asked over the top of the car as she got out.

Zack's eyes darted from Mandy, stepping onto the packed dirty snow on the road's shoulder, to Dawna, coming around the front of the car. His ear-to-ear grin wavered.

"Sure, Sergeant," he said. "Is this our new officer?" His rucksack jingled when he shifted it. Not loudly, but enough that Dawna saw Mandy give it a quick look.

"Officer Mandy Arsenault," Mandy said.

"Cool. Welcome aboard. I saw your picture in the paper." He put the rucksack on the ground, behind his legs and more carefully than Dawna would expect. It jingled again. He was wearing worn, but sturdy, Timberland work boots. One of three clothing items reported stolen. Size thirteens. Another was a glittery baseball cap, just like the one on Zack's head.

His eyes followed Dawna's. He inched sideways so his legs better blocked the rucksack.

"What're you drinking?" Dawna asked. "Looks cold for a cold day."

Zack looked at his giant clear plastic cup, almost with surprise. "This is an iced coffee with an expresso shot and some caramel thrown in. Don't you know drinking cold stuff on a cold day actually makes you warmer? It equals the temperature inside and outside."

It was clear that Mandy, bouncing on the balls of her feet, had something to say about internal temperature regulation. Or maybe she just wanted to say it's espresso, not expresso.

"Kind of an expensive drink for a guy on a budget," Dawna said. "Isn't that what you told me the other day? You had to sell your bike because you're living on a budget?"

"Gotta splurge once in a while, you know? Makes life worthwhile."

"Those sunglasses, aren't they"—she struggled for a second to remember the brand name—"Big Kahunas? Those are expensive too, right?"

"Oh, man. I don't know the brand name." Zack's face fell in what Dawna guessed was supposed to be disappointment and surprise. "I bought them wicked cheap from this guy, you know? He said he found them on the slopes and just wanted someone to have them who could use them."

"What guy?"

"Derek? Maybe? Hard to remember. Some guy I ran into at Pondside. Darren?"

"Someone stole a pair just like those from a car at College Garden Apartments."

"Oh wow. No way. That dude sold me stolen goods?"

"You mind if we look through your rucksack?"

"I don't know. I mean, it's not like I have anything bad in there, but it's my stuff, you know? I mean, don't you need a warrant?"

"The sunglasses give us probable cause."

"Maybe they're not the stolen ones, just similar." He took a big sip through his straw, his eyes skittering from Dawna to Mandy.

"We can easily tell," Mandy said. "They all have a unique serial number on the temple—that's the arm part. The gentleman who lost his gave the serial number to the investigating officer."

"If we can take a look, we can clear this up," Dawna added.

Zack's lip trembled. He handed them to Mandy.

Mandy pointed to a number on the temple. "Sergeant, I believe this is the same serial number as the stolen pair. I'd have to check the report, but it looks similar."

Zack handed Dawna his rucksack. "Okay. I guess you better look."

Inside was a fleece vest, the third item of clothing reported stolen. Under it were a pair of large, soggy, well-worn sneakers, obviously Zack's; a dozen lighters, gift cards, more sunglasses, and several pounds of loose change, among other items.

"Zack, you wait here," Dawna said. "I have to confer with Officer Arseneault."

He nodded, frantically slurping the last of his iced coffee. Probably afraid they were going to take that, too.

She signaled for Mandy to follow her to the other side of the cruiser. "This is your arrest. Nice bluff on the serial number. I'll call it in, and you can do the honors. Cuff him—in front, not back, okay? You can Mirandize him at the station."

"Got it, Sergeant."

Dawna ducked into the cruiser.

"Zack, we need to talk to you at the station, all right?" Mandy's high but all-business voice carried through the closed windows. "Are you carrying any weapons?"

"No, officer."

"Okay, put your hands out in front. No, don't throw the cup on the ground. No littering." Mandy opened the door of the cruiser and put the cup on the floor in front of the passenger seat. "Sorry," she whispered to Dawna.

"Am I being arrested?" Zack asked.

"When we get to the station," Mandy said.

"Okay, officer."

Dawna put the radio back in its holder as Mandy guided Zack into the back seat.

He looked at Dawna in the rearview mirror. "I guess there's a new sheriff in town, huh?"

"Spread the word," Dawna said.

****

Bernie should be doing the payroll, since it had to be filed by noon. She didn't have the mental energy. "Five minutes," she promised herself. She put her feet up on her desk. Outside it was gray and windy. She watched shoppers park in front of the Country Grocer, then leave the car running as they rushed in to pick up whatever it was people bought this time of morning in January. Other than that, the street was deserted.

Her cellphone rang. It was her insurance agent. So much for a relaxing five minutes.

"I have some good news and some bad news," she said.

"Are they both the same thing?" Bernie asked.

"I'm sorry?"

"Never mind. Bad news first, I guess."

"We're still waiting for the investigation to conclude before we can make a determination," she said. "I'm sorry, I know how stressful this must be for you. Arson is very hard to nail down, and the investigation can take awhile."

"What's the good news?"

"The bank's appraiser came in with a number far higher than what your property was appraised at when you bought it," she said. "It has to do with adjacent properties or something. It's higher than your coverage, which means that you'll get the maximum amount for the rebuild."

Bernie wasn't sure what it meant, but at least it sounded like it wasn't something she had to worry about. As she hung up, a round bundled figure pushed the door open. A burst of frigid air buffeted the papers on Bernie's desk before the door slammed shut.

Natalie Perry pulled back her hood as she approached Bernie's desk.

"Don't you have school?" Bernie asked.

"Teacher's day," Natalie said.

Bernie could never keep track of what happened with kids and school. She was happy not to have to. "I like your haircut."

"I got tired of braids," she said, self-consciously touching her bobbed black hair.

"Looks good on you. I hate hair stuff too."

"Thanks. I got tired of people calling me Pocahontas."

Bernie swallowed a little guilt. The "poker-hardness" joke with Tommy didn't seem as funny with Natalie standing there, lip trembling.

"Thanks for putting the stuff about the tribal acknowledgement in the paper, too," she said. "Dad says maybe they'll put it on their agenda to vote for next meeting, but not to get my hopes up."

Natalie put her knapsack on Bernie's desk, unzipped it, and took out a sheaf of papers, stapled together. "I have some more. I know you don't have kids write stories, but I have a story maybe you or someone could do. It goes with the acknowledgement."

She handed the papers to Bernie. Her large black eyes, always serious, burned.

The cover page, in neat block handwriting, said: "The Appropriation of Native Lands by Redimere's Forefathers, by Natalie Perry." There was a giant red C on the cover and, in what was clearly a teacher's handwriting "You worked very hard on this, and the writing is satisfactory, but your research needs another voice. There are two sides to every story." The last sentence was underlined.

"We were supposed to find something in Redimere's history and interview someone," Natalie said. "Hallowell did a story on the history of town hall and only talked to the mayor, and he got an A."

"Sorry. That's unfair." Bernie wanted to tell her to get used to it, but the kid would learn soon enough.

"I know I got a bad grade, but maybe you want my information? I saw the story today about the college building something on Mr. Ouimette's property. He told me for this paper that he was giving the land back to the Passamaquoddy Tribe. He showed me a story you had written where he said the same thing."

"I haven't been able to reach him to find out what happened. When did you talk to him?"

"In November. Right after Halloween."

"I'm going to do more once I can get hold of Normand. I'm talking to the people at the college about it tomorrow. I'll ask about that."

"They'll just lie." Natalie sounded older than her twelve years. "They've been lying to us for centuries. The newspaper should say so."

"I'll do my best."

"There's something else. Mr. Ouimette said to keep it secret, so I didn't put it in my paper. I'll tell you off the record."

Bernie smiled. "Off the record, sure."

"Petroglyphs." Natalie whispered it.

"What?"

"Petroglyphs. At the top of the hill by the quarry. Mr. Ouimette didn't want people to know because they'll ruin it. He said he'd tell tribal officials."

Bernie wondered if the college knew. There were other petroglyph sites in Maine, but she wasn't sure how protected they were. It could be an issue for the college's plans. Or maybe not.

"It's okay if you tell Mr. Ouimette I told you, but don't put it in the paper unless he says."

"Good call. You're right."

"You can keep my paper for now," she said. "My dad wants to put it in the mementos box, so I need it back sometime."

As Natalie left, Bernie's brother Sal came in, giving her a playful tap on the head as he walked past. "Go get 'em Nat," he said.

"I love that kid," he said to Bernie after the door closed behind her. "That story in *FOC* was wild today. I want to kick Kelley's ass."

"Thanks. But is there something I can help you with? I have to do payroll."

"Heard from the insurance company?"

"They can't tell me anything until the investigation is done. Arson's tough."

"Too bad for the cops they threw out all that junk science. They were going gangbusters until then. Remember the documentary we watched about the Texas guy whose kids died in a fire, and he was sent to the chair? It turned out he didn't do it? The science is bullshit?"

"Believe me, I've thought about it. Again, are you here for a reason?"

"I have a tip. Personal, not news. Chloe heard through the grapevine someone finally bought that land down the hill behind your house along Little Pond."

"Wow. Everyone's so interested. Pete's dad heard something about it, too, and the insurance agent just said something—the appreciation on my house went up. I don't think it's anything interesting, though. That easement expired with the deed. Something. I can't remember how it works, but it's no good now."

"Think about it. Whoever bought that land would probably buy your property. Bingo bingeray, your problems are solved."

"Not the biggest problem, which is there's an arson investigation going on. Until that's resolved, I don't have the brain capacity to wonder what'll happen with my land."

"Speaking of real estate," Sal said. "You know that Kelley's *Franklin On Call* office is in Grant's building, right?"

Bernie did. It was a one-story bungalow on Main Street. Fergus operated out of a room in the back.

"Chloe says he doesn't pay rent, gets the space free. Supposedly in exchange for advertising. Pretty good deal for Kelley, since rent's a lot more than what anyone would pay for advertising on that website."

"Advertising my ass." Bernie had felt for a while that there was some kind of collusion between the mayor and the feckless wonder. That just sealed it. Whether it just validated her suspicions or was information she could actually use, though, remained to be seen.

CHAPTER 21

BENJAMIN'S OFFICE WAS in an uninspired addition to an old train depot that housed a natural food store, a laundromat, and a variety of offices. His door was around the back, which involved navigating a narrow dirt parking area that was a minefield of frozen tire ruts and ice patches. The door was windowless and unmarked except for 3A in those shiny stickers people put on their mailboxes. Ringing the bell felt illicit. But that feeling disappeared when Benjamin opened the door and his giant eyes, downturned at the corners, practically melting down his large, soft face, lit up as his massive pillowy hand took Bernie's.

"It's so nice to meet you," he said in a slow, soft voice. Pete had imitated it for her many times. He'd been spot-on.

Benjamin led her through a reception area, tiny, barren, and empty, into a marginally larger office. A desk piled with folders and papers was crammed into a corner, but most of the room was taken up by three upholstered chairs surrounding a low coffee table. A box of tissues sat squarely in the middle, just like at Kermit's. Pete stood up as they walked in and kissed her on the cheek.

He was in shirtsleeves, his tie loosened, his suit jacket folded over the back of his chair. He looked rumpled and worn, his eyes rimmed red. He squeezed her triceps—she guessed in reassurance—before sitting back down. The gesture just made her more wary. Benjamin sat too. They watched her expectantly. The surge of good feeling she'd had at the warmth of Benjamin's greeting slid sideways. She didn't have a good experience with meetings that featured people oozing with serious intent silently eyeing her.

"Please sit," Benjamin said, indicating the empty chair. "We're checking in today to take the temperature of Pete's recovery from your perspective as well as lean in to some strategies. As you know, Pete has a lot of trauma to unpack. It sounds like you're doing a great job of leaning in and being intentional…"

As Benjamin talked, Pete sat stock-still, his forearms on his thighs, hands clasped, lips pursed, eyes on the table. He seemed unnaturally awkward and nervous. Not a good omen. Bernie had considered that the meeting could be an ambush. Benjamin facilitating a breakup, Bernie and her jigsaw-piece vacuuming and everything else too much for Pete. His constant pressure to make things permanent made that seem unlikely, but the ambushes in her life never jibed with her perception of reality. Isn't that what ambushes were?

"How do you feel Pete's recovery is going, from your point of view?" Benjamin asked, startling her back to the meeting.

That could explain Pete's nervousness, his quick look at Bernie, then back to the table. Maybe he, too, was worried about an ambush, about her emerging from the brush with a flamethrower of gripes and accusations.

What if she said the wrong thing and sent him spiraling further into whatever he'd been falling into the last several weeks? Benjamin's eyes, liquid blue pools of sadness that she was sure would spill over with one wrong word, didn't leave hers. *Son of sorrow.* Pete had told her that's what the name Benjamin meant. He'd said it fit perfectly. At the time she was impressed, as always, at the esoteric facts he could just pull from his head. Now she got it.

"He's doing great," Bernie said. "Really…great."

Benjamin's soft face crumpled, just enough to make Bernie feel guilty. He leaned forward, his eyes pulling her into deep, wet disappointment. She should've thought about this more. She hadn't prepared mentally.

"We need you to be intentional and authentic if we're going to help Pete," he said.

We? That's what she'd been afraid of, even though she'd been told by everyone—Pete, Chuck, Carol, Colleen, the few members of her family who knew specifics, the advice columns she'd Googled, *everyone*—that Pete was the one responsible for Pete's recovery.

"Let's set a foundation first," Benjamin said. "You are obviously two very caring and honest people who love each other very much. But you must learn to dialogue authentically. The biggest obstacle I see to authentic communication in your partnership is that you each fear hurting the other. That's commendable. But you *are* hurting each other if you can't be authentic about emotions and impactful reactions."

Once Bernie untangled the jargon, she couldn't disagree.

"All right, Bernie." Benjamin nodded to her and sat back.

Okay, authentic. Here goes. "A few months ago he was doing a lot better than last summer, or even last year," Bernie said, speaking slowly, trying to match Benjamin's measured calm. "He was lighter, like a veil had lifted."

Pete, silent, stared at the table.

"I know PTSD doesn't get cured"—she put air quotes around *cured*—"or fixed, but I expected linear improvement. The past couple months have been one step up, two steps back." She searched for jargon that would please Benjamin. "I'm tempering my expectations."

"What are your expectations?" Pete asked, terse.

"Pete, let's let Bernie unpack her thoughts at her own speed."

Thank you. It was the first time in her life anyone had acknowledged she needed that. This time of day, this type of situation, expressing thoughts she'd never said out loud and hadn't planned to, had stalled her brain into near paralysis.

"My expectation, or hope, maybe, is that Pete will stop being so hard on himself."

Benjamin sat back, nodded, and smiled. "Isn't this what we've been discussing?" he asked Pete.

"Yes." Pete's gaze had dropped down to his hands, which were still clasped, white-knuckle now. The tips of his ears were red.

"Thank you for your honesty about that issue," Benjamin said to Bernie. "We need to unpack Pete's anger, which is impacting you to a concerning level."

"I wouldn't say *concerning* level. I know it's a PTSD symptom. I don't take it personally."

Benjamin's eyes grew larger, wetter. The corners dipped closer to his cheekbones. "Let's not minimize it. You need to feel safe."

"I never said—"

"Pete and I have discussed immediate strategies that will allow him to navigate anger management more effectively." Benjamin's soft voice plowed through Bernie's startled objection. "We'll discuss long-term strategies going forward. In the present, we need to strategize on how you both can lean into the discomfort as Pete heals. It's important to hold space for Pete's pain but equally important to honor your emotional and physical space and well-being."

Pete's face was flushed, his knuckles whiter. She smiled at him. *It's okay. Hang in there.* He looked away.

"Pete, why don't you tell Bernie what we've unpacked?"

Pete took a deep breath. "Long-term trauma, when it's not addressed, grows. Like cancer." Bernie sensed he and Benjamin had rehearsed this. "My stepfather's abuse, losing my brother and my mom, all those years in homicide, some of the things that have happened the past two years…" He paused. "I feel like I'm consumed by it."

"Oh." It seemed like way too much to unpack. To sort out and hang up or put away, whatever you did with the stuff once it was unpacked.

His tone was less strained, almost conversational, now that he'd acknowledged the hard part to her. "I know it's not the only solution, but I feel like if I got more exercise, I'd feel better. I ran, swam, played basketball, hockey, worked out, lots of things, every day before this." He gestured at his leg. "I can't do anything. The gym isn't enough."

Benjamin added, "Physical activity can be a huge help for relieving stress, anger, and anxiety."

"Totally," Bernie said. The office was too warm. She was hungry. Her energy level was zero. She could barely get her head around the topics, so slow on the uptake. *Problem solved. Let's go home.*

"I'm not making excuses for my behavior," Pete said.

"What's your core emotion right now?" Benjamin asked Bernie.

Another one where the wrong answer would mess everything up. "Love. Hope?" *Are those even emotions?*

"Let me put it this way," Benjamin said. "What's your biggest question for Pete about his recovery?

No one told me there was going to be a quiz. She thought about it. She had so many. "You've seemed to have lost your—this is going to sound dumb—your joy? You've been—I know this is the wrong word—more uptight recently."

"Sorry. I didn't realize how I've been acting."

"It's not a way you're acting—it's a way you're being. Your aura or whatever. I know it doesn't make sense. I asked a dumb question."

"There are no dumb questions when you're revealing authentic feelings," Benjamin said. "In fact, that's very insightful. Pete's recovery is not a linear journey. Stress, physical elements, lack of sleep, and other issues all impact symptoms and behaviors. Night terrors are different from nightmares, as they're replaying something that actually happened—it's happening again without the benefit of waking filters. Those will ease, but for now, they're also a stressor as Pete relives trauma. There are other stressors, too, less tangible ones. The good news is that it's not like losing a limb. Symptoms fade, even disappear. Lightness and positive feelings can return."

"I'm sorry," Pete said.

"It's not something to be sorry for," Bernie said.

"As Pete's journey to better mental health continues, the power of Big T's—the big triggers that impact his night terrors, flashbacks, and anger—will lessen. Big T's become little t's. He'll be able to balance his anxiety better. Pete? There was something you wanted to ask Bernie."

Pete straightened up. Sat back. Took a deep breath. Looked Bernie in the eye. "Do I make you feel unsafe?"

"What?"

"Bernie?" Benjamin asked. He oozed gentleness. "Does Pete make you feel unsafe?"

"No. I would trust my life to Pete. I have, as a matter of fact."

"We need you to be completely honest if we're going to make progress," Benjamin said.

Bernie felt the same frustration as she had with the cops. *Why isn't the truth enough?* She damn well wasn't going to be pulled into a false confession, especially on this.

"I don't know how to say it any better. I have *been* with men I don't feel safe with. I know the difference. I know, now, you don't sneak up on someone in the shower who startles easily. Yesterday's thing? I knew even in the moment he was stressed and exhausted and I pushed it. I'm learning"—she tried to remember the jargon, so Benjamin would get it—"strategies to manage my emotional space."

"It doesn't matter *why* Pete is angry, it's the impacts of his behaviors on you that matter," Benjamin said.

"It devastates me that you don't feel safe," Pete said. "I could tell yesterday—"

"I *do* feel safe. Oh my god."

"Let's retreat and regroup," Benjamin said. "Let's establish if Bernie feels safe enough to continue the living arrangement and strategize on how that will work."

"*Continue?*" Bernie asked. "I'd move out for my safety? That doesn't even make sense. Pete, you get that, right?"

"I don't know." It was a whisper.

"Bernie, you shouldn't feel obligated to stay with Pete if his PTSD issues are increasing your anxiety or impacting your state of mind, aside from the threat of physical harm," Benjamin said.

Why did they have to keep going around and around? "That's not an issue."

"Pete, you had something else important to say," Benjamin said.

Pete shook his head, just slightly. "No, that's it."

"Pete."

He and Benjamin had a stare-down.

"This isn't what you signed up for," Pete finally said. "You shouldn't feel obligated to be my babysitter."

Benjamin shook his head and sat back. It was obviously not the "important thing," but it was important enough to Bernie.

"I never said I was." She didn't care that her annoyance, spiced with anger, was showing. She was being authentic. They weren't getting it. "What does anyone sign up for? It's not a fairy tale. I signed up for you. All of you." It probably would have had a better impact if her voice hadn't been rising.

Benjamin waved his hands. "Please, let's be intentional."

Bernie paused to get her annoyance in check. "I've been with guys who are financially abusive, passive-aggressive, withholding, indifferent, smelled bad, hogged the remote—all sorts of things that make relationships suck." She tried to make it sound gentle, the way she really felt it. "None of them, as far as I know, had PTSD. You are none of those things. PTSD is part of who you are. I could be with a guy who doesn't have it, but has one or more of those other things, and that'd be a lot worse. You are strong and loyal and brave and compassionate and empathetic. You care about me in a way I didn't know someone could. Our love is a constant revelation to me."

"That's, um..." Pete wiped his eyes with both hands, before rubbing them—shaking—on his thighs. "Thanks."

"You've unpacked your feelings in a very authentic way," Benjamin said. His eyes throbbed with emotion.

My work here is done. Bernie's stomach growled. *Let's go home and get some pizza.*

****

"Sorry I parked so far away, I don't know what I was thinking," Bernie said for the second time in less than a minute as they made their way around the building along the frozen, uneven dirt. The car was in the municipal lot, since she'd stopped at the Registry of Deeds first. It hadn't occurred to her to drive the five blocks to Benjamin's office. But as dark descended, the wind bit her cheeks, and Pete's leg gave a small jerk with each step, she realized it was a mistake.

203

"Why don't you wait in here and I'll go get the car?" she said as they came to the side door of the natural foods store.

"I'm fine." He took her hand in his, tight, though cushioned by his leather and her Gore-Tex.

"You're not being very authentic. I can tell your leg is bothering you. You're not even wearing a hat. It doesn't make sense for us to snail our way through this frozen tundra, like Perry or Scott or whoever starved to death at whichever pole. And please, I'm too tired and hungry to get a history lecture on which it was."

"I didn't want to lose an indictment because I had hat hair."

"Authentically? They'd think it was adorable and indict the shit out of every case you had." The cold wind whipped them as they approached Front Street. Her face stung with it, and her eyes watered behind her glasses. A pickup truck squealed to a stop, then revved its engine as they crossed the street, slick with blown snow. The second they were past it, the driver roared away with a blast of noxious exhaust.

"Where's a cop when you need one?" Bernie asked.

They started up the hill, Bernie forcing herself to meet his pace. Normally, he walked closest to the street, a protective habit that both warmed and annoyed her. Today, though, he stayed on her right, keeping her on the side of his bad leg. He gripped her hand, eyes on the sidewalk. They finally crested the hill, then inched across the parking lot to the car. As Pete got in, he adjusted his leg, trying to find a comfortable position.

"It's fine," he said.

"I didn't say anything. But since you brought it up, didn't Benjamin say we have to have authentic conversations? We're off to a great start."

"He said that, as a homework strategy, if one of us called for an authentic dialogue, the other had to honor that and be totally authentic, regardless of the feared outcome."

"I don't think that means we aren't supposed to try to be authentic the rest of the time." She turned onto Main Street and headed north.

"Speaking of authentic," Pete said, resting his hand on the back of her neck. He'd taken off his glove, and his warm skin against hers was an instant relaxer. "At least now we have a template for when we write our own vows."

"What the hell are you talking about?"

"What you said in Benjamin's office. Our love being a revelation? Etcetera? You've never said that to me. That's a great draft for your vows."

She looked over. He tilted his head. "Right?"

"Wrong. No way. Nope. Total deal-breaker."

"What?"

"Writing our own vows. That's not gonna happen."

"You don't think it would be nice to stand before each other on our wedding day and express to our family and friends why we're there?"

"No."

"That's the point, right?"

"I meant what I said, but I could barely say it with Benjamin facilitating. No way I'm going to stand up there in front of people and gush all that out. Gross. We'll stick to traditional vows or it's not happening."

"Okay." His hand gently rubbed the back of her neck. After a minute's silence, he said, "You're on board with getting married, then."

"I didn't say that."

"You said 'we'll stick to traditional vows or it's not happening.' "

"I meant *if* we get married."

"Let's have an authentic dialogue about it."

"Can we wait until we get home and eat? I'm tired and hungry and, believe it or not, talked out. That's a poor recipe for authentic dialogue."

"We should take advantage of the momentum. You know, unpack things."

"Haven't you had enough unpacking for one day?"

"I'd rather unpack it now than anticipate unpacking it later."

Her big box of feelings concerning their future, though, wasn't going to be easy to unpack. It wasn't ready. Thoughts that she hadn't been able to sort out for months had finally started to take form in

Benjamin's office. It was a tangled form, though. Benjamin's authenticity didn't leave room for the processing part. The tender navigation. The space for her emotional whatever.

"How about this?" she said. "We get a pizza, eat it, and then have an authentic discussion about whether it's time for an authentic discussion."

His thumb rubbed gently, back and forth, on her neck. It, combined with her meds wearing off, her exhaustion, and hunger, had a hypnotic effect that forced her to say things she shouldn't. She knew she should stop even as the words went from her brain to her voice box, but she couldn't. Kind of like vacuuming up a puzzle piece.

"I'm still processing. We won't have a satisfactory outcome if we talk now."

"That's a cop-out, Bernie. You've been processing it since July. It sounds like you've figured it out. Once I know what you're thinking, if there are problems, we can fix it."

"By 'fix it,' do you mean you try to convince me I'm wrong? I *am* living with you. I don't have any other place to go. My house is gone. Even though we're not married, or even engaged, you have it your way. Maybe you should quit while you're ahead."

"Don't throw the fire in my face." He gave her neck one last rub, then took his hand away. "I'm not happy your house burned down. I can't say it enough. You're smart enough to know that, anyway. By 'fix it,' I mean, find emotional space where we're both comfortable with how we feel and where we're at."

The taillights of cars heading north from Farmington snaked ahead of them on the two-lane road as it ran between woods and farm fields on one side, the Sandy River on the other. Bernie had driven this road hundreds of times, but tonight it felt impossibly long.

"What if it can't be fixed?" she asked. *You want authentic? Be careful what you ask for.*

Pete swallowed loud enough for her to hear. "I can't imagine what the problem would be that can't be fixed if everything you said in Benjamin's office is true."

"It is."

"Then I don't get it."

"Let's eat first, okay?"

They were going through New Portland, the ruins of the old mill black against the dark sky. They still had more than half an hour. She couldn't take it. She had to say more. "This is a general observation. I know you know it on some level. Women and men live in very different parallel universes. Right? We've talked about that, that a guy can go out for a run whenever he wants, park his car in a dark parking garage, all that stuff, without even thinking about it. Women don't have that freedom. Everything is a risk assessment."

"Of course I understand that. What does it have to do with our relationship? Unless you really don't feel safe with me and that was bullshit back there."

"It has nothing to do with how safe I feel with you. It's just part of my thought process."

They drove through the dark in silence.

CHAPTER 22

BERNIE MADE IT clear the authentic dialogue wasn't going to happen until they'd eaten the pizza and she'd changed her clothes. The pizza part was necessary. Switching out of her usual jeans and flannel shirt into pajama pants, long underwear shirt and his old 76ers sweatshirt that she'd taken as her own months before, was a stalling tactic, but also necessary as she worked out how she'd explain something to Pete that she couldn't explain to herself. She tried to stretch it out, but it still didn't give her enough time.

Pete's silence, his grim, gray face, added to Bernie's dread. She should've just handed him some line of bullshit and then shut up. There was no turning back as they sat on the couch, the empty pizza carton folded up and stuffed in the rubbish, the puzzle in front of them.

"Let's call a start to the authentic dialogue," Bernie said.

"Don't mock it," Pete said. "It's a permission structure for honesty that might be otherwise painful."

She'd had enough jargon for one day. Enough of thinking about their relationship too. The realizations that had started crystallizing in response to Benjamin's questions were too early. Too raw. The time was definitely not right. Pete's mantra for the past six months had been life is too short. He meant it. He was an evangelist on the topic. He daily, many times a day, told her he loved her. His actions made it clear he meant that too. His feelings for her and ability to express them were as authentic as hell. Earlier, in Benjamin's office, he'd opened up more, laid himself out bare. He deserved an equal effort. An authentic one.

But not this.

"Go ahead," Pete said.

She thought about it as she pretended to look for a specific elusive puzzle piece. "I love you as much as a person can love another person. That will never change. I also don't know if I'm ready to get married or even live with you full time, which if I did, we might as well get married, right? All of those things can be true. I'm as confused as you are. I told you, it's a work in progress. There's too much going on for me to mentally sort it out."

"There's always something going on. I could tell earlier you've come to a conclusion. Please tell me." He looked up from the puzzle. He'd said it gently, nonconfrontationally. Color had creeped up his neck into his face, though, and the freckles that were almost invisible unless he blushed peppered his nose and cheekbones.

"I haven't come to a conclusion, just reached another stage in my thought process." Before he could call her on copping out again—his head shake told her it was coming—she added, "I love you and love being with you. I love this house too. But I love my house. Loved. I love living by myself. It all just keeps going around in my head until I have to start thinking about something else."

Any pretense of doing the puzzle was gone. He put down the piece he'd been twisting around in his fingers and sat back, turned to face her. "Now that we're alone, no Benjamin, tell me. I know this isn't what you signed up for. The leg, the PTSD."

"The only thing about it that bothers me is that it hurts to see you hurting. I meant everything I said earlier. I know it's not a policeman's nature to accept an honest answer when you believe something else, but please accept that. This?"

She waved her arm around, taking in the house. "Our life together? I haven't, not one time, ever thought 'Gee, if only Pete didn't have PTSD I'd really like to live here,' or 'Gee, if only Pete's leg were fully functioning, that'd be the thing that would make me want to live here.' "

"Then what is it?"

This was the moment. Everything else was just the warmup. His eyes held hers with an intensity that forced her not to look away, as much as she wanted to. He could see right into her soul. The old look. No sadness. No uncertainty. Just determination. He was so sure he could make it right.

Just pull off the Band-Aid. "I know my life the past few years hasn't been anything anyone's going to mistake for awesome. I'm running a business in a dying industry on a shoestring. I never have money. I have no free time. My house was just a little bungalow, falling apart."

"Bernie."

"Let me finish. But I loved it. I loved my life. That doesn't mean I don't love you or our life together. It's not even saying I don't want to marry you."

He still had that confident, determined look. It broke her heart a little.

"I feel like since I moved to Redimere it's been the first time in my life I had some agency. Everything has been on my own terms. Every decision was mine. I could paint the kitchen orange and no one would—"

"You can—"

"It's not about specifics. It's the thing I was saying earlier about men and women in different universes. It's not just about my own house. It was having a life that was me. I know from experience that being in a couple—and yes, I understand this is what being in a couple is all about—means I have to give up some of that. It's been my experience that the woman gives up more agency than the man."

She could tell he wanted to mount a defense. She held up a hand to let him know that her pause wasn't so he could jump in. She had to figure out the best way to say it. Make him understand rather than feel defensive. "It's every relationship I ever had. Every *job* I ever had until I owned my own business. Fighting to be heard, and I know that may seem funny because I'm so fucking loud and talk so much, not to go on a tangent." She felt tangents assaulting her from all directions now that she'd started. She was exhausted. There'd been way too much opening up and raw emotion for one day. "All the things if I were a man that would impress people, or at least not be used against me. I have to fight to be me, something most men don't have to do."

"But that's got nothing—"

"Please try to understand what I'm saying. Look at how our relationship affects our jobs. For you, it's an annoyance. A mosquito buzzing around. Even if Ryan Grant or Fergus Kelley or whoever makes it an issue, it's not major. For me, it's a fucking wrecking ball. I know part of it is the different nature of our jobs, but that doesn't solve the issue. It's why I resisted going out with you in the first place. Remember? If we get married, or even just permanently live together, it's going to be that much harder to deal with. *For me*. Nothing changes for you. I'm not saying it's the biggest issue, but it's a big part of it. It's not anyone's fault, but it's there." She hadn't planned to say that much.

He wasn't trying to interrupt anymore. He stared at a puzzle piece as he rubbed it between his thumb and finger. She had no clue how much of what she'd said he understood.

"It's like…" She tried to think. "Say the world—life—is a city that's built for cars, and men have cars and women have bicycles. I'm trying to get around, navigating it all, trying not to get run over, keep up with the cars. It's exhausting. When I can park the bike and go into my house, I can finally relax."

"Oh." He didn't look up.

"I love you. So much. I want to be married to you, spend the rest of my life with you, but I wish I could do it without giving up me." Totally wrong words, but she didn't have the right ones. She wiped her eyes on her sleeve. "I warned you I hadn't figured it out."

He put the puzzle piece down. Carefully. "I didn't know."

"How am I supposed to explain it without you taking it in a bad way?"

"How else can I take it? You think being married to me would diminish you?"

"See? Like that. No. I don't mean I'd be diminished. I can't emphasize enough that I'm still figuring it out."

"That's what you meant by it can't be fixed." He said it quietly.

"I didn't say it *can't* be fixed. I said I'm *not sure*." She wanted it all back, as much as she'd meant it. "You don't seem to be hearing the part where I haven't fully processed it. I just lost my house and need to grieve that. Jesus, the embers are still smoldering over there."

"We could go to couples counseling."

"Yes, we could. But I have a burned house with a body in it to sort out, a newspaper to put out, a payroll to meet, and all that other stuff, and I don't have the mental energy."

"If it's important, though…"

"I am living here now." He'd asked for this. She'd warned him. "With you. In your house. Making a decision on marriage is not a top priority for me. Who knows how I'll feel once things settle down and I can focus? I told you it was a bad idea to have this conversation."

"No, it's good that I understand where you're coming from."

"Is it? I'm coming from the wilderness. It's not a destination." She took both of his hands in hers. "I love you. That's the bottom line."

"Where do we go from here?" His grip on her hands was tight. He looked bereft. She kissed him, but quickly, so he didn't have to decide whether he wanted to kiss back.

"We go to bed. Then we get up tomorrow and do it all over again. The same way we have been. Nothing's changed, Pete."

He nodded. Let go of her hands. "I'm going to work on the puzzle for a while."

Of course he was. Because no matter what she said, things *had* changed.

****

Bernie lay awake staring up at the skylight. She should've refused to have that conversation. There was no good way to explain it to him when she couldn't even explain it to herself. The Milky Way glowed brightly above. She marveled at how clear it was, even without her glasses, as she listened to Pete do the puzzle. Not that there was much to listen to. A sigh or cough, the soft rattle of puzzle pieces shifting around. The hiss of a beer bottle opening. A quiet word to the dog or one of the cats.

It was after midnight when he let the dog out, brushed his teeth—exactly two minutes. The light in the living room clicked off. He settled into bed, so careful, as usual, not to wake her. She braced for the inevitable wraparound, the arm around her waist, the leg over her thigh. It didn't come.

As much as it made her feel some nights like she was in a straitjacket—annoyed her that he always took such care not to wake her up, then glommed onto her in a way guaranteed to do just that—she was disappointed. She listened to him breathe next to her, feeling him there but, for the first time that she could remember, not touching some part of her when he lay down next to her. She rolled over and put her head on his shoulder, and his arm immediately went around her and tightened. She ran her hand up under his shirt until it rested in the hollow of his chest, where she could feel his heart beat.

"Are you awake?" he asked.

"It depends on why you're asking."

"It's not sex, if that's what you're worried about."

"Too bad, because if it was, the answer would have been yes. When the hell have I ever been *worried* about sex?"

He sighed. She lay quiet, feeling his heart, hoping he'd get to the point before she fell asleep, because now that she was pressed against him, she could feel it coming.

"I want to give you your space," he said. "I don't want to harass you or bug you. But can I say something in response to what you said earlier? Something authentic?"

"Sure."

"I'm not saying this to congratulate myself or tell you I think I'm some great guy, because I know I have a long way to go. It's more to just put into play the concept that I can change my assumptions and behavior. When I first came here, before we were dating or anything, remember how frustrated and annoyed I'd get with you sometimes?"

"Very well."

"The more I got to know you and understand you, the more I realized that it was my ego and the assumption you'd do things the way I thought you should at the root of that. I came to see that you're very good at your job, very smart. How I felt about things didn't have anything to do with how you felt or how you do your job. You were coming at it from a different angle and your mind worked differently. I had no right. It's not just your job, it's all of you. Understanding that, really seeing you, made me love you even more."

"You've never said that to me."

"I was saving it for my vows."

"Maybe less stuff about me being annoying."

He kissed her on the temple. "I guess I hoped you'd noticed that I'd evolved. But that's an ego thing, too, I guess. I don't have a right to get defensive and minimize your feelings, but it's like I was looking through a distorted lens and didn't even realize there *was* a lens. When I did, I started seeing things differently. Then tonight I find out there's another lens that I never knew was there. It's going to take time to adjust to seeing things from your point of view. That doesn't mean I can't."

"I appreciate the fact that you're willing to listen and understand. It's one of the many reasons I love you. I *do* need emotional space, without feeling pressure, to fully process my feelings." She raised up a little so she could look at him while she said it. "I can't emphasize enough, it's not like I felt one way about you yesterday and feel differently today. You get that, right?"

"Yeah, but I also get that you understand how you feel now in a way you didn't yesterday." Her hand, under his shirt, rose and fell as he took a deep breath "I'm afraid that now that you understand, it will change your feelings."

"Oh, Pete." She kissed him. His arm tightened around her. "Don't think this is some kind of end. If you feel like that, it's going to become a self-fulfilling prophecy. The fact I love you isn't going to change."

"Okay."

"I say that because I feel like you've had kind of a kicked-in-the-gut thing going on since we started talking about this tonight."

"If I do, it's just trying to adjust."

"Things will be better once we unpack our authentic feelings and give ourselves permission to explore our space or whatever."

He laughed. That was something at least. She rubbed his chest, finding comfort, as always, in the strength of his heartbeat. She lifted his shirt, then hers, and pressed back against him. "I like the way our skin feels against each other," she said.

"That reminds me of another authentic dialogue question that I wanted to ask but chickened out."

"The 'important thing' Benjamin wanted you to say earlier?" She'd been wondering what it was, if it had since come up disguised as something else. She didn't think so. He'd seemed so determined not to say it despite all the other sensitive topics they'd broached. It must be a real doozy.

"What? No. Forget that. It wasn't anything." He hesitated. "When you said the answer to sex would've been yes, was that your authentic answer?"

"Absolutely. Totally authentic. Let's get it on."

"That's not the question. I know you've never complained, but it's my experience that women sometimes don't, then I find out at the breakup there were issues. If you have any, you can say. I don't want it to be part of the problem."

"Who are these women throwing sex in your face? They must be nuts."

"Just Karen."

"I have no complaints. That's an authentic understatement. Do you have any about me?"

"God no. Except that your surprise-me-in-the-shower technique needs some tweaking."

"Ha ha. You said tweaking." She kissed him, long and soft. She slid her hand down his flat stomach, past the waistband of his flannel pants.

"Gee, you can't be that worried about it, considering you have a boner."

"I'm serious, Bernie. It can be one of those unspoken things that ends up putting a wedge—"

"Ha ha, putting a wedge."

"I don't even know how that has double meaning. As for my boner, you've been rubbing my chest and pressing against me and everything. What do you expect?"

She put her mouth against his ear and whispered, "I can see this is a Big T for you. Authentically. Let's lean into this discomfort you have that needs unpacking."

"I'm serious, Bernie," he said. "I'm trying to be authentic. Can we discuss this seriously? If there are issues—"

"Seriously," she said, not easing the pressure of her hand. "Every time we do it, I feel like we're making love. I know that's totally corny and something people say, and if you ever repeat it to anyone, I'll deny it, but you know I wouldn't say something that lame unless I meant it."

"That's how I feel, too, without all the qualifiers. But as far as technique—"

Oh my god. "Pete, if we had a problem, I'd say so, okay? The only problem we have now is that I'm going to give up and go to sleep unless we can find a way to authentically lean into this boner."

"I'm serious, Bernie. I know we have hurdles to cross, and this one I think is, I just want to make sure—*Geez, Bernie*—that this is one we can easily—" His sucked in his breath. "One we can tick the box on."

"Ha ha, tick the box." She whispered it against his ear.

"Okay. I get it." He pulled her on top of him, both of his arms tight around her. "Okay," he whispered. He pulled her in for a kiss.

It wasn't going to solve anything, but at least for the rest of the night, Bernie knew, things would be fine.

CHAPTER 23

PETE LEAFED THROUGH the week's reports piled on his desk, not really looking at them, the thin morning sun through the window behind him casting a shadow but not providing any warmth. He gulped down the dregs of his lukewarm coffee. It tasted like shit, but maybe at least it would jumpstart his head a little and get him on track.

One of the last things Bernie had said to him before he fell asleep was that they should wake up every morning glad they were alive and had each other, tackle the issues of the day, and not worry about their relationship. "We move forward, just like a shark." It was more than words, she lived by it. He wasn't sure how to do that.

He'd started a new notebook that morning, filled several pages with his confusion and sadness. He still couldn't find his old one, knew he hadn't misplaced it, but anything he said to Bernie about it would sound like an accusation. She must've done something with it. He was a cop, and those were the only two obvious answers. He always put it in his bedside table drawer. The dog and the cats didn't open the drawer and take it. He knew she wouldn't either. She'd probably been looking for something and absent-mindedly picked it up and put it in her bag or something. He'd just have to wait for her to find it. Fall all over herself with embarrassment and apologies. *Stop thinking about it. It's not a big deal.*

"Good morning, sunshine." She stood in the doorway, rosy-cheeked, bright-smiling and with two coffees. He was relieved that he felt that familiar and immediate surge of warmth and love. No lurking anger or resentment.

Bernie closed the door behind her. "I guess you've had enough coffee, but I brought you more." She sat down, putting a cup in front of him. "I also brought you some chocolate frosted doughnuts, and since they're my favorite, I'm going to eat at least one of them."

"I could use some fresh coffee," he said. "I needed a break anyway."

"You left so early."

"I didn't want to wreck your sleeping-in day by waking you up."

She gave him a long look as she took a bite of doughnut, leaving a fleck of chocolate frosting on her cheek.

"You've got a…" He leaned over the desk and wiped it off with his finger.

"Napkin," she said, and, before he could sit down, wiped his finger with the one she'd been holding. She held his hand longer than she needed to. He knew it was a message. She was going to be her normal self. Nothing had changed. It hadn't for her. She hadn't felt the world shift under her feet the night before as they'd talked. Felt it slide away.

"How's your morning been?" he asked. He could pretend. Doing anything else would screw things up even more.

"I came over to take a photo of all the loot you guys found on Zack Staples, though I'm surprised that you'd lower yourself to such a cliché move. But Vicki said Dawna had to run down to Farmington, so I guess it's off until Monday."

"The photo was Dawna's idea. Mandy's first arrest. It'd be a big deal if there weren't all this shit going on. I think she thought the positive publicity would be good, considering that the chief is such a bad-news magnet. Off the record."

"Wait, isn't that the 'Sexy Sheriff' guy? He's pretty hot." She gave him a big smile, eyes dancing.

"I'd be happy to never hear the phrase sexy sheriff again for the rest of my life." Her smile warmed him. "What else do you have going on today?"

"Going into the office, then I have a ten o'clock over at the college with Anthony Wilson, when he's supposedly going to tell me all about their plans to develop the Nakilot land."

"Why *supposedly?*"

"They've been cagey about it. The only reason they're saying anything is because I got tipped off and started asking. Their need to control the narrative is bad enough when it's something they've volunteered. With me forcing their hand, it means that I'm only going to hear enough to placate me. It'll be a lot of incomplete blah blah blah. Maybe not even the truth. It'll be interesting to see how they address the Passamaquoddy thing. Natalie Perry will have my head on a platter if I don't zero in on that. I still can't reach Normand Ouimette. What do you have going on?"

"This and that. The usual. Quiet day so far. Staff meeting at two, then I might head home early. Figure out something good to make for dinner."

"Speaking of eating, are you going to eat your doughnut?"

"I'm not hungry."

"What did you have for breakfast? I didn't see any dirty dishes, and the same dishes were in the drainboard that you washed last night."

"I had, um…"

"Coffee and aspirin. Just what I thought. Your funeral if you starve to death." She broke the remaining doughnut in half, put one half on a napkin, and pushed it across the desk. "I'm not leaving until you eat that." She picked up the other half, took a bite. "See? Easy."

He picked up his half, ate it in three bites, then wiped the frosting from his lips. "Happy?"

"Ecstatic." She finished off hers, too, getting more chocolate on her cheek. He leaned across the desk and wiped it off with his napkin as she chewed.

"I'd say my work here is done, but I have a thing," Bernie said once she'd swallowed. "You don't look in the mood, but can we talk shop for a second?"

"Sure."

"Just a heads-up," she said, her voice low. "I'd tell you at home, but I forgot to yesterday and I've already started, so I want to make sure you know. I know we usually don't discuss stuff like this, but I'm looking into Ryan Grant, not only whatever it is that's going on with the college project on Norm Ouimette's land, but—"

He held up his hand. "I don't want to know."

"I didn't want you to feel blindsided."

"Bernie, don't—"

"I'm not. I won't. I'm a professional doing my job. I'm not looking to do a hatchet job, just looking to see if there's anything there."

"I can't know."

"I know you can't. But I needed to tell you."

"Don't get involved on my behalf."

"If he were going after a police chief who I didn't have a relationship with, I'd be doing the same thing," she said. "I dropped the ball on fully looking into him when he forced the change in government, then ran for mayor. I was more focused on the vote, how things would change. It's not too late to do it now that he's going after the police department. Who's next?"

"It's not the police department, it's me," Pete said. "I don't want you to jeopardize your credibility on my behalf. I appreciate the fact that you want to fight, but if you go after him, you're giving him more ammo than he already has. It will hurt you more than me, which is already a problem with our relationship. You said it last night, and I get it. Doing this is a giant flaming example of that. It's the worst-case scenario. It won't end well." He'd been talking quietly but felt his voice rise at the end. It wasn't anger. It was fear. Couldn't she see that her loyalty and big heart were going to blow up her life?

"Gosh, so much for the evolved guy who appreciates that I know how to do my job."

"This is different."

"I know what I'm doing. This was just to let you know, not to ask for dispensation. You're the only one who knows about it besides Tommy, and it'll stay that way until I get enough for a legitimate story.

Believe, me, Tommy's already given me an earful."

Why does Tommy know? That somehow made it worse.

"I had a reason for telling Tommy. I'll tell you when we eventually talk about this after it's all over."

"I didn't say anything about Tommy."

"You didn't have to. I read your mind. Maybe you should both have some kind of dork duel to establish which one is the superior male and has the right to tell me what to do. At least it would keep you both off my back for a while so I could do my job."

"I'd like to think I'd win a dork duel with Tommy."

"I'd be rooting for you. What's so funny? It can't possibly be that I think you're a bigger dork than my brother."

He hadn't realized he was smiling. "No, I'm comfortable in my dorkiness. It's just that this is like old times. You doing something nuts and not listening to reason, but me wanting to kiss you anyway."

"I love how *listening to reason* means doing what you want me to," she said. "As far as old times goes, why did I never know you were wishing you could kiss me? That's information I could've used."

"I finally did, didn't I?"

She got up, came around the desk, took his face between her hands, and gave him a long kiss. "And I kissed you back. Don't you forget it."

****

Back in her empty office, Bernie looked at the two-page document Tommy had brought from Portland. It wasn't much. Wasn't anything, really. But it hinted at something. It was a photocopy of the first two pages of a lawsuit: *Ryan Grant v. State of Maine.* He'd sued the state after his real estate license had been suspended. The rest of the document was missing, so she didn't know any details. Tommy had told her she was lucky he'd found that much. The suit had been dismissed and Grant's license reinstated.

"I'll get you, you fraudulent fuck," Bernie said. She wasn't sure how, but saying it made her feel better.

She'd already exhausted all the channels she could think of. The suit was filed two years before Grant came to Redimere, when he was living

221

and working south of Portland. Long before much was online. A Google search hadn't turned up anything. She tried some real estate agent friends in the Portland area, but they didn't know anything. Or claimed they didn't. Real estate agents were a tricky bunch. Fun, but not always authentic. She was finding so many uses for that word.

She meant what she'd said to Pete. She was being careful. She knew how it could look. She wasn't going to do anything to make his situation worse or to make herself look vindictive. If she was going to take Grant down, it was going to be legit. *Give me something. Anything.* She wasn't always sure that prayers to the journalism gods who knew good must triumph over evil were answered, but she needed some sign on where to go with this.

Her phone rang. Julie Gower. Probably another letter to the editor. Bernie should just make her a columnist.

Bernie listened to the rhythmic rasp of Julie's breathing machine as she waited for her to get the wind for the next sentence after they said their hellos.

"I think I have a tip," Julie said. "This already would have stuck out to me, but the fact that *Franklin On Call* article was so off base just made it stick out more. The mayor said he's a Navy SEAL." The sentences came out slowly as she paused every few words to breathe.

"He brings that up a lot."

"Whenever I hear someone say they're a Navy SEAL, or CIA, or Special Ops, professions that people usually keep to themselves, I wonder. People brag more than they used to, so it's not like it's always a lie, but still."

"Me too," Bernie said. Yet, she hadn't with Grant. Until now.

"There's this group that looks into false Navy SEAL claims. I read about them in *The Washington Post.* Their thing is most real Navy SEALs don't go around bragging. I emailed them yesterday about the mayor, and they just got back to me. Want to know what they said?"

"Are you kidding me?" Bernie knew that no gift from the gods came without a karmic price, but she'd worry about that later.

"He's fake," Julie said. "A hundred percent fake. No military record at all, not just not being a SEAL. I gave them his name, date of birth, birthplace. They had nothing."

"How do you know his date of birth and birthplace?"

She paused longer than usual. "The internet isn't hard once you figure it out."

"Can I get the contact information for that group?"

"I can email it to you as well as the notes on my conversation with them and Ryan Grant's date of birth and birthplace and anything else I have."

"You've done great reporting work, so I'll pay you the base freelance fee of fifty dollars. I'm not sure when this will be in. I'm working on some other stuff, so don't want to publish it just in bits and pieces."

"That's fine. I'm just happy to help. I'd just as soon not be paid. Guys who lie about that really burn my butt. My brother Dave only joined the Marines because he didn't want to go to college and thought it would be a way to make money. He came back a wreck, then killed himself. No one has a right to claim they've done that service if they haven't."

After Bernie hung up, she walked around the empty office sorting her thoughts. She wasn't going to run a story on Ryan Grant that only said he was lying about having been a Navy SEAL. That would embarrass him, maybe hurt his chances for reelection, get him a few less real estate deals. Maybe. But that was it.

But where there was smoke, there was fire. If someone was going to lie about something like that, what else would they lie about?

CHAPTER 24

THE INTERCOM ON Pete's phone crackled. "There's an Imani Gilbert to see you." A baby whimpered in the background.

"Send her in."

"Them," Vicki said.

Imani came in, pushing a two-seat stroller, the baby from Wednesday in front, a toddler in back, both staring at him from bundles of coats and blankets with huge black eyes.

"Sorry about the stroller," she said. "I know it's not convenient for everyone, but I know no one wants me to just leave my kids home alone either."

"Not a problem." Pete went around the desk to move a chair out of the way.

Imani pulled the hood back from the toddler, revealing a head of curly brown hair popping with pigtails and bows. She unzipped her coat. "She's going to swelter and get fussy if I don't get some of this off her. It's just so cold out."

"I have some Goldfish crackers."

"That might help, actually."

Pete got the bag out and the toddler smiled, reaching pudgy fingers toward him. "Fish! Crackers!"

"May I?" he asked.

Imani was holding the baby, unzipping his coat as he squirmed and wailed. "Thanks, if you could."

Pete put a handful of crackers on the tray in front of the little girl. She grinned at him before grabbing some in her tiny fist.

"There," Imani said, sitting down with a sigh, the baby in her lap. "Winter is such a pain. Thanks for the crackers—that should keep her quiet for a while."

"Who do we have here?" Pete asked, smiling at the kids. The toddler, shoving crackers in her mouth, smiled back. He wiggled his fingers at her. The baby, who'd stopped squalling, looked at him with serious concentration.

"This is Echo. She's twenty-one months, and Drayton is ten months."

"Irish twins."

"So I'm told. Not that there's anything Irish about them. My mom was from Haiti, my dad was a Lewiston Frenchie, and their father is another Lewiston Frenchie."

"Jeremy isn't—"

"No, but he's better to them than their father was."

"And their father?"

"Not that it's any of your business, but he's down in Warren. For life. He shot some Somali guy. You'd think a man with Black kids would be less of a dick to Black people, but he wasn't. Don't ask what he was doing with me. That's not why I'm here."

"I'm sorry," Pete said. "I know it's not easy raising kids alone."

"I'm sure you do." She pointed at the photo of Bernie on the cabinet next to his desk. "That your wife? Do you guys have kids?"

"No, but I was raised by a single mother. My brother and I, so I understand to some extent." Did he? He felt all his certainties could go sliding out from under him with no notice after last night.

"I thought Chuck was your father."

"He is, but he wasn't around when I was growing up. We just reconnected." He didn't mind getting personal if it was going to draw her out, no matter why she was here.

"Chuck's a nice guy."

"Nice guys don't always do the right thing for their families," he said.

"Nice guys and not-so-nice guys."

"Have you found a babysitter?"

"I'm making do. I'm not leaving my kids alone while I work, if that's what you're implying."

"I'm not implying anything."

"Excuse me if I'm a little suspicious." She was angry now. "Your people have pulled me over twice since I moved here for no good reason. Once because my license plate light was supposedly out, when it wasn't. My car may be a shitbox, but I keep it in good condition. The other because I crossed the center line, even though the road didn't have a center line. Funny, when Jeremy drives my car, he never gets pulled over."

"I'm sorry about that," Pete said. "If you're being pulled over for no cause, it shouldn't be happening."

"*If* I am? Does your wife get pulled over?"

"If it happens again, let me know," Pete said. Bernie *did* get pulled over. Or used to. But it was for legitimate reasons. Now that she was driving his old car, he made sure the lights worked and the stickers were up to date.

"And you'll…what? Why don't you say something to your people now instead of waiting until it happens again?"

"I plan to."

Imani glared, unconvinced. He was about to ask her why she'd come by when Echo squealed.

"Go to sleep!" Echo said, waving her hand at Pete, a spray of mashed Goldfish dropping to the floor.

"You go to sleep," Pete said, in what he hoped was a funny voice.

She laughed. "No, you!"

"Okay," Pete said, and put his hands together, lay his head on them, and made blubbery sleep noises.

Echo laughed and threw more crackers on the floor.

"It's all well and good you can have this intellectual discussion with my twenty-one-month-old child, but I'm not that easy," Imani said. "Also, don't think you'll get what you want by threatening to take my kids away. They tried that after they arrested the kids' father. Told me they'd take them away and have me up on charges with Child Protective Services if I didn't tell them things. I told them to shove it. How many women do you guys threaten with that shit?"

"I don't do that with women *or* men," Pete said. He'd known plenty of cops who did. It was a standard tactic they used with women. "Why don't we talk about what it is you came here to talk about?"

She sighed, looking nervous for the first time since she'd sat down, but still defiant. "Jeremy told me you said you'd get him a lawyer. He's having trouble finding one. I'm sure you're on top of that."

Behind her anger and cynicism, Pete saw fear. He'd checked Tuesday and was told Jeremy had been assigned the attorney of the day for his arraignment, then he hadn't followed up.

"I told him that was nuts," Imani continued. "No cop who arrests someone is going to turn around and get him a lawyer. Even if you did, I don't know how we'll pay, but he said you said not to worry about it. He seems to have some kind of stupid belief you were telling the truth."

"I was." He wished he'd thought more about it. He wasn't sure how it was going to work. Maine was the only state in the U.S. without a public defender's office. There was a small roster of attorneys who did the work on a rotating basis, and Pete had vaguely assumed he could call one that he had a good relationship with and see what they could do. But he hadn't.

Imani watched him. It felt like she could see his wheels sputtering. Stopping. "You need to do something right away," she said. "The court told him the list is backed up and no one can take his case and he'll have to wait. In my experience, that means he's going to have to take a plea and go to prison because it's too much of a hassle to do anything else. That means a bad deal for him, a lot of money paid that we don't have, and all sorts of shit. They're going to transfer him to Wiscasset Monday. He needs someone like, today."

She was right about the plea. That's what happened when people couldn't afford to wait around in jail and didn't have bail. Even innocent people. At least Jeremy was there for a reason.

"I'll do it right now." He picked up the phone and punched in a number.

"I'd love to Pete, but I'm so backed up I'm never going to get loose," Kermit said after Pete told him the situation. "But I know someone who can. He's right here."

Before Pete could say anything, Tommy was on the line.

"Hi, buddy," Tommy said. "What's up?"

"Hi, Tom. I'm looking for a lawyer for a young local man. He's in Farmington, but he's being transferred to Wiscasset Monday and doesn't have representation, with the backup. You know how it is."

"I do indeed. What I don't get is why the police chief cares."

"I promised I'd help," Pete said, his eyes flicking to Imani's. Her bravado was gone, her eyes wide. Scared and vulnerable. "I arrested him Monday. I told him I'd make sure he was represented."

"I'd love to totally rip you for being a hypocritical asshole, but lucky for you I do care about the justice system working for people. Give me his particulars and I'll get down to Farmington this afternoon."

"I appreciate it. It's pro bono."

"Par for the course."

While he'd been talking, Pete had called up Jeremy's case on his computer. "Here's his full name, inmate number, charges." Pete read them off.

"This was the guy in the hostage thing? Not sure how it'll go over with the court that the arresting officer is my sister's boyfriend, but I'll cross that bridge when I come to it. I'll stop over and get the incident report from you before I go down."

Pete wanted to tell Tommy to get it from the DA when it was available, but Imani's eyes, which hadn't left his since he'd turned back from the computer, were a fierce reminder that now wasn't the time to get in a pissing match.

"The case was handed off to the sheriff's office, so it may not be an issue. They're not sharing much with me. For all I know, the state police may have it by now, so you'll have to go to them for the full reports. Or the DA."

"I can deal with that. See you soon."

Imani watched as Pete hung up. The two kids did, too, their eyes small replicas of hers.

"That was Tom O'Dea," Pete said. "He's up from Portland for a bit. In fact, he's renting a room at my dad's, so you may have seen him around. He'll talk to Jeremy today."

"Thank you. I'll find a way to pay for it." She smiled at Pete for the first time since he'd known her, wide and dimpled.

"He's taking it pro bono, so—"

"I know what that means. Thank you."

"Tom's a good guy. He's smart and he cares a lot. He'll do the best he can for Jeremy."

"Let's hope that's good enough," Imani said as she bundled her kids back up.

"Take my card." Pete wrote his cellphone number on it. "This is my personal number." He helped her turn the stroller around, then handed it to her. "Call me. For any reason, okay?"

She put it in her pocket. "Yeah. Right. Thanks, though."

CHAPTER 25

BERNIE WAS BRIEFLY blinded by the light coming through the floor-to-ceiling windows that faced both south and west in Redimere College President Anthony Wilson's office. When her retinas cleared, she saw Wilson detaching himself from a group of men standing around a large conference table across the room from the windows. He walked toward her, hand outstretched.

"Bernadette, so good to see you again." His gleaming white hair and gleaming white teeth were set off by the kind of tan you only see in Maine in January on people who had the money to spend the holidays somewhere expensive and warm.

"Thanks for taking the time," she said as her hand was crushed in his too-firm handshake.

"You know Ryan Grant, the mayor." He led her to the conference table.

"Of course." Bernie smiled and nodded. Grant nodded back.

"And Ken Parent? Our development partner."

"Sure."

"I know I said it the night of the fire, but things were pretty crazy," Ken said. "So again, sorry about your house."

"Thanks."

"We were very sorry to hear as well," Wilson said.

Too late, pal. Bernie smiled. "Thanks."

"Of course you know Ted Stone, communications director."

"Of course." Ted's hand, as always, was clammy with anxiety sweat. She didn't blame him. She guessed Wilson dressed him down about fifteen times a day.

"Sorry about your house."

"Thanks." Bernie wanted to tell them they could cut the crap. None of them had given it a thought until Ken brought it up.

Wilson nodded to the one guy she didn't know. "This is Bernard Harding, our new vice president for development. He just started this week. He goes by Bernie, so for the purposes of this meeting, you'll be Bernadette, since he's already Bernie."

"How about he goes by Bernard, since I'm already Bernie?"

The men laughed.

Bernie—the *real* Bernie—took some unnecessary notes so she could gather her thoughts. She was outmanned. At a disadvantage.

"I thought it best to have the mayor and Ken here so you can get all your questions answered," Wilson said. "A nice *positive* story."

Bernie gave him an innocent smile.

"I have a hard stop at ten forty-five," Grant said. "I have several meetings lined up. Important meetings." He looked right at Bernie when he said it.

She flashed the innocent smile again.

"Obviously, our project is in the very early stages. There is a lot we can't say," Wilson said. "But I will say it's a great example of public-private collaboration. We're grateful to the town for the part it's playing."

"I didn't know the town was involved." Bernie aimed it at Grant.

"The details aren't official yet. And as I said Monday, I wanted you to talk to President Wilson first, which is why I couldn't say more," Grant said.

"You were also the broker?"

"Yes. That's not a conflict of interest, by the way, if that's what you're thinking." He smiled.

"I wasn't thinking anything except I want to make sure I get the facts straight." She said it lightly. She knew how to act in a room full of men. Easygoing. Not difficult. Not annoying.

"We closed right before the year did," Wilson said. "It's a private transaction, so we're not releasing the details, including purchase price. You understand."

"Of course." *You bet I do.*

"The seller was Normand Ouimette?"

"We're not at liberty to say," Ted Stone said.

"Really?" Bernie asked. The men all frowned. "Sorry. Right." When she'd been in Farmington, she'd stopped in at the Registry of Deeds to see if she could find out who'd bought the land behind her house and also asked for the transaction on Normand Ouimette's land. They hadn't processed the forms for either yet.

"Our plans are aimed at not only expanding the facilities and options for our students, but also for the community," Wilson said. "We have a five-point project."

As Bernie listened to the plans for dorms, a hotel, ski area, and recreational trails, she knew it was just a giant information dump to distract her. Maybe pummel her into mental paralysis so she wouldn't ask uncomfortable questions. It almost worked until, forty mind-numbing minutes later, Wilson got to the fifth point.

He beamed his smile around the table. Bernie followed it. His two subordinates' faces were locked in nervous, compliant semi-smiles. Ken Parent's face was unreadable. Ryan Grant looked at his folded hands on the table.

"The community will be very excited to learn that we're going to honor the previous Native American heritage of the land. The ski and other recreation areas will be the Nakilot Ski and Recreation Area. The boutique hotel will be called Nakilot Redimere College Lodge. We can't think of a better way to honor the people who were stewards of the land before us."

I bet you can't. Bernie bent her head to her notebook so they couldn't see her face.

Wilson continued. "Nakilot is the Native American word for sunset. Sunset because, of course, we're in western Maine and get some spectacular sunsets over the mountain and the western mountains beyond."

They didn't invent Nakilot—that's what the land and mountain, really just a hill, were before they were stolen. A lot of people still called it that, including Normand Ouimette. She kept her face hidden.

"Of course," Ted Stone said. "The land has been used for commerce since the first white settlers came to Redimere more than two centuries ago. The quarry opened more than a century ago. The entire 146 acres was logged even before that. There used to be a sawmill there, logging and hunting camps. There was even a small textile mill on Nakilot Stream for a few decades early in the twentieth century. There's a precedent for the land being developed and used. A more modern precedent than that of the Native Americans."

"What Ted is saying"—Wilson waited until Bernie looked up—"is that we appreciate the first users of that land, but the precedent for it being used to support the commerce and economy of the region goes back more than a century. We're continuing that fine tradition of hard work and supporting our local economy through our best asset, our natural resources."

Ryan Grant continued the theme, almost as though it had been rehearsed. "This is definitely the most low-impact development this land could have. The previous uses were much less respectful of the geography and resources."

She was dying to ask about the petroglyphs. To push them about Norm Ouimette. But all that would do is cause problems. She'd ask Norm first. If only he'd call her back.

****

Pete was on his hands and knees with a tissue cleaning up drool-soaked Goldfish remnants, ground into the carpet by the wheels of the stroller, when Tommy walked in.

"The town's budget problems are worse than I thought."

Pete stood up, using the desk for support, ignoring the helping hand Tommy held out.

233

"I do what I can," he said. "Who can walk by food mashed into a carpet without cleaning it up?" He threw the sodden tissue into his wastebasket and sat down.

"I'm sure you've learned by now that an O'Dea can." Tommy sat down too. "Or at least a certain O'Dea, who I'm sure has told you"—his voice rose to a falsetto—"'I have too many important things to think about to be bothered by food on the carpet.'"

"I clean the mashed-up food from the floor, and she brings the joy and sunshine."

"Okay, I can see how this is going to go. You're in love and blind to the trail of food, hair, books, and chaos. God love you, man."

"You're not off to a great start for a guy who's here to get something from me."

"Since we're on a roll, you need to talk her out of that story she's planning on the mayor."

"I don't want to talk about it here," Pete said. "But I'll say this: You know I can't talk her out of anything. It's her job, she's going to do it her way."

"Shredding her credibility to write some bullshit hatchet job as payback for her boyfriend's getting in the hot stew isn't a great way to build her brand."

"I meant it when I said we can talk later," Pete struggled to keep his voice low. "It's not going to help if someone hears something through the walls and it gets all over town."

"We'll definitely talk later," Tommy said. "Because if you love her at all, you need to protect her from herself."

"Don't let her hear you say that. Let's get to Jeremy."

"Right. I know I could get the report the red-tape bureaucratic way, so I appreciate you making it available to me now. Also, I know it's not kosher, but can we have an off-the-record discussion about the kid and what happened Monday? Since we're doing each other favors?"

He was right. It wasn't kosher. Then again, kosher went out the window a long time ago.

"No problem."

****

Bernie's car was parked almost in the same spot she'd parked the other day when she'd talked to Joe Walsh, a reminder she'd done nothing with the information about Stephanie. She was opening her door, musing on that, when she heard someone shout her name.

Ken Parent, whose truck she now saw near hers—the distinctive bright red interlocking KP on the door—was walking toward her.

"I didn't want to say anything in there, but I was wondering if you'd made a decision on your property?"

"I can't do anything with the arson investigation going on. Why?"

"Just a heads-up. It's going to be a hot commodity. I heard someone bought the Perkins lot down by Little Pond. That's twelve acres of prime development land if they can get access through your property."

"Could be, yeah. It's a moot point right now."

"Sorry. I know you're still dealing with that, but just wanted to give you a heads-up, like I said. Once the word is out the Perkins parcel is sold, people will be nipping at your heels."

"Why would I sell it to someone else rather than whoever bought the parcel?"

"Real estate can be complicated."

Great, here we go.

"You own about half an acre, right, to the tree line on all three sides?"

"A little more. It's a nonconforming lot. It goes down the slope toward the lake a little." She loved how all these real estate and development guys knew as much about her property as she did.

"The simple way to put it is, while it's a small, nonconforming lot—which means, by the way, you can only rebuild on the existing footprint—someone could outbid the owners of the Perkins parcel on it, if the Perkins buyers even bid. The Perkins buyers may not want to pay full price for it, and someone else may buy it, then lease them an easement. Your lot would be great for a small solar array if the trees were removed from that western-facing incline, so whoever bought it from you could lease that out to a solar company too. It wouldn't be a ton of money, but nice change. So, it may just be cheaper for the Perkins developers to pay to lease an access easement and let someone else deal with your property."

"What's to keep me from dealing with my property? Maybe I'd want to do all that instead of selling." She wouldn't. But it also annoyed her that he just assumed she wouldn't.

He laughed, surprised. "You could. But wouldn't you rather take a windfall and not have to deal with complicated real estate matters?"

"I don't know. Like I said, moot point right now."

"When it's not, give me a holler, okay? I'd offer you a fair market price."

She watched him jog to his truck as she thought about it. She'd have to keep thinking about it for another couple of days before it made sense and she could figure out what to do once the investigation was done. She'd always assumed that the easement would be an issue that she wouldn't want to deal with and had something specifically to do with the Perkins' deed. It's why the property didn't sell. Ken made it sound, though, like she could do something about it.

If she could, even if insurance doesn't pay out, maybe her house burning down wasn't that bad a financial disaster after all. Dean Davis had offered to buy the land. Now Ken Parent.

That sparked another thought—which came first, the fire or the Perkins land sale? And did one have anything to do with the other?

CHAPTER 26

P ETE WISHED HE could skip the staff meeting, just go home and sleep for two days. Given all that was going on, though, he couldn't. He saved the worse for last—that he'd officially told the mayor the department wouldn't participate in *Real Rural Justice*.

"I'd think with the budget issues, the show makes sense," Brent said.

"I understand why people feel that way," Pete said. "But it would be a distraction that would outweigh any budget gains. You only started in August, and Tyler, in June. And Mandy, just this week. You guys haven't been here to see what we've been dealing with, but if no one's filled you in, Jamie or Dawna can catch you up. We're finally at full staffing, with good officers. We need to focus on being the best police department we can be."

"Shouldn't we all get a say?" Brent said.

"You're certainly welcome to express your opinions," Pete said. "But it's not open to a vote. I've made my decision and it's final."

"Then what's the point of talking about it?" Brent asked. He looked at Jamie and Tyler. Pete knew the look. *Come on guys, back me up.*

"Go ahead. It's good to air things out," Pete said.

"All they're going to do is shadow us. They won't get in the way. After a little while, we won't even notice they're there. I mean, look at *Cops*, right? It's been on since, what, 1989? Look at all it's done to show people what we can do. One reason I became a cop was from growing up watching *Cops*. It'll help people understand our job, what we're up against."

"I understand you have that impression," Pete said. "The reality would be different. People, both cops and the people you talk to, behave differently when there are cameras around. There are issues with getting release statements from everyone who's been filmed. The footage is edited in a way that won't show how we really do our jobs."

Pete continued before Brent could break in. "I'm also not comfortable with people who are having a really bad day, maybe the worst of their lives, being filmed while it's happening. The show also doesn't follow up. Someone who's arrested but isn't charged or they're found not guilty, will still look guilty of a crime to anyone who watches."

Jamie said, "You said yourself they sign releases, so they're okay with being on. Everyone wants to be on TV. Anyway, the TV people handle the releases, not us. We're just doing our jobs and they're tagging along."

"It's not that simple," Pete said.

"You know what this sounds like to me? This sounds like the editorial Ms. O'Dea wrote in the paper," Jamie said. "I mean, she *is* your girlfriend, so I get that, but—"

"This is not about me wanting to please my girlfriend," Pete said. "She does her job. I do mine. My decision is exactly what I've said. We've had way too much excitement the past two years. It's time to focus on being peace officers who protect and serve the people of Redimere and anyone who happens to be passing through. That's what we're here for. Not to be TV stars."

His tone stayed reasonable, but he was getting pissed off. He was about to shut down the discussion when Dawna spoke up.

"I believe the editorial in the paper focused on how the show, and these are her words, ignored the constitutional rights of people who encounter police and how *Cops* has a proven track record of not getting the required releases from everyone and of officers manufacturing evidence and arrests to make a scene look better, and other issues,"

Dawna said. "The chief is saying the cameras will be a distraction, so it's not the same thing. I agree. We'd be under a microscope. The police in this state have been fighting body cameras too. No matter how you feel about that issue, it hurts the argument against them if we have TV cameras following us."

"How can you ignore the money we'd get?" Jamie asked.

"The mayor has refused to say how much it is or where it would go," Dawna said. "The production company pays the town. There's no guarantee that the department would get any."

"See?" Brent said. "That's straight from the newspaper."

"That doesn't mean it's not true," Tyler said.

Mandy raised her hand. "May I say something?"

"Sure," Pete said.

"I read an article about *Cops*. The person watched hundreds of episodes in a few months, and it turns out it's pretty scary how much people's rights are violated. They talked to a psychology professor who said it was a bad idea to put cameras in situations like that. So..."

"There's more to police work than reading articles," Jamie said.

"The mayor told me that most of the money would go to us," Brent said. "He also said we waste money. Like these sweatshirts?" He pointed to his chest. Pete was well aware Grant hated them. They were top-of-the-line—thick fleece, with a collar and three-quarter zipper, navy blue with an embroidered Redimere Police Department logo. Expensive because they were well made.

"How much did these cost?" Brent said. "I mean, I know they're warm, but that's what our parkas are for. That's why the mayor's budget doesn't have the full amount in for our uniform allotments, because the department wasted money on these. The allotment already doesn't cover the full cost of two uniforms and a parka, so now we're paying the price."

"The money for the sweatshirts and the hats didn't come from the allotment," Pete said. It sounded like Brent was spending a lot of time listening to Grant's bullshit. "If that's an issue with the budget committee, I'll make that clear to them."

"I think we've exhausted the subject," Dawna said. "Agreed, Chief?" She was the only one who knew that Pete, who was tired of everyone shivering despite their long underwear, paid for the sweatshirts out of his own pocket. He wanted it to stay that way.

"Final thing," Pete said. "Just a reminder that traffic stops are for traffic and motor vehicle violations, or if the driver is known to have a warrant, or you know for a fact they're driving under suspension, that type of thing. If someone is obeying the rules of the road, they're not known to you to be in violation, and their vehicle isn't in violation, there's no reason to stop them."

"Sometimes you can just tell someone's up to no good," Brent said.

"No more random stops," Pete said. "On top of it, I want all stops logged, even if you don't issue a ticket or warning."

"What's the point of that?" Jamie asked.

"Fairness and accountability."

"Sounds like some politically correct bullshit to me," Brent said.

Jamie added, "What about stops for, you know, our top citizens?"

"If you're referring to mountain politics, we don't do that anymore, right?" Pete had never been happy with the long-held culture of letting wealthy or influential residents stopped for a violation, or something worse, like OUI, get away without a ticket or even a report.

Jamie looked at Brent, shrugged.

"No random stops, no mountain politics," Pete said. "Just good policing. Speaking of which, something else to keep in mind. I'm aware that we deal mostly with a certain segment of society. I know it can skew our judgment about people in general. This isn't a criticism, it's a reality that I fully understand and have lived. But this is a small town. We protect and serve all its residents as well as people just passing through. In the interest of our own sanity as well as good public relations, I'd like to see you all get out of the cruiser more and interact with people in general. For instance, if you're going to the store for a sandwich, walk, don't take the cruiser. Say hi to people. Stop in the stores. Pet dogs. You get it."

Pete's eyes met Brent's. Whatever Brent was going to say, he didn't.

"Everyone understand? Good. Have a good weekend."

****

Before Pete went home, he did what he'd planned to do Monday and hadn't had time to do since—stop by Bernie's house. He hadn't had a lot of homicide cases in Philly that involved arson, but he'd had enough to know what to look for. As a rule, the fires were set to destroy evidence or make it look like the person had died from the fire. Most of the time, investigators saw right through it. On the other hand, the fire, the water, the fact that firefighters were trying to save property and lives, meant it wasn't a carefully preserved crime scene. A lot was destroyed or trampled. Or missed.

As he drove past Dean Davis' house, he was glad to see the guy didn't appear to be home. He was confident that if anyone else saw him there, in uniform, they wouldn't question it. He didn't have to answer to the Dean Davises of the world, but if anyone was going to make an issue about it, it'd be that guy.

He ducked under the crime scene tape and made his way across the little dooryard that in warmer months was an untamed mass of perennials. Now the parts not covered by snow were a frozen wasteland of brown and gray, torn up by truck tires, heavy hoses, and booted feet, soaked then frozen over.

The bedroom end was little more than a pile of charred beams and rubble. It was easy to see, though, where the body had been found. In the back corner, the tangle of metal and springs that had been Bernie's bed was surrounded by a partially cleared area where they'd looked for evidence.

The last time Pete had been in this room was the night they got back together after their month-long breakup in June. When he woke up that morning, the sun slanting through the windows, the smell of early summer wafting through the screen, he'd felt reborn. He'd had visions of endless summer, waking up in that bed beside her. A few days later, he had his accident and the vision disappeared.

The room was reduced to garbage, the acrid smell of the fire still thick. He was blindsided by a wave of pain that left him bereft. *Feel it, acknowledge it, move on.* "Okay Benjamin," he said. He was here to be a cop, not to add to the load of self-pity he'd carried around all day.

It was obvious that the room, the little left of it, had been ground zero for the fire. It had been incinerated. If not for what was left of the bed frame, there'd be nothing. It had since been cleaned up more by the investigators—scoured for evidence, not out of any altruism—given how Bernie, shaken and shocked, had described the crime scene photos to him.

It didn't surprise him that George Libby had waited until she and Kermit met with him without Pete. While Pete and Tommy squabbled like schoolboys in Pete's office, Libby had made sure Bernie got the full effect of what fire can do to a human being.

When he'd first pushed the photos in front of her, she told Pete, she couldn't make out what it was. She was overwhelmed by the destruction. But then the true horror emerged.

"It was like one of those pixelated pictures where you're supposed to see the horse and carriage or whatever if you look long enough," she told Pete later. "But it wasn't a horse and carriage, of course."

Libby helped her by pointing to what she eventually figured out was the bed frame. As she continued to stare at it, she realized that there was a body, contracted into a fetal position, arm, leg, and rib bones giving it away among the black and gray. She could make out teeth in the blackened head, mostly skull, but with some scorched-black skin and hair.

"It looked like she was screaming," Bernie said.

"She wasn't," Pete told her, trying to be reassuring. "That's how they always look."

"I told him I didn't know what he wanted me to say," Bernie said. "He said, 'I wanted to make sure you knew exactly what happened in your house. What that fire did to a human being.'"

As Pete stood in the debris, the late afternoon sunshine glinting off the backyard snow, his rage at Libby flared. The only reason he'd shown Bernie the photos was to get a reaction—maybe she'd blurt something Libby could use. It was also to stick it to her and show her he was the boss. Pete knew. He'd done it himself with suspects often enough.

If what was left after the fire held some clues, they were gone. Pete knew that, too. It had been a week. Still, he had to come and see for himself.

He made his way to the more intact part of the house, if it could be called that. The roof was gone. Anything visible under the snow was charred or black with soot. He slid on snow-covered ice and almost fell. He should've guessed it would be there—the house had been drenched by fire hoses for hours. Long icicles hung from what remained of the beams. Bernie's furniture and other belongs were unrecognizable—squat dark ghosts of her former life. The worst was the bookcase—floor-to-ceiling, wall-length—that she'd built herself after she moved in. He ran his finger along the spines of a row of books. With some effort, he pulled out the *Riverside Shakespeare*, a textbook from college that she'd kept. It had been the most expensive one she'd bought, but she kept it because it had all his plays, his sonnets, annotated not only by the editors, but by her. He tried to pull it open, but its thin pages were stuck together, the words a dissolved black mass. He'd thought earlier maybe he could save some books, bring them home to her. He saw now how impossible that would be. They were frozen chunks of disintegrated paper and cardboard. She was desperate to see what was left of her house, but he recoiled at the thought of her seeing this.

After their talk last night, he'd felt a renewed need to visit here. Try to feel some of what she'd felt. He still didn't understand, but the ruined books, a chronicle of her life that dated back to her childhood, through college, the two decades of her adult life before he'd met her, broke his heart.

He stepped into the screened porch off the kitchen, the one part of the house still relatively intact. The bright sun off the snow blinded him, a surprise. It had always been dark with the tall pines that surrounded her small yard. He put on his sunglasses. The reason it was so bright was because the trees beyond her property line were gone.

The garden shed that had been at the back, snug against the woods that marked Bernie's property line, was all alone in front of a backdrop of silver winter sky. Pete pushed the door open, a struggle against the knee-deep snow. He wasn't wearing boots, and the cold wet seeped through his shoes and plastered his pants to his legs.

A couple yards out, the walking got easier, the snow flattened by the feet of firefighters, then investigators. Their steps had worn a path to the garden shed, the site of the gasoline cans discovery. He followed but then veered off into deeper snow so he could look down the hill to the lake, a couple hundred yards beyond. The sharp pine smell of recently felled trees was stronger here than the acrid fire smell. Piles of trunks dotted the slope among the stumps, waiting for stripping and loading. The sun glinted off something by the lake. He moved a step sideways so there'd be less of a glare. It was a white pickup truck with a maroon logo on the door. His breath caught, a stab of panic paralyzing him. But it was quick. He did his breathing exercise and examined the trigger, Benjamin's soft coo of encouragement helping melt the anxiety.

He made his way back to his car, trying to categorize the trigger. A pickup truck. So what? He saw them every day. A million times a day. The trigger danced away. He wouldn't push it. He'd wait for it to disappear forever, which some of them did. If it came back, he'd worry about it then.

CHAPTER 27

THE MIDAFTERNOON LIGHT was already fading when Bernie drove down Loon Lane Saturday, but she could make out two figures on the ice in front of Pete's house and signs of some kind of project. She pulled in between Pete's Charger and Sandy's pickup truck, feeling the hours of being normal, shopping in Augusta with her sister and sister-in-law, fading just like the weak sun.

Dubby and Sandy's dog, Heidi, rocketed around the side of the house to greet her.

"Let's see what nonsense your daddies are up to."

At first she didn't understand what she was looking at, it was so unexpected. A channel, about five feet wide, had been cut in the ice, stretching from the shore out about a hundred yards. The two men were securing what looked like a giant chainsaw to one of the fire department's rescue sleds. Blocks of ice were scattered and stacked off to the side.

"What's this?" Bernie asked.

"A swimming lane." Pete gave her a hello kiss, then added, with a big smile. "Neat, huh?" His eyes shone, his face ruddy from the cold.

"Jump on in, the water's fine," Sandy said, pulling the sled with the saw to where they stood.

"Neat is not the word I would use," Bernie said.

Sandy gave Pete a quick look that Bernie interpreted as *I told you so.* He grabbed the sled pull. "I'll put this by the truck and you can help me load the saw in after."

"I told you about that article I read, right?" Pete said. "About ice swimming?"

"I foolishly told myself it wouldn't be logistically possible for you to do something like this."

"The fire department has that saw for ice rescues, so it worked out great."

"Great is not a word I would use either." They'd been walking to the car as they talked. Bernie handed him several bags of groceries. "I hate these plastic bags, it's like they put two items in each one, so you have a million that are all going to be part of that plastic island the size of Texas pretty soon."

"It's part of my plan," Pete said.

"Polluting the ocean with single-use plastic?"

"My exercise regimen. Before I hurt my leg, I swam every day. Every single day until there was ice on the water, then as soon as ice-out came, I was back out."

"It's dangerous," Bernie said. "Being in the water when it's that cold? What if you have a heart attack? What if something else happens and you can't get up on the ice and get out?"

"We've thought of that. We're going to put pylons around the edges, with a cable, so I can grab it if something happens. Also, we stacked the ice blocks so they'll block the wind. We're going to make a cover, so it doesn't freeze over, but until we do, I can probably break it up before I go to bed and again in the morning."

"Gee, you've thought of everything." *Except your freaked-out life partner who's never going to sleep as long as that hole in the ice is out there.*

Pete put the grocery bags on the counter, then took her chin in his hand, tilting her face up to his. "Look. It's going to be fine. I promise." He said it softly, but that didn't make Bernie feel better.

"It's dangerous." After he hurt his leg he'd told her a story about how, last May, the night before he broke up with her, he swam to the middle of the lake, and thought about how easy it would be to just sink down and not come up.

"Don't worry," he whispered, reading her mind. "After that, I swam every day until I hurt my leg and never had that thought again. It scared me straight. You know that. It's why I told you about it."

"It's hard to not think about it."

He cupped her face in his hands, wiping tears from her cheeks with his thumbs. "Exercise is going to make me better. It'll help with stress and anger and everything. I don't have those thoughts anymore, but even if I did, this is better than therapy."

"I know." She wiped the rest of her tears with her sleeve. "Speaking of which, there's something I need your help with."

"Sandy," she yelled as they went back outside.

He came around the house. "I was starting with the pylons. Everything okay?" She knew it was obvious she'd been crying.

"We're good," Pete said, too cheerfully as far as Bernie was concerned.

"I need you to help with something in the car," she said. "Both of you."

"You're staying for supper, right?" Pete asked him.

"Am I?" Sandy looked at Bernie, raised his eyebrows.

"What? I'd ban you just because you're encouraging this foolishness?"

He gave her his heart-melting smile.

"It doesn't mean you're off the hook," she said to him quietly as Pete continued to the car. "If something happens to him, I'll kill you."

"Got it." He hugged her around the shoulders and smiled wider.

"Don't look so happy."

She lifted the car hatch higher and waved her hand toward the interior. "Voilà."

"A punching bag?" Pete asked.

"I even got bags of sand for it. You're supposed to put the sand in, then put rags and stuff around. There's a thing that explains the whole thing."

"Fantastic," Sandy said. "I get dibs once we set it up."

"Where are we going to put it?" Pete asked.

247

"Sorry you're so underwhelmed. I was trying to think of exercise things for you, and this seemed good. I got gloves too. A guy at the store helped me. Unlike you, he was very enthusiastic."

"I'm not underwhelmed. I'm overwhelmed that you did this for me. Thanks." He kissed her on the cheek.

"It'll go in the utility room. I looked up how much space we need, and there's enough if we take my chair out. The beam in there is load-bearing so it should be fine to hold the weight."

"If we move your chair, you won't have a reading space."

"I can read fine in the living room, and we can put the chair in the bedroom in the corner by the window. I'll just find something smaller for my bedside table. So I can read there, too." She could tell he wanted to argue. "It's fine."

Sandy rested the box on his shoulder while Pete piled the two bags of sand on top of each other and lifted them. "Let's take these around to the back door."

Bernie was putting away groceries when the guys came into the kitchen.

"I got yellow for the cabinets," Bernie said. "A nice subtle buttercup, not some kind of screaming Yellow Submarine."

"You're painting the cabinets?" Sandy asked. "Didn't you paint them when you bought this place?"

Pete shot him a look that Bernie interpreted as *shut up, stupid.*

"Pete suggested it, since I like color." He'd suggested it the night before, casually, like it wasn't a big deal. It was a gesture that made her sad more than hopeful. On the other hand, she found painting relaxing, so she wasn't going to argue.

"How about another shade of beige to match all this?" Sandy waved his hand at the surrounding palette of white, beige, and gray.

"Yellow's great," Pete said. He took two beers out of the fridge and joined Sandy, who'd moved to the couch and was bent over the puzzle.

Sandy picked up a puzzle piece. "What's this, aqua? Why don't you paint your cabinets this?"

"Don't give her any ideas."

"I don't need people to give me ideas. I have plenty of my own. Weren't you guys going to finish the pylons? It's getting dark."

"I have a rescue spotlight in the truck," Sandy said. "That reminds me. I have some stuff from your house."

"What stuff?"

"Not much. There were a couple things under the bed. I wiped the soot and crap off, and they seem okay. I left them at the station, in my office. Remind me Monday. I'll bring it over to you at work."

"Under the bed?"

"Yeah. The fire burned the body and most of the mattress, but it flashed over enough that there was an air pocket created by the box spring. That's the layman's version. They took what was left of the box spring and mattress for the investigation, but I guess they didn't care about what was underneath."

"It's a crime scene," Pete said. "What the hell are you doing removing things?"

"I was with the insurance adjuster." Sandy never seemed bothered by Pete's snippiness. "They didn't want to do it without someone from the department there. I called Libby to double-check it was okay, that they were done. I assumed they didn't need those things."

"That's quite an assumption."

"I knew this piece went in the ocean part." Sandy tapped it into place. "Libby was done. I thought it would make Bernie feel better if she had some of her things."

Bernie stepped in before Pete could snipe back. "When was this? If it's not a crime scene, why hasn't anyone told me?"

"You know cops," Sandy said. He leaned back, stretched out his long legs, and took a longer pull on his beer, his eyes dancing at Pete.

"You've just lost your puzzle privileges," Pete said. Then, to Bernie, "They won't release it until the insurance agency is done."

"It sounds like they are, right? I want to go look. It's *my* house."

"I wouldn't recommend it, sweetheart," Sandy said. "It's a mess."

"It's *my* mess."

"When Libby says it's okay, I'll go with you," Pete said.

I don't need anyone to go with me. She bit it back. "Sandy, that reminds me. Did you see anyone filming on their phone the night of the fire?"

"Couple. I didn't pay much attention."

"Do you remember talking to anyone about it being arson?"

"I don't know. People say all sorts of shit to me, and I don't really listen. I'm trying to work, you know?"

"Check this out." She got her laptop and showed Sandy and Pete the Redimere Raw video that caught the audio of someone mentioning arson, implicating Bernie, and Sandy telling the guy he was needed on a hose.

"Sorry, doesn't ring a bell," he said. "Must be one of the volunteers. People always speculate about arson, so it's probably nothing."

Bernie wanted to ask him to think hard and remember, but he was already back fiddling with the puzzle. Pete too.

****

Bernie got started painting the cabinets right after breakfast Sunday. She worried that Pete thought it meant more than it did, like it would make her feel like she belonged there. She was tired of worrying about what he thought. She promised herself to take a day off from it.

"It's not that I don't like color," he said as he hovered, watching her remove the doors. "It's just that I'm never sure what to do with it."

"One great thing about painting is that you can change it if you don't like how it turns out," she said. Small potatoes, she wanted to add, when compared to the smoldering pile of rubble a few miles away on School Street.

"I still can't find my notebook." He said it tentatively, like he was afraid of how she'd react.

"It'll turn up. Along with that gift card." Before she'd left for Augusta the day before, he told her to take the Barnes & Noble gift card her parents gave him for Christmas and buy herself some books. Her mom would kill her if she found out that Bernie had used Pete's gift card to buy something for herself. She'd also be hurt in her Italian way, thinking Pete hadn't appreciated it. They'd compromised that Bernie would buy Pete some books that she'd like too. Then he

250

couldn't find the card, which he was sure had been in the same drawer as his notebook.

"I wonder where they are."

"They're not in this cabinet." She waited for him to move out of the way. "You have those gloves on, why don't you go box?"

He jabbed the air, then posed in a classic boxing stance. "Did I ever tell you that I did a year with the Police Athletic League boxing club? I think I was around nine."

Of course not. "At least you'll know what you're doing."

"Not really. I sucked. I was scrawny and scared of getting hit." A couple more jabs. "I watched a YouTube video last night, though, so I'm all set."

"Also, the bag doesn't hit back."

"I stopped being scared a few years later, with my stepfather. I traded it for being pissed off."

"Go get 'em, Rocky," she said as he disappeared into the utility room. She wasn't sure what else to say, she was too surprised he'd brought it up. He rarely, almost never, talked about the abuse he'd suffered at the hands of his stepfather. She sometimes couldn't resist tracing the cigarette burn scars on his hip and lower back with her finger. He didn't jerk away anymore, but talking about it was off-limits. Maybe it was like the out-of-the-blue suggestion that she paint the cabinets—an effort to bridge that confusing and yawning gap between her love for him and a life in his house. Painting helped her think, so wondering gave her something to work on.

Half an hour later, he danced into the kitchen, his gloved hands raised over his head. "Pete is biiiigggg. Pete is mean. Float like a butterfly. Sting like a beeeeee." He sang it to the tune of the theme from *Rocky*, bouncing on the balls of his feet.

"I believe the words are 'Gonna fly now.' You're getting Rocky and Muhammad Ali mixed up."

"You can't out-*Rocky* me. I lived in Philly for half of my life."

"I'm more of a Muhammad Ali gal."

He danced around her on his toes, jabbing gently in the air. "I *am* the greatest," he said in a not-too-bad Muhammad Ali voice. "Float like a butterfly, sting like a bee. His hands can't hit what his eyes don't see."

"Don't make me regret getting you that," she said through her laughter. This was that lighter side of him that had disappeared recently. Was this all he needed? Maybe, but it couldn't possibly be this easy.

Pete stopped dancing and took her face between the boxing gloves and kissed her. "I love you, baby."

"Just don't start calling me Adrian."

"I'm going for a swim."

"In boxers and a T-shirt?"

"Swimsuit." He walked to the bedroom.

"Shouldn't you wear a wet suit or something?"

"The idea is to let the body experience the water and cold. It's about acclimating. That's how you get the benefits."

"Great."

"I know! It'll feel good. Maybe when we build the addition, we can add a sauna. I already want to upgrade the outdoor shower. That'll be nice, right? For both of us."

He came out wearing a swimsuit and water shoes. He laid a beach towel, a heavy long-sleeved T-shirt, and flannel pants on top of the pellet stove. "Nice and warm for after."

"Great." She laid a cabinet door across two kitchen chairs, carefully protected with layers of newspaper.

He came up behind and put his arms around her, his post-boxing body hot against her back. He rested his chin on her shoulder, pressing the side of his face against hers. "I want you to feel like it's your house too. If you decide to live here. I was thinking about it and figured it's okay to talk about that, right? Even with the way things are? Instead of avoiding topics. Right?"

"It won't matter if you die of a heart attack under a foot of ice."

"That's not going to happen," he said. He kissed her cheek, then danced away toward the slider. "Because I *am* the greatest," he said in his Muhammad Ali voice. "I float like a fish and swim like a loon."

"Great."

"Anyway, the ice isn't nearly a foot yet. You can easily break through it to get me out. Use the garden shovel, okay? Or maybe a tire iron."

"Ha ha."

"Seriously, Bernie. This is going to be really good for me. Don't worry, okay?"

"Okay." She sanded the door in front of her with unnecessary concentration and energy.

"Bernie."

She looked up. This new version of him still caught her off guard, even after six months. He was the same compact coiled spring, but thinner, less wiry. The lopsided, splotchy baseball-sized scar on his left leg was white against a swollen thigh so different from his chiseled right one it looked like it belonged to someone else. His hand was on the slider handle, waiting, impatient.

"Okay?" he asked.

The white expanse of lake behind him blended into the gray sky. She couldn't see the dark gash of the swimming lane from where she stood, but she could feel it. Felt it deep in the pit of her stomach.

"How long do you think you'll be out there?"

"Not long. I have to acclimate over time. You read the article, right? I'll try one lap after I immerse for a couple of minutes to adapt." He'd spent most of the last twelve hours, the waking ones, enthusiastically preaching the benefits that the article touted. Beyond heart, lung, and immune system strengthening, there was also a huge antidepressive factor. A cure, the thing he'd been looking for.

The words in the article that had stuck with her were *shock, hypothermia, cardiac arrest, death, drowning*. Unsaid was the fear that always hovered, that he was hiding his darkest heart from her. That someday he'd go into the lake, or into the woods, and not come back.

Despite all that, she'd been noncommittal. She wasn't going to say no to something he put so much hope into.

"I need to know you're okay with this."

"The article *did* say that people in good shape were most likely to benefit, and you're in good shape from the gym."

"Right. Like I showed you." He didn't have to do fifty plank-straight push-ups to prove it, but he had the night before. Then he walked on his hands across the room. "Okay, enough," she'd said, laughing, and he'd collapsed in laughter too.

"Knock 'em dead, Rocky." She smiled, hoping it looked encouraging.

He opened the door, then raised his hands over his head. "Na na naaaa," he sang as he danced onto the deck, which he'd cleared of snow the night before, along with a path to the water.

Bernie refilled her coffee mug and took it to the slider to watch. The temperature gauge mounted outside the door said twenty-five degrees. It was in the shade, but the silver winter sun wasn't going to make a difference on the lake. Dubby joined her, whining softly. "No, you can't go out with Daddy. One idiot in the water is enough for my nerves."

Pete walked to the edge of the water as though it were an August day. A thin layer of ice had formed overnight. He waded in and pushed at it with his hands, breaking it as he entered. Once he was waist deep, he went under. Bernie held her breath. He came up quickly, gasping. He smiled at her, gave a thumbs-up. Went under again. This time he stayed under for ten seconds—she counted—and came up without gasping. He walked in until it was up to his shoulders, then stood, moving his arms back and forth just below the surface. Small waves lapped onto the thick ice on either side of him.

"Get it over with," she said. Dubby, his tail slapping against her leg, watched Pete with his usual doggy joy and devotion, stubby legs marching in place, as though he were imagining swimming too. "I hope you have some Saint Bernard in you, or Labrador, whatever kind of dog can jump in freezing water and save a life." Poopoo had come to the door to watch too. "You too," she said to the cat.

Pete's feet came up in the air, and he floated on his back. Then he flipped in the water, a sleek, pale dolphin, his back arching up, then flattening. He swam with strong, sure strokes, the thin layer of ice breaking as he swam.

When he got to the end of the lane, he held onto the edge for a few seconds, then the safety cable. Even from a distance, she could see he was taking deep breaths. She fought the urge to open the slider and call to him. He plunged back in and swam back just as surely as he'd swum out. He emerged from the water and walked back to the house.

He smiled as she opened the door for him, a stupidly happy Dubby-type one. She couldn't remember the last time she'd seen that smile.

"That looked fun."

"It was great." He put his arms around her and squeezed, then kissed her.

"You're getting me wet and cold."

He was shivering, his skin pebbled and slightly blue. The shivers started as small tremors but within seconds became quakes. She wanted to envelop him, force her body heat into him. Instead, she handed him the warm towel from the top of the pellet stove.

"The article said this would happen," he said through chattering teeth. He stepped out of the water shoes, pulled off his trunks, briskly dried off, then wrapped the towel around his shoulders. He pulled it tight with one hand as he reached for the clothes.

"Lean on me and I'll put the socks and pants on," she said. He held her shoulder as she pulled on the socks and then worked the flannel pants up his quaking legs, fast past the scar that was bright blue and throbbed with his heartbeat.

"See? No problem. Everything's fine," he said.

"I'm just trying to keep you alive, bud."

"I know."

She looked up, expecting the same big smile. Instead, his eyes shone with tears. He wiped them with the towel, then took the shirt from her. "That's just endorphins."

"Okay."

"Seriously, Bernie, it was great. It felt so damn good. I was prepared for the shock of the first few seconds, after reading the articles, but it wasn't as bad as I expected. Once I was past that, it really felt good. Not just swimming again, but the cold too. I can't describe it. Not just physically invigorating, but like the best drug I could take."

He rubbed his hair with the towel as he stood in front of the pellet stove. "I'm going to do this every day. Maybe twice a day." He walked into the kitchen where she was putting the kettle on to make coffee.

"There's a couple sawhorses in the shed," he said. "It's okay to use the chairs, but the sawhorses may be easier."

"I didn't feel like dragging them in here through thigh-deep snow."

"That reminds me, what were you doing in the woods back there?"

"The woods? Behind the shed? Nothing. The only time I've been out there since the last storm was to get the stuff for the table puzzle thingy. Straight to the shed and back. The snow's too deep for detours. Why?" *What did I do wrong this time?*

"Come with me." He seemed confused, not mad or even annoyed.

"This"—Pete pointed out the back door to a line of deep holes, basically a trench, that came around the house from the dooryard—"was me and Sandy bringing the punching bag in. The line from the shed to here was you Wednesday, right? What's that?" He pointed to two rows of deep holes that skirted the shed to the woods behind it. They intersected the path Pete and Sandy had made, ending at the kitchen window.

"I don't get it," Bernie said.

"It wasn't you. It wasn't me."

"Was it there yesterday?" she asked.

"That's when I saw it. I assumed it was you. Was it here Wednesday?"

"I don't know. I would've noticed, right?"

"Maybe. Maybe it just didn't register or you thought it was me."

"Maybe." She was pretty sure that could've happened.

"At first, I thought maybe you'd brought the dog out here, but he wouldn't have been able to plow through the snow. I was curious, because it seemed odd."

Two can play at that game, Mr. Detective. "See how mine are different from the others? Since I'm shorter, my legs drag in the snow up to my thighs. My track is more trench-like. The ones you guys made are more like holes, because you're taller. I bet that's Sandy's since he's six-three and you're five-ten. His are the most like holes since he can lift his legs higher. Those ones are obviously you, since the right leg is more of a hole and the left more of a trench. The mystery ones are more like Sandy's. From someone tall."

"Thanks, Holmes." Normally he'd punctuate it with a smile, but his eyes were on the snow.

"I'll add one more thing, Watson. Whoever did it walked back in the same tracks he made coming, which is an obvious thing to do, but you can tell because the holes are mishappen and longer."

Pete stood in the doorway with his arms crossed, his gaze on the path in the snow to the woods.

"Someone was here." He said it the way a detective would, with interest, rather than the fear that Bernie felt creeping in. "It would've been since the last major storm, so some time since New Year's. He came down from the road, through the woods. That's a steep climb, and even though the snow isn't that high because of the tree cover, the rocks and undergrowth make it difficult. It looks like he went to the window, maybe this door too. It's hard to tell since the area around the door is cleared away and we all tramped it down."

"Someone broke in?"

He examined the strike plate on the door, a little over a year old and still shiny. "No tampering that I can see. You locked the door behind you Wednesday, right?"

"Of course I did."

He didn't say anything.

"Remember? I had to unlock it for you and Sandy yesterday."

"Right."

"Even if someone didn't come in, they were creeping around, looking in the window."

"It's probably nothing," Pete said. He added, reassuring this time, "Don't worry. I'll make sure we're safe. We already have the security lights. I'll get an alarm system. Today."

CHAPTER 28

BERNIE WASN'T THRILLED that a trip to Augusta meant Pete would be gone for hours, the only security being Dubby and Heidi's dubious protective instincts. At least Heidi, Sandy's dog, looked the part. Anyone peeping in a window would see a large German shepherd who looked like she was on permanent alert. Dubby, a burly ball of fur on too-short legs with flopping ears, didn't have the same effect.

"At least you two won't be critiquing my painting technique," Bernie said to the dogs, who'd settled at the edge of the kitchen to watch. Her anxiety had gone from low-level to whatever the worst DEFCON was. When Pete and Sandy had left in Sandy's truck, Pete assured her that the fact that both their cars were in the dooryard would deter any lurkers or creepers.

"This obviously happened when we weren't home," he said.

When she looked up from where she was painting the cabinet doors, all she could see out the window over the sink, the only one on that side of the house, was the deep green of pines with gray sky above. Someone looking in, though, could see the small kitchen and living area, like the set of a play. Ibsen, she decided. *A Doll's House.* All laid out like one, with her a little round doll with two fuzzy toy dogs. She tried tacking a blanket over the window but lost too much natural light, so she took it off. Her desire to have the cabinets come out right and prove to Pete the color was okay was greater than her fear. She wasn't sure if that was a victory.

"In *A Doll's House*, Ibsen pioneered a new kind of realism and moral criticism, but the final act, which is supposed to show Nora as a hero, is also laden with misogyny," Bernie told the dogs. It was the opening line of a paper she'd written in college. Funny how she couldn't remember when her credit card payment was due, but could recite something she'd written more than two decades before. She'd gotten a C because the professor, a faux hippie who was much more of a square than he realized, disagreed with her on the misogyny.

"They all do," Bernie said as Dubby and Heidi, snouts on their paws, looked on.

"In the play, the husband thinks he's on the moral high ground, and—spoiler!—the wife, Nora, commits fraud to help him out. She pays it back, but it's too late, and he blasts her for it, so she leaves him. But *she's* the one who's considered destructive by people who analyze that stuff for a living," Bernie said. "What the hell is *that* about? You tell me."

Her life with Pete wasn't an Ibsen play, was nothing like one. She knew that. Still, she couldn't shake the feeling that she was bringing down his house, yellow cabinets and all.

"When Ibsen was on his deathbed, some friend came to visit, and the doctor told the friend that Ibsen was doing much better. You know what Ibsen said?"

Heidi raised her eyebrows.

" 'On the contrary.' Then he died. Those were his last words."

Dubby yawned.

"Maybe I almost flunked that class, but whenever there are Ibsen questions on *Jeopardy!* I know the answer. I even beat Pete on a Final Jeopardy question about Ibsen. A rare victory. If Pete were on his deathbed and someone said he was doing much better, he'd agree and jump out of bed and start doing push-ups just to prove it. *Then* he'd drop dead."

Heidi sat up and rotated her ears.

"Sorry. Bad joke."

Her cell buzzed.

"Just checking in," Tommy said.

"I'm doing an Ibsen lecture for the dogs. Putting that $50,000 education to work."

"The fun never stops over there, does it? I always found Ibsen depressing. Incomprehensible too. Sounds like you've finally lost your shit. What little shit you had left."

"I just may have."

"I'm inviting myself over. Our cable's out, and I want to watch the NFL playoffs. I know Pete must be an Eagles fan, so I figured, you know."

"Packers. He's originally from Wisconsin, remember? He and Sandy went to Augusta on a shopping trip. Don't make some sophomoric joke about them being gay lovers or something."

"Like I'd do that. All I care about is his manly TV."

Tommy arrived half an hour later with a twelve-pack of beer and a hot pizza.

"Where do I put this stuff?" he asked as he settled on the couch, slice in one hand, beer in the other. "I don't want to mess up the puzzle. That part with the Greek letters still isn't done? It's so obvious." He put his beer on the end table and reached for a puzzle piece. "This one—"

Bernie picked up the cover for the table frame. "Release the piece."

"But—"

"Release it."

He did. She put the cover on.

"Whatever. Geez. Don't want to upset Pete, for chrissake."

"That's not it," Bernie said, even though it was. "You have pizza. It's messy."

"I see he's letting you paint the cabinets.

"He's not *letting* me do anything. I'm *choosing* to paint the cabinets."

"What's he really doing in Augusta on a Sunday when the Eagles and Packers are playing in a wild card?"

"Getting an alarm system. We may have an outdoor lurker."

"Way to bury the lead."

Bernie brought him to the back door and showed him the disruption in the snow.

Tommy took it in. Bernie could feel his mental calculations. "This is serious shit, Bern. Someone came out of the woods and looked in your window. Who knows what else. Good thing I came over."

"I'm a big girl, I don't need a babysitter." She shut the door, and they walked back to the living room.

"Since Pete's not here, this is a good time to talk," Tommy said. "Tell me why I was looking for court records about Ryan Grant."

"He's the mayor. In fact, he's the guy who pushed for us to have a mayor. We were fine without one. When I wrote about him before the election, I didn't go deep enough."

"Why now?"

"There's a lot going on. Development projects that he's involved in. He's throwing his weight around a lot more recently. It seems like time to check in."

"Throwing his weight around as in going after your boyfriend."

"Even if Pete and I weren't dating, even if I didn't even like Pete, I'd be going deeper on Grant. Why is the mayor so focused on the police chief? Town residents, voters, and taxpayers deserve to know."

"Are you kidding me? No way that was holding." Eyes still on the TV, he said, "I know you mean it, but will anyone else know that? Using the paper to go after your boyfriend's enemy could make you look really bad. You live here. You're painting the cabinets. Soothing his troubled brow, no doubt. You've done such a great job of building up that newspaper, and its great reputation, too, even outside of Franklin County. So, what the fuck are you doing?"

"I'm doing journalism. If people don't like it, they can kiss my ass."

"And cancel their subscriptions."

"If there's nothing, fine. No story. If there's something on Grant, people will focus on that, not on the fact that Pete's my boyfriend."

"What do you think you're going to find?"

"I don't know."

"Grant doesn't have any kind of record. Those two pages from a dismissed lawsuit about his revoked license, that I'm told was the result of some ex suing him for business fraud, were all I could find. It was dismissed. Both suits were. You're going down a slippery slope to try to paint him as anything bad when he looks perfectly fine to everyone but you."

Bernie got a beer out of the fridge and a slice of pizza and sat down in the recliner. "Thanks for the Tommy-splanation. He's also a fake Navy SEAL."

"Humiliating for him if you just go with that, but it'll just look like tit for tat. He goes after your unstable boyfriend, you out him as a guy who brags a little too much."

"Claiming you're a Navy SEAL when you're not goes beyond just bragging, and it's also a red flag for a serious personality issue. Just as important, he's got his fingers in a lot of pies around town. Any pie that has to do with development and money? His fingers are in it. He and the college are tight as wet jeans on that development on land that's supposed to be going to the Passamaquoddy."

"For chrissake, Bernie, don't go after the college too. It's like you're hell-bent on crashing and burning."

"I'm not *going after* anyone. I'm doing journalism. Haven't you been listening to me at all?"

"I've been listening. I just hope you know what you're doing. Oh geez, look at that." He sat back in disgust as the Packers celebrated a touchdown.

She *did* know what she was doing. Maybe she was on shaky ground with regard to her relationship, her burned-down house with its tragic victim, her always precarious bank account. Some weird stalker lurking around their neighborless house. Still, she felt strangely at peace as the football game danced in front of her to the soundtrack of Tommy's moans and groans. Her life may be a chaotic mess, but she knew what she was doing where it counted.

****

Pete and Sandy were nearly back in town when Pete's cellphone rang.

"Hey, Chief, sorry to bug you." It was Jamie. "Dawna's visiting her aunt in Bangor and we have a little bit of a conundrum here at the station."

"Be there in ten minutes," Pete said. "Want to drop by the station for a conundrum?" he asked Sandy.

"Sounds like fun."

When they got there, Jamie, Tyler, and Brent were sitting around the office, drinking coffee and talking about that afternoon's NFL games. Tyler was the only one in uniform.

"What's up?" Pete asked as he and Sandy settled into chairs.

"I responded to a report of a subject threatened with a gun over by Pondside Convenience," Tyler said. "By the time I responded, both subjects were in the parking lot at the Pour House. To make a long story short, a gentleman was leaving the gas pumps at Pondside, and there was a vehicle blocking his way with a girl driving. She was just sitting there doing something in her car, so he beeped. She responded by making an obscene gesture and yelling obscenities out her window. Then she peeled out of the parking lot."

"Whose account is this?"

"Oh right. His. Hers is similar at this point, only from her point of view. She makes it sound less like she was being offensive. Anyway, he's behind her on Pond Road, and they both have to stop for a train. While they're stopped, with her in front, she exits her vehicle and proceeds partway toward the gentleman in the pickup, shouting obscenities. When she gets close enough, he doesn't know what she's after, so he picks up his gun, which was in his console. It's holstered and not loaded. He doesn't take it out of the holster, just holds it up so she can see. She shouts an obscenity and goes back to her vehicle. By now the train is gone and the gate is going up, so he peels past her, toward the Pour House. She follows him. They both at this time call 911. The gentleman stays on the phone with dispatch, because this crazy lady is basically tailgating him. He's driving around the Pour House parking lot, which, you know how big it is, so even with football on, it's half empty. He parks there, waiting for us. She's parked at the other end. He'd yelled to her that he'd called us, and she was like, 'Good, so did I.' I check in with him, then her, advise them both to sit tight. Jamie arrives around then, and Brent too. We discuss the incident—"

"I'm on standby today," Jamie said. "I heard it on the scanner. Brent's off, but he did too. I radioed dispatch to advise we didn't need backup from state or county. It was obvious it wasn't much of anything."

"We split up and I go and talk to the girl," Tyler said. "She was pretty much hysterical. Jamie goes to talk to the gentleman along with Brent. I advise her to calm down and I'll come back and talk to her when she's ready to talk—"

"When you say girl—"

"Oh right." Tyler's face pinked up. "She's someone we're familiar with. Amber Gagnon. We busted her for drunk and disorderly in September. She has some similar priors. She's twenty-six, lives over to the Beehive, so that tells you something right there."

"I remember her." Pete laughed. "I'm the one who booked her. I was still on crutches, and she said, 'Who the fuck are you, Tiny Tim?' "

The guys laughed.

"Oh yeah," Tyler said. "And you said, nice as could be, 'No, I'm the police chief, and my name is Pete, tiny or not.' "

They all laughed again.

"And the gentleman?" Pete tried not to say it with irony. He'd never thought about the police tendency to call every man a gentleman, even those who'd committed horrific crimes, until Bernie had gone on a rant about it. As with most things like that, she was right. He'd never said anything to his staff, though. Or another big peeve of hers, using "advise" instead of "told." No point in nitpicking about trivial shit.

"William Sawyer, thirty-five, lives in West Vineyard. Spotless record," Tyler said. "Not even a parking ticket."

"If we issued parking tickets, which we don't," Pete said. They all laughed again. Except Sandy, who'd been listening quietly.

"The girl was pretty much out of control," Jamie said. "A real handful. She was crying and not really coherent. It seemed like she just wanted to give us a hard time. William was calm and cooperative, so the three of us took his statement first. Or rather, I did, with Tyler and Brent there too."

Tyler nodded. "Yeah, then her story, when we could get it out of her, is she had her kid in the car seat. He's like two, and he'd spilled something, so she was trying to deal with him, so it pissed her off when the gentleman beeped at her. She said that when he showed the gun, it really scared her, especially with her kid in the car."

"But why did she follow him if she was so scared?" Brent said. Jamie and Tyler nodded.

"What did she say?" Pete asked.

"She said that she thought he was dangerous, threatening her with a gun, so she called it in and followed him until we could get there, so we'd be sure to get the right guy. Something like that," Tyler said.

"We thought that was kind of bullshit," Jamie said. "She seemed like she just wanted to give him more shit. Us too."

"So, the question is?" Pete asked.

Tyler looked at Jamie, who nodded, then he said, "Do you think what the guy did, holding up a holstered gun, is worth a threatening with a dangerous weapon charge? The way I see it, and the three of us discussed it, he was more trying to de-escalate a situation, since she was so off the handle. He was trying to calm her down."

"What does the threatening with a dangerous weapon law say?" Pete knew he sounded like the pedantic professor his Philly coworkers had mocked him as, but Tyler was twenty-two and green as grass. He wanted him to make thinking things through a habit.

Tyler pinked up again, the color running to the roots of his slicked-down blond hair. Forget twenty-two; he looked twelve. "If they intentionally or knowingly place another person in fear of imminent bodily injury. Us three talked about it, and it seems like, since he didn't even point the gun at her, and they were both in separate vehicles, and *she* followed *him*, she really wasn't in fear of imminent bodily injury. She didn't seem scared, just out of control."

"How did you leave it?"

"We advised William we'd get back to him. We didn't charge him. He's a local guy, with kids of his own, which is another thing. He's not going to seriously threaten someone with a baby in the car, right? He said he understood and wouldn't go anywhere."

"And Ms. Gagnon?"

Tyler laughed and shook his head. "She was yelling at us that we needed to arrest him. I advised her that maybe we'd arrest her if she didn't calm down. Since she had priors, it wouldn't go over too good."

"That shut her up, more or less," Jamie said. He, Tyler, and Brent laughed.

Sandy uncrossed his legs, sat up straighter. He gave Pete a wry smile.

Pete turned to Brent, "What do you think?"

"Since I wasn't on duty, just went when I heard it on the scanner, I tried to stay out of it. I chatted with William a little, though. He's a responsible gun owner. You know, hunts, that kind of thing. Very cool and calm guy."

"What do you think, Jamie?"

"There really isn't enough to charge threatening. I mean, you can bring it to the DA, but it just seems like she was haranguing him, and he was trying to calm down the situation. He didn't point the gun or anything, like Tyler said. She didn't seem scared, just, you know, wicked emotional. Also, I was thinking, when she approached his vehicle at the railroad gate, he had no idea what her intentions were. He was probably the scared one, right? Pulling the gun was more self-defense than anything else. He was the one in imminent danger."

"Tyler? It's your case."

"I agree with the guys. William was calm and no problem. The girl was a total pain in the ass. If we charge William, he's in the paper as being charged and everything, and there goes his reputation. His wife works at the nursing home, and his kids are at school, and are people going to give them shit? It doesn't seem like it would be fair if he's found not guilty later."

"Sounds like a non-situation," Pete said. "Just a couple of people getting pissed off for a few minutes. No one got hurt, or was likely going to, except maybe getting into an accident with all the yelling and finger waving. Let William know we're not charging. No reason to bring it to the DA. She'd say the same thing."

As they walked back to the truck in the gathering dusk, Sandy said, "Are you going to run that by Dawna?"

"I wasn't planning to. Why?"

"I don't know. Different perspective, maybe?"

"Dawna would agree with me. Anyway, I already made a decision and discussed it with the guys. I don't see the point in revisiting it. It wouldn't go down well with the guys, for one thing. Dawna wasn't even there to see the behavior or talk to the people involved."

"Maybe Bernie, then? Not to change your decision, just get a different point of view?"

"Bernie and I don't talk about everything that happens on our jobs. She's not a cop, so her perspective on something like this doesn't matter. I'm just going to leave it where it is."

CHAPTER 29

"I FEEL WEIRDLY OPTIMISTIC today," Pete said to Bernie as he toweled off from his swim. "Really good. Like things are looking better than they have in a long time."

"That's just endorphins." The heat of the coffee mug she handed him stung his cold hands. "Both my Irish and Italian DNA and deep incurable Catholic background tells me that if you feel that way, you're going to be punished."

"I don't remember the nuns teaching me that."

"Really? I thought you were a straight-A student."

He sat down to a plate of scrambled eggs and thick wheat toast that she'd made while he was swimming. She was going along with the swimming as though it didn't bother her, a big relief. He knew she'd get used to it.

"I was reading this article about Mount Everest." She joined him at the table. "They just leave most of the bodies up there of the people who die. Did you know that? Climbers go past these frozen dead bodies. There's even this lady from the 1970s. She's kind of leaning on her elbow. Her brown hair still whips in the wind."

"Are you making conversation or telling me this for a reason?" He met her eyes, large and liquid brown behind her glasses. Anxiety on steroids.

"I'm just saying that things can seem really good, like you're doing something wicked awesome and kicking the shit out of the bucket list, but you don't need frozen dead bodies along the path to let you know there's danger ahead."

Pete swallowed a mouthful of toast, trying to cover up a laugh. "Bernie, I'm just going to work today, like I have every day that I've been physically able to for twenty-three years. I'm going to fill out a lot of paperwork, make executive decisions, give pep talks to rookies, have nice conversations with Dawna, engage in public service, come home, and make dinner for the woman I love. I don't anticipate one frozen dead body along the path."

"The article said that the hikers, even though they'd heard about the bodies, were still shocked and shaken to see them. Even though they knew they were there, they didn't expect them until they saw them."

"I know your anxiety is amped up. I totally get that. But today is going to be a great day. Both of us are going to have a great day, right?" Usually, she was the one who made the optimistic morning speech.

When he left, he hugged her extra tight. She melted against him, warm and soft. It always took his breath away, how good she felt. He kissed her. He hadn't felt this positive for a while. He couldn't remember how long it had been, since he still couldn't find his notebook. Even that wasn't bothering him as much. He gave her a final squeeze. "Like a shark, baby."

****

That unusual extraordinary good feeling lasted about twenty minutes, right up until Pete went into the kitchen to heat up his coffee.

Dawna and Mandy stopped talking as he entered. Mandy looked away, guilty, maybe a little defiant. Dawna gave him her we-need-to-talk look.

"What's up?" Pete asked.

"We were just talking about the road rage thing yesterday, the lack of charges," Dawna said. She and Mandy exchanged a glance.

"No one else is here," Pete said. "You're free to tell me whatever you're thinking."

"Did you look at the statements?" Dawna asked.

"No. Since there are no charges, I wasn't planning to."

"I did. William Sawyer's is very detailed, and the impressions of his demeanor and comments, very positive. Amber Gagnon's is short and negative."

"Okay."

"It seems like Amber was given short shrift. Maybe the guys were swayed by a guy they could relate to as well as by negative feelings about an emotional woman."

"Did Sandy say something?"

"Sandy? What's he got to do with this?"

"Never mind. I talked to the guys at length. It sounds like they did a thorough job."

"I'd expect that," Dawna said. "I don't think they deliberately took his side, but I think they had some cognitive bias."

Cognitive bias. Bernie had brought that up recently too. They must've read the same article.

"Cognitive bias is the tendency to make assumptions based on personal experience," Dawna said. "A guy, for instance, will see it from the guy's point of view. A white person—"

"I know what it is," Pete said. He'd had to look it up when Bernie was going on about it. "Mandy, what do you think?"

"I'm not sure." Her face, set in angry defiance, and her tightly crossed arms told him differently.

"It's okay," Dawna said. "He really does want to know."

"I feel like they made assumptions about Amber based on how she was acting," Mandy said. "Even though I'm a cop, as a woman, if a guy on a country road with no one around shows me a gun, I'm going to feel threatened, possibly terrorized. Isn't that what the law says? Not what a bunch of male cops think about it, but how the victim felt."

"She followed him," Pete said.

"Because he pulled a gun and she thought he was dangerous," Mandy said. "She thought she was being a good citizen. It's not like she got out of her car after that and went after him."

He swirled his coffee, watched his distorted reflection break and fade in the darkness.

"I read this article," Mandy said. Tentative.

What's with all these women reading all these fucking articles? "Go ahead."

"They did a study where they asked women if they'd rather run into a bear if they're alone in the woods, or a man. Something like 87 percent of the women said bear."

"I don't think a bear is the right choice. Not all men—"

Dawna cut him off. "With all due respect, Chief, it's not about what you think. It's about what a woman in that situation thinks. The bear thing aside, you've seen enough in your career to know what happens to women at the hands of men, right?"

She was angry. It wasn't like her to show him up in front of another officer. He took a deep breath. Held it. *He did know.* She was angry because she expected him to get it.

"Why don't you get me the report and statements. Have Tyler see me when he gets in. He's in at eleven, right?"

Dawna nodded.

"Thanks, both of you, for speaking up. I appreciate your insight."

****

Bernie wasn't one of those people who thought genders should conform to specific colors and scents, but Pete's addiction to the mango-peach-coconut body sugar was bugging her. She was used to his pleasant soapy and woodsy scent. Now he smelled like an overly sweet fruit punch that spilled on the couch and you could never get the smell out. Before work, she stopped at the Maine-made store. There had to be a better scent for him if he was going to use the stuff.

The jars of body sugar were along the wall, jammed in between a display of loon salt-and-pepper shakers and a bunch of whittled wooden sculptures. She had to get to work, so didn't have a lot of time for her decision. She settled on cinnamon-cedar. It smelled good. Manly.

As she was twisting the lid back on the jar after the smell test, the small wood sculptures caught her eye. They were familiar. It came to her fast, since she'd taken photos of similar ones when she wrote her first Normand Ouimette article. They were his craftwork.

She brought the jar to the counter. "Do you have information on the artist who makes those wood sculptures? I'd like to contact him."

"We have cards for all of our consigners," the woman said. She rifled around in a box under her counter. "Except that one, I guess. I can't find anything."

"You must have his contact information, right?" Bernie said. "So he can get paid and everything?"

"We do, but I don't. This is a co-op, so no one is really in charge. We rent the building. The board, probably? Bev Dulac?"

Bernie left with her jar of cinnamon-cedar body sugar and the feeling she was finally going to find Normand. She knew Bev. Could talk to Bev. Bev was on top of things. She'd know where he was.

****

Pete was fully immersed in the budget when Bernie knocked on his semi-open door around noon.

"Still feeling awesome?" she asked.

"Of course not."

"That's my boy. Good check-in, but I'm also here on business. I was just taking some photos of that stuff they got from Zack Staples. Have you looked it over?"

"Not yet."

"Do you have a minute to look?"

Not really. But she wouldn't bug him with it unless there was something going on. He followed her to the conference room, where Zack's loot was artfully displayed on the table, Dawna standing by. He'd read the report but still wasn't prepared to see it in all its pilfered glory. Three fanned-out rows of gift cards were laid above two fanned-out rows of lottery scratch tickets. They framed, on one side, an extra-large Ziploc bag of coins and piles of wrinkled paper currency, sorted by denomination, mostly ones and fives, but twenties too. There was a vinyl wallet, with the cash pulled out enough to see it, as well as a brass money clip with a few twenties folded in it. On the other side of the money was a row of sunglasses and a variety of small items.

"See anything you recognize?" Bernie asked.

"Your vase." Pete picked up a shot glass-sized cobalt-blue glass vase with twists of bright yellow, red, and orange. One of Bernie's sisters had brought it back from a trip to Venice. It was usually on the windowsill in their bedroom.

"Anything else?"

He picked up the money clip, just now seeing the small Philadelphia Police Department emblem. On the back was engraved, "In grateful acknowledgement of twenty years of exemplary service."

"And there's this." Bernie picked up a gift card. It was for Barnes & Noble with $50 written in Sharpie in Bernie's mother's handwriting.

He shook off the rising red mist. "Where's my notebook? It's the size of a steno pad. Blue cover."

"There weren't any notebooks," Dawna said.

He took a deep breath. Met Bernie's eyes, then Dawna's. "I want to talk to that son of a bitch."

"He's already been transferred to Wiscasset," Dawna said.

"Call them and tell them to get him back to Farmington."

"They'll say if we want to talk to him, we have to go to Wiscasset."

"Fine. I'll go to Wiscasset. He was *in our house.*"

"Chief—"

He called up cop mode. "Let Wiscasset know I'll be there tomorrow at eight. I have a meeting with the mayor today I can't miss."

"Now we know who our creeper was," Bernie said. "Funny, it doesn't make me feel any safer. I didn't even notice the vase was missing. He probably just threw your notebook away or something when he realized it wasn't worth money."

"Why would he take it in the first place?" Pete said.

"Zack's got some explaining to do," Dawna said.

Pete's eyes met Dawna's. He knew they were both thinking the same thing. Zack Staples wouldn't branch out into breaking into homes, wouldn't go to Pete's house, struggle down that steep hill from the road, without some incentive.

****

As much as she wanted to dig more into the Zack Staples case, particularly finding out when he'd been in the house and how he got in, Bernie trusted that the police department would be on it. She had other fish to fry.

Glad the newsroom was empty, she sat down at her desk and got out her phone. First fish was her friend Carol.

"Hey, you know Rita Chandler, right? You mentioned she was helping you with that back-pasture sale. I've tried calling her a couple times, but her voicemail is full. I know she's in Cabo—wherever the hell that is—but do you know when she's coming back?"

"Next week. We're meeting her the day after she gets back. Good thing too. Ken Parent has been putting on the pressure. He really wants to buy that parcel, but Vince isn't sure we should sell."

"Speaking of Ken Parent and everything, have you talked to Norm Ouimette recently? I know Vince did some forest management for him last year. I can't reach him, either, but I see that his sculptures are on sale at the Maine store."

"Vince has been trying to get him too. He was supposed to do some more forest management for Norm, but now with the college buying the land, he's not sure what's going on. Norm never said anything. Someone told Vince that Norm's spending the winter off the grid at his parents' old camp up in Coburn Gore. Maybe he's hiding out—that college project isn't popular since it screws over the Passamaquoddy."

"Last time I interviewed him, we talked about his camp," Bernie said. "Not for the story, just that I discovered we have a mutual thing about the Arnold Expedition, and it's up there near Arnold Pond."

"Vince went up there fishing with him once. Great place, but rustic. I think it had an outhouse, no septic. No electricity, either. I'd be surprised if he was spending winter up there."

"You never know," Bernie said. "Normand is pretty self-sufficient."

Bernie made another call, this one to a real estate friend in Portland who'd been in the business for ages and knew everyone.

"I've heard around that your brother was asking about Ryan Grant for you, too," the friend said after Bernie told him what she was after.

"Glad to hear he left a small footprint," Bernie said.

"You know how word gets around." After some hemming and hawing, the friend confirmed that, yes, Ryan Grant had ripped off a female business partner, who also happened to be his soon-to-be-ex wife, and he briefly lost his real estate license. He'd really done it, deserved to lose his license, but had wiggled his way out of it and there was likely no paper trail this many years later.

"Looks like he's up to something similar here," Bernie said. "Possibly, at least. He split with his partner Rita and I've heard she might have something on him."

"I guess a leopard doesn't change its spots," her friend said. "Just be careful. He managed to slip out of the one down here, and if he can do that, who knows what else he's capable of?"

"That's what I'm trying to figure out."

Tired of making calls, Bernie walked over to the post office, where Bev told her she hadn't heard from Normand in a month, she was holding his mail, something he'd requested, but she thought he'd be back by now.

She then went on a long monologue about his land. One story was he'd sold it and left town so he wouldn't have to face the embarrassment of going back on his word, the other was that he'd lost it because he owed back property taxes.

"It's not taxes," Bernie said. "He wasn't on the list in last year's town meeting report, and he'd have to be way behind for that to happen."

Bev agreed. "Neither thing sounds like Normand. If he's up in Coburn Gore, he needs to give someone a call and let us know what's going on."

Bernie stopped by Rita Chandler's and stuck a note in her door asking her to call as soon as she got back. The vague message Rita had left before she went on vacation had started to form a life of its own in Bernie's head.

If she couldn't track down Normand, Rita was the next best bet.

She headed to Normand's land. The college's, actually, she

conceded. She knew he wouldn't be there, but she wanted to get a feel for it, walk around, let her thoughts coalesce.

There were two roads in, the one that wound next to Nakilot Stream and led to his house, and the one at the northwest end that went to the top of the hill, with a view of the quarry. She figured the house one would be more passable with the snow, but as she turned down the private road, she had to stop because it wasn't plowed.

She turned around, backing into the snow and spinning the wheels, then headed toward the other entrance. She knew that would be a bust, too, unplowed and steep, but she'd check anyway.

The back road *was* a bust, but not because of the snow. A shiny new gate had been installed where it forked off from another side road. A generic no trespassing sign, crisp and clean, rather than battered by the weather, was affixed to it. The road beyond had been plowed, but by a small blade, not a large town plow. Just wide enough for a pickup truck to pass through. Tire tracks showed under a thin coating of snow.

She pulled over to the side and turned off the car to think. She could strap on her snowshoes and hike up. It wouldn't be the first time, or even the twentieth, she'd nosed around on land she shouldn't be on in pursuit of a story or to satisfy her curiosity. She couldn't, though. She'd promised Pete that her trespassing days were behind her. His argument had been mostly that it wouldn't be a good look for the police chief's girlfriend to get busted for trespassing. She'd wanted to argue, but didn't. His calm laying out of the facts didn't hide his underlying panic. Obviously, there was more to it.

An ancient pickup truck coming down the other fork of the side road stopped next to her. It was Corliss Gower, the mother of Julie, her Navy SEAL tipster.

"Hi dear, everything all right?"

"Just enjoying some peace and quiet," Bernie said. "I was thinking of going up the hill, but I see there's a gate."

"New owners," Corliss said. She didn't look happy. "The college has been after Norm for the land for years. They got it somehow."

"Have you talked to him recently?"

"Haven't seen him in a couple months. Hope they didn't drop him to the bottom of the quarry or something." She winked and drove off.

Great, something else to worry about. Bernie tried to relax and enjoy the quiet, just like she'd told Corliss she was doing. It *was* peaceful. Nothing but snow and woods. No traffic, even on the main road a little ways behind her. The day was cold, but the earlier gloom and wind had eased up, and the sun was out, warming the inside of the car.

As she watched the massive pines that crowded the road sway in the breeze, the unease about that idiot Zack Staples being in the house, going through their stuff, was a constant hammer. It could've been worse. Zack, who was a familiar Main Street presence, was harmless.

The problem was, she found it hard to believe he had the energy and initiative to break into a house that far out of town. Then there was the fact that no one just walked into Pete's house. The utility room back door stayed locked. So did the slider. The front door was unlocked if one of them was out and the other was home, but when they were both in, that stayed locked too, unless it was summer and it was open. In that case, the screen door stayed locked.

One time, before she'd moved in, they were watching *Dateline*, and Bernie started riffing on one of her peeves—cops always said if there was no sign of forced entry, the victim must've let the killer in.

"Doesn't anyone but me leave their door unlocked when they're home?" Bernie asked.

Pete had fixed her with his cop stare. "No." She got the message.

He also insisted that she lock her car when she was at work, though she forgot to do it half the time. She'd tried harder to remember once the crime spree started, but she wasn't perfect. *Ohhhh.* The pile of Zack's loot included keys. She rooted around in the console. No spare house key on its mini-flashlight keychain.

There was no cell service here, but she texted Pete. He'd get the message when she got into range. "Check the keys in the Zack stuff to see if there's a house key on a key chain with a green mini-flashlight."

She almost apologized for being an idiot, but then figured she could do that in person later.

CHAPTER 30

BERNIE KNEW CELL reception had returned shortly after she turned onto the main road and her phone started buzzing and pinging, a frenzy of texts and voicemails.

She pulled over.

A text and two voicemails from Pete. "Call me." The last voicemail added, "Where the hell are you?" They were all terse, but it was definitely the tersest.

There was a text from Carrie. "Doing chief story. Need guidance."

A voicemail from Dawna. "Call me after you talk to Pete."

One from Sandy that said, "Don't freak out. Everything will be fine." All telling her not to freak out was going to do was make her freak out. He knew that. Which made her freak out even more.

She texted Carrie back. "I'll call when I know more. It'll be ASAP."

She called Pete.

"Where are you?" he asked. His voice was calm but strained.

"Out of range. On a story. What's going on? My phone blew up, and I was all like, 'What the hell happened to Pete?'"

"I'm fine."

"There's evidence to the contrary."

"I got suspended."

"The council can't—"

"Not the council. Grant."

"What happened?"

As Pete gave her a brief rundown, she watched Ken Parent's truck turn onto the side road and pull up to the gate, the maroon lettering across the white cab bright against the backdrop of dark trees and snow. He got out of the truck and unlocked it. If she hadn't been having this conversation, she'd race over there and ask if she could follow him up.

"We can talk more when you get home." Pete took a deep breath. "Soon? I know you can't just leave work—"

"I'm the boss, I do what I want. I have some stuff to wrap up, then I'll be there." There'd been times when she knew he needed her, but she couldn't remember him ever coming right out and asking.

Pete exhaled. "It's okay. Honest."

As they talked, Bernie watched Ken drive through the gate, get out of the truck, close and lock it behind him. She was far enough away she couldn't see his face, but she could tell by the way he looked up that he'd seen her car. It was probably just the effect of the conversation with Pete, but it gave her a chill.

"How much do I tell Carrie?" she asked.

"I can't say anything while it's pending, but Grant showed me a news release he was sending out right after our meeting, so it's out there. The council is going to discuss it at an executive session tomorrow night. I can email her a general statement, that I've done nothing wrong and will fight for my job."

The wind had picked up again and buffeted the car. The only sound besides the rustling trees was a group of crows, circling and cawing off to the west. She was getting cold. She wanted to say something to sustain him until she could get home. She had nothing.

"I'm sorry, Bernie."

"For what?"

"Adding to what's already been a shitstorm of a new year."

"This isn't your fault. It's that asshole Grant. If anything, I'm energized. I might go right over there and punch his smug face."

Pete laughed. "Jesus, don't do that."

"You've done nothing but be a really good police chief and better person. You're the one who doesn't need it."

"Don't pick up any food on the way home, I got some scallops at Walt's. I'll sauté them in some butter and garlic, maybe make that broccoli-cauliflower cheese bake to go with it. What's wrong?"

"Nothing." She snuffled and wiped her nose on her coat sleeve. "That sounds great."

"I was afraid for a minute you didn't like scallops anymore."

"Long day. I'll be home in half an hour."

After she talked to Carrie, she sat in the car for a couple more minutes, getting her head into a place for a safe drive home now that it was getting dark and any snowmelt from the sun had frozen, making the roads slick. She was pissed off, frustrated that every time Pete seemed to be getting better, something kicked him in the head. The fact that through it all he'd told her he was making supper touched her in a way that all the "I love yous" in the world couldn't.

She loved him too. Fiercely. There *was* something she could do to help. She was already doing it. She turned the key, put the car into gear, and skidded on the icy road as she hit the gas pedal.

Fuck you, Ryan Grant. Bernie O'Dea's coming.

✻✻✻✻

Two hours earlier, Pete had sat in front of Ryan Grant's desk, prepared for the worst. He didn't have to wait long.

"I'm suspending you indefinitely," Grant said. No "Hi," no "How ya' doin'" no "How about this weather?"

Grant had insisted Dawna come too. She was told to wait in the outer office. Pete knew then the meeting wasn't going to end well. Still, hearing it out loud was a shock.

"I have the right to have my management representative here."

"He's AWOL, as usual. I'm told he took a day off to go ice fishing."

"On what grounds am I being suspended?"

"What we discussed at last week's council meeting apparently had no effect on you. In the week since, your actions make it seem like you almost want to be fired. You're lucky it's just a suspension, which I'm doing in deference to the council, but you won't be coming back."

"What actions?"

281

"Where do I start?" Grant made a show of searching his memory. "First of all, there was your attack on Sean Speck. Then you tell your staff that you won't consent to *Real Rural Justice* even though you and I never had our final discussion on it. We agreed that we'd talk about it and that it was my call, not yours."

"We didn't agree to that."

"To top it off, the third strike, so to speak, came today. Do you know who Clark Sawyer is?"

"Yes."

Grant stared at him, unblinking. Pete realized that, like a chastened schoolkid, he was supposed to recite what he knew.

"He owns Sturgis Fabricating. He owns a lot of land. He lives in a very large house on a hill overlooking the lake."

"He's also not a guy you want to piss off. He's the father of William Sawyer."

"Who we charged with terrorizing this morning."

"Bingo. Imagine the phone call I got. Clark Sawyer is not only an important citizen of this town, he's also an important businessman. Here you are, overruling the arresting officer to charge him for defending himself against a crazy, drugged-out bitch. Hell, the guy should get a medal for not shooting her on the spot."

"I assume you told him it was police business and I'd be happy to discuss it."

"Do I have to remind you that I'm your boss? Your business is my business. Important citizens like Clark Sawyer, and by default, his family, are given a certain amount of respect."

"The police chief runs the police department. And if by respect you mean a blind eye when they violate the law, those days are over. They have been since I took this position."

"You are a loose cannon, mentally unstable and a danger to the citizens of this town. Case in point, when you told Officer Anderson you were overturning the decision not to charge, your explanation was that men are cars and women are bicycles. What the hell does that even mean?"

If that was Tyler's takeaway from their lengthy discussion, Pete despaired for the kid's future. "Good lord."

"Are you saying that's not what you said?"

"The short version is that I felt we didn't give Ms. Gagnon a fair chance to give her account. I called her this morning and discussed what happened. She hadn't been heard. I explained to Officer Anderson that we have to listen and consider the point of view of the victim, particularly when they don't share the same background or gender. I used a metaphor to illustrate it, that women have to navigate different dangers than men do and may see the world around them differently. As peace officers, we need to recognize those dangers from their perspective."

Grant's face had gone from pink to red to purple as Pete spoke. "I was told you're shoving politically correct bullshit down the department's throat, but I'm surprised you're actually admitting to it. You're saying that women should be treated differently? That girl is a known drug user and hooker, and she was probably high during the whole incident and when you talked to her this morning. Girls like her get off on drama and attention."

Pete had heard that criticism of women since he was a patrol officer, just one more thing he hadn't given a second thought to until recently. He took a deep breath. Let it out. Made sure his tone would be normal before he spoke.

"She was perfectly lucid on the phone, though angry and frustrated, which is understandable. She works nights cleaning houses. We've never charged her with prostitution or even had her on our radar for it. She's been charged twice with drug possession, but not in the past three years. She's working hard and trying to raise a kid."

Grant snorted. "Save the lectures and condescending tone. You may think you're in the driver's seat, but both of us know how unstable you are. I can't just tell the council you're mentally ill, another PC issue. I can't make your shrink give me his notes, but I have inside information that I'm sure you don't want out there, for instance, published in *Franklin On Call*."

"I'm not worried." Grant had to be bluffing. Dawna, Sandy, and Bernie were the only ones who knew just the tip of the iceberg as far as his mental health went. None of them would say a word. "Whatever my mental health challenges, they're not extraordinary. They're being treated, and if I thought I was a danger to this town, or to anyone, I would have resigned."

Grant raised his eyebrows. Gave a knowing smirk. "You're a liar. I know for a fact you think you're a danger to Bernadette. I wonder if she knows?"

He's trying to bait me. "Leave her out of this. You have no idea what you're talking about."

"*You* have no idea. Keep that in mind on your paid time off. I'm going to call that sergeant in here, and you'll relinquish your badge and sidearm. The sheriff will temporarily take authority of the department."

Pete stood up as Dawna came in. Their eyes met.

"It's okay," he said.

"Sergeant, please take his badge and sidearm, then escort him to his vehicle, bring him to his office, allow him to get his personal effects, and make sure he's off town property. He's not allowed on any town property without an express invitation until this is resolved. Report back to me once you're done."

"My gun is at the office," Pete said to Dawna.

"Of course it is," Grant said.

Pete held his badge out to her. She didn't move to take it. Their eyes met again. He nodded. She took it.

****

When they'd walked to town hall earlier, it hadn't occurred to Dawna they'd have to walk back with the news slipping and sliding on the wind around them, into the stores and offices and houses they'd pass. At least Pete seemed okay. Back straight, head up. No dead man walking here. No walk of shame.

"The council will sort it out. He doesn't have a case. He wants to be king, not mayor. He doesn't like that I won't play along," he said, like she was the one who needed support.

"Let's hope."

"Do you ever feel like you've been dropped into some bizarro world, and when you think you finally understand the language and culture, you find you don't have a fucking clue?"

"Grant?"

"Everything. Every fucking thing."

The door of Dunkin' flew open as they passed.

"Chief, got a minute?" It was the assistant manager.

Dawna almost said no—Grant made it clear he didn't want any detours—but Pete smiled and shrugged. "Sure."

Three women, one of them Vanessa, gathered around a table with an open box of a dozen doughnuts and a flower arrangement with a sign sticking out of it with a big happy face and the words "Thanks So Much!"

"I know it's not a lot to thank you with," Vanessa said, coming around the table toward Pete. "But you saved my life. Thank you." She hugged him, then kissed him on the cheek while the assistant manager snapped a photo. The handful of customers applauded.

"Let's get another one with the chief and the staff, with the doughnuts and flowers," the assistant manager said. She handed Dawna her phone. "Will you do the honors?"

Dawna took the phone. The women couldn't know what had just happened a couple doors down. The moment meant a lot to them. She wasn't going to spoil it.

They squeezed together. Vanessa put an arm around Pete and kissed him on the cheek again. Dawna hit the button. Pete's smile was sheepish, his face red.

"Thanks, ladies. I was just doing my job. I know that sounds corny, but that's what it was. Vanessa's the one who deserves all the credit. You were very brave."

"I couldn't have been brave without you there," she said, wiping her eyes. "You're my hero."

"No, I'm ju—" Before Pete could finish the sentence, she enveloped him in a big bear hug. Dawna saw him take a deep breath.

The other women joined in and he disappeared, just the top of his ski cap showing above the bright polo shirts and permed hair.

"Okay, ladies," Dawna said. "We have to get back to the station."

The women gathered the flowers and doughnuts and pressed them on Pete. "Your coffee is free here for the rest of your life," the assistant manager said. "We have that right from the owner."

"I don't know what to say. I'm humbled."

Dawna took the flowers and let Pete carry the doughnuts. She couldn't control what people would remember, or say they did, about his walk from town hall once the news was out, but she sure as hell could make sure it wouldn't include him carrying a giant bouquet of flowers.

"That was nice of them, but I feel like a total fraud," he said once they were walking again.

"You're not. It wasn't your place to tell them you've been suspended. They won't hold it against you when they find out. Or rescind your free coffee for life."

"There's that."

"Brent's the one who told him about charging Sawyer," she said.

"You could hear us?"

"Not you as much, but Grant's pretty loud. I could hear most of his end of the conversation."

"Brent didn't waste any time."

"No, the minute Tyler told him, he was on the phone to Grant. He went into the kitchen to make the call, but you can hear a lot of what goes on in there from my office. He talks to Grant a lot."

"Lots of thin walls in this town."

When they got to Pete's office, he unlocked his top desk drawer, took out his gun, and gave it to her.

"I'm sorry, Chief." There was so much more she wanted to say.

"Don't be. Please. The sheriff likes you. I bet he'll let you call the shots. You're going to do a great job. Don't forget, this is temporary. I'll be back."

He was calm, matter-of-fact. Unhappy, but still the strong,

confident man she'd relied on almost from the minute he walked in the door of their old office in the town hall basement more than two years before. He'd never not had her back. He'd never let her down. It was her turn to return the favor. "You can count on me."

"I know."

She walked him silently out, glad no one was there to see it.

****

Dawna had always thought Ryan Grant was an okay guy. A little full of himself, a little condescending, particularly to a large woman like her who was twenty years his junior. A little too willing to boast about his military service. But she'd seen enough of it to know it came with the territory, and it didn't make him a bad guy. As she sat down in front of his desk after watching Pete drive out of the public safety complex parking lot, she wondered what had changed.

Grant wanted a report on what happened after she and Pete left. She gave him the short, unemotional version, leaving out the coffee shop stop.

Grant then launched into the monologue that she'd expected, ticking off the points on large, manicured fingers. The sheriff was in charge, she was just his Redimere representative.

A crew from *Real Rural Justice* would be in town to shoot some preliminary B-roll by the weekend. She was to welcome them and give them as much access as they needed.

The charges against William Sawyer were being dropped.

Even with the sheriff in charge, he, Ryan Grant, was her boss. If she remembered that, they'd get along fine.

She kept her questions and comments—and there were many—to herself.

"We're both former military," he said. "You a Navy Corpsman, me a Navy SEAL."

He let it hang in the air, she guessed so she could muse on the obvious difference between the two branches.

"We both understand chain of command. I hear you were decorated twice during your service. So was I. We both know what it takes to operate under fire, and that's sticking to the plan and following orders."

She nodded. She knew it wouldn't help to mention that in the actions that had resulted in both her Silver Star and Meritorious Service Medal, she'd thought outside the box and done things that she probably would've been reprimanded for if they hadn't saved lives.

"I know that you're loyal to Novotny," he said. "I respect loyalty, but you don't know the full story. He's dangerous. Don't forget your loyalty is to me now."

It almost killed her, but she nodded.

CHAPTER 31

B ERNIE THOUGHT OF HERSELF as optimistic. She approached each day as a fresh chance for things to work out great. Sometimes that feeling was gone in minutes, sometimes it took longer. Tuesday morning it was gone in seconds. Maybe nanoseconds.

When she woke to the ringing alarm at five-thirty, two hours before sunrise, Pete's side of the bed was empty. In the living room, his flannel pants, long underwear shirt, wool socks, and beach towel were on the pellet stove. The back deck light was on, and she could make out the dark gash in the white ice of the lake, but couldn't see Pete's churning arms, his bobbing head.

"Where's Daddy?" she asked Dubby, panting happily beside her. She didn't have her glasses on. Once she did, she could see the gash in the lake more clearly, but still no Pete.

She opened the slider. "Pete?" Nothing. "PETE!" Still nothing. She ran across the icy deck, slipping in her stocking feet, then into the snow between the deck and lake, noticing, but not caring about, the icy wetness seeping through her socks. The swimming channel, ink-black, was calm. Not even a bubble. *Shit.* Should she dive in? No, better to go out on the ice, around the perimeter, to see if she could see him. Dubby was already doing it, dancing on his cold paws and marking clumps of snow with pee. She stepped onto the ice, her legs trembling. The water in front of her exploded.

Startled, she jumped back, slipping and landing on her butt.

Pete's head popped out of the water.

"Hey," he said, gasping. "What are you doing out here?"

"What the hell are *you* doing?" She got up as he climbed out next to her. She punched his shoulder. "You scared the shit out of me." It was a sob, which pissed her off even more.

"What's going on?" He was genuinely puzzled. "Let's get inside before we freeze to death. Look at you, in your socks in the snow."

She wanted to snap something back, but it would be another sob, so she said nothing.

"I didn't see you," she said as Pete closed the slider behind her and Dubby. He stripped off his swim trunks. "I didn't know where you were."

"I did a lap underwater." He toweled off, then pulled on the warm clothes, a routine he had down to perfection. "I'm sorry I scared you."

"Fucker." She went into the kitchen and poured coffee from the carafe into two mugs that were waiting on the counter. His arms went around her. He hugged her tightly from behind, kissing her neck.

"I really am sorry," he said. "It didn't occur to me that you'd think anything about it."

Of course it didn't. "You are freezing."

"Why do you think I'm hugging you? Trying to warm up." He squeezed her tighter. "My little oven-hot muffin."

"You're going to spill my coffee."

His hug tightened. "My warm little loaf of Italian bread, all plump and crusty on the outside, but warm and soft underneath."

"That's not working." She pulled away but kissed him on the cheek as she did. She was still pissed off, but she wasn't going to start his suspension with a fight. "You'll have to settle for this." She handed him the mug. "I have to get ready for work."

As she got dressed, her phone pinged with a text. It wasn't even six yet. It was from Sal. "*FOC* assholes at it again. Dragging you in."

"I guess there's already something on *Franklin On Call*," Bernie said to Pete. She took her laptop out of her bag and called up the story.

She read it out loud.

Police Chief Suspended, Termination Imminent
Girlfriend's Arson, Murder May Be Linked

By Fergus X. Kelley

REDIMERE — Police Chief Pete Novotny was suspended with pay Monday, a move Mayor Ryan Grant said is a preliminary step toward permanently removing him from the position.

Grant said Novotny's suspension is "the culmination of a long record of malfeasance and incompetence on Novotny's part."

Grant said that there are "serious issues with Novotny's mental health." He said that he will reveal those when the time is right, but first must talk to the Town Council and consult legal counsel. The council will meet tonight at 7 in council chambers and plans to discuss Novotny's suspension in executive session.

The house of Novotny's romantic partner, newspaper editor Bernadette O'Dea, burned in a fatal arson overnight on Dec. 31, which is also under investigation. A body found in the burned house, which state police investigators say was murdered, is likely O'Dea's tenant, Stephanie Woodbury, who rented the house after O'Dea moved in with boyfriend Novotny.

Grant would not comment on whether O'Dea's arson is related to Novotny's issues. "That remains to be seen."

"That stupid headline doesn't even make sense." Bernie said. "It makes it sounds like I was murdered. What the hell is Grant trying to do to you?"

"He can do what he wants to me, but I told him to leave you out of it." Pete went into the bedroom. "It's beyond the pale. I'm going over there."

"You can't," Bernie said, following him. "You're just going to make things worse. You can't get involved or they can fire you. Don't you see? He's trying to bait you."

Pete sat on the bed, his head in his hands.

"Pete."

He looked up. To her relief, his eyes were dry. "You're right. I can't do anything. But Grant's pulling you in, it's just totally—"

"Beyond the pale?" Bernie said. "Not the words I'd use, but yeah. It'll be all cleared up and Grant will end up on the losing end. I'm sure of it."

****

Pete walked in the door at the *Watcher* at six that evening balancing aluminum-foil-covered plates, snow clinging to his ski cap.

"Snowing again," he said, giving her a kiss as she stood up to greet him. "I thought I'd join you, if that's okay, since we've hardly talked."

"Let's go in my office."

"That fella's a keeper, Bernie," Guy called after her.

"What he said." Pete put the plates on her desk. He reached into his coat pocket and pulled out two paper-towel-wrapped sets of silverware. "I made meatloaf, and there's the broccoli-cauliflower casserole from last night. Piece of apple pie for us to split for dessert. There was only one left."

"Tommy ate most of it Sunday," she said.

He took the foil off the plates and set one in front of Bernie, who'd sat down at the desk, then one on his side. "Still warm," he said. "Forgot drinks."

"Check the fridge. I'll have a can of seltzer. Any flavor."

He pulled off his coat and ski cap and gave her a big smile. She was standing close enough to him to feel his body heat radiating through his flannel shirt, smell the combination of that stupid mango-peach-coconut body sugar combined with his normal pine and soap. There was a big heart drawn in the sweet sauce on her meatloaf slice. Something in her snapped. Shattered like a hard covering, and whatever the soft and warm good it was hiding spread through her. She was too tired to figure out a metaphor for it. Definitely *not* a plump loaf of Italian bread, though. Something deeper and stronger.

"What's wrong?" Pete asked as he sat down. He put a can of seltzer next to her plate, then wiped a tear from her cheek with his finger.

"Long day." The feeling hadn't been a bad one, just surprising. "I love you."

"Amazing what a little meatloaf can accomplish."

"That's what you're wearing to the executive session?" she asked.

"I'm not invited. Remember?"

"There are too many things to keep it all straight."

"Even though it's an executive session, so not for public consumption, Gert told me she'd shut down any discussion of you, your house, Stephanie, anything, if it came up."

"Thanks. You'd think he'd have enough with his vendetta about *Real Rural Justice*, and that bullshit about the Sawyer guy, and you being a tree-hugging woman-lover, etcetera etcetera blah blah blah."

"I sound like a real monster."

"A monster for justice," Bernie said.

"I just want to move past this and get back to work."

"Hopefully you won't smell like an overripe remains barrel at a fruit orchard when you do."

"What, the body sugar?"

"Why aren't you using the new jar?"

"Why have two open jars of it? This is fine."

She knew she was obsessing about trivia. It was easier. She took a big mouthful of meatloaf and closed her eyes. She opened them to Pete giving her that look that meant he was going to say something she wasn't going to like.

"What?" she asked.

"I talked to Dawna today. She said you asked her if she knew anything about Brent making some kind of deal with Stephanie."

"I did. At some point. I can't even remember when now."

"I know she promised not to say anything," Pete said. "She tried not to, but I made her."

"It's okay. Events have overtaken that."

"Between us, I have serious concerns about Brent. Where did you hear about the thing with Stephanie?"

"A guy who worked with her at Sturgis. He didn't know any details, just that Dean Davis complained, Brent came over, and that was that. Stephanie agreed to something so she wouldn't be charged."

"It's not like there would've been charges if Davis was just complaining about cars parking in the road or noise or something."

"Pot maybe?" Bernie shrugged. "I don't know what she was really up to and what people have just made up."

"Dawna's going to ask Brent about it," Pete said.

They ate in silence. Pete's eyes stayed on his food. He was thinking. She wondered which thing he was thinking about.

"Speaking of too many things, did I tell you that Stephanie was taking in lodgers?" she said. "One, actually—that guy from work, Joe Walsh. Who knows what the hell she was up to? There seem to be a lot likelier suspects than me. Maybe Brent will be up-front with Dawna and we'll find something out."

"Maybe pigs will fly out of my butt."

Bernie laughed. "Hopefully not before we can get to the pie. I'm too hungry to deal with that kind of crisis."

****

Gert Feeney called Pete after the executive session. "It's not kosher, but I don't give a damn. If Grant won't play fair, there's no sense pussyfooting around and pretending everything's business as usual."

The upshot was that Grant wanted Pete fired. The council favored Pete three-two but didn't take a formal vote because they had to do that in a public session, and they weren't ready. The town's municipal attorney said that since Pete had been appointed under the previous form of government, a case could be made for Grant not having the right to fire him.

"The phrase long, protracted, expensive lawsuit was bandied about," Gert said. "The rest was the usual bullshit."

When he asked if Bernie's arson had come up, Gert said it hadn't.

"Thanks for that," Pete said. "He shouldn't be dragging her into this. It only hurts her, not me as far as my job goes."

Carrie, who'd sat dutifully in the hall as the council raged behind closed doors, texted him about half an hour after he hung up with Gert asking for a comment.

Pete texted back, "While they didn't take a vote, I appreciate the council's continued support. I plan to be back behind my desk soon." It was long for a flip phone, but he wanted Grant and his followers to know he was paying attention.

He texted Bernie saying he'd heard from Gert. He asked for an ETA, but she didn't respond. It was her late day, and if she wasn't answering, she was busy. Probably hadn't even seen the text. He'd developed an anxiety thing around Bernie not being home. He couldn't tell her, of course. He'd been trying to identify triggers, but it wasn't as easy as Benjamin made it sound. He could hear Benjamin's gentle encouragement. "You're blocking, Pete. Ease up. Let the block dissolve. Picture it." It didn't work.

He called Bernie's desk phone. She picked up on the first ring.

"Sorry to bug you. Just wondered if you had an ETA."

"You're not bugging me. What time is it? Oh Jesus, quarter after eleven. Shit."

"Everything okay?"

"No, just a lot to do. Maybe an hour? Don't wait up, okay?"

"I'm reading, so I'll wait. I want to fill you in on the executive session."

"Carrie said they didn't take any action. How did you hear about it?"

"Gert filled me in."

"Wow, rules violation. Good for Gert."

"She said Grant left you out of it."

"That's a relief. Gotta go. See you in a bit."

"Hey, Bernie?"

"Yeah?"

"Drive safely. The snow's pretty slick."

"You got it. I'll text you when I leave."

He didn't feel like going back to his book. It was too late to box or swim. Dubby, who'd rousted himself from sleep in front of the pellet stove when he'd heard Pete say Bernie's name, danced around his legs.

"Want to go out?"

Dubby launched into a jumpy, twirling frenzy.

"I thought so."

The night was quiet. The snow was coming down harder, hard enough that he couldn't see the lake just yards away. He wondered if his suspension meant he wasn't first on the plow schedule anymore. It was a perk he'd balked at when he'd bought his house, not wanting to seem like he was getting special treatment. But the town manager had explained that he was on the emergency list, that they didn't want him blocked in if he had to get somewhere. Pete wondered if Ryan Grant had told public works it wasn't necessary now. Maybe he should call Bernie and tell her that the road wasn't plowed. It was less than six inches, though. She'd laugh. She'd also be annoyed since he'd already told her to drive safely.

Dubby, snow sticking to his fur, ran to the back door. Pete took one last look around. All he saw was snow and the dark shadows of pine trees towering above him. Quiet. Safe.

"Everything's fine," he said to the dog as he opened the door. "She'll be home soon."

CHAPTER 32

I T WAS MIDNIGHT when Bernie locked the back door of the office and made her way down the wooden staircase to the parking lot. Normally this time of year she went out the front door and walked around the building and down the driveway, but the break-in at Pete's had made her paranoid. The fact Zack Staples was safely behind bars didn't make her feel any better. She had no idea what was going on or who to trust. If someone was watching for her to leave, she wanted to at least make it hard for them. She left a dim light on in the back of the office, so anyone going by on Main Street would think maybe she was still there. Who'd be going by on Main Street this time of night and looking at her windows anyway, except for someone who wasn't minding their own damn business? She turned off the motion light over the stairs before she walked out the back door, so she wouldn't signal any lurkers.

The parking lot looked empty, but it was hard to tell with the falling snow and no moon. She adjusted her bag on her shoulder and gripped the railing with one hand. In the other, she held the box Louise Babb had given her with her documents in it. Louise had called that afternoon to ask if she had everything she needed. It was the third time she'd called about it since she'd left the box for Bernie. Bernie had told her she'd take it home tonight and go through it. She tossed the plastic bag Sandy had given her with some stuff from her house in it too, without even checking to see what was in it. She was surprised at her lack of curiosity, but the thought of seeing some piece of crap that was probably made even crappier by the fire depressed her. The box wasn't big, and it wasn't heavy, but it was awkward to carry it with her heavy bag slipping off her shoulder as she made her way down the snow-covered stairs. She adjusted her grip, gazing down through the snow and dark. All was quiet.

The snow kicked by her feet fell silently to the ground under the steps as she descended. Aside from the faint *beep-beep-beep* of a plow backing up somewhere, followed by a metal blade scraping snowy pavement, the night was quiet. The white lump of her car, next to the snow-covered dumpster, was just visible in the dark. The rest of the parking lot was shadows. Nothing moved.

When she got to the bottom, she scanned the backs of the buildings that lined the parking area and the bank of the river. The windows were dark and, she hoped, empty. Even if someone was looking, they'd have trouble seeing anything since she'd turned the light off. She was at her car now, anyway. She was safe from whatever it was she was afraid of. Her car, covered with the snow that had fallen in the eighteen hours she'd been at work, was untouched. The thought of clearing it off made her want to weep with exhaustion.

She slid into the front seat, putting the cardboard box next to her. She turned on the car, cranking the heat and defroster as high as they would go. She'd have to get out and at least clear off enough to ensure she didn't drive into a tree on the way home—one tree vs. car accident in a lifetime was enough—but she'd let the heating system do some of the work for her. As she waited for the heat to take effect, she opened the box. Might as well begin checking so she could tell Louise tomorrow everything was in order. She didn't want to turn the dome light on, so she found the flashlight function on her phone—something she always forgot existed—and unzipped her coat, using it to shield the light. She didn't want to be lit up like a snow globe in the dark night.

Inside, in no particular order, were papers, brochures with the description of the grant requirements, printed-out receipts, bank statements, bids from contractors, printed-out photos of the work she'd had done. Some of it was in manila folders that she stacked on the seat as she took them out. You'd think the town's files would be more organized. It looked like Louise had thrown everything that had anything to do with her grant or the program in general into the box. The thought of going through it with any kind of attention made her brain explode.

When she picked up the folders to put them back into the box, something small and heavier than paper slid out onto the floor.

At the same time, her cellphone rang. Pete.

"Hey, I'm just on my way," she said. "Gotta clear off the car. I'm warming it up first. I was going to text you once I was about to hit the road."

"I would've done it for you when I brought dinner, but it was still snowing pretty hard."

"It's the thought that counts. I'll be home in about fifteen minutes, twenty tops, depending on the road. Sorry I'm so late. You don't have to wait up." As she talked, she fished around under the seat, trying to find what had fallen. Candy wrappers, a crushed Dunkin' cup, two losing scratch tickets. It was hard to feel around down there given the tight space and the constriction of her coat. She pushed the seat back for more room.

"Are you okay? What's going on?"

"I dropped a glove under the seat."

"I'll let you go, then. Be sure to clear the headlights and brake lights, okay? Back window? Don't leave any ice on the windshield."

She wanted to protest, but she didn't have grounds. She'd peered through a lot of frosted-over windshields in her day, hoping that no one was coming from the other direction. "Yep."

"I love you. Drive safe, okay?"

"Yep. Love you too."

She moved off the seat as much as she could to look under it, scanning the floor with the phone flashlight. She saw something glint. It was her spare house key, on its mini-flashlight key chain. One mystery solved. She angled her phone higher. Leaning against the bottom of the console, partially under the seat, was a black checkbook. Was it hers? She was always misplacing them now that she didn't write checks that much.

It wasn't hers. It belonged to Ryan Grant. An account with a large national bank. The nearest branch was in Lewiston, an hour and a half away. It was the kind of checkbook with carbons for each check—she used one herself since it was easier than recording checks in the register. There weren't any blanks, but his name and address were printed on the carbons. It was a personal account, the checks were for utilities, a men's clothing store in Portland, groceries. The dates were mid-2009 into early 2010, so a year old.

What was it doing in her docs box? She should probably return it to him. Sometime. She wasn't in the mood to do him any favors right now, though.

****

Bernie didn't like driving in the snow, so she was glad, given how tired she was, that no one was on the road. It wasn't her own driving she was worried about, it was everyone else's. At least a plow had come through recently, but snow was still falling, and it was cold out, making the road slick.

Her mind kept drifting, not only to the checkbook but to the key under the seat, which meant Zack Staples hadn't used it to enter the house. She was too tired to figure any of it out. She just wanted to get home.

Through town, Main Street was straight, but as she headed east toward the intersection with Pond Road, it twisted along the river, dipping and weaving. Her car slid slightly, but she reminded herself that she had good tires. Pete, ever vigilant, had made sure.

She braced as she approached the steep, long downhill curve where the road left the river behind and angled to Patten Pond. It snapped south at a forty-five-degree angle, with the elbow of the curve right at the entrance to the boat landing at the end of the lake. Careening down the winding hill, knowing that sharp turn was at the bottom, made her nervous even in broad daylight and good weather. She shifted to second as her headlights illuminated the giant yellow signs with black arrows that warned of the curve, still invisible in the falling snow. The car slid sideways as the hill got steep. Even though she knew better, she hit the brakes, and it slid toward the shoulder, a narrow strip that separated the road from a deep ditch and then towering pines. At least it was piled high with plowed snow, a bumper she'd either get stuck in or that would bounce her across to the other side of the road. She pushed the gas gently, letting the car recover, silently thanking her older brother Pat for teaching her how to handle a skid. She scraped along the piled snow, then straightened. She kept her mind on the road ahead, not the slick, steep curve. She tried not to think about the articles she'd put in the paper chronicling accidents here. An eighteen-wheeler that had taken a wrong turn, never should've been on the road, that plunged into the lake in a driving rain, killing the driver and passenger. A car full of high school kids that missed the turn after a homecoming party and did the same. She tried not to write the headline in her imagination about her own demise. Would it be full of irony? The newspaper editor who'd been the recorder of so many fatal accidents at this spot meeting the same fate? She was never good at getting irony into headlines. She hoped Guy would play it straight.

She recalled something else her older brother had told her. If your car ever plunges into water, remember POGO. Pop seat belt, open window, and GO. She considered opening her window, to get that part out of the way, but she didn't want to take a hand off the wheel.

As she neared the bottom, she still couldn't see the curve and its final warning sign or the big blue boat landing entrance sign. She knew they were there, though, at the break in the trees, the lake just yards beyond. The car slid again. Maybe, if it slid through the entrance and across the small cleared area between the entrance and the lake, the ice was thick enough to keep her car from going in. She'd put a story on the page hours earlier in which the Maine Warden Service warned people not to drive on the ice yet. At the time she'd laughed. "You'd never get me out on the ice in a vehicle," she'd said to the room.

"There's some more irony for you," she said now.

She gently touched the brakes even though she knew she should gas it a little. The car fishtailed, a slow one since she'd shifted down to first. She braced again, trying to picture what she'd do as it slid toward the lake.

Then her headlights picked up a glow of dark blue and gold though the snow. A Redimere police cruiser. It looked like the big SUV, not the sedan. It was blocking the entrance. *Thank god.* At least she'd hit that and not end up in the lake.

She took her foot off the brake and turned the wheel. The car skidded around the turn, sliding sideways toward, then past, the cruiser. Its logo flashed just feet away through her peripheral vision.

As her car straightened, blue lights came on.

"You've got to be kidding me."

She pulled over as far as she could into the snowbank at the side of the road. The cruiser pulled up behind her. She couldn't tell in her rearview mirror who the lone driver was. Eventually—they always make you wait—a figure holding a flashlight at shoulder height walked toward the car.

She lowered the window.

Brent looked in. "Please turn the engine off, miss."

She turned it off. She didn't know him as well as the others, but she knew he knew who she was. Still, she wasn't going to play the I'm-your-boss's-girlfriend game. She hoped it was implied.

"Where you headed, miss?"

"Home. I just finished work."

"Do you know why I stopped you?"

"No."

"You were driving erratically. May I see your license, registration, and insurance card?"

No shit, it's twenty degrees out, snowing, and I was coming down a steep, winding hill. "Snowy night, you know?" She gave him what she hoped was a winning smile. With his flashlight shining in her face, all she could make out were dark eyebrows and humorless eyes below a navy-blue ski cap with the Redimere PD logo. She took off her gloves and fumbled in her bag for her wallet. After handing him her license, she easily found the registration and insurance card. Pete had paired them for her in a small vinyl folder since she was always losing or spilling coffee on them.

He studied them way longer than he needed to.

"Can you please step out of the car?"

"Is something wrong?"

"Please step out of the car, Ms. O'Dea."

She didn't want to, but she knew cooperating was the key to getting home. This was obviously the latest salvo in the war on Pete, though she didn't expect it from his own department. If she was a jerk, that'd just make things worse for him.

Brent stepped back as she got out of the car, slipping in her sneakers—she hadn't bothered with boots since she was going to spend all day and night indoors. She grabbed the side of the car to right herself as he watched.

"Have you been drinking, Ms. O'Dea?"

"No. I've been at work for eighteen hours."

"Are you impaired in any way?"

"I'm tired and want to go home to sleep so I can do it all over again in six hours." She felt her cellphone buzz in her pocket. She knew it was Pete. She wondered how Brent would react if she took it out and said, "Home in a few, sweetie, just as soon as I'm done being hassled by one of your officers."

"Please recite the alphabet backward."

"You guys really make people do that?" The blue lights of his cruiser pulsed, making everything around them, including his unsmiling face, throb with an unnatural blue glow. They were making her dizzy.

"Please recite the alphabet backward," he repeated.

"Z. Y." She had to think for a second, doing it forward in her head. "X. W? U? T? No, wait. V. Before the W."

"I believe you're impaired." He aimed the flashlight through the window. "What's in the box?"

"Tax documents."

"I'm going to ask you to proceed to the front of the vehicle so I can conduct a search."

"You don't have my consent."

"I don't need it if I have probable cause."

Okay, buddy. You're hassling the wrong gal. "I don't consent to a search. You don't have probable cause. There is nothing in plain sight, no drugs, paraphernalia, or weapon, that allows you to search without consent. Think I'm impaired? Do a Breathalyzer."

He stood, silent, the light focused on the box.

"No? I didn't think so. I'm going to get in my car and drive home. If you have an issue with that, follow me. You can explain it to my partner, the police chief."

Brent lowered the flashlight and handed back her vinyl folder and license.

"Please drive safely, miss." He walked back to the cruiser.

Bernie got back in the car and put on her seat belt, her hands shaking so much it took a couple tries to click it. *What the fuck was that?* The cruiser's high, bright headlights lit her up, and the blue flashing lights continued to throb. She pulled into the road. She watched in her rearview mirror. When he didn't follow, she drove twenty miles below the speed limit the three miles home.

CHAPTER 33

A S EARLY AS WAS CIVIL, Bernie, with Kermit's blessing, called George Libby. She didn't want to get Sandy in trouble, but she'd taken a look at the stuff from her house, and it wasn't hers.

"There's a BlackBerry and some jewelry," Bernie told Libby. "It was under the bed. I guess it's Stephanie's, though I had no clue she had a BlackBerry. Last I saw, she had a flip phone. Once I saw what the stuff was, I just put it back in the bag. It's kind of sooty, and I don't know what water might have done to the BlackBerry—"

"I'll have a trooper come and get it from you."

"I also found my old flip phone in a drawer in my desk here at work. Under a bunch of stuff."

"We don't need it anymore."

Bernie was surprised, annoyed too, that she'd wasted so much angst on something that no longer mattered. She was also surprised that he didn't give her an earful, but he sounded distracted, almost disinterested.

"Is my house still a crime scene?"

He sighed, that long despairing one that she was used to. "Not much of a house now, is it? We're done. But the insurance company isn't. I don't know if the fire marshal is. You'll have to talk to them."

"If Sandy found that stuff, don't you feel like maybe you should look again?" Even though it went against her best interests, she was curious.

"I don't tell you how to do your job, don't tell me how to do mine."

"Makes sense. But my job is to ask questions even though this is an off-the-record conversation. So, ya know, doing it."

Libby laughed, another surprise. "I have a question for you. Did you know your tenant was renting a room out?"

It startled Bernie. Then she remembered that Dawna had likely passed it on. "I just found out the other day. I had no idea before that."

"Raises some possibilities."

"It does." It hadn't felt to her like Joe Walsh was involved, but Libby was the cop, not her. "Am I off the hook? Or is that trooper going to arrest me when he comes to get that stuff today?"

Libby laughed again. "Remains to be seen, Bernadette. Stay on your toes."

****

By late morning Pete had swum, boxed until he was soaked with sweat and it felt like his arms would fall off, walked the dog the mile up to the road to get the newspaper from its tube, read every story in the *Lewiston Sun-Journal*, cleared the driveway, cleared off the Charger, done the laundry, folded it and put it away, dusted, vacuumed every room, changed the two litter boxes, cleaned the refrigerator, then tried to work on the puzzle. It was no use. He couldn't sit still. He was about to go for another walk when Dawna's Jeep pulled into the dooryard.

"I talked to Brent," she said as she settled in on the couch. "As far as pulling Bernie over last night, he said he didn't recognize her at first and then truly believed she was impaired. He made the point that we were told no one got special treatment. I called bullshit on that. I'm not sure what his motive was. He seemed kind of shifty, but maybe it was just to make a point."

"If it was, he isn't going to be with this department very much longer," Pete said.

"I also asked Brent what was going on with Bernie's tenant. You know, the deal that guy told Bernie about. He told her he'd give her a break if she became a CI."

"We don't do confidential informants. You need a policy for that, a vetting—"

"I told him. He said it was an informal thing since he believed she was selling pot and also had a lot of shady characters around."

"I can't believe a word that guy says."

"On the non-Brent front, the crew from *Real Rural Justice* is arriving Friday to film some preliminary stuff. It's supposedly not for broadcasting, but just for them to get a feel for things. Grant signed the contract with them Monday right after he suspended you. I'm not sure if you were aware of that. If you're back by Friday…" She shrugged.

"I won't be back until at least after the council meets Tuesday. Once I am, I'm shutting that down. I don't care what it takes."

"Good. I don't have any say, since I'm just filling in. Mandy asked if she could opt out, but Grant's making it sound like all members of the department are required to sign the release or we could lose our jobs. I'm going to run it by the town attorney, but he's off for a few days, so we're stuck until then. I'm supposed to meet with the producer, but it's just so they can find out about the logistics of the shifts and things like that."

Pete tried to adjust his focus, dissolve the anger that was building, the frustration of being powerless. How big a mess was Grant going to make before Pete could get back?

"You okay?" Dawna asked.

"Fine."

"Be honest."

"I feel…discombobulated."

"You're just at loose ends. Stressed out about Ryan Grant, the stuff with Bernie. You want to be at work, take care of business, but instead you're just listening to me talk about it."

"Makes sense."

The wind off the lake had picked up, and snow was spitting hard against the picture window and slider.

"Roads are going to be a mess later," Pete said. "Probably should put on someone extra."

"Already have," Dawna said.

****

Bernie called Kermit before she left for home Wednesday evening.

"I'm thinking I'm not going to get arrested for this thing," she told him. "When that trooper picked up that stuff, he barely looked at me. I felt like saying, 'What am I? Chopped liver? Don't you know I'm an arson and murder suspect?' "

"But you didn't say it," Kermit said.

"Of course not. I'm not stupid. Have you heard anything?"

"Turns out no one talked in detail to your neighbor, aside from your reporter. I nailed him down that it was a silver smallish SUV he saw, not a green one. He couldn't even say for sure what the model was, just assumed it was you. I let Libby know. He was grudgingly grateful. Since they've determined the fire was set shortly before it was discovered just around eight, you're *alllmossssssst* off the hook. Libby did posit that you could've borrowed someone else's car as a cover and made a point that your alibi—watching TV with your boyfriend—is still suspect. Especially since said boyfriend is in trouble himself."

"They're idiots. Anyone could've borrowed a car, not just me, or someone with a silver SUV could've used their own. Now that they know she was renting out to people, it's a whole new ball game, which Libby knows. And Pete's not in trouble, at least not for anything he's done wrong. He's the victim of politics or something."

"Even so, think hard about ways to prove that alibi if you can. I know you already have been"—he cut off her yelp of protest—"but keep thinking. You're still the lowest-hanging fruit they have, even with the lodger thrown in. You know how it goes. It's what they can bring to a grand jury to get an indictment, not necessarily what the truth is."

****

Bernie opened the door to the smell of frying onions. "What's for supper?" she asked as she walked to the stove and kissed Pete on the cheek.

"Shepherd's pie, but with ground turkey, since we just had meatloaf."

"Sweet potatoes instead of yellow," she said, looking into a steaming pot. "We're not going on some kind of health food kick, are we? Because this is the absolute wrong time for it."

"I just thought I'd mix things up. How was your day?"

She got a beer out of the fridge and went to the couch. "Oh, you know, status quo. Got a newspaper out. Talked to the cops and my lawyer about my arson and possible murder charges for my tenant's homicide. The usual. You?"

"Kept busy," he said. "Oh, I almost forgot." He went to his coat and took something out of the pocket. He handed her two scratch tickets. "Walt said you usually come in and buy a couple on Friday, but you didn't last week."

Bernie felt her face burn. "Oh. Right."

"What?"

"Isn't this the part where you lecture me on what a waste of money they are and if I just saved six dollars a week and invested it, how rich I'd be? Blah blah blah?"

"Don't you think I would've done that a long time ago if I felt that way?" He went back to the stove.

"I thought I was hiding it. My dirty shameful little secret."

He laughed. "Baby, I'm a trained investigator. How many times do you think I saw those scratch shavings on your clothes, your coat, and in the car before I figured it out?"

"Now I'm even more embarrassed."

"Don't be. Look at the money I spend on beer. I pay extra for cable so I can watch the Celtics and Bruins. Why would I judge you?"

"Why indeed?"

"Look," he said, walking to the couch and standing in front of Bernie. She'd put a newspaper on the coffee table—no shavings here!—and was scratching one of the tickets. "You obviously have an issue. What is it? Authentically?"

"I've rarely gotten a positive reaction for buying scratch tickets."

"I'm not Steve, if that's the problem."

"You're not. Sorry."

"That looks complicated."

"It's the crossword. I like it because it takes, like, ten minutes, so it's more satisfying than just scratching something off in ten seconds. You get eighteen letters. You don't know until you scratch them off what they are. I do one at a time. Then you scratch off the corresponding letters on the crossword. Prize depends on how many words. Three is three dollars, four is five dollars. The top prize is $30,000, which could be a house downpayment or a new car."

"Depends, after taxes."

"Killjoy."

"Looks like you have at least one word."

"I try not to pay attention until I'm done. That way I can enjoy the hope. They give you all the vowels, so I don't worry about those. Usually it's one letter—N or R most of the time—that you need to make the difference. J is useless."

Pete leaned over, arms crossed, studying the ticket. Bernie stopped scratching so he could see. "By the time you get half the letters scratched, you can probably calculate what your odds of winning would be," he said.

"*You* probably could. I can't. Nor do I want to." She went back to scratching.

"Ultimately, the letters don't matter," he said. "It's just a construct. It's either a winning ticket, or it's not. It doesn't matter if you scratch them off or even scratch off the right ones, right?"

Bernie stopped scratching. "Okay, I get it. You just want to sap every ounce of fun out of this for me and destroy my lottery dreams."

Pete laughed. He sat down next to her. "No, I just think it's interesting how it works."

"Sure you do. I won three dollars. Now I can pay you back."

"They're both on me."

"So I'd have to split any big winnings with you? Like if I win $30,000 on the other one?"

"No. They're a gift."

"I guess if you lose your job, it'd come in handy to pay the bills. I'd definitely donate it to the cause, since I'm living here rent-free and you gave me a car and everything."

"Bernie," he said gently. "What's mine is yours. Money isn't a problem, anyway."

"I know." She started scratching the second ticket. "J. Figures. Wasted letter."

He leaned his head against the back of the couch and closed his eyes. Put his hand on her back. "I'm not going to lose my job. I'm confident that Ryan Grant, whatever his issue, isn't going to win."

"Good versus evil," Bernie said. "Even if you did lose your job, there are lots of things you can do. You're smart. You have an Ivy League education, law degree, you're white, attractive, have all your hair, and have a penis. The world is your oyster."

He laughed and rubbed her back.

"I was thinking, too, that you could finally achieve your dream of being on *Jeopardy!*"

"That's not my dream. Maybe your dream for me."

"Actually, my mom's for you. If you don't want to encourage it, why do you two text every night about the Final Jeopardy answer? You're like a couple of teenage girls with a copy of *Tiger Beat*, with all that giddy giggling."

"I don't think I've ever giddily giggled in my life, but I like having that with your mom. You're always welcome to join in, you know."

"Right. Then I could feel even dumber than I already do. On the other hand, I just won another three dollars. Living the dream, baby." She waved the ticket at him. "Just need to double-check. Sometimes I miss a word. We might be five dollars richer, not three."

"You're not dumb. You even beat us a couple of weeks ago. I'm trying to remember."

"Naw, that's not—" She was hunched over the coffee table, running her fingers across the crossword. She turned to Pete.

"What?" he asked.

"I *am* dumb. Dumb as a fucking tree stump."

"Bernie—"

"No. Listen. How did I not remember? Maybe with my house burning down and tenant being killed and all, it slipped my mind."

"What?"

"New Year's Eve!" She reached for her phone and scrolled through her texts. "Jesus, I text a lot. On New Year's Eve, remember? Final Jeopardy. I got the answer and texted you and Mom with it, which proves I was here right before eight."

Pete sat forward and watched her scroll. "I forgot too. Holy shit. The 1912 speech that said the Bull Moose Party comes from the roots of these, people's hard necessities."

"I can't believe you forgot it happened but can quote the clue word for word." She continued to scroll. "Grassroots! Here's the text. 7:57 p.m. I would have to have been watching to send that. I can't watch TV at home and set a fire across town at the same time. Even if Libby tries to say I was watching at my house, Stephanie didn't pay the cable bill and they cut it off in November. Anyway, it's not like someone who's setting a house on fire is going to be like, 'Hey, I can catch Final Jeopardy while I'm pouring the gas.' "

"How did I forget about this?" Pete said.

"Maybe you blocked it out of your mind because I beat you on a Final Jeopardy answer."

"In all fairness, you sent the text faster because it's easier to text on an iPhone, but I sent a text seconds later with the same answer."

"What is 'I have an alibi'?" Bernie grabbed Pete's face and kissed him, hard. "I have an alibi, baby!"

Pete laughed. "Considering they had your phone for two days you'd think they would've checked your activity at the time of the fire."

"It doesn't matter now. I'm calling Kermit. I'm off the hook."

****

By midday Friday, Pete had made a decision. He couldn't just sit around and let things happen to him. Bernie had been right all along about going after Ryan Grant. But it shouldn't be up to her. This was his battle. There had to be something on the guy. The problem was, he was in an iffy position. He was suspended. He couldn't go poking around asking people questions about the guy who'd suspended him.

Most people.

Fifteen minutes later, he was sitting in Sal and Chloe's cluttered kitchen.

"I'm experimenting for the restaurant," Sal said. "How does brisket quesadilla with a horseradish sauce and caramelized onions sound?"

"Great." Pete could feel Chloe's tension buzzing at him from across the table.

"Is this about Rita?" she asked.

It caught Pete off guard. "Rita?"

"Rita Chandler? My boss? She was going to go to the attorney general, but maybe she went to you guys instead? It was right before she went to Cabo. I'm not sure what I can tell you. I don't know a lot about it."

Pete went with it. "I'm not sure what I want to know. Whatever you can tell me about Rita would be great. A lot of odd stuff going on."

"Odd stuff!" Richmond, the toddler, yelled it as he ran in from the other room, a Lego brick clutched in each hand. His bright red hair stuck straight up, stiff with some gooey substance. He stuffed a fist and Lego into his mouth, then stumbled forward.

Chloe, not missing a beat, caught him before he hit the floor. She took the Legos. "You know you're not supposed to play with these."

Richmond began to wail.

This is why we talk to people at the station.

"Sal, could you?" she asked. "And while you're at it, see if you can get more of that Fluff out of his hair."

"Yeah, I guess this can keep a couple minutes." He took the pan off the stove and picked up Richmond, who cried and kicked, his chubby bare legs flailing in the air. "Sounds like it's time for someone's nap." The wails receded up the stairs.

"Sorry about that," Chloe said. "Corrina styled his hair with marshmallow Fluff and we can't seem to get it out. Sal wants more kids, and I'm like, 'Are you nuts? I'm forty-two, and three is enough.' It's not even that they have to be his own biological kids. He just wants a family like he grew up in. I'm like, 'No thanks.' Sorry. What did you want to talk about again?"

"I'm just trying to figure out what's going on with Ryan Grant. I thought since you worked for him, and work for Rita, you may have some thoughts. I'm fishing, to be honest. This is totally off the record. I shouldn't even be doing this." He shrugged. He was at her mercy.

"It's okay, we're family. I really empathize, actually. It makes me mad, because you're a good guy and he's jerking you around. That stuff in that article? I mean, wow. But I don't know much, just, like I said, Rita was going to the AG and I'm pretty sure it had to do with him. I don't know what connection there'd be to you, unless she told your department, and so he's doing some kind of end game or something. I don't know. I'm not good at that stuff."

"Rita hasn't come to us about anything. If Ryan Grant was doing some kind of fishy real estate deal, the AG's office would deal with it, not a department like ours."

"I assume it's a real estate deal, but I don't even know that," Chloe said. "Rita said the less I knew the better. Whatever it was, it pissed her off. She was always kind of pissed at him, even when I first started working for both of them at the agency that's his now. She hated his little side deals."

"Side deals like what?"

"I'm not totally sure. She was professional and didn't say much, and he'd stop talking when I walked in. Of course, he was really nosy about *my* stuff. Like I found out he was asking around about where I was when I had showings or meetings. One time—" Her blush came back. "Okay, I know this is nuts, but I asked Dawna to check my car to see if he'd put a tracker on it. Did she tell you? It was like two years ago."

Pete shook his head. "Before my time, probably."

"He hadn't, but that's how paranoid he made me. Rita split with him last spring, both in the relationship and the business. I stayed with him at first because I have three kids to feed and I knew it would be a pain to leave, because *he's* a pain and I was doing all the shit work, but I finally left at the end of summer when Rita asked if I'd come work for her. I was so happy and relieved. She's awesome. Ryan was making the big money, leaving me to sell the $60,000 houses in the flats or deal with rentals. The no-money stuff. Rita is much more generous."

"Whatever she was bringing to the AG, if she stopped working with Ryan last spring, what would it have to do with him?"

"No, it was recent. I'm really sorry, I just don't know." She *did* look sorry. "She said the less I know, the better. Whatever it was, someone came to her with it. Someone Ryan had ripped off, I think. The person wanted Rita's advice."

"Could it have been Normand Ouimette?"

"Possibly. I know Bernie's wondering that, too. But I honestly don't know. I don't want to speculate and send you guys off on the wrong track."

"But Rita definitely was going to the AG about something."

"Definitely. I thought she was going to before she left for Cabo. She said she had everything she needed. She left the day before New Year's Eve, so I'm not sure if she got to it. You know how that week between Christmas and New Year's is. Everything is all topsy-turvy."

"When's she coming back?"

"A week from Monday. The 24th?"

"Have you talked to her at all since she left?"

"No. She was very clear. She needed a break. She said she wasn't going to look at email or answer her phone or anything. She said there wasn't anything that couldn't wait until she got back. Except that thing she was reporting to the AG's office. She definitely said that couldn't wait. Maybe she did report it. We don't know she didn't, right?"

CHAPTER 34

THE WHEELS OF BERNIE'S car churned ineffectively despite the ultra-expensive snow tires Pete insisted on. She'd tried to reverse up the steep hill once she saw her progress was blocked by snow, but the clutch slipped, and she had to drift back down, the smell of burning clutch filling the car. She tried to turn around, but there wasn't room. Now she was stuck.

Hours before, when she'd left Redimere, her plan had seemed so simple. She'd drive up to Coburn Gore and find Normand Ouimette. Easy-peasy. She didn't know exactly where his camp was, but it couldn't be hard to find. Coburn Gore wasn't even a town. It was barely a thought, a wilderness of woods where Route 27 crossed into Quebec. It had a small border station, a gas station and store, and a network of tote roads tangling around in the woods. When she'd interviewed Normand the previous fall—a freewheeling, lengthy conversation—they'd talked a lot about his camp. It was off La Croix, a gated road, the last turn before the border. Bernie knew she'd be able to get in, because Normand had groused that the gate, put there after 9/11 for border security, was always open because of the camps and logging operations, even though everyone who had property beyond it was supposed to have a key.

There was a big storm coming, but it wasn't supposed to do much more than spit flakes until early morning, so that wouldn't be a problem either. Bernie had batted away that nip of apprehension as she drove north, the one she always promised herself that she'd listen to. Of course, just like all those other times, she didn't keep that promise. She had to find Normand, now more than ever. She'd driven up here to do it. The opportunities, especially this time of year, were few. She didn't know when she'd get another chance.

She didn't bother with the GPS on her iPhone. It wouldn't work past Carrabassett Valley. That was fine. There was no substitute for a map and using your head. Pete always said it. She always agreed.

She found La Croix easily in her *Maine Atlas & Gazetteer*. The gate had been open, the road plowed, though with about a six-inch covering of snow rutted with tire tracks. It went along Horseshoe Stream. Normand's camp—he'd showed her on a map—was off a tote road past where the stream and road parted company. She remembered thinking at the time, all those months ago, how easy it would be to get there. *Easy-peasy!* She thought the same thing as she'd cruised up Route 27. She'd be home before supper.

She'd made a deal with herself just in case it wasn't that easy. She had a time limit. If she didn't find the camp by then, she'd go home.

The time limit passed long before she got stuck. Long before she drove deeper into the woods, past where the last set of truck tire tracks turned into a clearing full of giant piles of felled trees. The tracks disappeared, but she kept driving. The thick tree cover kept the snow on the road from being too deep for the car. She'd gone down half a dozen possibilities, gotten stuck, gotten unstuck. Turned around when the road ended at trees or the snow got too deep. She knew Normand Ouimette would be down the next road. She couldn't give up now.

Now, hours after she left home, it was too late to regret not listening to that little voice that told her to err on the side of caution. She'd just have to remember next time.

The pre-storm darkness had become night-falling darkness as she rocked the car from reverse to first gear and back, trying to get unstuck. She tried to ignore the burning clutch smell, the grinding noise it made when she tried to reverse.

Once she got unstuck, she'd drive back to Route 27 and ask at the store if they knew Normand. They'd have to. It was the only store for miles. She should've done that to start with. Once she was out of here. She didn't even know where "here" was. There were no landmarks, only giant old-growth woods and snow. She *was* going to get out. She wasn't going to be one of those people who froze to death in their car after eating year-old ketchup packets to stay alive. Or worse, died of exposure foolishly hiking out for help.

Before she'd become stuck at the bottom of this steep grade, she'd driven down a wide clearing that had less snow than some of the roads she'd been on, going east by her assessment. She checked the map for anything that seemed like it might be it, but there was nothing, of course.

She'd used the compass app on her phone earlier, but the battery died. Likely because of the lack of service and all the roaming it was doing. She was hitting all the stupidity high points. When Pete lectured her—and he would—she'd deserve it. She almost longed for it at this point. It would mean she'd made it home.

She put the car in neutral and put on the parking brake. She kept the engine running, though part of her was wondering if she should conserve gas. She had almost a full tank. She'd worry about it later. It was too cold out. She'd want a warm car to get back into after foundering around in the snow.

The snow was deeper than she'd expected. It was tight against both sides of the car and in front, though not that deep on the road she'd been on—if that was what it was. She struggled through thigh-deep snow, opened the back hatch, and pulled out the snow shovel. She usually had some pieces of cardboard to put under the tires if she got stuck in a slippery spot, but Pete had put them in the recycling. He'd been getting antsy about how cluttered the car was. She wanted to tell him not to mess with her system, but didn't want to rock the boat. *What the hell had she been thinking?*

She tried to dig the snow out from behind the tires with the snow shovel, but it was too packed in and frozen. She got the large garden shovel that she also kept in the car for times just like this. Well, not exactly like this. She began chipping at the snow. It was slow progress, and tiring. Her gloves—nice, thick, padded Gore-Tex—were soaking wet. So were her jeans. There was snow in her boots. It had also fallen from the trees onto her neck and into her coat. She'd left her hat in the car but didn't want to plow back through the snow to get it. She tried to clear the snow out from under the car's carriage and slipped, landing flat on her back. She rolled over and the cold stung her bare skin where her coat rode up. It burned. *Don't cry, you'll only make it worse.*

She got up and leaned against the car. She had to keep her wits about her. Figure out what to do. "Another fine mess you've gotten us into," she said. No one laughed.

An engine rumbled somewhere in the distance. She'd have to remember to put emergency flares on her list of things to put in the car. She scrambled through the snow back into the car and leaned on the horn, flashed the brights on and off. Even though she was facing dense woods, maybe there'd be a reflection. She stopped honking to listen. The engine was louder. Bright light reflected on the trees in front of her. She got out of the car to watch a set of big, bright headlights bump their way toward her. She almost wept with relief. As the headlights approached, blinding her, she smiled and waved. *Hi! Nice to see you out here!* It wasn't until they stopped, feet away from the back of the car, that she panicked. No one got out. Here she was, in the woods, miles from any other person, standing in thigh-deep snow. There they were, behind those bright headlights.

Waiting.

****

Pete called Bernie, but it went to voicemail. She'd said she had to go out of town on a work-related thing but she'd be back by late afternoon. It was still early, but it was getting dark. The wind had picked up, and light snow was falling on and off, the coming storm percolating.

"Come on, Dubby, let's go outside." The dog had been pacing, occasionally whining. Very out of character.

Dubby took off up the road the second he opened the door. Pete

319

called him and whistled, but the dog hurtled forward in a blur of white and brown fluff. Pete cursed himself for not putting the leash on, but Dubby was usually good about sticking close, then letting him do it when they got up to the main road.

Pete made his way up Loon Lane quicker than he'd been able to since before he hurt his leg. The swimming was helping. But he still wasn't quick enough to keep up with the dog. When he got to the top, where Loon Lane met Pond Road, Dubby was sitting next to the row of mailboxes, looking north, panting.

"What's that all about, boy?" He got the mail, then clicked the leash on the dog. Dubby looked up at him with large, questioning eyes. "Don't worry, Mommy will be home soon."

It took a couple of tugs, but Dubby finally got up.

"Think Mommy wants pizza for supper?" Pete asked the dog, who was marching purposefully ahead of him, pulling at the leash as they neared the house. When he said *Mommy*, Dub's ears went up. "I think she does. Maybe Walt will have a nice bone for you, since you're being such a good boy."

In the house, Dubby sat and looked expectantly at Pete.

"I don't have the bone yet."

He tried Bernie again. Right to voicemail. "I'm going to pick up a pizza, okay? So don't stop for anything. Dubby misses you." He paused. "So do I. Hurry home, okay? The storm's not supposed to be here until tomorrow, but it's getting ugly out. I love you."

He knew it was PTSD. He and Benjamin had talked about it the day before, how Pete had had a panic attack waiting for Bernie to get home Tuesday night.

"It's not a premonition," Benjamin had admonished, his big sad eyes holding Pete's, trying to make sure he understood. "It's anxiety."

Pete took a deep breath. "She's okay," he told Dubby, who'd stretched out in front of the pellet stove but was watching Pete, snout on his paws. "She'll be home soon."

CHAPTER 35

B ERNIE TRIED TO GET comfortable on the hard plastic chair, where it seemed she'd been sitting for hours. It didn't help that the room smelled like her Catholic elementary school—whatever that cleaning fluid was they used, laced with judgment and fear. She burned with humiliation. Getting stuck in the snow was bad enough. Finding that the headlights belonged to a giant tanklike SUV driven by two members of the Royal Canadian Mounted Police was at first confusing. Then mortifying.

She somehow, in the deep snow and woods, had crossed the border. The Mounties were polite but not amused.

One of them drove her car, which they extricated with ease, and she rode in the back of the SUV to the customs station at Coburn Gore, where the equally unamused agent called the Border Patrol. Then she'd had to explain, for the third time, to an unhappy Border Patrol officer, when he finally arrived, what she'd been doing and how she'd had no clue she'd crossed the border. It didn't get more convincing with the telling, apparently.

"Do I look like a drug runner? Human trafficker? Terrorist?" she asked him.

"You'd be surprised."

As he looked at her address, he asked if she knew the Redimere police chief. Knew him? She sure did! In the biblical sense. Which she was smart enough not to say.

"Can you call him? He'll vouch for me."

The Border Patrol officer went to an inner office to make the call. She could hear his voice, but couldn't hear what he was saying in a conversation that lasted way too long.

"Guess this is your lucky night," he said when he returned. "He not only vouched for you, he's coming to get you."

"Why can't I just leave?"

"We're confiscating your car."

"Confiscating?"

"Protocol. You broke the law. Count your blessings. You could be on your way to a federal prison cell right now. You owe your boyfriend a big favor."

"I broke the law in *Canada*. They were nice enough to bring me back across the border instead of sticking me in some Canadian gulag. I don't get why you guys care."

He rolled his eyes and went back into his office.

As Bernie waited for Pete, nothing to do but watch the minute hand on the clock slowly make its way around the large white face and black numbers, she reflected on what an idiot she was. Not for the first time either. She could imagine how he was going to react. She'd almost rather walk the sixty miles home.

Traffic through the crossing was slow. Just an occasional trucker coming south out of Quebec who the customs guy—an older man, slightly nicer than the border officer—chatted with in rapid-fire French. Bernie was awful at French in school. Still, she tried to imagine the conversations.

"Who's that loser lady sitting over there in the chair?"

"Oh, just some idiot who crossed the border, says it was an accident, got stuck in the snow, and had to be hauled in by Mounties."

"Sacre bleu!"

The guy's badge said Customs Officer Gagne, but he'd told her to call him Roland, had given her a coffee and a packet of those vending machine peanut butter crackers that she'd never liked. The coffee was tepid and tasted like plastic. The crackers were stale and coated her mouth with a residue that she couldn't get rid of. All part of her penance.

It was almost eleven when Pete walked in, shaking snow out of his hair. She stood up, waited to gauge his mood before speaking.

If he wasn't so gray and pale-looking under the fluorescent lights, he could've been one of the truckers in his open parka and jeans, boots glazed with salt and sand. No hat or gloves.

"You okay?" he asked. He seemed neutral. Didn't hug her, but she was just as glad. She didn't want to be any more on display for the two strangers than she already was.

"Yeah. You know." She shrugged. What could she say?

The border agent came out of the office with a big smile. "Pete, how ya doing?"

"Dennis. Good to see you."

They shook hands. All very manly.

"Why don't you come in here?"

Neither looked at Bernie as they went into the office. Whatever. If being treated like an idiot was more penance, she'd take it. As long as Pete got her out of here, it was fine.

She couldn't hear what they were saying. She could hear the low rumble of Pete's voice, but mostly what she heard was the other guy's voice. Dennis. There was a burst of laughter from both of them. She felt a stab of betrayal. *Whatever it takes. You have no right to anything.*

After about fifteen minutes, they came out. Dennis had his hand on Pete's back, as though they'd just shared a deep, but manly, conversation. They shook hands.

"Thanks," Pete said. "Again, I appreciate it."

"No problem, Pete. Happy to help."

Pete turned to Bernie. "All set?"

"Stay out of trouble, miss," Dennis said, and not in a friendly way.

Pete had been there twenty minutes, tops, but the car was coated with snow. She hadn't realized how hard it had started coming down.

"Thanks," she said as she got in.

"I had to call in a favor to keep you from spending the night in their lockup in Rangeley." He turned on the car. "Should be warm in here in a minute. Just have to clear it off."

As he meticulously cleared the windows, the headlights, the taillights, she watched his face, pale, expressionless. She was tired. Hungry. Her meds had worn off hours ago. She was stricken with that familiar feeling that she'd totally fucked up and he was going to hate her for it.

As he pulled onto slick Route 27, fat wet snowflakes almost immediately covered the windshield. He turned the wipers on.

"Sorry. I know you're mad."

"I'm not mad."

She glanced sideways. His eyes were on the road, his gloved hands on the steering wheel. She'd always admired the way he could drive in a storm as casually as if it were a perfect sunny day. Tonight, with the wind whipping the Charger and snow piling on the windshield between every swipe, it was no different. Unless she looked closely.

"You have that strained, temple-throbbing mad look about you."

"I'm not mad," he repeated, this time gently. "I'm just..." He paused. "Exasperated. I wish you wouldn't do things like this."

"I'm not sure what 'things like this' means, since this is a first for me. It certainly wasn't on purpose."

"Would it have killed you to let me know where you were going?"

"It didn't occur to me. I thought I'd be home before supper. I was just doing my job. It's not like I have to check in."

"That's not the way it turned out, though, is it? Getting lost in the middle of nowhere. The car getting stuck. Illegally crossing the fucking border. What the hell were you thinking?" His voice rose with each sentence.

"I wasn't thinking any of that or it wouldn't have happened." His I'm-not-mad phase had been predictably short.

"Jesus, Bernie."

"I appreciate you coming to bail me out, I really do. But I don't need this paternalistic bullshit."

"It's not paternalistic." She could tell that the anger she knew, *just knew*, was under the surface was boiling up. "I just wish you'd think."

"It *is* paternalistic. You sound like my dad or something. Getting *exasperated*. That means I'm doing something you don't find reasonable and you're frustrated about it, right? I'm not doing something the way you would do it. Or you want me to do it. *Because I don't think*. Like I'm some kind of inferior being. Sounds like paternalism to me."

"It's not that I think you're inferior. It's that here I am, driving through a snowstorm to pick you up and having to call in a favor to keep them from hauling you to spend the night in a cell. I think I have the right, don't you?"

"As I said, I appreciate it. I needed help. I don't deny that. My issue is with the fact that your reaction is that I'm some kind of naughty child who won't behave when I was doing my fucking job."

When he didn't say anything, she continued. "I don't tell you how to do your job. You strap a gun to your belt every day and walk out the door into god knows what. I know Redimere isn't a hotbed of crime, but every fucking person out there has a gun, half of them are on drugs, and the other half are nuts, and the other half will just shoot at anything for the hell of it." Her voice was rising into that pre-cry territory, but there was nothing she could do about it. "I watched through that window as you talked a guy with a knife down, expecting any minute he was going to go nuts on you."

"But he didn't. And that's three halves." She saw him in her peripheral vision turn to her. She caught a smile. He squeezed her thigh. "Half of the people in Redimere? You had three halves."

She kept her eyes on the driving snow out her window as the car climbed up the narrow curves, with the long drop down to Chain of Ponds below. She knew it was there, right out her window, though she couldn't see it.

"My job is different than yours," he said. "With yours, there's the expectation that you're safe. You're not putting yourself in harm's way. Cops, that's what we do. You know that."

The car slid a little toward the guardrail, but Pete righted it without any reaction or change to his expression.

"It's not just your job. Forget your job. I don't tell you not to go hiking by yourself, despite the fact you almost died doing it. I didn't get mad—didn't get *exasperated*—when you and Sandy dug that channel of death in the lake even though I know that less than a year ago you went out swimming with the intention of not coming back. You didn't check with me or ask how I felt about the ice swimming. You just did it. Whatever my feelings are, I didn't tell you not to, because I know I don't have the right."

Pete didn't say anything, his face a white mask, focused on the road.

She knew she should shut up, but she couldn't. "I have that expectation, too, that my job is not dangerous, except of course for the real threat of journalism-induced obesity, high blood pressure, and bad eyes, but sometimes shit happens. You have the right to feel however you feel about it. I'm not comparing jobs or feelings. My point is that every time I turn around, I have some guy—whether it's you or Sandy or Tommy or two twelve-year-old Canadian Mounties or your Border Guard buddy Dennis or whoever—lecturing me like I'm a little kid. If I were a guy, no one would be doing that. You said that you've come to understand more about me and how I do my job. I guess that only goes so far."

"This is different."

Was he even listening? She took off her glasses and wiped her eyes on her sleeve. "The difference is, in your job and life in general, you have the expectation you can do what you want despite how I feel. But I can't expect the same in return."

"I care about how you feel about what I do."

"I know you do. But you still do what you want, right? No matter how I feel. It doesn't occur to you not to. Yet I'm expected to take your feelings and opinions about how I should behave and act into account and adjust my life appropriately. This isn't an attack on you. It's been true of every guy I'm related to, every guy I've worked for, every guy I've ever dated."

Bernie was exhausted. She'd emptied her tank. She leaned her head on the window, watching the snow rocket by, any view of trees or mountains obliterated. They rode in silence, the wipers whapping, the swish of tires on the snow-covered road, the hiss of the heater the only sounds.

He finally let out a long breath. "I guess my issue is that I don't get why you always have to do everything the hard way."

"Okay. Now I see what the problem is." Her voice cracked.

"What?"

She could feel his eyes on her, but hers stayed on the window. She felt defeated. Sadder than she'd felt in a long time. "You think I see more than one way."

****

It was long after midnight by the time they got home. Bernie was exhausted and dispirited. Loon Lane hadn't been plowed, and Pete, who she knew took pride in never showing driving stress, swore as he maneuvered the mile down to the house.

"Guess being suspended means I've lost my plow privileges." His first words in half an hour.

"Assholes," Bernie said. She felt bad about her rant, though she didn't regret it. It was more that she knew even as she was ranting that there was no point. All it would do was add to his anxiety, make him feel like he couldn't win with her. Maybe he couldn't. She was too tired to know.

Dubby charged when she walked in the door, dancing circles around her and yipping as she took off her boots and coat. "What's gotten into you?" She kissed his head, then gave him a tummy rub when he rolled over.

A pizza box was on the counter, top open, an untouched pizza inside. It was her favorite, pineapple and bacon, which Pete had some kind of philosophical prejudice against. Yet he'd bought one for their supper.

"I can heat that up," he said.

"I'm not hungry." She let Dubby out the slider. "I'm pooped. I'm just going to bed."

She changed into an oversized long-sleeved T-shirt and crawled under the covers.

"I'll put it in the fridge for tomorrow," Pete said from the kitchen. As though it were just another night. As though everything were normal. "We're probably going to lose power tomorrow if this storm is as bad as they say. At least it'll be a chance to see how the generator works."

"Great."

"I told Sandy I'd help set up the warming shelter in the morning. I don't care if I'm suspended, they need the help. I'll have him pick me up so you won't be left without a car. Though it'll probably be too bad out for you to go anywhere. Still, you shouldn't be stuck down here if you need one."

She listened as he did the dishes. He said something softly that she didn't catch.

"What?" She'd been half asleep.

"Sorry. Talking to the cats."

She listened as he brushed his teeth—exactly two minutes, just like any other night. The living room light went out. He got undressed in the dark, trying to do it quietly. Folded his clothes and put them away in the dark. He never tossed them on a chair like she did. He climbed into bed, curled up next to her. As always. Rested his bad leg on her thigh, put his arm around her, and pulled her tight.

"I love you," he whispered. He pushed her hair away and kissed her behind her ear.

"Me too," she mumbled. She did. So much. So why did she feel such despair? Normally she'd tell herself she'd feel better in the morning. Normally she did. Tonight felt different. She listened to him breathe, steady and soft, already asleep. She stared at the window, the snow a moving white curtain blown against it by the wind.

****

Bernie woke to the sound of Pete moving around the house. It was still dark. She fumbled on the side table for her glasses, and the red blur of the clock numbers formed into 5:43. *Ugh.* She pulled the covers over her head. A few minutes later the bed sagged next to her.

"I know you're awake under there."

"Oh yeah? How?"

"I'm a trained detective." He pulled the blankets down so he could see her face, leaned down, and gave her a kiss. "Good morning."

He was dressed in heavy lined Carhartt pants and his police department sweatshirt.

"Why are you up and dressed so early?" It was Saturday, a day they usually slept late, by Pete's definition—sometimes as late as seven thirty!—snuggling and enjoying not having to go to work.

"Sandy's going to be here in a couple minutes. We're going to check the people on the Neighbors and Friends List," he said. "You know, the elderly, disabled—"

"I did a story on it. Several."

"Then we're going to set up the warming center at the school gym." His hand was still on her cheek, which he'd cupped when he kissed her, his fingers drawing gentle lines along her cheekbone as he gazed out the window. He had more to say. She hoped he kept it to himself. It was too early to deal.

"Is that okay, with you being suspended?"

"I don't give a shit. As far as Ryan Grant is concerned, I'm a community volunteer who's helping out. If he doesn't like it, he can shove it up his clammy white ass."

"Whoa, did you turn into me overnight? Is this some kind of *Freaky Friday* thing where we've exchanged bodies?" She was more awake but still not ready to discuss last night. If she could string this out long enough, he'd have to leave and she'd be off the hook. She sat up against the headboard.

Pete laughed. "Remember, you can use my car if you need to. Though it's already pretty bad out. You probably won't want to."

Oh, right. Her car. "I appreciate you trusting me with the Charger even though we both know that there's no way I'm taking your baby out into a blizzard, so it's a win-win for you."

He laughed again, but it faded fast. His green eyes locked on her with that intensity that she knew all too well. "Look. I want to say something."

She tried to generate an eager-to-hear-it expression, though she was cringing with shame inside.

"I know it sounds like bullshit, but I *am* trying. I honestly am."

Not what she expected. "I know." His eyes held hers. She felt the sting of guilt. How hard was *she* trying?

He let out a long breath that she hadn't noticed he was holding.

"It's like learning a new language," he said. "One I feel like I should already know."

"At least you're good with languages."

"Yeah." He squeezed her hand. "I don't mean to make things so hard for you. But look, last night…"

Here it comes. There's always a but.

"I know it's not fair, but I have a big favor to ask."

"Okay."

He took another deep breath. "Until I get there, please indulge my fears."

She had no clue what he meant, but she knew what he needed to hear. "I can do that. I want to."

"Thanks." He kissed her again, this time long and slow. He tasted like toothpaste and coffee. Underneath was the faint smell of mango-peach-coconut. Her heart lurched. She grabbed his arms and pulled him in closer.

"I love you," she said, when the kiss ended.

There was a knock at the door.

"Gotta go." He gave her a quick, light kiss and stood up. "If the power goes out, the generator should go right on. Turn off any lights you're not using. It's supposed to be enough for the fridge and everything else, but I don't want to take chances. I'll give you a call when I can to see how you're doing."

"Probably going to sleep a little more."

She pulled the covers back over her head. She listened as he opened the door. He and Sandy talked quietly, but she could hear snippets, the word *she* seemed prominent. Then, a burst of laughter, reminding her of her humiliating wait as Pete and Dennis talked about her while she sat in that hard plastic chair. *Et tu, Sandy?* The door shut and she was alone. She burrowed further under the blankets and quilt.

When she finally got up, it was lighter out, but it was a gray, shadowed light. Wind and snow battered the house. She looked out the window, but all she saw was a whirlwind of white. No lake, no trees. The cats had been draped over and around her as she slept, and now they twisted through her legs, tripping her up as she walked toward the kitchen.

"Didn't Daddy feed you?" When, she wondered, had she and Pete started referring to each other as Mommy and Daddy to the pets? She was glad her brothers hadn't picked up on it. Dubby snored in front of the fire, not acknowledging her. Good. The thought of opening the door for him exhausted her.

The thermal carafe was on the counter, heavy with coffee when she picked it up. It was next to a plate covered with tinfoil. She lifted the foil to see three pancakes, chocolate-chip by the look of them, and three sausages. There was a note from Pete in his neat block printing: "If these are cold by the time you get up, no more than two minutes in the microwave should do it. I love you." He'd drawn a happy face in a heart. "Boy, Daddy is laying it on thick this morning," she said to the cats as she opened a can of cat food. "Mommy does not deserve it."

She weirdly didn't feel like eating. She felt sluggish and heavy. In the bathroom, she took her temperature with the digital thermometer that she'd bought the previous summer, when Pete was in such danger of infections after his accident. She was normal. "Not sick," she told the cats, who were grooming themselves in post-breakfast ecstasy.

She went to the desk, where her phone waited. She almost wished she hadn't plugged it in to charge the night before. She didn't feel like dealing with whatever might be on it. She turned on the notifications and it came to life, lighting up, buzzing, and dinging like some crazy carnival game. Twenty-three texts, twelve voicemails. Her first thought was someone must've died. But of course, it wasn't that. It had been all about her, out of touch and oblivious. They were all from the night before, about a third of them from Pete, asking where she was, his tone getting more desperate with each one. The others were from people he'd apparently called looking for her.

A voicemail from Tommy summed them up. "For chrissake, let Pete know where you are. He's bugging the shit out of me."

There were several voicemails from Sandy, the last around eight-thirty. "Pete's having a serious panic attack. I'm going over even though he doesn't want me to. Please, just check in with him, okay?"

She already felt shitty about being so bitchy after he'd driven through the snowy night to get her after yet another one of her stupid epic fails. Now she felt something deeper. Painful. Beyond guilt. The way she'd feel if she'd physically slapped him across the face.

She scrolled through texts as she went back into the bathroom with her clothes from the day before. Her jeans and shirt weren't that dirty, but she could smell her fear and stupidity, the plastic chair and stale crackers and fluorescent lights. The polite anger of the Mounties. The condescending annoyance of Dennis. The judgy sympathy of Roland. Her phone slipped out of her fingers into the hamper, down the side past Pete's wet towels from his morning shower. As she dug to get it, she smelled vomit. She pulled out a towel at the bottom that was sticky with it. The only times she'd ever seen (or, rather, heard) Pete throw up were few, after particularly bad nightmares or panic attacks.

Indulge my fears. The stab grew more painful. *Please.* She replayed the night before, frame by frame, looking for any indication that he hadn't just been mad, or exasperated, or whatever reaction he usually had to her stupidity. He'd been pale. Quiet. But totally in control.

What the hell is wrong with me? The guilt and remorse nearly doubled her over. She'd been planning to eat even though she wasn't hungry. Check in with Carrie to plan storm coverage. Do some work on the laptop. But she felt so exhausted she could barely drag herself back to bed. She pulled the covers over her head. She slept so soundly that two hours later, she didn't register the ding and pop, then dark silence as the power went out.

CHAPTER 36

"BERNADETTE, WAKE UP." Bernie thought she was dreaming. It was dark, she couldn't see. Ryan Grant was telling her to wake up. "Bernadette, wake up."

It wasn't a dream. She emerged from under the covers to see Grant sitting feet away, in her reading chair. She screamed.

"I'll wait until you recover," he said. She couldn't see his expression in the dim light filtering through the window, with the storm raging behind him. She reached for her glasses.

"What the hell are you doing?" She sat up and pulled the blankets up to her chest despite the fact that she was wearing Pete's old 76ers hoodie over her long underwear top. The violation went way beyond Ryan Grant seeing her in her pajamas. She looked at the side table for her phone, but it wasn't there. "I'm calling Pete," she said anyway.

"Why don't you hold off until you hear what I have to say?"

Bernie couldn't understand why he was acting as though this was a normal encounter. She considered calling his bluff, getting out of bed and marching into the living area to find her phone, calling Pete, or just continuing on until she got outside, getting in the car and driving off. But Ryan Grant was a big man, all chest and shoulders and neck. She was soft as an oven-hot muffin, as Pete sometimes told her. He meant it as a compliment, but right now it felt like an indictment. Her only option was to see how it played out. Call it by ear.

"What do you want?"

"First, I suspect you have something that belongs to me. That's why I originally came here. I didn't think anyone was home."

"So you broke in? If you think I have something of yours, why not just ask?" Dubby jumped up on her bed as she talked, rolling over on his back for a tummy rub.

"Not much of a guard dog you have there. I didn't break in. The door was unlocked. What I'm looking for isn't something I want to draw attention to." He unzipped his parka. She was annoyed he hadn't taken off his boots, but, of course, he wouldn't. He shouldn't be here.

"It's still illegal entry."

Grant smiled. "Let's not quibble about semantics. Give me what belongs to me and we're half done."

"I don't know what you're talking about." Bernie figured it was the checkbook, but why wouldn't he say? It had seemed innocuous, but if it were, he would've just asked for it, not illegally entered the police chief's house, then take a huge chance by engaging with her rather than leaving when he saw her there. She'd have to give it to him, but she wanted to know more first.

"Where is that box Louise Babb gave you?"

"Right here." She leaned over the edge of the bed, her head inches from his large knees, reached under, and pulled it out.

"Hiding it."

"No, there wasn't anywhere to put it. This is a small house. I didn't want to clutter things up."

Grant reached for the box. She thought he was going to snatch it from her, but he surprised her by waiting for her to hand it to him.

"Be my guest. I haven't looked through it thoroughly, but all it is are documents related to my grant funding. Every single thing Louise could think of to throw in there."

Grant rummaged through the papers, lifting out the manila folders to check inside.

"How can you tell if it's there if you're not even looking to see what the documents are?" Obtuseness, she knew, would help her case.

"It's not a document," he muttered. It looked like he'd reached the bottom of the box. "Dammit. Where is it? Did you take anything out?"

"No, I haven't had time to deal with it. I just opened it and looked to see if the stuff I needed for my taxes was there, and that's it. You know, Ryan, this is really weird. You coming in here like this, accusing me, looking through my stuff. You know I'll tell Pete. I don't get what's going on." It wasn't getting easier to play it straight. She wanted to scream at him to get the hell out.

"You won't tell Pete. That brings us to the other thing I wanted to talk to you about. When I saw you were here, I almost left, but I've been wanting to talk to you about something else, a private conversation. Off the record. This seemed like a good opportunity."

"Pete could be home any minute."

"No he won't. I saw him and MacCormack a while ago, and they have a full plate. No worries on that part." He leaned forward, his forearms on his large thighs. "I've heard you're asking about me, both personal things and nosing around about the Nakilot deal, and you're going to have a story Thursday."

"Yes." She could've denied it, but what would the point be? "I was going to call you later in the week for comments."

"There won't be a story beyond what we talked about in President Wilson's office."

"That's for me to determine."

"I want to offer you a deal. You lay off me and that project, and I'll call the chief back to duty and get off his back."

Bernie had a split second of temptation. It would be so easy. Then rationality roared back. "Sorry, no. I'm sure Pete will be back on the job soon without me compromising my journalistic principles."

"Get off your high horse." His disgust seemed genuine.

"You get off yours. You're not even a real Navy SEAL. You got sued for fraud after you ripped off your partner and lost your real estate license. I don't know what you did to get it back, but I'm sure it was underhanded." It was a stupid gambit, she knew it. Not even a gambit, because that implies thought and planning. She was just spewing her whole case out to him, not leaving any aces behind to play later.

Of course, it didn't work.

He took a piece of folded paper out of his pocket. "I'm not even going to respond to any of that. I don't have to. I have this." He waved the paper at her.

Nothing was going to change Bernie's mind. Grant didn't have to understand it for her to feel it. Live by it. It wasn't about her and her personal life. Her commitment to truth and accuracy, the cornerstones of what she did, was as sacred as a doctor's Hippocratic oath.

"Let me read a little bit." Grant shook the paper open with a flourish. He cleared his throat, an actor about to recite his big line. "Just a sampling. 'My pain is so overwhelming I can't distinguish between physical and emotional. Everything's black. My world narrows to a pinpoint. It's too small and far away for me to ever get through. I feel like I'll never get away from it. At times I feel like I'm not living. Not even subsisting.' I'm sure you're familiar with this."

"I have no idea what that is." She had a feeling though. A deep, sinking one. She was glad she was sitting down, leaning back against the headboard, the dog draped over her legs. Just enough support so Grant couldn't see her collapsing inside.

"Don't tell me you didn't snoop in your boyfriend's diary. Let me read you some more."

"*No.*" Bernie didn't mean to, but she shouted it. "I haven't read it and don't want to hear it. Those are his private, personal feelings, just for him and his therapist. How did you even get that?"

"I'm not in a position to disclose my source, but I have the original notebook. The deal I'm offering is you back off, I reinstate Pete, leave him alone."

"You'll give back the notebook?" She knew there were holes, but was too panicked to see the specifics.

"I keep it as insurance. If you don't hold up your end of the bargain, Fergus Kelley starts publishing stories about this. Do you really think the citizens of this town want a police chief who, let's see, 'can't distinguish between physical and emotional' pain? That's just one passage. I believe you when you say you haven't read it, because you wouldn't be here, all cozy in his bed, if you had. There are some not very flattering things about you, things about sex that would humiliate him, and some very, very dark thoughts and scenarios."

"Pete was asked by his therapist to write down everything, particularly the thoughts and feelings that frightened him or were an issue. No one else is supposed to see it. I'm sure you have thoughts you wouldn't want anyone else to know, that come, then go away, and you're like, 'Wow, what the hell was that?' "

Grant was sitting back, expressionless, either thinking out his next move or just waiting for her to shut up. When she did, he said, "That doesn't matter. What does is that I have this. I've copied the entire thing, and it's in a place where, even if you sic your boyfriend on me, Fergus Kelley will know how to get it. I know your wheels are spinning right now on how you can shut me down, how you're going to tell Pete and put an end to this, but do you really want to risk it?"

"Do *you* want to risk it?" Bernie knew his plan couldn't work, she just had to figure out the logistics. She was bad at anything that involved complicated strategizing—chess, figuring out the final wager on *Jeopardy!*, personal relationships.

Grant laughed. "I've thought this all out, Bernadette. Yes, I'm taking a risk, but I have that covered. Who's to say that you didn't anonymously give Kelley the copies of the notebook yourself, plant it on me to make me look guilty as a way to get back at me for going after your boyfriend?"

"That's ridiculous. No one would believe it."

"Really? But they'd believe that I'd somehow come into possession of it? How? What's more plausible? Even now, you're trying to figure out how to protect him. I've noticed you haven't replayed your journalistic ethics card."

Bernie had nothing.

"My original plan was to accuse you of fraud on your grant award. It would've been easy to fake some documents, especially since yours were lost in your fire. The fire helped, too. Someone who burns her house down for fraudulent purposes, what's to keep her from defrauding the town out of $100,000?"

Bernie had an epiphany. "*You* burned my house down."

Grant laughed. "Why? What would I have to gain? Now you're just grasping at straws, which tells me I have you where I want you. I could see you idiotically fighting the fraud charges, and even if you won in the end, it would likely cost you enough to lose your business. It was tempting. But this isn't a long game, it's a short one. I decided this worked better. I know what your Achilles' heel is." He waggled the paper at her again. "If this gets out, not just this page, but a month's worth, it could send Pete right over the edge, couldn't it? It would destroy his career. Destroy him, too. What's a little compromise on your journalist ethics compared to that?"

Bernie closed her eyes. She wanted this to go away. When she opened them, Grant was still smirking at her, waggling the paper.

"I don't want to play your games. What you're doing is wrong on every level. You can't win."

"Can't I? I already am. I'm sitting next to your bed, the power out, by the way, since I turned off the generator, so that fancy surveillance system didn't capture me. No one around for miles, a blizzard raging. If something happened to you, who's going to know it was me? Say you slipped and fell in that hole in the ice trying to get your dog? Isn't it easier to just take the deal?"

CHAPTER 37

PETE TEXTED BERNIE a couple of times, then left a voice message. He knew where she was. Everything was okay. He was ashamed of his panic attack the night before, embarrassed that Sandy had rushed over. The fact Bernie had actually been in possible danger made him feel inadequate, not vindicated. He wouldn't repeat that today. She was home. She was fine.

"Still no answer?" Sandy asked.

"She's probably sleeping in. That was an ordeal last night. She's pretty tired."

They opened a metal cot, one in a long line in the school gym. Pete rolled out its thin mattress, put the folded sheet, blanket, and pillow on top.

"I could probably lie down on this and take a nap myself," he said.

"Do you want to go home?" Sandy asked.

Sandy was being careful with him. Pete wished he wouldn't. He, of all people, knew the helpless terror when a loved one was in danger, when you can't help. How it echoes and pings through the rest of your life.

"I'm okay. It's just normal concern. She was unusually lethargic this morning. Maybe she's coming down with something."

"At least she can drive out if she has to." Sandy had given the public works director an earful earlier about how he had to use the blade on his truck to get to Pete's, an occupied house on a public road.

"Even if no one's home, someone lives there," he'd said.

Surprisingly, Ryan Grant, who'd been nearby, had agreed. "Get someone down there ASAP, Don." He'd nodded at Sandy and Pete, as though they were all pals, as Don Littlefield, the public works director, shook his head and shot Grant a dirty look. Pete suspected Grant had originally told him to leave the road alone.

That had been hours ago. "It's probably snowed in again," Pete said. "I'm sure she didn't go anywhere, anyway. She was very...I don't know."

"I'm taking you home, buddy," Sandy said. "Don't take it personally, but you need to be there, and she needs you there too."

Sandy drove fast in the blowing snow, the red lights on the front of his truck flashing. He expertly skirted downed limbs and hanging wires.

"No crews out yet with this wind," he said. Power was out for most of the county. Some of the houses they passed showed dim lights. They'd hear a symphony of generators if the storm weren't howling so loudly. Others were dark. Pete pictured the residents bundled up inside, wondering to each other how long the outage would last, if they had enough batteries and water to make do, debating when they'd give in and go to the warming center. Most would go a day or more before they'd make that concession.

"Glad I finally got a generator," Pete said. "Nothing worse than no power for days on end."

Sandy turned down Loon Lane, which, as predicted, had filled back up with snow, but wasn't so bad he had to drop his blade. As they came down the hill, Pete strained to see the lights of the house through the storm. Suddenly they were in the dooryard. The house was dark.

"She must still be asleep," Pete said.

He opened the door to a cold house. The pellet stove, which ran twenty-four hours a day this time of year, was silent and dark. The breakfast he'd left for her was on the counter, just as it had been that morning. Dubby ran up to greet him, silently dancing around his legs.

"Why isn't the generator running?" Sandy asked.

"Bernie!" He didn't take time to take off his boots or coat. He was in the bedroom in four strides. In the dim light from the window, he saw a lump under the covers, surrounded by three startled cats. He pulled the covers off and they scattered. Bernie blinked at him, confused.

"What's wrong?" she asked.

"Jesus," Pete said. He sat down on the bed.

"What's wrong?" she asked again, sitting up. "Just tell me." She looked from Pete to Sandy, who was standing at the opening in the partition.

"I'm going to go check on the generator," Sandy said. "Your carbon monoxide alarm looks like it's working okay, nothing there, so we're good on that."

"Carbon monoxide?" Bernie asked.

Pete hadn't been thinking about carbon monoxide. He hadn't gotten there yet. All he'd been thinking was something was horribly wrong. He took a deep breath.

"Pete? What's going on?"

"Why didn't you tell me that the generator didn't go on?" He fought to sound calm.

Bernie looked confused. "I don't know."

"I'm not criticizing you. I just want to figure out what's going on. The door was unlocked too."

"I never opened it. I didn't even let the dog out."

"You went out."

"I did?"

He pointed to dried remnants of footprints on the rug, the white of dried moisture on the hardwood floor.

"Oh." Her face crumpled. "I must've. Sorry I didn't clean it up."

"I don't care about that. Are you okay?" He put his hand on her forehead. It didn't feel overly warm.

"I don't know." She started to cry.

"Hey, hey." He put his arms around her. "It's okay."

The generator roared to life. Sandy came back in, blowing on his hands. "Shit, it's cold out there. Someone turned off the master."

"It was on this morning," Pete said. "I checked."

"Ohhhh," Bernie said. She'd put her glasses on and her eyes were giant brown pools of guilt. "Why am I so stupid?"

"What?"

"I forgot. I did go out. Sorry, I'm just so tired. I let Dubby out, and I guess I forgot what you told me about the generator. I wanted to make sure it would go on and I must've accidentally turned it off."

"I'm outa here," Sandy said. "Glad everything's okay." He rolled his eyes at Pete.

"Don't be mad," Bernie said. "I know I'm using up my reserve for stupid things. It's been a stellar twenty-four hours."

He didn't know what to say. At least she wasn't crying anymore. He wasn't mad, just confused. She hadn't seemed herself this morning, and now, though the words were all Bernie, she was even less like herself. He got it, she was afraid of how he'd react. This was his fault.

He hugged her again, felt her stiffen in his arms. "You're tired and stressed out. It's been a rough couple of weeks. It's all okay now. Let's heat up those pancakes."

****

By early evening, the storm had died down. The power wasn't back, and word was it wouldn't be until at least Tuesday. Trying to act normal when things had taken such a stunning, abnormal turn was exhausting Bernie. She wasn't sure how she'd maintain it. When Pete woke her up, she'd at first thought Ryan Grant's visit had been a bad dream. Felt that relief the way you do when you have a dream that you're sitting down for a college final but haven't gone to class all semester. When you wake up, the dream was almost worth it because the relief is so sweet. The feeling, though, died fast. She had to figure out how to explain things. The footprints didn't help. Smudges, actually, too unclear to tell they'd been made by a foot twice the size of Bernie's. Who else could've turned off the generator but her? She wondered what the surveillance footage would show if he looked at it. Ryan Grant driving up and turning off the generator? Likely not. It was snowing too hard for the camera aimed at the dooryard to show anything. She knew there'd be lies. She just hadn't anticipated them starting so soon. She hated lying in general because trying to remember details took up space in her head she could use for other things. Lying to Pete made her feel sick, even when it was for his sake. It wasn't lost on her that she'd turned into Nora from *A Doll's House*, even though she already knew the lesson—doing the bad thing to save your man only made things worse for you. But Pete wasn't that awful husband. And her life didn't suck, like Nora's did. *And anyway, this was real life, not a depressing play, right?*

Bernie's ruminations as she washed the dishes were interrupted by Pete's cellphone ringing.

"I thought you were suspended," she said after he hung up from a long, involved conversation with someone from the sheriff's department about road closures.

"It's relative."

She'd had one win—getting him to turn off the police scanner as they sat down to eat. It had been humming in the background since shortly after he'd arrived home that afternoon. Normally she'd want it on, too. But her head was already buzzing, and its static and beeps and bursts of urgent conversation ramped up her anxiety.

"Maybe you can get out the guitar?" Bernie sat next to him on the couch. "A little Sexy Sheriff serenade?" It would keep her from having to talk. She could tell he was already suspicious that something was up with her.

His phone buzzed again. He shrugged apologetically. "It's Imani Gilbert. I wonder what she wants?"

Bernie watched his face go from mild curiosity to serious cop as he listened to a recitation that went on for several minutes. Bernie couldn't hear the words but heard Imani's voice, fast and urgent.

"They'll be there soon," Pete said. "Keep the door locked—"

There was another burst from Imani.

"Okay. Close the window. But—"

A brief pause.

"No, Imani. Don't—"

There was a loud burst of static.

"Imani! Imani!" Pete pulled his phone from his ear and looked at it. "Shit. Disconnected."

"What's going on?" Bernie asked as he pushed redial.

"I don't know. She said someone was prowling around and it sounded like they were trying to break in."

"Fucking epidemic in this town," Bernie said.

"She's not picking up. I better go over."

"Didn't she call it in? I heard you say something like that."

"Something's wrong." He pulled on his boots. "I'm going over."

"I'll go too. I just have to change." She was still in her sleeping clothes.

"Stay here, okay? I don't know what's going on. I'll call Dawna from the car."

Bernie didn't really want to go, but she didn't want to stay in the house alone either.

He squeezed her shoulders and gave her a quick kiss, pulled on his hat, and opened the door. A burst of wind and snow blew in. "Brent and Mandy are on tonight. They'll likely be there by the time I get there, and I'll just turn around and come home."

She listened to Pete's car roar to life, his tires spin as he roared up the road. He must've barely cleared it off.

Bernie turned on the scanner and was met with a wall of static instead of the usual Franklin County dispatch chatter. It cleared long enough for her to hear the dispatcher say "copy" followed by "possible 10—" before static drowned the rest.

She called Carrie. "I hate to bug you after you've been working all day, but there's something going on at the Beehive. Pete got a call from a woman who lives there, and he's on his way over."

"They called a signal 1000 like a minute before you called."

"Must've been right before I turned on the scanner. If they've called for radio silence, it's something big."

"I'm already in my car," Carrie said. "I'll let you know."

Bernie went to the back door and looked out at the empty dooryard, the snowy road with Pete's fresh tire tracks. Dubby squeezed past her and sniffed the new snow in a delighted frenzy, aiming shots of pee at one pile, then the next.

The clouds had cleared, and the Milky Way sparkled above. There was no wind, not even enough to rustle the trees. Bernie wished she could go back in time, even just twelve hours, when the worst thing in her life aside from her house burning down and tenant dying was that she'd humiliated herself by driving over the border on a wild-goose chase, sending her fragile boyfriend into an epic panic attack. Now she'd sold her soul to Satan so that he wouldn't spiral further. She already regretted it. She should've just come clean to Pete. He would've figured out a way to shut Ryan Grant down.

Far off, a siren wailed. Bernie took a deep breath, Pete style. Held it. Let it out. She called the dog and went back inside. The scanner spit out static, the occasional sound of a voice, a fraction of a syllable, before it was swallowed up. She kept it on anyway. She itched to call Dawna and find out what was going on, but she knew she'd just be a nuisance. She was going to have to sit and wait to hear from Pete or Carrie. It wasn't something she was good at.

Even with the door shut and the generator running outside, she could hear the siren, then another one farther away.

She *was* an idiot, but she didn't have to keep being one. When Pete got home, she'd tell him about Grant's visit. He wouldn't fall apart because Grant had his notebook. He'd relish the fact that the guy had made a huge misstep. He wasn't going to collapse in a heap of fear and panic, he was going to figure out what to do. Sure, she'd have to eat shit, but she deserved it. She felt better already.

****

Pete's car fishtailed around the corner of River Road, sliding in the snow. He'd made it there in record time, his certainty growing with every second that he was driving to a disaster. It wasn't panic and anxiety, wasn't PTSD. It was good old-fashioned police instincts.

The street was quiet, the only light, with the power out, was a floodlight illuminating his two officers. He skidded to a stop behind the Redimere Police Department's SUV, parked in front of the hulking apartment building. Let himself believe just for a second that things were okay.

Of course, they weren't. He approached Brent and Mandy, huddled in front of the building, lit up by the strobe from the *Real Rural Justice* crew's camera.

"That better not be on. I don't consent to be filmed," Pete said to the man holding it and the guy next to him. They were both bundled in parkas and scarves. He couldn't see their reactions. He'd deal with them later.

"What's going on?" he asked Mandy and Brent.

They looked small and cold, pale in the light from the camera.

"She had a gun," Brent said. His voice shook. "She had a gun and wouldn't put it down."

"Who?" Pete, with effort, flipped the switch that turned off his rising panic and turned on cop mode. "What happened?"

He started toward the last doorway in the building. The one that led to Imani's apartment.

"The girl—"

"Brent, shut up," Mandy said. "Chief, a minute. Please." She took Pete's arm, tugging him past the steps, away from Brent and the *Real Rural Justice* crew. "You gentlemen stay there," she said to the TV crew.

"Don't worry, I didn't let them mic me up," she said when they were out of earshot.

"What happened?" Pete asked, his eyes on the dark windows of Imani's apartment.

"Brent shot the woman who lives in that apartment. She's dead." Mandy's voice shook, but she looked at Pete with sharp, unwavering eyes.

Brent's voice cut through the cold air. "Mandy, you better be telling him the truth."

Mandy ignored him. "He claims she had a gun. There's no gun in there. Those TV guys were filming. I'm not sure what they got."

"Her kids," Pete said, moving toward the door.

She took his arm, firmly. Even through his thick coat, he could feel the iron grip of her small hand. "Chief, with all due respect. Please listen. They're asleep. I checked on them. Dawna's on her way. I called Franklin County dispatch. They issued a code 1000. As long as they're okay we need to stay out of there."

"I can't do that."

She didn't take her hand off his arm. "Chief, I know I'm in danger of being insubordinate, but it's already a Charlie Foxtrot here. If you, being suspended, go in, it could make it worse."

Her small face looked up at him with resolve. No fear.

"You're right." His panic was gone, logic taking over. It was a relief, locking in to the routine of a crime scene, following procedure. Emotion burned somewhere deep under it, but he could deal with it later and ignore it now.

He walked back to Brent. "Give Mandy your gun and get in the cruiser. Back seat, please."

"But—"

"It's standard when there's an officer-involved shooting," Pete said, hyperaware of the camera's light hot on the back of his neck. "We want this to go by the book, right? Better for you and everyone involved."

"You're right." Brent's gun was still in his hand. He handed it, barrel-first, to Mandy.

"If you have any evidence bags in the cruiser, put that in one, okay?" Pete said to her.

Mandy followed Brent to the SUV.

Pete saw movement out of the corner of his eye. He'd been too focused on Brent and Mandy to notice, but though the night was still silent, dark shapes hovered in windows down the row of apartments. A few people had come out onto the front stoops. Here and there the ember of a cigarette bobbed.

"Everyone please stay inside. Don't go anywhere. Someone will be by to talk to you later," he called out.

He heard a ragged voice. "Where the fuck else are we gonna go? Dumb shit." It was more for her neighbors than for him.

"Pete."

Chuck stood on his porch, no coat. Pete was close enough to see the concern on his face. He had a split-second urge to run to him, have him fix things. It was an emotion he hadn't felt for nearly forty years. It was gone just as fast, to his relief.

"Stay over there, inside, okay Dad?"

His father stayed on the porch. *Fine, if he wants to freeze to death.* He was glad Tommy was in Portland for the weekend. That's all he needed, both of them standing there, watching him.

Pete looked again at the dark, empty windows of Imani's apartment and the ones above it. It was cold, the kind that made your cheeks go numb and eyes water. It didn't bother him. He thought of Imani, determined and smart, ready to take on the world. Dead in seconds. Her kids, asleep, no clue their mother was gone. Cop mode slipped a little. He took a deep breath. Held it. Let it out slowly, one-two-three-four. *Please just let me do this.*

His father still stood on the porch. "Dad, please go inside, okay?"

Chuck stood for a couple seconds more, wavering, then turned and went in the house.

Pete walked toward the cruiser, where Brent stared from the window, his face white.

"Turn the cruiser on so Brent doesn't freeze to death," Pete said to Mandy. "If there's a bottle of water in there, give him some." He was likely in shock, but Pete didn't add that. The less said, the better, with the TV cameras rolling.

"What now?" Mandy asked, coming back from the cruiser, blinking in the bright camera light.

Pete let out the breath he'd been holding. "We wait."

****

Bernie lay in bed, listening to Pete breathe just feet away on the other side of the partition. Every once in a while she heard the quiet sift of puzzle pieces, but otherwise, nothing. She must've slept, but it didn't feel like it. She put on her glasses. 2:47. She went into the living room.

"I can't sleep," Pete said before she could say anything.

"You have to try before you know you can't. If anything, that hour-long shower you took should've made you sleepy." He'd been in almost catatonic distress when he'd walked in the door two hours earlier. He seemed better now, more or less. She wished Benjamin was there on the couch, gently guiding Pete through whatever his core emotion was. Bernie was not equipped. Leaning in wasn't going to cut it.

"I know I can't. I don't have to try." He picked up a piece—she knew it was random—and scanned the puzzle as though he had an idea of where it should go.

She sat down next to him. "I can't sleep either."

"Looks like you made a lot of progress on the giraffe herd," he said.

"I finally figured out the yellow and dots were a different shade than the beach umbrellas. Once I had that down, I separated them into two different groups, and I was off to the races."

"I see you re-sorted some of the piles."

"I made one with all the pieces I could find that had human faces and another one with animal faces. I figured at this point, it's more logical than sorting by color." *Why are we talking about this stupid puzzle?*

Pete put down the piece he'd been holding and picked up another one. "Did I ever tell you why I became a cop?"

No. "To help people?" It seemed like the logical answer.

He made a noise somewhere between a cough and a bitter laugh. "That's turning out great."

She rubbed his back. "You help people every day."

"That doesn't count for much when one is shot to death while she's on the phone asking me for help. By one of my own fucking officers."

"It's not your fault."

His hand shook. He put down the puzzle piece. Took a deep breath.

"Imani dead, her kids—" His voice broke.

"Pete." Bernie put her arm around him and squeezed. "It's not your fault." She knew how empty it sounded, but she couldn't think of anything else.

"What do I do?" He wiped his eyes on his sleeve. "How do I fix it?" He turned to her, his face inches away, white with fear. It was a plea, like he expected her to know the answer.

"Maybe it's not up to you to fix it," she said softly. "Bad things happen. You can only do your best, which is more than what a lot of people do." She felt like her stupid platitudes, as much as she meant them, were making it worse.

"Even if that were true, none of it matters if someone was killed on my watch for no fucking good reason."

"It's not your fault. There was nothing you could've done. You can't change what happened. You're human, Pete."

"It's hard," he said with a sob. "So many people dead, all for nothing. It's just been so hard, and I don't know what to do."

She pulled him to her, pressing his head against her chest. "I know. I know it hurts. I know it sucks to feel so bad, but it's because you care. You can't control the outcome, you can only do what you can, and sometimes the outcome really, really sucks. You've helped people. So many people. More than you know."

"I failed too many people." She could barely make out the words as she held him tight. His hands clutched her shirt, hot on her back. "I need—" He sobbed. "I can't do it alone."

"I know. It's okay. I know. I'm right here."

CHAPTER 38

BERNIE WOKE TO AN empty bed and the smells of coffee and bacon. The room was dark. The red blur of the clock numbers came into focus. 5:58. The sun wouldn't be up for more than an hour. If this was a normal Sunday, she wouldn't be either.

Pete appeared at the partition, fully dressed, khaki pants and his Redimere Police Department sweatshirt. He'd shaved, and his wet hair was neatly combed. The smell of mango-peach-coconut mixed with the bacon and coffee. She swallowed a quick bubble of nausea.

"If I didn't know better, I'd say you were wearing police chief casual for some bizarre reason. What's going on?" Even as she asked, she knew it was a stupid question. This was not a normal Sunday. If things were ever going to be normal again, it wasn't going to be today.

"I have to go to Farmington to talk to someone from the attorney general's office about the shooting. I made you breakfast," he said, his normal morning-cheerful self.

"Smells good." She felt heavy and slow. She was determined, though, to try to act as normal as he was. She'd felt useless as he'd sobbed just a few hours before, ineffective and helpless. Her one small victory had been finally convincing him to go to bed.

"Look," he said as he watched her struggle with her mukluks. "I don't want to sound paternalistic, but will you be okay alone here today without a car?"

"You're not sounding paternalistic. I need to go to the office to make sure the generator is working and the system didn't crash and to get ahead on coverage. I have plenty of work to do. You can drop me off."

"I have to be in Farmington by nine."

"That's fine." She followed him into the kitchen. "I guess being on leave doesn't count for something like this."

"I'm still the chief. One of my officers shot someone. Added to it, Imani was on the phone with me when she was shot. They have a lot of questions."

"Didn't they talk to you at the scene last night?"

"Yes, but now they want to talk to me more." He smiled at her. *All normal. Business as usual.* "They don't care that I'm suspended, apparently."

"How did you sleep?"

"Right through."

She met his eyes. "Hmm. Doesn't sound authentic." She poured maple syrup over her eggs, bacon, and pancakes.

Pete put a mug of coffee in front of her, then sat down across from her with his own plate.

"I had a nice swim. It perked me right up."

"It's below zero out."

"Added benefit." He smiled again. "I'm in one piece and ready to rock and roll." He was trying to reassure her that his meltdown was over. He was *fine.*

"Humph." Her mouth was too full of pancake to say more.

"I'm good, Bernie. Really. Thanks for listening last night."

"That's what I'm here for, right?"

"Right. But it was heavy."

"You ain't heavy, you're my lover." *Man, I need more coffee.* "Gross. Yuck. Forget I said that. Sorry. Ugh."

He laughed. "I *do* love you."

"Good."

"Authentically? It really helped that you were here, but I don't want you to think…" He faltered. "I could be by myself if I had to. I don't want you to worry about that. I'd be sad, but I don't want you to think I'm a basket case that you have to take care of. I was upset. Now I'm okay."

She chewed as she thought about how to respond. Should she call him on his not-complete authenticity? She imagined Benjamin's melty sad face. She needed it to channel the right words. She knew he wasn't okay. Her shirt had dried, but in her mind it was still plastered against her skin like it had been a few hours ago, soaked with his tears.

"I know that was hard for you last night. After my house burned down you said you were with me 100 percent, no matter what. It goes both ways. I'm with you like that too. You can be however you are, and I'll be right there. I don't want what I said last week to make you doubt it."

"I know."

Sooner or later she'd have to confess her deal with Ryan Grant and let the chips fall where they may. But there was no way it could be now.

****

Bernie spent the morning going over the shooting coverage with Carrie and Guy. They hashed over whether to put in the story that Pete had been on the phone with Imani, but decided that unless the AG released that information publicly, they wouldn't. Guy was adamant that the only reason they knew was because Bernie lived with Pete, and given his status, it would open a can of worms that would be hard to contain. Carrie agreed, with no argument. Bernie had argued for complete transparency, but when they disagreed, she was relieved.

"I'm just going to run the college's information on the Nakilot story and leave out the parts about how fishy the sale seems to be, given Normand Ouimette's intentions," Bernie said. She tried to sound casual, but both Guy and Carrie looked surprised.

"I know you don't have a lot of details," Guy said. "But what you've got is solid. It's no secret what Norm's plans were. It's no secret no one can nail down why they changed and that he's not around. Going after the college and Grant on not revealing details is a good call. We

353

talked about that Friday and you were gung ho. Grant's possible conflict as both mayor and broker is also legit. We talked about this."

Bernie knew this was going to be hard. She just had to get through it. She channeled the thought of Pete the night before, his distress. She couldn't begin to imagine what was in that notebook. She pictured it in Fergus Kelley's slimy hands. He'd be drooling at the prospect of running stories on the mentally unstable police chief.

"I'm not comfortable with it until we talk to Ouimette," Bernie said. "There's a lot of innuendo and speculation. It's a big deal and we open ourselves up for a lawsuit if I get it wrong. Anyway, between the shooting and the storm, we're tight on space."

"You added four pages," Guy said.

"That was for the storm. Who knew we'd have a police-involved shooting too? On top of it, we don't want the good stuff about the Nakilot deal to get lost in all this other news. It'll play better in a week or two, when this has died down."

Carrie had already sat down at her computer and put her headphones on, leaving the discussion to Guy and Bernie.

Guy stood in front of her desk with his arms crossed. "What's going on Bernie? You're not backing off are you? It's a good story."

"Not at all." Her face burned. "I'll put in this week's that Norm had planned to hand his land over to the Passamaquoddy and that they've said they haven't heard from him lately, but the other stuff can wait."

"Okay." He shook his head. "Your call." He went back to his desk.

She felt like the world's biggest asshole.

She put her feet up on her desk, watching out the window as a steady stream of people descended on the store, squeezing through the openings Walt had cut in the massive snowbanks lining the street, heartily greeting each other in that way people do the first day of a power outage, before grim discomfort takes over. It wasn't going to work, lying to Pete. Lying to Guy. Not doing her job right. She couldn't tell Pete, though. Not after last night. The most important thing was having his back, not her discomfort.

Her cellphone rang. Louise Babb from her cell, not town hall. Which made sense, since it was Sunday. Bernie took the phone into her back office.

"Ryan wants to know where the checkbook is," Louise said. "You have it, right?"

"Thank you for finally mentioning it. I was beginning to wonder if I was in some crazy weird other dimension or something. I have it, but I don't know why it's such a big deal. He even came to my house yesterday—Pete's house—and walked right in and woke me up looking for it. I played dumb, and he believed me, I guess. Don't tell anyone about that, by the way."

"I won't, believe me. Have you looked in it?"

"Yeah, just his personal stuff. Groceries and things like that."

"You have to *really* look. Where is it?"

"My coat pocket. The inside one. I stuck it there last week, so I'd have it to give back to him."

"In the sleeve, there are twelve deposit slips, all for $9,900, for between mid-2009 and January 2010." Louise paused, waiting for Bernie's reaction.

"I know that if deposits are for $10,000 or more, the bank has to report to, um, Treasury? I can't remember. So that would indicate deposits that he wanted to be under the radar?"

"Correct. It's shady," Louise said. "You ran that campaign donation story during the mayoral election, right? All his donations put together didn't equal even one of those payments. So, what are they? If you look at the slips you'd see there's no indication where the money came from. Someone needs to find out. You gotta follow the money."

"I'm not Woodward and Bernstein," Bernie said. "I'd have to think about how I could even do that. It's a dead end if we don't find out. If someone was just handing him cash, there's no way to track it down. For all I know, he has a benevolent aunt somewhere who's sending him pin money. I can't subpoena bank records. What do you think it is?"

"I think that it's payoffs for favors granted of some type. Kickbacks maybe? I don't know. You're the reporter."

The reporter who can't go after Ryan Grant. "What did you tell him when he asked where the checkbook was?"

"I told him I hadn't seen one. Things were chaotic when we moved his office into the new addition. I found it behind a file cabinet right before you asked for your docs, and I figured it was a good way to get it to someone who could do something."

"If you can think of any way to find out where the money is from—without doing anything illegal, please—let me know. Meanwhile, I'll try and figure it out too." It was likely a dead end. If Louise did find out anything, Bernie'd figure out then what to do with the information.

****

When Bernie got back to her desk, there was a manila envelope on her keyboard.

"Ryan Grant dropped off that info you were looking for," Guy said. "I'm heading out, okay? See you tomorrow, bright and early."

The envelope was light. No notebook in it. Not that she thought there would be. Grant wasn't going to have a change of heart.

"I'm going too," Carrie said. "Our power's out, so I'm going to my mom's, in Milo. I can work from there. I'll be back tomorrow."

Bernie walked to the front window and looked out. The street, snow piled high on either side, was empty except for the cars in front of the store. No Ryan Grant hovering around to watch her read its contents. Still, she brought it to the couch out back before she opened it.

It was two pages, both filled with Pete's neat block lettering, the faint lines of notebook paper barely picked up by the copier. There was no note or message, of course. Grant wouldn't want a paper trail. She was surprised he actually dropped it off himself, though he often dropped stuff off. If it came to it, he could always claim he was dropping off a news release or something.

Bernie didn't want to read it. It felt like a violation. It *was* a violation. But she had to have some idea of what she was dealing with.

The top page started in mid-sentence:

—covered with blood. He'd slashed her throat. His bloody handprint was on her leg. From the way she was positioned, it was obvious she was hiding under the bed and he'd dragged her out. When I got home, my pantleg was covered with blood from kneeling in it and I hadn't even noticed. Karen wasn't happy I'd ruined those pants. That sticks out to me.

With her, the mother and other girl dead downstairs, we just got to work. The father shot himself in his car a couple miles away before we could track him down. It's not something I forgot, but not something I thought about much over the years. When I got called to the Wings' house Thursday, the little girl, 8, same age as the one under the bed, was bleeding out. She'd been kneeling on the sink trying to cut her hair and fell. She was using big fabric scissors, sharp ones. It wasn't the same thing, was it? I think I started having a panic attack, but then shifted into cop mode. The dad was home with the kids, and he was frantic. He was no help. I held a clean towel to her neck and talked to her until the ambulance got there. It was maybe five minutes. They'd been in Farmington and were just getting back. The dad wanted me to drive her to the hospital, or to meet the ambulance, but the way she was bleeding, I didn't want to move her. It was a decision I had to make. Which thing would be more effective? She was bleeding heavily and there was no other help, so I made it and didn't second-guess myself. I talked to her and tried to keep her calm. She wanted to talk, which was good, it meant she was still with us, but I told her not to, because it would make her bleed more. I kept talking. Telling her how brave she was and what a good girl she was being and how much she was helping me and her dad. Anything to keep her calm and positive.

> After, I drove home to change my uniform. It was covered in blood. The legs, the shirt. A bloody mess. Bernie was home so I made a joke. She went along with it, but I could tell she wanted to know. I wanted to tell her but I couldn't. Maybe deep down afraid of being dismissed? I know that's not fair to Bernie.

"No, it's not," Bernie said. *Was* she dismissive? She'd have to try not to be. She was so focused on separating their jobs that she was careful what she asked about. He brought stuff up, and she eagerly engaged, but he hadn't brought up the girl who'd cut herself with the scissors at all, except to make that joke about his bloody uniform being just another day at the office. He sure as hell hadn't told her about the horrific triple murder from years before. She kept reading:

> I didn't think I was affected from the call Thursday. Grace Wing. No T's that I felt. That night I had my worst night terror ever. The child under the bed was alive in the dream and kept turning into Grace. Looking at me. Wanting me to save her. I knew she was dying. Her father had slit her throat. Dragged her out from under the bed and slit her throat. There was so much blood. In the dream it was up to my thighs. I knew I was screaming when I woke up. I'd wet the bed I was so terrified. I couldn't believe it. Bernie was so kind, but I knew she was terrified too. I wanted to tell her. I couldn't. Couldn't. Couldn't. Couldn't. Can't. Scale of 1-10 T level? 11+.

Bernie put the pages back in the envelope. She wanted to burn them or something, but she might need them later. Evidence against Grant if she could figure out how to bring it around to that.

Her cellphone rang.

"Did you read what I sent you?" Grant asked.

"Yes."

"I don't think the citizens of Redimere want to know how their police chief feels when their children are injured. Or that he wets the bed. Do you?"

She wanted, irrationally, to tell him that you're only a citizen of a country or state, and she was fucking sick and tired of people referring to town residents as citizens. Anything but what he wanted her to say.

"No. I don't."

"I just want to make sure we still have a deal. I know I sprung things on you yesterday and you were sleepy."

"We have a deal."

"Good. As a good faith effort, I'm going to lift Novotny's suspension. I hope I don't see anything online or in the paper when it comes out Thursday that's going to make me regret it."

"You won't."

Bernie had to sit still and get her blood pressure under control before she made her next call.

When Tommy answered, she asked if he still had a friend in the AG's fraud division.

"I'm not sure," he said. "We dated a little, and she got annoyed because she didn't hear from me for a while. The shooting wouldn't come under fraud anyway."

"It has nothing to do with the shooting. I'm working on a story, and I need someone to run a hypothetical."

"If you call her, that'd be weird. Tell me, and I'll give her a call."

Bernie, without naming names, told him about the deposit slips and what would be needed to get a fraud investigation going. She wasn't good at Grant's type of games, but if she could prove he took illegal payoffs from someone, she had leverage. She knew she'd blow it if she tried to cut a further deal, but she could play along until the AG's fraud division nailed his oversized ass.

CHAPTER 39

"HOW WAS THE MEETING with the AG?" Bernie asked as she got into the Charger.

"Not bad. Same questions, different day." Pete could already tell how things would go with the investigation. It would take a while, then they'd determine Brent was justified. As Bernie often pointed out, all they have to do is say they were in imminent danger. It's like they learn the phrase at the police academy. It's not that he didn't want to concede that to her, it's just that he was exhausted.

"How are you?" she asked.

"Fine."

"Authentically?"

He laughed. "A little shaky."

Bernie seemed better than she'd been the day before, but quiet. After they got home, they sat on the couch, her curled up reading, him half watching football, fighting the urge to curl up himself. He finally gave up the fight and lay down, his head in her lap.

"Gonna use this nice soft pillow."

"You're going to take a nap? What about football?" She smoothed his hair, then rested her hand, so warm even through his shirt, in the hollow of his chest.

"Just getting comfortable. The Packers won yesterday, so this isn't vital."

She turned a page. Then she surprised him by closing the book and putting it down on the puzzle.

"Do you need to get up?" he asked.

"No. But I've been wanting to ask. What happened last night? If you don't want to talk about it, that's okay. I know you're probably talked out, but I'd like to know. As someone who loves you, not as a newspaper editor."

"I don't mind." He rolled onto his back so he could look at her. He was struck by how sad she looked, pale behind her usual peaches and cream.

"What I'm going to tell you, I've only told the AG. Chuck was there and he's been bugging me for details, but I haven't told him or anyone. Don't tell Tommy."

"This is just between us."

"Imani told me she thought she heard someone on the stairs in her building. You know how they have four separate entrances?"

"Yeah."

"The apartment above hers is empty, and the one above that belongs to a couple who are out of town. She checked the hall. With the power out she used her phone to light it up, but it's a flip phone, so not a lot of light. She didn't hear or see anything. The door to outside was unlocked, so she locked it. She called dispatch. They said they'd send Redimere PD, but Brent and Mandy were finishing up another call, so it'd be a couple minutes."

"No sense of urgency," Bernie said.

"She thought she heard something but didn't see anything. No one seemed to be there. It wasn't like someone was breaking in, so, you know. She felt something was wrong, though. After she called dispatch, she looked out back. She thought she saw someone with a small flashlight or using the flashlight on their phone, looking up at the apartments. I looked when I was there, and that parking lot was deep snow. All the cars were covered with snow. Someone had definitely been walking around, though, but not cleaning off a car or anything. Imani didn't want to call dispatch back after she saw the person, since they'd made it clear they were busy. So she called me. I gave her my number that day she came to the office."

"Oh, right."

"While we were talking, there was commotion outside. It turned out to be the TV crew arriving with Brent and Mandy, but she didn't know that. She had the window open, anyway, because she'd been smoking before she heard the noise. So she went to the window."

"Oh no."

"Yeah. Brent saw a flip phone and thought gun." It had played on a nonstop loop in Pete's head since Saturday night. Imani, confused. Brent yelling for her to put down the gun, then shooting, not understanding she was blinded by his powerful flashlight.

"Jesus."

"He was shouting, you know, 'Police, put down the gun.' I don't think cops realize that people who aren't holding a gun and are confused don't even understand what they're yelling." Bernie had said that to him before, when they were watching a documentary on TV. He'd disagreed at the time, but she was right. She didn't say anything now, no *I told you so.*

He added, "You can't even make it out on the TV recording. Or really see her that clearly."

"Will the fact it's all on a TV recording hurt Brent's case?"

He appreciated that she was being diplomatic, but he'd almost rather she was her usual cynical self, telling it like it is. "Brent had the TV crew wait on the street, maybe fifty feet away, so they'd be out of range of any gunfire. They weren't, of course, if she'd really had a gun and decided to shoot them. But they didn't get a clear view of her in the window, all you see is a dark silhouette that's not moving when he yells. If anything, it'll help him."

Her hand, soft and warm, had taken his while he was talking. She kept holding it when he stopped. "I'm so sorry, Pete."

He woke up an hour later, his head still in her lap, her hand still holding his. A new football game had started. She was engrossed in her book. He didn't let on he was awake.

****

Pete was grateful to see Tommy waiting for him at the corner of River and Main when he drove there to pick him up late Monday morning. Even though he could see the Beehive as he pulled to a stop, it was better than driving by it. He wasn't sure what size T it was going to be and wasn't anxious to find out.

"Thanks for helping out," Pete said as Tommy climbed in. "Bernie couldn't leave work for this long, but boy she wants her car back."

"I bet. How are you doing?"

Tommy sounded like he meant it. Pete was reminded, once again, that Bernie's brother, for all the crap, still had the same DNA she did. The same heart.

"Fine."

"I'm glad to hear it, because now that we're stuck together for an hour, it gives me a chance to debrief with you on Jeremy's case. I already got an earful from Chuck about how you're not talking about Imani, though anything you tell me would help, since Jeremy is shattered, as you can imagine."

"I can't say anything with an investigation going on, as much as I'd like to help Jeremy out."

"I thought maybe you could tell me off the record. I could swear him to silence."

Pete laughed.

"What's funny?"

"You're like Bernie. Relentless."

"She's not totally relentless, because when I asked her what happened, she said she wasn't talking. When I said I could read all about it in her newspaper, she said all she's going to print is what's released publicly, which doesn't even include you being on the phone with Imani. Chuck and most of the people at the Beehive know that, you know, so it's out there. Yet, she's still not printing it."

"It's her decision."

"She must love you a lot, because if it was anyone else, she wouldn't hesitate for one second to have a front page exclusive."

"I'm aware of that." Pete navigated the car around a tree branch tangled in wire. "This storm damage is going to take weeks to clean up. Once we get to Route 16, it may be a little better, but it's going to be slow going."

"More time to talk," Tommy said.

"Too bad about the Patriots yesterday. Did you catch the game? I say Packers all the way, and it's not just because I'm a fan."

"Yeah? They'll have to get by Pittsburgh first. They're going to crush the Jets next week. Jeremy's devastated about Imani. There's no way she had a gun. He needs to know."

Pete flashed the blue lights under his grill and was waved forward by a power company crew.

"I'm impressed," Tommy said.

"That's why I did it." He said it jokingly, but was embarrassed that it was true. Normally he'd stop, just like anyone else, but he'd wanted to show Tommy he could.

"Whatever you tell me won't go farther. I'm not going to use it in Jeremy's case. You have my word as your brother."

"It's not that I don't trust you. I just can't say anything."

"Jesus, you're a tough nut."

"No matter what your sister may say, I'm not Jesus, either."

Tommy laughed, genuine and merry. "Yeah, she calls you that all the time."

They hit Route 16 and Pete sped up.

"Has a woman ever called you paternalistic?" Pete asked. Friday night seemed like a long time ago, but Bernie's words had been weaving in and out of everything else.

"Probably. Why?"

"I'm just trying to figure it out."

"They have a lot of little tools in their little verbal toolboxes. It's just one of the things they say."

"Yeah." Pete wasn't convinced.

"Anyway, I consider myself a feminist."

"Me too."

Pete pulled over to let a line of utility trucks pass, then pulled back on the road.

"But do you think maybe—"

"Nah," Tommy said.

Another mile or two went by before either spoke.

"Bernie was there when you talked to Imani," Tommy said. "It's not even like you're defying the AG's request that you don't talk. I've seen plenty of cops jibber-jabber to the media after an officer-involved shooting. It's always to bolster their side of the story, but still. I don't get why she's not putting it in her story."

Pete felt the criticism behind it. "I didn't tell her not to. I told her to do what she had to. I don't want to stand in the way of her doing her job, no matter what the story. Her job is hard enough as it is without her worrying about me."

"Then I don't get it."

"Look. Don't tell her we talked about this, okay?"

"You got it."

"She thinks it'll look bad for me. All people will see is that I was on a phone call with the woman who was shot by one of my officers. I'm suspended, it's seven-thirty on a Saturday night, and I'm on the phone with a woman whose partner I arrested two weeks earlier. At the *moment* she's shot."

"Yeah. The optics suck."

"She's protecting me."

"She's got it bad for you. Stubborn as hell, too. Once she decides something you can't move her."

"I want her to be able to do her job. I didn't ask her to protect me. I don't need to be protected."

"You're with the wrong gal, then, buddy."

****

"Your car is parked out back," Pete said to Bernie when he and Tommy walked into the newspaper office Monday afternoon. "There's still no on-street parking."

"Pete let me drive the Charger home," Tommy said.

"You're like a little kid who got to play with the big boy's cool toy," Bernie said.

"What's your point?"

"It's nice to see the bromance is blooming."

"I wouldn't go that far." Pete handed Bernie her keys and gave her a quick kiss. "I got a text from the mayor. He wants me to stop by ASAP. We'll see what that's all about."

"Maybe good news," Bernie said. It had better be. It would mean that Grant was keeping his end of the bargain.

After Pete left, Tommy said, "I wanted to fill you in on what my friend with the AG said."

No one seemed to be paying attention, but Bernie still didn't want to talk in front of them. She led Tommy back to her office.

"Bottom line, in your hypothetical situation, is that a bunch of deposits like that, while they may raise some eyebrows and are red-flagish, won't trigger an investigation. You need more. I mean if this were a real thing, not some hypothetical."

"I'm not telling you what this is about. I have to figure it out first."

"Maybe I can help."

"I wish."

"Seriously, Bernie. Run it by me."

She had a burning need to tell someone. It had to be someone she could trust, and the fact he was a lawyer didn't hurt. She wouldn't tell him everything, of course. Nothing about the deal. But she could tell him about the checkbook.

"Grant has obviously committed some kind of fraud," she concluded. "I just don't have any way to find out who's paying him off."

"It's a small town. There are some obvious possibilities."

"Believe me, I've gone over it. The most obvious one is the college or Ken Parent, since he's done a lot of work for the town, though the public safety complex was way before Grant was mayor and had any clout. He also built that new addition to town hall. The dates on those deposits start before the election and then after it. So who knows? I'll have to think about it."

Tommy stood up to go. "Be careful. If someone's paying off Grant, it means there's much bigger money involved, and that can get someone like you hurt."

"Don't worry. I'm not going to do anything stupid. I've used up my quota of stupid for 2011."

****

Bernie had overlooked something. It had taken almost a week for the lightbulb over her head to spark to life. Her box of tax documents was mundane, just flimsy cardboard that had once held a ream of paper with a bright Post-it stuck on top, "O'Dea grant documents." Yet Brent had been focused on it during her traffic stop a week before. He'd wanted to search her car with her standing in front of it, where she couldn't see what he was doing. It didn't make sense, but you had to follow the evidence, as Pete always said.

Who knew she had the box? Louise Babb, who'd called her three times asking if she'd checked its contents. One of those times was the day Brent pulled her over. Bernie had told her it was at the office but she'd bring it home that night.

It's weird how one seemingly unrelated thing rolling around your brain can lead to another and open up a huge insight. Saturday, before Imani called and everything went to hell, they'd been watching a rerun of *Jeopardy!* The clue was "Mapmaker's MacGuffin." Without thinking, Bernie said "Mountweazel."

Pete laughed. "You're just making things up."

The contestant didn't know the answer.

"It's mountweazel," Alex Trebek said in that way Bernie liked— slow, savoring the word. Just like she would. "Mountweazel. A false decoy entry on a map or reference work to guard against copyright infringement." He said it as though it were something he just naturally knew.

Bernie remembered it because it was one of those rare times she knew an answer that Pete didn't. He'd even apologized for doubting her.

Now, she thought about the coincidence of Brent pulling her over, his flashlight playing on that box. Her brain skipped to how, after the fire, Ryan Grant knew Louise told Carrie that Fergus Kelley said Grant was going to go after Pete for the fire. Once she sorted out the players in the jumbled game of telephone, there was only one way.

On that map of seeming coincidence, Bernie was going to plant her own mountweazel.

She punched in Louise's town hall number, got voicemail, which made it even easier. "I've got a favor to ask. Please don't tell the mayor. Can I get copies of any documents related to *Real Rural Justice*?"

Then she called Louise's cell. Left another voicemail. "I left a message on your office phone. Hold off on that, okay? And don't tell anyone I left it." She could trust Louise. Had for years. The fact Louise had handed that checkbook off to her meant that she trusted her, too.

CHAPTER 40

THE FIRST THING Pete did Tuesday morning was throw out the bag of Goldfish crackers. He would probably never eat one again. He sat at his desk, much as he'd left it a week before, including the budget printouts, front and center, his reading glasses on top as though he'd just left for a cup of coffee.

Vicki, who'd earlier greeted him with a warm smile, stuck her head in his door. "There's someone here to see you. Corey Wing and his daughter, Grace?"

His chest constricted. *This is not a trigger.* He drew in his breath. Smiled.

"I hope we're not bothering you," Corey said. "Grace wanted to say thanks."

The girl smiled shyly. She had a gauze bandage around her neck but looked pinker and much more energetic than she had the day before New Year's Eve.

"How are you, Grace?"

"Good. I brought you something." She held out a crayon picture with three figures—a girl with a big smile and a large white neck, a gray cat, and a man in blue with brown hair. "Thank you!" was written at the top of the page, with hearts around it. Down the side, next to the picture, the final words crammed in to fit: "I am happy you saved my life. Love, Grace," followed by X's and hearts.

"This is beautiful," Pete said. "Thank you. I'm glad you're better."

"She insisted on bringing it over," Corey said. "She saw your photo in the paper last week. I tried to explain the story was about you being suspended, but she wouldn't shut up about it. I called to find out where we could find you, and they said you were reinstated."

"That's my cat, Phillip," Grace said, leaning against Pete so she could look at the picture with him. "I didn't have room to put my family, but that's our house. I made it summer so the sun could be out."

"It's a great picture," Pete said. He cleared a space in the middle of his bulletin board and tacked it up. "Now I have something happy to look at."

"I brought something else too." She looked at her dad.

"The picture wasn't enough," Corey said. He held out a sheaf of stapled papers. "She made a book."

"A graphic novel," Grace corrected.

"Great." Pete took it from Corey.

"Can I give you a hug?" she asked, shy again.

"Sure." He got on one knee, his bad leg quaking. She wrapped her arms around his neck. She felt tiny, a baby bird, even in her heavy, too-big coat. He drew in his breath at a flash of her on the bathroom floor, blood everywhere, his hand pressing the towel to her neck. She kissed him on the cheek with a big *mwaw* and let go.

"You smell like Kool-Aid," she said. "Want to see my stitches?" She reached for the gauze.

No no no no, for god's sake, no.

"No honey," Corey said, gently pulling her hand away. "Remember, the doctor said you have to leave it alone."

"I had twenty-seven stiches. That's a record for our house."

"Let's hope no one breaks it," Corey said.

"I'm glad you're okay," Pete said. He put his hand on top of her head.

Corey nodded, his eyes wet. "We really appreciate what you did. My wife said to tell you too. If you hadn't come along, I don't know what…" He looked down at his daughter, who was watching him with bright, interested eyes. He shrugged.

"I'm glad I could help."

"Mom's mad at Rita's friend," Grace said.

"He doesn't care about that, honey," Corey said.

"No, it's okay. Why's she mad?" He didn't like to shut down kids when they had something to say, but it also felt like something he needed to know. Already knew, maybe.

"You probably don't remember," Corey said. "When you got there, I told you I hollered over to the neighbor's friend for help and he ignored me. Got in his truck and took off. My wife is obsessing about it. It doesn't make a difference since you showed up right after, but you know how women are."

"How are women?" Grace asked.

"Right," Pete said. A photo flashed in his memory, too quick, then was gone. It wasn't the years-old memory that roared back, shredding his sleep that night, triggered by Grace's injury. It was something new. Gone before he could grab it.

"How are women?" Grace asked, more insistently.

Corey turned red.

"Smart and observant," Pete told her. "I'm so glad that you have the chance to grow up to be one."

****

The mountweazel worked. Bernie was just settling at her desk Tuesday morning when Ryan Grant called.

"Louise tells me that you want the documents related to the TV show. I won't release them unless you file a Freedom of Information Act request."

"I guess I'll reconsider," Bernie said. He didn't know that the message on Louise's phone was a trick. The fact that it had worked—he'd just confirmed that he was recording Louise's calls—didn't mean he wouldn't retaliate if her writing about the show violated their deal.

"Just so you know, the production company has gone back to New York. They'll be back when the weather is better." All business, no hint of the underlying threat.

"I'll hold off. There's a lot going on, with the shooting and all."

"I thought so," he said.

After she hung up, she got the manila envelope from her desk drawer, not wanting to, but unable to stop. She took out the latest message from Grant.

Pete gave it to her, in its unmarked envelope, the day before when he'd returned from the mayor's office to tell her he was back on duty.

"Grant asked me to give you this. A news release or something."

It takes a special type of asshole, Bernie thought, to have the object of your evil be an unwitting tool in it.

She'd read it so many times since then she had it memorized. She wished she'd stop, wish she'd never seen it. Grant hadn't included a note, of course. The message was clear, though. This one was personal.

> I know part of my healing is to tell Bernie how much I need her. How my downward slide began when she told me she was moving back to her house. I just can't. I can't. I CAN'T. It's too much on her. I CAN'T. I know if I did, she'd move in, marry me, whatever I wanted. I don't want it on those terms. I know my anxiety about losing her is irrational. I know I'm not losing her if she doesn't live with me. That's not what it feels like, though. I know I conflate it with my fear something will happen to her. I almost watched her die twice and couldn't do anything to help. It gives me more nightmares than anything else that's ever happened. I know I have to manage my feelings better, but how do I manage how much I've let her down? I'M A FUCKING MESS AND NO USE TO ANYONE.

It hurt. It made Bernie sad. It made her feel guilty. All of that and so much more. Feelings she couldn't decipher. She understood why he wouldn't tell her. He was right, too, that now she knew, she didn't want to let him down. Then there was this: She'd moved in without even thinking about it when he needed help because of his leg. Being with him because he needed her like this was even more important, no matter what terms he preferred. He'd never have to know this was why. She'd have to think more about it, figure it out.

First things first. Once she solved the Ryan Grant issue, she could focus on solving the Pete issue.

She needed to solve the Grant thing fast, too. Pete had asked her earlier how her investigation into the mayor was going. She'd told him she was dropping it for now, there was too much going on with the shooting and everything.

He didn't look like he bought it, but didn't say anything. She was weak. She couldn't keep this ruse up forever. He was going to find out. She wasn't worried about herself, but every envelope from Grant convinced her more that Pete's mental health was in danger, and it was up to her to keep things from blowing up.

****

It was almost midnight and Bernie was packing up to leave for home when her cellphone rang. Probably Pete looking for her. Either that or Ryan Grant calling to taunt her.

It was neither. "Hope I'm not calling too late, but I have some news," George Libby said. "For you, not for publication."

"That's fine. I have enough news for publication this week."

He chuckled, which didn't make Bernie like him any better. He had a lot more ground than that to make up. "That BlackBerry in your house belonged to a Rita Chandler. Do you know her?"

"Yes." It was the last thing Bernie expected. "Stephanie stole it from her?"

Libby sighed. "We identified the remains through her dental records, and they belong to her. Turns out that jewelry was hers too. Her sister ID'd it."

"Wait, that's Rita?" She'd been so focused on the body being Stephanie, or not Stephanie, she missed the obvious point that it could be someone else she'd feel sorrow for. "When did this happen?"

373

"Today. We just got the paperwork wrapped up now, and I thought you'd appreciate knowing."

"Does this mean I'm off the hook?" Saying it made her feel guilty. *Sorry, Rita.*

"We have to examine every possible suspect. You were no more a suspect than anyone else."

"Funny, it didn't feel that way."

"In any case, there were some incendiary—pardon my pun— messages on her BlackBerry from her ex."

"Ryan Grant?"

"Yes."

"He burned down my house too?"

"We don't know. It's interesting that her body turned up in your house, though we don't think that's necessarily where she was killed. We also have reason to believe you're not the arsonist. But we're not charging him with the arson, only Rita Chandler's homicide."

"What reason do you have to believe I'm not the arsonist?"

"I'm not at liberty to say. We arrested him at his home this evening for the murder. We'll have an official news release tomorrow."

She called Pete, too full of the news to wait until she got home.

"I don't know," he said. "If what Libby told you is all they have, I find it hard to believe the DA would charge murder. Texts to her? You know how flimsy that is."

"Yeah, but at least it takes away all my motive stuff, right? So whoever did it, they can't make a case against me." Unsaid was the second biggest thing—at least now she'd likely never have to tell Pete about her shameful deal with that piece of crap Grant.

****

"I've got good news and bad news," Dawna said, sitting down in front of Pete's desk Friday afternoon.

"Are they both the same thing?"

"I'm not sure how I'm supposed to answer that."

"Sorry, something Bernie says."

"They kind of are, actually." Dawna was relieved Pete was back. He seemed energized from his time off. It made her feel the same way. "I think this will be a good way to end your first week back. The bad news isn't too bad, and it's not your problem."

"Great."

"You're right about Ryan Grant not killing Rita. They're close to dropping the charges."

"I was hoping I was wrong. If he didn't do it, who did? And also, that asshole shouldn't be on the loose. At least he's been locked up and out of our hair for three days."

"Well, the good news may keep him in there for longer." Dawna probably should've told Pete earlier in the week, but she wanted to make sure Libby was going to consider it as important as she did. "We uncovered evidence that he may be the arsonist."

"Whoa. What've you got?"

"It was Mandy, actually. She was reviewing Pondside Convenience video to help with the Zack Staples case. On New Year's Eve, Ryan Grant filled two gas cans there around seven-thirty."

"Good for Mandy."

"To follow up, we re-checked his alibi. He got back from Lewiston around seven and was at a New Year's Eve party here in town by eight-thirty. Plenty of time for the arson. The cherry on top is that the hostess said he smelled like gas. He told her he'd filled up on his way over, at Pondside, and got some on his coat."

"Plausible."

"He only shows up on their surveillance filling those gas cans, not putting any in his car. And it's the only gas station in town."

"That's a relief. I just want that off Bernie's back."

"I feel the same way."

"Speaking of Rita," Pete said. "I asked a friend in the AG's office if Rita reported anything about Ryan Grant. It turns out no, she hadn't filed anything."

"She must not have had the chance."

"Or changed her mind."

"I know you feel bad about never getting to talk to Zack."

"Because I was suspended." The fact that he laughed when he said it was a good sign. Dawna laughed, too.

"Well, now Zack's lawyer says he'll talk, so I'm going to go down there Monday. See what he has to say," she said. "I'm thinking since Grant's been arrested, Zack knows some things and wants a deal."

"Here's something to ask him about. Chloe, Sal's girlfriend, told me that Grant had this weird habit, as she called it, of keeping keys for the property he sold. She called me today. It was something she'd just remembered. I passed it on to Libby. I was thinking since Grant was the broker on my house, that could be how he got in. Grant was the broker on Bernie's, too, so if he's the arsonist, there you go."

"Wow. You'd think that's something Chloe would've mentioned before. I mean, it's unethical if nothing else."

"No kidding. It's all working out, isn't it?" Pete gave her a big smile.

"It is. Anything new with the shooting?"

"You know how it is. AG's got it now. Thank goodness they got an injunction to keep the TV footage off the air. I've made the case that Imani was on the phone with me and there was nothing to indicate she had a gun or was about to shoot anyone, but you know how it is. It doesn't matter if she had a gun, just what Brent's perception was. If he felt she did, and felt he was in imminent danger, then…"

"Which he says was the case."

"Yeah." Pete looked like he had more to say, but she could practically see him flip the mental page. Instead, he said, "You know, I've watched that video several times, and I swear there's someone in the second-floor apartment. I pointed it out to the AG's office, but they're just focused on the part of the video that shows the shooting."

"No one lived upstairs, right?"

"Right. I even went over and checked it out. Looked like maybe a squatter had been there. I'm sure it's nothing. Just kind of bugging me."

CHAPTER 41

PETE WAS CLOSE to done for the day Friday, feeling good about his first week back. Dawna's news, as she'd put it herself, was the cherry on top. When his desk phone rang, he almost didn't answer, he was almost out the door and he didn't want anything to wreck his good mood. *Why do I always feel like I'm one phone call away from everything going to shit?*

When he saw Eli Perry's name on the caller ID, he picked up.

"I tried to get Dawna," Eli said.

"She just took off for Sugarloaf for the weekend."

"Maybe you can help. I know this isn't an official police duty, the only reason I was calling Dawna is because she's Natalie's cousin, kind of her surrogate mom, you know? But I'm trying to track Nat down. She was supposed to check in at three, and I haven't heard from her. I tried her cell and got voicemail. I'm in Skowhegan. I know it's just been an hour, but she never misses a check-in. She knows the only reason she has that phone is to check in. She'll lose it otherwise."

"No problem. I'll let you know when I scare her up." It would be dark soon. It was cold out, and, as always, there was a threat of a storm in the air.

Pete tried Natalie's cell and left a voicemail telling her to call her dad, and him too. Then he called Sal. Chloe's son, Hallowell, Natalie's friend, told Pete that she probably rode her bike up to the quarry.

"She was supposed to come over and play Risk, but she had some stupid thing to do, so that's probably where she is. It's that stupid Native American stuff she's obsessed with," Hallowell said. "I'm not supposed to say, but she wants to take pictures of those petroglyphs. She saw in the paper they're going to blow them up."

Pete texted Jamie, who was on patrol, that he was looking for Natalie and if he saw her to call his cell.

Jamie called him. "Is something up?"

"No, her dad's just worried, I'm sure she's around somewhere, just keep an eye out and let me know." *Nothing to worry about.* So why did he feel like there was?

****

It was spitting snow and the afternoon was growing dark as Pete drove through the open gate and turned up the road to the quarry. Someone had been up, and maybe down, ahead of him. The road's packed-down snow was marked with tire tracks. He got out to look closely, and, sure enough, there was also the thin line of a bike track, the same basic shape as the fat all-terrain tires Natalie had proudly shown him a few weeks before. There weren't two bike tracks, though, so she was still up there.

The road wound to the east, around the bulk of the part of the small mountain, just a hill, really, that had been ripped away for the quarry decades before. Glimpses of the sharp geometrical unnatural towers of rock near the bottom of the road gave way to a tunnel of pines as he wound his way up, but he could still feel the rock's dark presence. The road briefly got steeper, then he was in a clearing. It wasn't as dark without the trees. The weak glimmer of setting sun to the west still glowed on the upper parts of the quarry walls, spread out below, and dimly lit the spectacular vista of the western mountains beyond. An endless carpet of rolling pine in between.

The clearing was empty. "Natalie?"

Crap. Bernie was going to meet him at his office so they could go to dinner in Farmington. In his concern about Natalie, he'd totally forgotten. Now he had no service. He texted, "Looking for Natalie, back soon. Let yourself in." He knew it was likely it wouldn't go through until he was back down the road, but that would be soon.

The clearing wasn't big. Natalie was a little girl with a bicycle in the snow and it was dark. She couldn't have gone far.

The snow was windblown, crisscrossed with tire tracks, the same ones as on the road, but there was no sign of a vehicle.

"Natalie?" He said it loudly. Nothing came back except the wind through the trees and a low call from an owl. "Natalie?" Louder. Nothing.

He turned on his flashlight and went to where her bike track entered the clearing. It was accompanied by small footprints, which meant she was walking by the time she got there. There were larger footprints, too, in various places around the clearing. Pete followed Natalie's to a narrow opening in the tangled bushes. The snow around it was trampled, too disturbed to make out details. He pushed through the bushes. "Natalie? It's Chief Pete."

His flashlight picked up a spark of metallic blue. Next to the trail, shoved into the undergrowth, was Natalie's bike.

"Natalie?" He yelled it.

He went down the trail, the snow churned up too much to tell if he was following her footprints or something else. An engine, somewhere off in the distance, came to life. *Funny how sound carries when you're up high.* Other than that, it was just the wind. After a few yards, the terrain became uneven, the path narrow, skirting around rocks, some discarded from the quarry, some natural formations. Then the trail edged steeply down. He'd come to the back end of the hill. The snow on the trail was untouched. He'd gone too far.

"Natalie?" As loudly as he could.

He backtracked and saw that the disturbance, tracks or whatever they were, went between a thick grove of bushes. The opening was no more than a deer trail. He pushed in. After a few yards, the bushes cleared. In front of him was a rock wall. His flashlight shown on smooth, natural rock, not the sharp cut rock of the quarry.

At first he thought he was seeing graffiti. It was easy to miss in the disappearing light. It was the petroglyphs. Little round faces dancing across the rock, punctuated by other stick figures depicting animals and other shapes. If he were on a hike, it would've been an astounding and delightful discovery. He would've run his fingers over them. Sat with them for hours, not wanting to leave. All it did for him now was confirm Natalie was likely nearby. She had to be.

"Natalie!"

He heard shuffling, rustling. He realized he'd been hearing it since he'd seen the petroglyphs, but thought it was the wind, which had picked up.

"Natalie!"

This time the rustling was accompanied by a muffled cry. He pushed aside the undergrowth to his right to meet large frightened eyes above a duct-taped mouth.

She shook her head.

Why? That was his only thought before everything went black.

****

No one was around when Bernie let herself in at the police department. She texted Pete. "I'm at your office. Getting hangry." She added a smiley face.

She sat down at his desk. "Ugh, budget." She flipped through the computer printouts, but they were too boring to distract her. She scanned his shelves. Police procedural manuals. Nothing even remotely interesting. She shuffled the printouts around again. Underneath, there was a thick stapled bunch of papers. The top one said, in crayon, "The Adventure of Grace Age 8 and Her Cut and the Police Chief Saving Her Life By Grace Wing."

"Plot *and* character. Excellent." It was obviously the work of a kid, crayoned words in speech bubbles squeezed and hard to decipher. Definitely better than the budget.

The story started out as a snowy day with dad and little brother, watching videos and eating cereal. The plot got dark fast, though. As the father dealt with some issue with the toddler, Grace decided to cut her hair. She used her mother's fabric scissors, since they were big and sharp and would cut a lot. She kneeled on the bathroom sink so she could see in the mirror.

Then she slipped, cutting her neck. The drawing of that scene was particularly graphic, bright red crayon lines of blood everywhere. Bernie recognized the story. Grace was the child who was injured the day before New Year's Eve. The one whose blood soaked Pete's uniform. The one he'd written about in his journal.

Bernie would have to keep an eye on this kid and hire her at the paper in a few years. The story was dramatic, and Grace had an eye for detail. The frantic father, the wailing baby brother, the obtuse neighbor. The police chief, when he arrived, was larger than life. Bernie tried, not quite succeeding, to keep Pete's version, the horrific scene from his night terrors, from overtaking what she was looking at.

Her phone rang. Sal.

"Did Pete find Nat?"

"Is that where he is?"

"I guess she went up to the quarry to take photos of the petroglyphs before they, as Hallowell put it, 'blow them up.' I left a message on his cell, but this is kind of important, so can you—"

"Oh geez. We had a classified ad in the paper this morning. You know how they're required to put one in when there's going to be blasting?"

"No."

"Well, they are. It was put in by Nakilot Partners LLC for the summit. Natalie came in after school today, all upset. She didn't get why I didn't have more about the Passamaquoddy angle in the paper, then on top of it, her dad saw that classified ad and mentioned it. For a twelve-year-old, she made a great case. She thinks I'm on the college's side now. Hard to explain news decisions to a kid. She's obsessed with the—"

"Petroglyphs. Yes. But—"

"I've got Tommy trying to see if there's a way to file an injunction before it happens, though I don't know on whose behalf it would be filed. I obviously can't do it myself. Since I can't find Normand Ouimette, I've got a call in to the Passamaquoddy officials he was dealing with, but haven't heard back. The blasting is next week."

"Bernie, can you please shut up a minute?"

She realized he'd been trying to interrupt her. "Sorry, I'm very hungry."

"Tell Pete if you can reach him that Hallowell says some guy was bugging Natalie last time she went up there. She said he was creepy and she was scared of him. He got the impression she wasn't going to go back up there because of it, but I guess the call of the petroglyphs is a strong one."

****

For a second, Pete thought he was swimming in the lake. Underwater, quiet and very cold. Then he realized with startling clarity that he was in an ever-growing pool of freezing water in the front seat of his Charger. Instinct kicked in. He had a minute or less to get out of the car. That's if the windows would work. He reached to unbuckle his seat belt, but he wasn't wearing one. It would waste time to remove his boots, coat, or anything else that would drag him down. He wasn't that deep in yet. He just had to get out.

As he reached for the window button, desperately hoping he could lower it, movement in the back seat caught his eye.

It was Natalie, her mouth duct-taped, her hands behind her back, her legs taped too. Water rushed in her open window, covering the seat and rapidly rising.

He slid over into the back and ripped the tape off her mouth. He wouldn't have time to undo her arms and legs.

"Take a deep breath and hold it," he said. She did, her terrified eyes not leaving his. "We're going to get out. It'll be okay. Just do everything I say."

She nodded.

"When you're out the window, go up as much as you can." He lifted her toward the opening. Her clothes were wet and heavy as he pushed her against the force of the rushing water. The car was underwater, but it hadn't filled up yet. That was changing fast as the torrent filled the window opening, pushing Natalie back against him. He braced his legs on the seat, wrapped his arms around her and pushed through the deluge.

He managed to vault them through it, then found the window's edge with his foot, and tried to launch upward toward the ice. The hole that the car made was a few feet to their left. He pushed Natalie in front of him, up and toward it. Her soaked clothes and inability to use her arms and legs made it hard to keep her on an upward trajectory.

At least the cold didn't bother him. If he just told himself he was ice swimming, just another morning on the lake, they could do this.

Save the kid. Save the kid. It was his only focus. Using the sinking car for leverage, he pushed again, this time with both feet. With one big heave, Natalie was halfway through the hole, the top of her body on the ice. The car beneath his feet dropped away, but he had enough leverage for one more push as it sank to get his head and shoulders above water too.

He had one arm around her—his nearly numb hand gripping her soaking wet coat—and one arm flat on the ice. He tried to pull himself up, while continuing to push Natalie farther onto the ice.

"Try to wiggle up onto it." It came out in gasps, but she understood. She squirmed farther onto the surface, dolphin-kicking her bound legs as he tried to get a better grip on her without letting go. The effort sent him backwards and under, his coat and boots dragging him down. Underwater, he wrapped his arms around her legs and gave a mighty kick, propelling himself upwards. It worked. He felt her squirm onto the ice above him.

He gave another kick and his head and shoulders were out of the water. He spread his arms on the ice. One more to heave himself up. He'd done it a couple times in the lake, but he'd been wearing swim trunks and water shoes, exhilarated from his swim. This felt nothing like that. His clothes were heavy, his bare hands—he had no memory of losing his gloves—had no feeling. He took a deep breath and summoned whatever strength he had left and gave one more kick.

It worked. He was lying on the ice next to Natalie. "We're going to be okay," he told her. She nodded. She was shivering, her teeth chattering.

He had no idea if the ice was thick enough to support him standing up, but they had to get off of it. He tried to undo the tape around her wrists, but his fingers were useless. He knew once the adrenaline wore off, he'd start shaking from the cold, too. He had to do whatever he could now, before the cold overtook him.

"There's a knife in my pocket," she said, barely audible as she trembled with cold.

Pete felt around in her waterlogged coat until he found a Swiss army knife, along with a flashlight. With some effort, he cut the duct tape around her wrists and legs.

"I know you're cold," he said. "We're going to get out of here and it'll be okay. Try to concentrate on that, not on being cold."

It was dark now. The one saving grace was that whoever had pushed them over, he hoped, wouldn't be able to see that they were out of the car. The wall of the quarry that loomed nearest to them was just twenty or so feet away. It was hard to see in the dark, but when he'd looked down earlier, he remembered seeing a ledge jutting out from that side. There had to be more than just the dark vertical barrier that seemed to surround them. They'd get there, find the ledge, then he'd figure out where they'd go next.

"Let's go. On our tummies in case the ice is thin."

"That man is going to come back."

"No he won't. Even if he does, it's dark and he won't see us. I won't let him hurt you, Natalie." He knew if she thought about it, she'd know how empty a promise it was. Whoever it was had managed to knock him out and put him and Natalie in the car and push it over the quarry edge. Still, he meant it with everything he had in him.

"Let's go, quick, okay?"

They belly-crawled toward the wall, Pete helping her along with one arm, using his other to move himself. There was a ledge, about a foot above the ice, but it was smaller than he'd thought. Maybe two feet at its widest, disappearing and then re-emerging along the rock.

He helped Natlie, quaking from the cold, work her way onto it, then he scrambled on next to her.

The quarry walls rose above him. In front of them was a long stretch of white, the hole where his Charger had broken through barely visible in the dark. He couldn't see the other side, but from above, it had looked less like a vertical wall. There'd been trees, a slope going down to the white expanse of ice. If they could get over there, they could get out and to safety. The ice seemed thin, though. He'd heard it cracking below and around them when he and Natalie moved across it. He had to make a decision. They wouldn't last long on this rock ledge in soaking clothes, the cold wind howling.

Natalie was shaking so hard he was afraid she'd fall back onto the ice. "Try to curl up a little, keep some body heat," he told her. He put his arm around her. It wasn't going to be nearly enough. They had to go, but his adrenaline was gone. Whatever had driven him to get them both out of the car, out of the water, across the ice, had sapped him. They had to go. He didn't even have minutes to decide. They had to do it now. He was shivering as hard as Natalie by now. He moved to straighten his legs, stand up, but they wouldn't work.

"Are we going?" Natalie asked.

"Yes," Pete said. He stood up on the ice, holding himself steady against the wall. He willed himself to stop shaking. It only half-worked.

"Try to stand up," he said to Natalie. There was no way he could carry her. He took her quaking arm and she managed to get up, then fell to the ice.

"It's okay," Pete said. He lifted her and held her against him. "Just lean against me, and we'll go slow."

Holding her tight against his right side, the one with the strong leg, they began inching their way into the darkness. Natalie's flashlight worked, but she'd panicked when he turned it on, afraid their attacker would see it. He knew where he was going, anyway. Straight across. He tried to ignore the cracking sounds as they shuffled through the snow. It wasn't that loud, he told himself. Sandy always said ice makes that noise, don't worry about it.

Their progress was excruciatingly slow. Natalie, for the third time, slipped from his grasp, falling in a heap. "I'm sorry," she said, more faintly this time than she had the time before. "I'm trying."

"I know," Pete said. He tried lifting her back up, but her legs gave way. He picked her up, cradling her in his arms, took one step, and fell forward into the snow. In the distance, somewhere, a faint engine started up. He could hear an owl above the wind. They were incredibly close to civilization. Too close to die. Pete wouldn't let it happen. Not to Natalie, not to him. If only he could get his body to understand.

CHAPTER 42

BERNIE LOOKED AT HER phone, in front of her on the desk, every ten seconds, hoping Pete would call or text. She considered driving to the quarry, but that would just complicate things. Everything was fine. Pete probably had to walk up because of the gate, and it was just taking a while.

"Let me know the second you're back in range," she texted.

She flipped through the book, not really paying attention, the blood, words jammed into bubbles, exclamation points, secondary characters—it was a confusing blur. All colored by the chilling words in Pete's journal. As she put the pages down, though, something nagged at her. Something in the blur stood out. Tripped something in her brain. She picked it up and went through it again.

There it was, a man, Grace's dad apparently, hanging out a window of the house yelling "Hey! You! Mister!" at a house next door. An arrow pointed down at the house with the words "Rita's House" jammed next to it. There was a pickup truck, larger than the house, with a man standing next to it. The truck had a big maroon KP on the door.

"Who's on duty?" Bernie asked the empty room.

She texted Sandy, her hands shaking. "Where are you?"

"Fire station."

"I'm in Pete's office. On my way over. We have an emergency."

****

Sandy had assured Bernie everything would be fine, but she didn't believe it as she hung on for dear life in the cab of his pickup. The way he was driving, she was pretty sure he didn't believe it either. They roared through the open gate at the bottom of the quarry road, the truck fishtailing as Sandy took the turn too hard.

She was happy to see Jamie's blue lights behind them. Dawna was minutes away. She'd been on her way to a ski weekend, but turned around when Sandy called.

It was dark, and the road that twisted up the hill seemed to take forever, though Bernie knew it was less than a mile. When they got to the clearing at the summit, there was still a faint glow in the western sky, but other than that, night had fallen.

"His car's not here," Sandy said.

Bernie catapulted out of the cab.

"Pete!" There was no answer. Nothing but the wind.

"Maybe he went back," Sandy said. He had his cellphone out. "No service up here. You get anything from him?"

Bernie had been obsessively checking. "No."

She walked toward the edge overlooking the quarry.

"Careful, sweetheart. It's slick up here."

It was too dark below, a deep black hole. A bottomless pit.

Sandy's flashlight played around the empty clearing.

"What's this?" Bernie asked, though it was obvious what it was. Tire tracks going off the edge. She wouldn't believe it though. It couldn't be real. Sandy came closer with the light, and they came to life in deep, stark relief.

"I don't know." Sandy said. His voice shook. He knew as well as she did.

"And this?" A few yards away, two dark shapes transformed in the bright beam into a Redimere PD ski hat and a big green Maglite flashlight, just like the one Pete carried in his car.

"I don't know," Sandy said quietly. He went to pick them up.

"Don't touch those," Bernie screamed.

He jumped, startled, but backed away.

Bernie didn't understand. Yet, she did. She went back to the tire tracks that ended at the edge.

Blue pulsing light lit up the clearing. It took her a second to realize Jamie had arrived. Part of her said it didn't matter now, but another part screamed that it did. This couldn't be what her head was telling her it was. Somehow, Jamie would read something different into it. There'd be an obvious explanation she and Sandy had overlooked.

"Too dark to really see down there." Jamie's voice caught on the final syllables.

"This isn't happening," Bernie said. "This didn't happen." It came out too high, hysterical. She needed to stay calm, figure it out. She couldn't. She was rocked by a terror that left no room for anything else.

Sandy grabbed her from behind, his arms tight around her, squeezing her against him. "Stay away from the edge, Bernie." His heart pounded through his coat, her coat. She couldn't breathe. Her legs gave way, but Sandy's steel grip held her up.

"He wouldn't do that," she said. "He wouldn't. This didn't happen."

"I don't know," Jamie said.

"No, you don't," Bernie screamed. Jamie had been on that mountain when they rescued Pete the previous summer, but he'd never understood. "He wouldn't do this." The sound of her voice made her ears hurt, filled the western sky. Sandy and Jamie, faces white, looked at her with a helplessness that made her wish she could scream louder.

Headlights swept across them, too bright. Too big to be Dawna's Jeep.

"Oh, thank god you're here," Ken Parent said, approaching from his truck. "No reception up here, so I went down to call it in. Nothing anyone can do now, though."

"What did you do?" Bernie screamed at him. She struggled in Sandy's arms, but he held her tight.

Ken shook his head. "Bernadette, I tried to help, but I was too late."

"Help what? What happened?" Jamie asked.

"I was down near the bottom, doing some surveying, and saw that little girl ride up on her bike. She comes up here, no big deal. Though it's really not safe for a kid. Then, a couple minutes later, I saw the police chief's car go up. At first I didn't think much of it, but then, when no one came down right away, it just didn't feel right. A guy up there alone with a little girl."

"Bullshit," Bernie screamed.

"Honey." Sandy squeezed her tighter. He was shaking.

Ken was way too calm. She wanted to tear herself from Sandy's arms and rip him to shreds.

"When I got up here, I saw he had that little girl bound up in duct tape and was putting her in the back of his car," he continued, speaking to Jamie. "I yelled to him, 'Hey, what're you doing? Stop.' But he just got in the car and drove over the edge before I even knew what was happening."

"Liar!" Bernie screamed. "It was you!"

"Bernie," Sandy said.

"No!" She struggled to free herself, didn't even know what she'd do once she did. Sandy's long arms enveloped her. So tight she could hardly breathe. Ken looked at her like she was insane, but she knew she was the sanest person on that summit.

"We'll have to see about all that," Jamie said. "I need to radio down."

Another set of headlights lit them up.

They watched silently as Dawna approached them.

"We think the chief went over the side with Natalie Perry in the car," Jamie said, voice trembling. Ken started talking, but Dawna silenced him with a quick, "Not now, please."

She looked at the tire tracks. Looked over the edge.

"I want everyone back away from this edge," Dawna said. "Everyone move way back. Don't step on the tire tracks."

They all shuffled back. Bernie hadn't wanted to look over the edge again, anyway, but as Sandy pulled her back, away from it, away from Pete, it felt wrong.

Dawna shown the flashlight around the clearing. Its beam caught the ski cap, the Maglite, neatly nestled together.

"It was him," Bernie screamed, struggling and frantic in Sandy's arms. "Those are just placed there. Look at them. Just neat on the ground. He did it."

"Please step into the back of the cruiser, Mr. Parent." Dawna spoke quietly, with no emotion.

"Wait," he said. "I'm a good Samaritan here."

"I just need to talk to you further. Jamie, please call this in. Sandy, get Bernie somewhere warm and safe, okay?"

"He did it." Bernie yelled it again, sobbing. She had to make Dawna understand. "He did something. Not Pete. He did something to Pete and Natalie. *He* did something." Her ability to articulate was gone. *This is not happening.*

"We'll take care of it, Bernie. You need to go." Dawna nodded at Sandy. "Mr. Parent, please get in the back of the cruiser. Sandy, once you get Bernie safe, we'll need a recovery"—she looked at Bernie—"a rescue, crew."

Sandy half-steered, half-carried Bernie to his truck as she struggled in his arms. "No, sweetheart. Okay? No."

Bernie was in the passenger seat, seat belt firmly around her, before she realized it was happening.

"He's not dead," she said to Sandy as he drove down the hill. "He can swim in icy water. You know that. He got out. He saved Natalie. We have to find him. They're cold." She knew as long as she believed it, it would be true.

"I'm going to bring you to Chuck's house. You can wait there with him and your brother."

"No." She unbuckled her seat belt and reached for the door handle. "I'm not going anywhere. I have to find Pete. He's down there somewhere."

Sandy put his arm across her as he pulled over and stopped the truck. He leaned past her to buckle her seat belt, his wet cheek against hers as he fumbled with it. She was convulsing with sobs now, unable to talk. He gave up on the buckle and put his arms around her. "I know, sweetheart. I know."

"We have to find him," Bernie said against his shoulder. "It's too cold. We have to find him."

He was sobbing now too. "I know. I know."

****

Pete sat in the snow, surrounded by darkness, signaling with the flashlight, a high-powered one Natalie had pilfered from her father's toolbox. At least it was fully charged, had a good, strong beam. It was all he could do. He could barely move. Natalie, enveloped in his arms,, couldn't at all. She trembled uncontrollably, her lips blue. He'd tried to lift her, but his bad leg couldn't bear any weight. The rest of him wouldn't stop shaking. All he could do now was try to keep her warm and keep pushing the button. He forced his thumb, no feeling in it at all, not to stop. He had no idea if anyone would see the light, but at least the sky had cleared, stars beginning to emerge. He knew there were some houses through the woods on the other side of the quarry, and North Road beyond that.

Natalie had panicked when he told her he was going to signal for help, but he assured her that the man in the truck wasn't coming back. Even so, when he heard a motor, his instinct was to stop. He put his panic aside. It was their only hope.

Natalie yelped, stared at him in terror from a blue-white face.

"It's okay."

He flashed the light as the engine got louder, a bobbing light approaching them across the snow-covered ice. The dark shape was too small to be a truck. It had just one small light. A snowmobile.

"What the hell are you doing here?" the driver, a woman, asked.

"Take her," Pete said. "I can make it on my own."

"I'll take both of you," the woman said. She was off the machine, leaning over Natalie. "This child is half dead. Let's get her in here."

She, with as much help as Pete could give, lifted Natalie into a trailer with sled runners hitched to the back of the snowmobile. The woman took off her coat, a too-big man's Carhartt, and tucked it around her. "That'll have to do," she said. "We'll be warm in no time, honey."

392

"Climb on behind me," she said to Pete.

Through chattering teeth, Pete said, "We'll be too heavy."

"Nonsense. The ice is fine."

"I heard it crack." Pete had been focused on keeping Natalie alive and reassuring her, on getting them out of there. Now that she'd be safe he felt a panic he knew was irrational growing in him. He was freezing, shaking. Knew he wouldn't last even an hour in his frozen clothes on this windswept ice. But the thought of getting on the snowmobile and crossing it paralyzed him.

She pointed toward the end where the Charger had gone through. "Over there, it's fed by a spring, churns the water up, makes it harder to freeze. It's fine here. I've lived here all my life. I know this ice."

Pete could barely stand. He desperately wanted to get on the snowmobile. He just couldn't. He could see the machine plunging with the three of them through into the freezing water. He wouldn't be able to get out this time. Wouldn't be able to save Natalie, or this woman.

"I can make it myself," he said, his voice shaking with the cold.

"I know you've been through something," the woman said. Even in the dark he could see she understood. "You're in shock. But if we don't get this little girl somewhere warm right now, she'll be dead. If I leave you here, so will you. I lost a son. I'm not going to leave someone else's son here to freeze to death."

He tried to take deep breath, ease the panic, but his chest was tight, heavy. He had a flash of the frozen bodies on Everest, Bernie's latest obsession. Of himself, frozen here, forever.

She took his arm, a strong, firm grip. "Come on, let's get onboard and get home."

She put one leg over the machine, her arm guiding him. He sat down behind her.

The machine roared to life. Above the engine, she yelled, "Hang on tight, son. We're almost home."

CHAPTER 43

PETE WAS DESPERATE to call Bernie. To call Eli Perry. At the moment, though, he was powerless. Corliss Gower, their rescuer, had left in her pickup truck to get help. Her phone hadn't worked since the power outage. Neither had the Wi-Fi. Pete wanted to go with her, but he could barely stand, was still shaking from the cold.

He sat on the couch in layers of too-big flannel and wool, wrapped in a blanket. Corliss had heated up chicken soup and hot chocolate. Pete was shaking too much to lift either without spilling it.

Natalie lay wrapped up next to him, her eyes, when they were open, still wide with horror. He'd heard her tell Corliss the man knocked out Pete, he put them both in the car and made it go over the side. She'd lowered her window because of POGO—pop the seat belt, open the window, and GO.

"I could only do one of those things," she'd told Corliss. She managed to get her elbow on the window button as the car hurtled toward the ice.

Now she was silent. Pete kept a hand, stinging with frostbite, around her ankle—he'd had to burrow through two blankets to find it—to monitor her pulse and let her know he was there.

When Corliss led him through the door, Natalie in her arms, she'd said to her daughter, "Here's your Sexy Sheriff."

"Sorry I'm no help," Julie said now. Each word was punctuated with a rasp from her breathing mechanism.

"Help will be here soon," Pete said. "It's okay."

"I knew it was trouble. Norm wouldn't have sold his land to the college," she said. "Mom's been going back and forth with that Parent guy. He told her Norm's land was taken for taxes, but that's not true. The college was after it for years."

Pete listened to her slow recitation, happy to have her talk so he wouldn't have to. He could barely think. The pain in the back of his head, where he'd been hit, pulsed. His hands and feet burned. He was exhausted, his mind foggy. "What do you think happened?" he asked, more to keep awake than anything else.

"Something happened to Norm. Probably at the bottom of the quarry, just like Parent wanted with you."

"You're sure it's Parent?"

"It's him," Natalie said. "KP. On his truck. He told me if I went up there again he'd throw me in the quarry. But I had to go, because he's going to blow up the petroglyphs. He took my camera."

When Natalie said "KP on the truck," Pete felt the familiar sharp pain in his chest that came from more than just his cold-constricted lungs.

"No surprise," Julie said. "Mom told him about the petroglyphs. He said there weren't any. I'm sure he wanted to get rid of them before anyone saw. Norm had photos. I bet they're gone, just like Norm."

"Where was the truck?" Pete asked Natalie. He wanted to press the trigger. He needed to know how he was so easily fooled.

"He had a place he hid it. I looked when I got there, and it wasn't there. I heard it when I was taking the pictures and tried to hide, but it was too late."

His chest tightened more. He closed his eyes. Tried to breathe through it. He'd passed the truck that day on the way to Grace Wing's house. Ken Parent, turning off her street, looked straight ahead, no friendly wave. It seemed off, but not significant. He'd forgotten about it, but it had attached itself in Pete's head to his waking nightmare, his night terror. He hadn't been able to see it past the horror of blood, of little girls with giant gashes in their necks. Now it was clear. Bright. High-definition. He opened his eyes. Natalie and Julie were watching him. He tried to calm his breathing, look like he wasn't in the grip of a panic attack. It eased slightly.

He squeezed Natalie's ankle. "We're okay now."

"My dad is going to be so mad."

"Your dad is going to be very happy you're alive."

Natalie tried to sit up, but Pete, with a hand on her shoulder, gently eased her back down. "You need to take it easy." He focused on breathing, as the panic faded.

Her bright eyes roamed the large room. They lit on the large whiteboard next to Julie. It was next to an extended keyboard that was hooked up to two monitors.

"You have a lot of stuff."

"I need to since I'm stuck here," Julie said.

"What's the math?" Pete asked. Strings of numbers, color-coded with notes, filled the whiteboard. He didn't have the focus to make it out.

"That's not math," Natalie said. "It's IP addresses."

When Pete didn't respond, she said, "Computer addresses."

Julie laughed, a loud rasp. "You're smart. Maybe you can be my assistant."

Natalie smiled, deep dimples emerging in her cheeks, which had regained some of their color. "You're Redimere Raw."

Julie laughed again. "You're *really* smart."

They were interrupted by a commotion on the front steps.

"Too soon for your mom to be back," Pete said. The panic rose, but so did his adrenalin. "Does she have a gun?"

"There's a shotgun in the closet by the door."

It was Ken Parent coming back. He had to protect Natalie and Julie. Pete struggled to get up, but his legs gave way, and he fell back. He fought his way back up, cursing his shaky legs, his throbbing head, lungs that weren't working right.

The front door burst open, and before he could make the mental switch from fight to relief, Bernie was in his arms, sobbing. "I knew you got out. I knew it."

Corliss and Sandy were behind her.

"I had to follow these two flashing my lights for about two miles before this one finally pulled over," Corliss said.

Pete held Bernie tight. He buried his face in her hair, wet from the snow, tangled from the wind. "I'm sorry," he whispered.

"Holy shit, Pete," Sandy said. He'd been crying too.

"Everything's okay," Pete said. "It's okay."

CHAPTER 44

"WHY ARE WE UP this early?" Bernie asked. Pete had slept soundly, but she'd lay awake most of the night, making sure his heart was beating and that he was breathing. Now, at 6:30 a.m., on a Saturday no less, he was energetically pulling on his jeans.

"Up and at 'em," he said.

He'd refused to go to the hospital with Natalie, had insisted he was okay. Dawna thought he might have a slight concussion and mild frostbite, but he said he was fine. Bernie didn't believe him. He wouldn't let her help him shower, though he seemed too shaky to do it himself. She'd hovered in the bathroom, just in case, but he refused to turn on the water until she left. *He was fine.* He'd collapsed into a deep sleep shortly after he was done, smelling like mango-peach-coconut that didn't hide, at least to Bernie's senses, the cold dark odor of the quarry. Of terror.

Now it was like it hadn't happened.

"I don't understand what's going on." Bernie sat up.

"Dad wants us over at his place. It's urgent."

Pete rarely referred to Chuck as Dad. It was a tell. He wasn't as okay as he was acting.

"At least let me have coffee."

"We'll have it there."

When they got to Chuck's, it took Bernie a couple of seconds before she recognized the guy on the couch. He'd lost weight, was unnaturally pale with large dark circles below his eyes. Normand Ouimette held out a hand to shake, but she hugged him.

"I found this guy asleep on Imani's couch this morning when I went over there to get some of her belongings to bring down to her mom," Chuck said.

Norm was living in the empty apartment above hers, and she was bringing him food. Even with her gone, he was afraid to come out.

"I've filled him in. He doesn't have to be afraid anymore," Chuck said.

"Where were you when I went over there and checked that apartment the other day?" Pete asked. "I *knew* I saw someone in the window before."

"Sorry," Normand said. "I hid in a closet. I was scared to death you'd find me. I don't know who to trust." He said to Bernie, "I want to talk to you before anyone else. I don't know what's going to happen. I want it on the record."

Bernie set her phone to record and took a notebook and pencil out of her bag.

It started with Ryan Grant.

"I needed help with the conservation easement. He was so great when I bought the land." Normand had dealt with Passamaquoddy officials, but Grant took that over in October when Normand asked. In December, Normand got an eviction notice. It was, of course, the last thing he expected.

"From the college?" Bernie asked.

"Nakilot Partners LLC. I thought it was a mistake. Then Ryan didn't return my calls. I called the Passamaquoddy guys I'd dealt with, and they didn't know anything about it. They'd been waiting to hear from me. That's when I called you."

"Sorry. I got a new phone."

"I also called Rita Chandler. I hoped she could figure it out. Meantime, I got an anonymous letter telling me if I didn't get out, I'd be burned to death in my bed."

"You didn't report it?" Pete asked.

"No. When I say I don't know who to trust, I mean it. I'd figured out by then the mayor defrauded me. Who knew who else was involved? I trusted Rita, though, and she said she'd get to the bottom of it. She's the property manager next door and set me up in an empty apartment. She knew Imani and said she'd keep quiet. Rita gave her money to get me food, but had to keep the water and electric off or the owner would ask questions. Imani let me use her bathroom, so that was okay. I parked my truck out back. It's got a lot of miles on it, some rust. No one was going to notice it there."

Bernie agreed. The dirt parking lot behind the Beehive was full of beaters and rust-buckets, whatever its tenants could afford. No one would look twice at one more hard-used vehicle back there.

"They had to know I was gonna make a stink. I knew I'd be in for it. Some accident would happen to me." He made air quotes around *accident*.

"Rita got word out that I'd gone up to my camp at Coburn Gore, to keep them from looking for me while she got the AG to get an investigation rolling." He laughed. "They bought the Coburn Gore thing, Rita said. No way I'd be up at that camp this time of year. You can't even get to it. Joke was on them."

Pete's hand found the back of Bernie's neck, gave a little rub.

"Was the college involved?" Bernie asked, hoping they chalked her red face up to the little house, crammed with people, being so warm.

"I don't think so. They've been after my land ever since Wilson became president, and I always told them no, I'm not selling, but I don't think they'd resort to fraud. Maybe not ask too many questions if someone else did, though. They didn't care a fig about Passamaquoddy heritage. The land abutted theirs, and they offered a ton of money, but there was no way."

"Chief, I need to tell you this," he said. He'd been matter-of-fact as he told his story, but now his voice shook. "Ryan Grant was sneaking around out there the night that cop shot Imani. She was petrified he'd find me."

****

There's an old saying in the legal profession that Bernie always liked. "First to talk, first to walk." When more than one person is involved in a crime, the one who blabs to police first usually gets the best deal.

Bernie, as she sat in Pete's office Monday on her lunch break, foodless to her dismay, and listening to Dawna's latest update, wasn't sure if Ryan Grant, the piece of crap who'd burned down her house and defrauded Normand Ouimette, was going to get a good deal. Still, it would likely be better than the one for Ken Parent, the piece of crap who not only helped defraud Norm and burn down her house, but also killed Rita Chandler and tried to kill Pete and Natalie.

Once Grant knew they could put Ken Parent at Rita's around the time police believe she was killed, he couldn't shut up, Dawna said.

Grant admitted to being at the Beehive when Imani was shot, but swore up and down that he did not have Brent shoot her.

"I've talked to Brent," Pete said. "I believe him when he says he had no idea Imani had anything to do with Grant, or that he was even there. Grant had Brent do him a lot of favors, he called them, but said that Brent wasn't in on anything to do with Norm, or anything else that Parent and he were up to. He'd just ask Brent to do things, like pull Bernie over to get that box. He used Brent's antipathy for me as a lever. I guess it worked. The shooting though was just one of those..." He shot Bernie a look.

She drew in her breath. She'd thought about it a lot, and agreed that it didn't make sense Brent would shoot Imani for Grant. But the reason he did was just as bad. He saw a Black woman with something in her hand and pulled the trigger. She and Pete had talked about it. He'd even agreed with her. Kind of. He also insisted until you were in that situation, you couldn't know what you'd do. She felt like it was something he had to say, more than something he believed deep down. She didn't push it, though. Everything, all the emotional stuff, had become very raw again.

"Back to Rita's homicide," Bernie said to Dawna.

"It's great you remembered seeing Parent's truck on Rita's street when you were going to the Wing house the day before New Year's

Eve," Dawna said to Pete. "It was just what they needed to get Grant to open up."

"Backed up by graphic artist Grace Wing," Bernie said. She caught Pete's eye. He'd told her that he associated Grace's injury with "a bad case in Philly" and it had become a big T, big enough to include Ken Parent driving by. She couldn't tell him, of course, that she knew all about Philly.

Dawna continued. "The whole thing—the arson part—started with Parent and Grant deciding to buy the Perkins lot behind your house at the low price it had been listed at for years. Grant had figured out a way to untangle the easement thing, and all they needed was your property to make it work. It'd be a really valuable piece of development land for them."

"Too bad they just couldn't go about it in a normal way," Bernie said. "Arson seems a little extreme."

"Grant told Libby he'd offered to buy your house when you started renting it to Stephanie, but you weren't gonna budge."

"I forgot all about that. I didn't take it seriously. Brokers are always telling people to list. He sure as hell didn't mention the easement or anything. Though, I remember now he did when I first bought the house. In one ear and out the other."

"The arson was Ken's idea, if you believe Grant," Dawna said. "But Grant figured that they were doing you a favor, you'd be better off anyway since your house was, and these are his words, not mine, a shitbox and you had somewhere else to live."

"Better off if you ignore the fact that I could be charged with arson."

"Grant paid Stephanie $5,000 to leave town, with Parent splitting the cost, keep her mouth shut, and never come back. Brent helped him do the deal," Dawna said. "Grant also says he had no idea Parent was going to kill Rita. They found out she was asking about Normand's land and Ken went over to talk to her. They thought she'd react better to him, since she and Ryan were going through such a nasty breakup, and they also knew she'd talked to you, Bernie, because you called

Parent to ask about it. They didn't want to mess up the sale to the college, which they were closing on the day she was killed. It was big money."

"He went over to kill her," Pete said. "No doubt in my mind. If it were my case…never mind, it's not."

"Then they had to get rid of the body," Bernie said. "No one ever thinks that part out."

Dawna nodded. "Since they were going to torch your house anyway, they figured, just throw Rita in. Grant said people would think it was Stephanie. Parent had left Rita's body at her house, knowing no one would come by. Grant drove her to your house in her SUV, silver, of course. He didn't want any sign of her remains in his pickup, or for anyone to see his vehicle at the scene. Anita Wing, Grace's mother, saw Grant's pickup there on New Year's Eve when he was there to get her body. It was in the driveway from a little after seven-thirty to a little after eight. She wanted to go over and give him hell, but her husband stopped her. She thought it was the same one she'd seen the day before, a white pickup with a plow blade. Grant's just doesn't have the logo."

"Too bad he wasn't smart enough to realize there were cameras at Pondside when he got the gas," Bernie said. "In his own vehicle."

"Or to shut up about it while your house was burning," Pete said. "It was Grant and Parent talking on that Redimere Raw video."

"How do you know that?" Bernie asked.

Pete smiled. "As you know, contributors to Redimere Raw are anonymous. I happen to know who the administrator is, and I am confident they are telling the truth when they say they don't know who sent it in. The Major Crimes unit, though, was able to enhance the audio enough that Sandy and I could identify the voices."

"How do you know the administrator of Redimere Raw?" Bernie was annoyed he'd kept this tidbit from her.

He made a motion like he was zipping his lips. "I'm sworn to secrecy."

"Grant also caved on the kickbacks, once the AG's office confronted him with the deposit slips," Dawna said. "Parent started paying him off before the election, helped make sure, with his connections, that Grant became mayor and continued to pay him off. That's where Grant went off the rails."

"The potential was always there," Bernie said.

"It's funny," Dawna said. "Libby actually admitted to me that he was using Grant as a source at the beginning, but he was off base." She handed Pete a bulky envelope. "He asked me to give you this. He said to tell you that when he saw what it was, he made sure no one read it."

Pete opened it. "My notebook. With copies. Where'd this come from?"

"They found it when they searched Grant's office. He said he paid Zack Staples to go in your house to find something that would cause trouble."

"This could've ended up being a mess. Boy that guy didn't like me."

"Actually, it was because of Bernie," Dawna said.

Oh no. Bernie didn't plan to tell anyone about her deal with Satan. Figures that Satan would spill the beans.

"Bernie was asking about the Nakilot land," Dawna said. "Grant said he knew she'd figure things out. This was right at the same time as the arson, so I feel like that was probably as vindictive as it was 'practical,' if you want to call it that. Going after you was the one thing that would distract Bernie, give her second thoughts."

"What a jerk," Bernie said. *If they only knew.*

"He was pissed about *Real Rural Justice*, but he would've just fought you on that and left the other stuff alone."

"His whole vendetta against me was to stifle Bernie?" Pete said. "That backfired, didn't it? It just made Bernie go after him harder." He smiled at Bernie. "Boy did he read you wrong."

"Did he ever." She was sure it wasn't decency that kept Grant from revealing their deal, just him not wanting to seem even more of a jerk.

"I'm sorry, Bernie. I wish I'd realized," Pete said.

Bernie shrugged. "The result was the same either way, right? It didn't matter which one of us he was after."

****

When the door of the office opened Monday night, Bernie was engrossed in finishing up an edit on her computer and didn't look up. It was getting close to seven, too late for most visitors, and she assumed it was Pete, hot pizza in hand, arriving for his ride home.

When she looked up, though, it wasn't Pete. Fergus Kelley was standing in front of her desk, with his usual condescending smirk and a large manilla envelope in his hand. Bernie, as of late, had developed an aversion to large manilla envelopes. One clutched in Fergus' hammy fist accompanied by his smirk sent her warning bells into overdrive.

"Let's make a deal," Fergus said.

"You've got to be kidding me. How dare you even come in here?"

"How dare I?" Fergus asked, pulling up Guy's chair and sitting next to her. "This."

She reached for the envelope, but he didn't hand it over. "I'm not giving it to you. Take this instead." He handed her a sheet of paper. It was a content-sharing contract. He'd be allowed to choose up to three of her stories for his own website every Thursday, with the exception of her lead story, and she could choose the same amount of his after he'd had his pick of hers.

"Pretty fair deal, I think," he said.

"Why the hell would I sign this?"

"I'm having trouble meeting my content quota," Fergus said. "I'm up here in the middle of nowhere. Content sharing is becoming more common now. Journalists working together."

"I'd be dead in a ditch before I'd share content with you."

"I knew you'd say something like that," he said. "But I have this. It worked for Ryan Grant. It'll work for me." He opened the envelope and took out a sheet to show her, then jammed it back in. She didn't need to see Pete's neat block printing, the faded notebook lines, to know what it was.

"Grant left a copy for me," Fergus said. "I haven't heard from him since he was arrested, but he never said to get rid of it or anything. So…" He shrugged.

Bernie read through the contract again.

"It's non-negotiable," he said. "It doesn't say it in the contract, but once you sign, I'll give you this." He held up the envelope.

"How do I know you didn't make another copy?"

"I'm a man of my word. But if you need more, I used Grant's copier, and now his office is locked up. The copier at the post office has been broken for months. I don't have access to one unless I drive to Farmington, which I don't have time for."

Bernie couldn't believe she was considering this. She'd vowed after making the diabolic deal with Ryan Grant that she'd never do anything like it again. But Pete's notebook, the raw, searing pain, was kryptonite.

"Novotny's a big hero now, with surviving that plunge into the quarry—which still doesn't pass my smell test, by the way—saving that kid in the process, bringing down the mayor and Ken Parent. This could lay it all to waste in a day," Fergus said.

Her head spun, lit on topics, tried to process the very important information in front of her, sort out options. It wasn't landing on anything and she didn't have time to wait for it.

"You can stop pitching," she said, pulling the paper toward her. It was just sharing content after all. Sure he had no credibility and his stuff was shit and she likely wouldn't use it, but it said right in the contract the *Watcher* would be credited on her articles. It sucked, but not as much as blowing up Pete would.

As she spoke, the door opened, bringing in a cold blast of air and Pete carrying a pizza.

"What's going on?" He put the pizza on the counter.

She and Fergus probably looked like a pair of guilty teenagers caught with a joint, or something more shameful. If a genie had given her one time in her life when she could have a poker face for two minutes, this was it. But even if she did, Pete wouldn't buy it. She and Fergus wouldn't, under any circumstances, be sitting shoulder to shoulder at her desk for any good reason.

"Can I look at that?"

It was disconcerting, Pete, in uniform, demanding the contract. Her brain switched. *This is Pete.* She handed it to him. She didn't want to, but she didn't have a choice.

Pete read it. "I don't see any benefit for Bernie."

"Just a little journalism deal between two colleagues," Fergus said. "State of the industry, you know how it is. New era."

"What's going on?" he asked her. Quiet, almost gentle. He green laser stare, though, told her he meant business.

About a dozen responses zipped through her head. He wouldn't believe any of them. The truth, though, wasn't an option, She just couldn't. He couldn't know she knew what was in the notebook. Worse, he'd know Fergus did. He'd been agitated enough that Ryan Grant had seen it, that had been clear. He'd put on a good face since the quarry, but he was having nightmares almost every night.

"Okay, Bernadette," Fergus said, standing up. "I'll leave that contract with you to get back to me. No rush." He waggled the envelope at her.

"You're not leaving until I know what's going on," Pete said.

"You're going to assault me like you did Sean?" Fergus asked, though with no bravado. He was larger than Pete, but a lot of it was gut. Pete could probably have him on the floor and in cuffs in seconds.

"No. You're trespassing, since you're prohibited from stepping foot in this office. I can take you in for that, book you, mess up your night, or you can tell me why you're here harassing Bernie."

"He's not," Bernie said.

"He obviously is. I can tell just by looking at you." He took a step toward Fergus.

Pete's body language said he was in control. He wasn't going to touch the guy. Fergus had no way of knowing that. Unsurprisingly given the lackluster, cowardly piece of crap he was, he caved.

"Ask her about her deal with Ryan Grant. I was just looking for the same consideration."

"He's trying to extort me with information that was illegally obtained," Bernie said. "You can charge him with that, too."

"You're both bluffing," Fergus said. "You don't want this made public, which would happen if you charged me."

"Give me that." Pete held his hand out for the envelope.

Fergus hesitated, but knowing defeat when it slapped him in his no-longer-smug face, finally did.

Pete took out a page, read it while Bernie's heart sank and melted at the same time.

"I wasn't really going to write about that," Fergus said. "Just trying to keep my job."

"Get out." Pete was calm, level. His expression hadn't changed.

Fergus looked from Pete to Bernie, unsure of what to do.

"Get. Out."

Fergus was out the door faster than Bernie knew he could move.

"What did he mean about a deal with Grant?" Pete asked. He wasn't mad. Not even exasperated. She tried to gauge what he was—concerned? It was hard to tell.

He stood in front of her desk, the envelope in his hand. She could've pointed out the pizza was getting cold. That it was a long story. She could tell him when they got home. But it was time to pull off the Band-Aid.

She told him about Grant's visit the day of the power outage, the deal they'd struck, the pages he sent her in the following days to keep her "on track."

"Why didn't you tell me?"

"I was in shock after it happened, but once that wore off, later that day, I was going to. Then Imani got shot, and…"

"And."

She opened her desk drawer, handed him the envelope with the other pages. "I read them. I'm sorry."

He read each one as she waited, wishing she were anywhere else. Even more, wishing she could have that cold, bizarre afternoon back. He folded the two envelopes and put them in his coat pocket. She braced for whatever was coming.

He held out his hand. She took it and rose from her chair. He pulled her into a hug. "It's okay. The pizza's getting cold. Let's go home."

CHAPTER 45

PETE HELD THE remaining puzzle pieces in his hand, easily fitting them into the right holes. Dinner was on the stove. A nice quiet January Wednesday afternoon. He hoped he wasn't going to blow it up.

"Don't you want to watch the big puzzle finish?" he asked Bernie.

"No." She didn't take her eyes from her book. "You know how much I hate it when someone bugs me when I'm reading."

"I have an authentic dialogue thing."

She put down her book.

"What I'm going to tell you has nothing to do with PTSD. It's about us."

She looked wary. He smiled, but her expression didn't change.

"You're going to argue, but hear me out, okay?"

"Not a great start."

"I'm going to resign. I'll give them enough notice so they can hire someone. I'm going to strongly recommend Dawna. They'll still be short-staffed, so I won't leave immediately."

"Oh." Now she was confused. "Why? Everything's fine now."

"I've thought a lot about our future. The impact on your job."

"Oh no. No no no no. Don't quit your job on my account. Please." Her voice rose with each *no*, then her body, until she was off the couch, like she wanted to flee.

"Sit down, okay? Hear me out." He waited for her to settle. "I know how you said maybe it can't be fixed. I'm not doing this as some kind of quid pro quo or grand gesture to convince you or fix it."

"I can't deal with you quitting a job you love because of me."

"It's not because of you. It's because of us. If I don't, it'll destroy our relationship. Look at your stress, your anxiety. This is one thing I have control over that I can fix. I care much more about being with you and your well-being than I do about being a cop."

"You do now, but what about later? I can't ask you to do that. You'll end up hating me."

"I'll love you forever. You're not asking. You've never asked. Every week, you make concessions at work because of me. You never complain, barely bring it up. You back me up all the time. If nothing else, the past couple weeks…"

She turned red.

"You put everything on the line to have my back. Heroically."

"I don't know if I'd put it that way."

"I do. Bernie, I've been a cop for nearly twenty-five years. I could do it for the next twenty-five just out of habit. Benjamin and I have talked about it. I can continue to do it while working on my issues. It won't hurt my recovery. I'm good at it. I like it. I'm not in love with it, though. I'm in love with you. It's the easiest decision I've ever made."

"What will you do? Just those few days you were off work, you were going nuts. What about money? I was already broke, and now I have that smoldering pit of debt."

"Maybe I could work for Kermit. I could take the Maine bar or be an investigator. Money's not a problem. You know that."

"You have all the answers, don't you?" Her resistance seemed to be fading a little. He'd expected to get some, knew it would take her some time to process. He just had to make sure she heard him. Understood.

"I started thinking about it after we talked after the appointment with Benjamin. Then there was the Coburn Gore adventure and what you said that night. I've thought about it a lot. I've hashed it out with Benjamin. I know you well enough to know what you'd say."

He could see her wheels turning, feel her processing it.

"Are you presenting this to me as a done deal? Looking for my blessing? What?"

"If you don't want me to quit, I won't. But I can't imagine you really want me to stay. Take away all the other stuff, all your concerns. Just think about your job, how you'd feel about it I weren't police chief."

She was about to protest. He could see it. Then she shook her head, physically shook it away. A smile started, and it grew until she was laughing. "Authentically? It'd be…like Christmas every day."

****

It was just a coincidence, Pete knew, that he'd been at his desk trying to sort the loose ends that he had to tie up in his final weeks on the job when Sandy stuck his head in the office door. "We've got a situation."

"I've had enough situations for January," Pete said. "Come back next week."

"Since I'm your ride home, and it's on our way, you can't avoid it," Sandy said. "The guys were cutting the hole in the ice for the Polar Plunge, down at the boat landing, and there's a car down under it."

It turned out to be one loose end he hadn't even considered.

He and Sandy arrived just as a gray late-model Chevy Malibu was being towed up the boat ramp, a cascade of icy water spilling from its crevices.

"Those are Arkansas plates," Pete said. He didn't have to see the plates, though, to know the car. He'd seen it for months, every time he drove by Bernie's. He'd seen it drive into his dooryard that cold Thanksgiving weekend day. He'd been watching for it ever since, not fully convinced Stephanie was gone for good.

Yet here she'd been, all the time. He and Bernie driving by her every day.

A few days later, George Libby called to tell him what they'd found.

Stephanie had been in mid-text to Bernie at 4:57 p.m. on Christmas Eve. They theorized that as she was texting, her car had missed the turn at the bottom of the hill on Pond Road, rambled across the entrance to the boat landing and the few yards of grass that separated it from the lake, and plunged into the water. It would've stayed there, as the ice formed over it, until spring if it weren't for the Polar Plunge.

The text was typed, but not sent: "$$$$$ C Ya Im outa here."

"The $5,000 in cash that Ryan Grant paid her off with was in her bag," Libby told Pete. "Twenties and fifties."

CHAPTER 46

THE AFTERNOON SUN glinted off the bulldozer as it pushed the last of Bernie's house into a pile. Another piece of big machinery picked up the charred timbers, the pieces of roof and wall, and underneath it, the other pieces of her life. It dropped its load into a dump truck.

She hadn't wanted to watch, but found herself walking up the hill anyway. She waited to feel devastated. She told herself that in the month since her house was lit on fire and destroyed, she'd had little time to mourn it. Now that she did, she only felt a mild sadness. More wistfulness than anything else.

The life she'd had there, the one she thought she'd go back to, had ended eight months earlier. She'd thought of it as home. She'd missed it. She hadn't noticed that large parts of her had moved on.

She turned to see Pete walking up the hill. He still limped, but his stride was strong, his face lifted toward hers. He smiled as he got near, that big smile that said he was so happy to see her.

"Looking for my ride," he said. "How are you doing?"

"Good. Better than good, actually."

"I stopped by the office and they told me you'd walked up here. I wasn't sure what I'd find."

"Oh, ye of little faith."

They watched the last pile of debris go into the dump truck, then stepped aside as it rumbled onto the road.

"That's it," Bernie said.

"You sure you're okay?"

"I am." She kissed him on the cheek. "Authentically speaking, very okay."

He held out his hand as they started down the hill.

She took it.

She looked back at the dirt patch, brown snow pushed aside, basement filled in. Nothing, where there had once been something. She turned back to Pete. "Let's go home."

—30—

ACKNOWLEDGEMENTS

I'd like to thank my excellent readers, Rebecca Milliken, John Radosta, Kathy McGrath Fitts and Elizabeth Milliken. Their suggestions were a big help in making this book better.

Betsy Judkins, of Maine Woods Editing, did a fantastic job. Her skill and professionalism also made the book much better. Any errors, mistakes or grating editor's choice issues are mine alone.

Nicki Beauregard was a big help with medical questions and Chris Grimes with insurance as it relates to arson. It's great to have experts to talk to, but sometimes a writer has to go rogue, so any errors or literary license in either the medical or insurance aspects of this book are mine alone as well.

Neighbor and friend Anthony Wilson generously donated to the local Neighbors Driving Neighbors auction, winning the right to have his name used in this book. Anthony was given a choice of characters, and chose one much less savory than the real Anthony. I appreciate his good humor and generosity.

Speaking of neighbors, mine are much nicer than Bernie O'Dea's, and a big thanks goes to Kris and David Viens, who make my life much less stressful than it could be under other circumstances. Definitely the best neighbors ever.

The Final Jeopardy clue and answer on December 31, 2010, came from the excellent website J! Archive. Bernie's "mountweazel" clue is a figment of my imagination, which is not to say it's never been a *Jeopardy!* clue.

Can't get enough of Bernie, Pete, and Redimere?
Check out
The Bernie O'Dea Reader's Companion

Everything you wanted to know about Redimere, its residents, and the Bernie O'Dea mystery series, but didn't know how to ask. Includes character bios, renderings of Bernie and Pete's home, FAQ's, photos of real-life Redimere-area settings, maps, and more, including 60 pages of unpublished story.

Visit maureenmilliken.com

ABOUT THE AUTHOR

Maureen Milliken, author of the Bernadette "Bernie" O'Dea mystery series, is a longtime journalist who worked for daily newspapers in northern New England for more than three decades. She's a member of the Mystery Writers of America and Sisters in Crime, and blogs with other Maine crime writers at Mainecrimewriters.com. She co-hosts the Crime & Stuff podcast with her sister, Maine artist Rebecca Milliken. She lives in central Maine.

For updates and news, visit maureenmilliken.com
or maureenmillikenmysterywriter on Facebook.